D0908281

PARTY TRICKS

PARTY TRICKS

Geraldine Bedell

St. Martin's Press ✄ New York

Library of Congress Cataloging-in-Publication Data

Bedell, Geraldine.
    Party tricks / Geraldine Bedell.—1st U.S. ed.
        p.   cm.
    ISBN 0-312-18154-X
    I. Title.
    PR6052.E293P37   1998
    823'.914—dc21   97-39440
                                                            CIP

First published in Great Britain by Hodder and Stoughton Ltd, a division of Hodder Headline PLC

First U.S. Edition: March 1998

10   9   8   7   6   5   4   3   2   1

For Charlie

Acknowledgements

With thanks to Elaine Bedell, Clive Brill, Sue Fletcher, Carol Heaton and Charles Leadbeater.

Chapter One

I SPECIALISE IN TRIVIA. This is not necessarily what I would have chosen, but it does at least explain how I came to find Tony Bagnall, MP, in his office at the House of Commons, hanging from the ceiling pipes.

I no longer specialise in death. There was a time when I was always jumping on planes and heading for some strafed landing strip or fortified airport; when I spent weeks on end in borrowed rooms – even, once, in a tent – tapping out reports of death by starvation, war and indifference; when I won awards and didn't specialise in trivia at all.

But I'd put that behind me, or thought I had – and so when I arrived at the House of Commons to meet Simon Healy that wild, bright Wednesday morning in March, I only expected to find out how he'd met Hester Allan. The most excitement I anticipated was a few discrepancies between his version and hers.

The wind tore through the trees, scudding little white clouds across the sky. I threaded past the tourists to the St Stephen's entrance and made my way through the security check and inside the building, where the vast, severely empty space of the ancient Westminster Hall opened beneath my feet, the hammer beam roof arched overhead. I was sucked up the warm, wide, dimly lit corridor.

The Commons this morning, too early for many MPs to be in evidence, was cavernous, hushed and solemn. I sat down on one of the green leather benches in Central Lobby and leant my back against the sandy stone, taking in Pugin's riot of stained glass, mosaic and gold. A pair of high heels click-clacked across the floor: a woman in a suit met a man in a suit and exchanged quiet words under the fabulous ceiling. No one took any notice of me; the place was too conscious of its own dignity to pay outsiders any serious attention.

The man they called the real leader of the Labour Party came down to meet me himself.

It was years since I'd seen Simon Healy face to face, and he'd changed. Not so much in looks: he was still rather short, slim, and tidy-looking, except for the lopsided gaze which made you suspect he might be able to see more than most people, or at any rate differently. The eye operation he'd had last year had only been partially successful, and it was still never wholly clear where his attention was fastened, or which eye it was advisable to catch. People who disliked Simon Healy – and there were plenty of them – put it about that he'd asked the surgeons not to correct the defect completely, on the grounds that the squint enhanced his reputation as an enigma. Personally, I'd always found it rather disarming.

What *had* changed was something you could only describe as presence. When I'd known him before, he didn't have it. Now he did. Then he was a junior researcher at the BBC; now he was one of the most famous politicians in the country. The *most* famous unelected politician. Many scenes, people said, existed solely so that Simon Healy could be behind them. This was a man of whom myths were made. The squint story was typical, and almost certainly spurious. For some reason, people needed to believe that Simon Healy was a sort of younger, facial-hair-free, and less libidinous Rasputin.

So Simon Healy, the most artful, effortless spin doctor in the history of media manipulation, was credited with more extraordinary and disturbing achievements than were humanly possible in one, as yet, rather brief life. He was supposed to decide where George Dalmore's children went to school, to approve Penny Dalmore's choice of hairdresser and outfits, to write George's speeches and decide where he gave them.

It had always been obvious Healy was a man with a future, even when he was a junior researcher and I was a temp secretary on a university vacation. For a start, he had so much *past*. He'd grown up in a household steeped in left-wing politics. His mother was the first woman to lead a trade union; his father was the left-wing barrister Mark Healy, who was notorious for taking on unwinnable civil liberties cases and then winning them. When Simon's parents gave parties, cabinet ministers came. Plots to oust prime ministers were devised around the family's dining table.

Even back then at the BBC, he'd been almost exhaustingly dynamic. But he hadn't had this air of cool authority that surrounded him now like a little impenetrable cloud. I had gone back to university, and Healy had become an excessively young producer. He'd launched the most popular political programme in the BBC's history. And then, at the age of twenty-eight, he had bewilderingly (to everyone else) decamped to work at John Smith House in some not-quite-specified promotional capacity. Crazy, or what? This was a man who could have been a future director general.

But far from being the unhinged move of someone too successful too soon that it was widely held to be, Simon Healy's move into politics turned out to involve the transformation of George Dalmore into the most popular Labour leader this century.

If Labour won the election – which now looked pretty much inevitable – then Simon Healy, thirty-four years old, short and with a disconcerting habit of seeming to look in two directions at once, would be crucial in shaping the government.

George Dalmore's Labour-led Britain, styled by Simon Healy, would have little in common with any previous Labour regime. There would be no great role for the trade unions, no talk of comrades or collectivism. The atmosphere would be individualistic but caring; efficient, but with flair, style and élan. It would be a government for people who wanted to get on in the world but not trample all over everyone else in the process. That was the idea, anyway.

Healy's many enemies, including some in his own party who may have owed the size of their majorities to him, observed sourly that this might leave the next Labour government looking remarkably similar to the last Conservative one. Healy's enemies would have liked nothing more than to see him make some hideous mistake and consign himself to political oblivion for ever.

But Healy didn't seem to make mistakes. He appeared to have convinced a majority of voters that a Labour government would be more successful with the economy, and, at the same time, more tender with their anxieties about health and education than the Tories. What's more, this Labour government wouldn't be riddled with sleaze.

I knew all this because Simon Healy's career had been public property for years. Mine, on the other hand, had not, so I didn't expect him to remember our brief encounter at Television Centre more than ten years earlier.

He shook my hand, smiling with what might have been warmth of recognition, or mere politician's politeness, and asked if I minded making a detour to drop a note into another office. I said not at all, and followed him at an incredibly brisk pace through an inner lobby and up a sweeping staircase.

'I wanted to do this,' he said, knowing I understood how rarely he gave personal interviews, 'mainly because I remember your first reports from Iraq. When everyone still thought Saddam Hussein was on our side.' He shook his head. 'Brave journalism.'

'Foolhardy,' I said.

He smiled. 'You decided not to go into television, then?'

'Yes. Six weeks was quite enough to put me off.'

'Were we so vile?'

He hadn't been vile at all. He'd been kinder than everybody else put together. He'd taken me out to lunch several times and offered advice on getting in to the BBC, even help with my application if I wanted it. But I was telling the truth. I'd felt weary just thinking about television's top-heavy structures, wanted to be out on my own, me and a laptop, no committees. I'd fallen for the old-fashioned rackety romance of newspapers.

We turned a corner. 'How long did you manage to stay in Iraq after you'd written those reports?'

'Two months. They made it clear I wasn't wanted.'

'No doubt.'

'They didn't quite know what to do with me. Execution would have suited them. But it seemed a bit extreme.'

'It's a pity the Government didn't take notice of what you were saying.'

'They did. Eventually. Though by then it was a bit late. Three years later I was quoted by the Foreign Secretary twice in three weeks.'

'But by then, presumably, you must have been in East Timor?'

I was impressed. He had a better memory of my career than my editor. This, of course, was why he was so good.

'Yes. I'm afraid I missed the Gulf War.'

'Plenty of other people covered it.' He smiled. 'I hope this won't embarrass you, but your reports from East Timor convinced me that we – the Labour Party – ought to have a policy on Indonesia.'

'It seems rather a long time ago now.'

'I expect so. It was moving stuff, though. Memorable journalism. It must have been hard for you – afterwards.' He met my eye, to emphasise he knew what had happened. 'Sam Sheridan was a very fine photographer.'

We turned a corner (I was thoroughly muddled by now: too many corridors, staircases and swing doors) and paused. Healy fished an envelope from his breast pocket and knocked on a door labelled 'T. Bagnall, W. Mosey'. When he received no answer, he tried the handle; he seemed surprised when it turned.

'I'll leave this on his desk,' he said, entering the office while I waited outside in the empty corridor.

How long, I wondered idly as I waited in the corridor, did it take to learn your way around these passages? Would we have to walk a lot further before we got to wherever we were going to do the interview? Would we do it in the Leader of the Opposition's offices? How could I get Healy onto the subject of the latest sleaze allegations?

T. Bagnall. W. Mosley. The first name rang a bell. Terry . . . Toby? . . . No, Tony Bagnall. I'd read an interview somewhere, in connection with some new job. Chairman of some committee on Europe. A pro-European backbench group. He was middle-aged and old Labour, very different from Healy in his slick suits, slicing his way through the House of Commons corridors.

The sound, which began as something between a cry and a cough and ended as a strangulated yelp, brought me back to the present. But then there was no sound; only a silence more disturbing than the guttural noise preceding it. I stepped forward uneasily, and peered round the door.

Simon Healy was in the office, leaning against a filing cabinet with his hands over his face. The rest of the cramped room was dominated by two desks, facing one another and littered with papers. There were two chairs, one for each desk, but one had been kicked aside, so that Tony Bagnall could hang himself.

Tony Bagnall was – had been – a bulky man in his early fifties. Though his body hung limply from the ceiling, he seemed to fill the room, too solid to be anything but earthbound, too fat to be suspended above our heads, shifting slightly in the currents of air.

He had come out to kill himself this morning in a grey suit, a white shirt, and his Transport and General Workers Union tie. He'd taken off his shoes to climb on the chair and left them tidily on the floor.

His wool socks were grey. His face was grey as well; his head lolled horribly to one side, eyes bulging, mouth red. His expression had already ceased to be human; his face had become simply the face of a corpse with a broken neck.

I don't think he had been dead long. There was a smell in the room that was not the smell of decay but of sweat, faeces and urine.

I had seen corpses; I'd seen people dying alone, and in fear. But death in war, death brought about by soldiers, struggled against, was different from this methodical suicide, a planned and lonely self-destruction amid the privileges of the Palace of Westminster.

Simon Healy was clutching the envelope he'd meant to leave in the office, and staring at Bagnall's feet, which were swaying slightly.

I took in the desks, the overflowing wire baskets, a bookshelf stuffed with box files, stapled reports, folders, all looking urgently in need of attention – much of it, now, probably of no consequence whatsoever; the mullioned windows, the cold blueness of the sky beyond, the worn carpet.

'Let's get out of here,' Simon Healy muttered, grabbing my wrist and pulling me towards another door beyond the filing cabinets. I stumbled behind him into another narrow room, similar to the one we'd left but tidier. 'Secretaries' office,' he explained, steadying himself on the desk, and pushing a chair away with his foot so I could sit down.

The image of Tony Bagnall's chair, kicked aside, swam before me and I knew I was going to be sick. I reached for a wastepaper bin I could see beneath the desk, and heaved, tasting a sour trail of vomit. I didn't have a tissue, and had to wipe my mouth with the back of my hand.

Simon Healy picked up the telephone and punched out a number, asked someone to come.

He seemed to have to explain about three times that we'd found the MP dead, that we were in his secretary's office next door, that it was absolutely imperative that someone came to cut him down. When he replaced the receiver, he was shaking his head, appalled.

'Was there a note?' he asked suddenly. 'Did you see?'

'The police will find it if there was. Is someone coming?'

'I'll look,' said Simon. 'There might be a note.'

I stared at him.

'Elise . . .'

I didn't know who Elise was, but I had the strong impression Healy had gone mad. Whoever the dead man was, there was nothing anyone could do to help him. If he had left a note, someone would find it. Let them; we'd had enough.

I looked at a slime of vomit down the side of the wastebin and wanted to get out of the room, to be outside, half an hour earlier, in the wind.

But Simon had gone back into the office, and a second or two later, when he emerged, he was clutching a piece of paper.

Chapter Two

A MIDDLE-AGED WOMAN with untidy grey hair and a sensible skirt shouldered her way through the door, laden down with a briefcase and a couple of bulging carrier bags.

'What's going on?' She put down her bags, looking from one of us to another.

Simon pulled out a chair and presented it to her. She sat automatically.

'This your office?' the sergeant asked.

'This is Susan Halliday,' Simon explained, the briefest hesitation betraying that he was having to make an effort to remember. 'She works for Bill Mosey, who shares the office next door. Susan, I'm sorry to overrun your office like this. This is Helen Clare, a journalist, and Sergeant Lyon. I am afraid Helen and I found Tony Bagnall dead next door a few minutes ago.'

'Tony?' She stared at the communicating door.

'He hanged himself.'

'Tony? . . . No . . .' She couldn't believe it.

'Do you know – can you think of any reason why he might have done that?'

Susan Halliday shook her head, wide-eyed. It was too much to take in; the muscles around her mouth were loose; she was trying not to give way.

'He wasn't depressed?' Simon persisted. 'He hadn't seemed – I don't know – different lately?'

'If you don't mind, Mr Healy, CID will be here in a minute,' one of the policemen said, 'and I'm sure these are questions they'll want to ask. If you and Ms Clare wouldn't mind perhaps going along to the Leader of the Opposition's office, and they can see you there?'

Healy collected himself. 'Of course – I'll have to plan what we're going to say to the press, anyway, and someone will have to tell Elise . . .'

Susan Halliday was fingering her blouse and staring distractedly into the middle distance. Suddenly she said: 'Where's June?'

'Who?'

'June Lennox: Tony's secretary.' She waved at the desk opposite. 'She should have been here by now.'

'What time does she usually arrive?' the sergeant asked.

'Ten o'clock. Always. I sometimes pop into the shops on my way in, but . . .' Susan Halliday put her head in her hands and seemed to be in some distress.

'If there's anything I can do, or George . . .' Simon offered, while the policeman patted her shoulder awkwardly, and nodded at Healy and me to indicate that it might be more helpful if we waited elsewhere.

'I suggest three interviews, one for the cameras, one for radio, and one to the Press Association. I'll handle the papers,' Healy said, as he led me briskly along dark-panelled corridors towards George Dalmore's office.

'That poor woman. She must feel if only she'd got there an hour earlier . . .'

'Once this gets out of here, and it may be out already, there'll be reporters all over. They won't leave you alone. You're young, female – well, I don't have to tell *you*. The point is simply that it'll be much easier if you make up your mind right at the start how you're going to handle it and whom you'll talk to, and stick to your plan.'

He opened a door at the end of a corridor and ushered me into an ante-room where a young woman was sitting over a computer.

'Morning, Simon,' she said cheerfully. 'My God!' Her expression changed. 'Is something wrong?'

'Sal, this is Helen Clare – she works for the *Sunday Chronicle*. This is Sally Elliott, who keeps George's diary and generally runs his life. Can we use George's office?'

'Sure. He's not coming in until three. He's at that conference.' Sally got up from her desk. 'What's happened?'

Healy told her and she clapped her hand to her mouth.

'Whatever for? How awful. He always seemed so respectable.'

'Can you get me a biog?' Simon asked. 'I'll need it if I'm going to talk to the press.'

'Yes, I'm sure I can . . . and you should drink sweet tea, you know, for the shock.'

She disappeared to find a copy of Bagnall's CV. When she came back, she also brought two cups of thin, sugary tea. I sipped at one experimentally; it made me feel sick again.

Then she perched on the edge of George Dalmore's table and insisted we tell her what had happened.

'Bloody hell!' she muttered, when Simon had explained.

He frowned. 'Someone ought to tell Elise. The news will be out before we know where we are. The police, the secretaries . . . Gossip spreads like crazy in this place. We won't keep this secret for five minutes. Oh, Christ! She's in bloody Bradford.' He pressed his lips together. 'George. George'll have to do it over the phone.'

Sally looked at her watch. 'He'll have started his speech. We won't get to him for at least three-quarters of an hour.'

Simon paced the floor, polished shoes steadily measuring out the carpet. 'Someone has to tell her. I don't think we can even wait three-quarters of an hour.' He looked at us. Or he may have been looking at the door. The straying eye made it difficult to tell. 'Friends . . . They must have had friends? In the Commons?'

Sally looked at him helplessly. 'Maybe. I wouldn't know where to start.'

'Christ!' Simon muttered again. He looked at us with an expression of alarm, and then left the room.

Sally exhaled noisily and sat down. 'Poor Simon. What a horrible thing to have to do.' She stared into the middle distance. 'I don't know anything about Tony Bagnall, that's the trouble, and I doubt he does either. Isn't it awful? He's dead, and we can't even think who his friends were.' She bit her lip and appeared to pull herself together. 'Which paper was it you said you worked for?'

'The *Sunday Chronicle*. Today. I'm freelance.'

'Were you supposed to interview Tony Bagnall?'

'No, I was seeing Simon, for a feature called "How They Met". He's doing it with Hester.'

'Poor Tony. No one was really interested in him. Though he must be newsworthy now. More than he ever was alive. I suppose I just thought with this new role . . .'

'I don't really know much about the Brussels Group.'

'It's a backbench thing. Pro-Europe. Hasn't ever been important, though I think Bagnall hoped he might be able to make it count: he kept ringing up the papers offering them interviews.' She sighed. 'Poor bloke. He hadn't made much of a mark here otherwise. It was his last hope. Simon, of course, is another matter entirely.' She swung her legs. '*Everyone*'s interested in Simon.'

'I've found the CID officers,' Healy said, coming back into the room followed by a man in his late forties and a rather younger woman.

'How was Elise?'

He winced. 'Poor woman. Horrible to have to hear it on the phone.' He rubbed at his temples with his thumb and fingers, forehead in his hand. 'We must make sure George calls her later. Which reminds me,' he added to Sally, 'would you mind calling in on Susan Halliday in a while? She looked traumatised. Now,' he turned to the police, who had introduced themselves as Detective Inspector Trewin and Detective Sergeant Blake, 'how can we help you?'

We rehearsed for them our discovery of Bagnall's body: Simon's detour to the office, the limp dead weight creaking on the length of new rope.

'And why exactly was it you were visiting Mr Bagnall's office?'

'I wanted to deliver a note confirming that George Dalmore was planning to visit Bagnall's constituency.'

'Is that something you'd normally do? You wouldn't telephone, or send – I don't know – an e-mail, or get one of the secretaries to do it?'

'I might do any of those. In this case I was rather hoping I might see him. He'd very much wanted George Dalmore to come up to the constituency . . . –' Simon hesitated. 'He'd been having a bit of trouble with his local party.'

'What sort of trouble?'

Simon sat back on the sofa and crossed his legs at the ankles. 'You'll probably appreciate that members of the Parliamentary

Labour Party often have differences with activists in their constituencies.' The inspector nodded, pen poised. 'In the past these invariably involved activists being more left-wing than their representatives in Parliament – you'll remember all the trouble we had with Militant in the early eighties. In this particular case, the dispute, if that's not too strong a word, was slightly different. Tony was an old-fashioned socialist, who came up through the trade unions. He didn't have much time for fashionable causes: he was openly antagonistic to George Dalmore's attempts to modernise the party. He thought we were selling out.'

I can't be sure, but I think Detective Sergeant Blake may have smirked.

'He was a smoke-filled-rooms sort of politician, if that makes any sense. Some people – and I probably would have been one of them, to be frank – would have been happy to see him leave Parliament. There was a feeling in some quarters that he was a bit of a relic from another age, although of course he was only in his mid-fifties. But increasingly his constituents were taking that view as well. Northern Labour Parties are often thought of as bastions of tradition, but Bagnall's area of Bradford wasn't like that. They're very keen up there on party reform, great supporters of what George has been trying to do. Tony Bagnall was concerned they might try to replace him with an alternative candidate – probably an Asian woman.'

'Wouldn't that have suited Mr Dalmore?'

'Oh, but think of the press coverage.' Healy smiled. 'The dispute would have been interpreted as a race row, the Party would have looked divided. Never a good thing in politics. There would have been racial slurs in the tabloids – you know the sort of thing: Asian conspiracy to take over the constituency – which would have provoked an anti-racist backlash, which in turn would have upset middle England, the very people the Labour Party needs to win over. George wouldn't have wanted that at all.'

'How upset do you think Mr Bagnall was about all this?' DS Blake asked.

'Do you mean would he have killed himself over it? I don't know. I have no very clear idea what he was like, to be honest: I couldn't gauge how much it might have mattered to him. Other people – his secretary or his wife or his close friends – would be able to tell you better than I can what he felt about it. But my sense was that the dispute was at an early stage; George's visit was supposed to prevent things from coming to a head.'

Sally knocked and put her head round the door. 'Call for Helen from her paper,' she said. 'D'you want me to tell them you'll get back to them?'

I nodded, but DI Trewin said I could take it if I wanted. He had a couple more questions specifically for Simon.

Sally showed me into an adjacent room – obviously Simon's office, from the memos and letters awaiting his attention. This was the room from which he must have called Elise Bagnall, for his jacket was on the back of the chair. Sally put the call through.

'Peach, what a relief to get hold of you,' Dan said. 'Look, there's a rumour someone's topped himself at the House of Commons. A Labour bloke, we think. While you're there, can you ask Simon Healy what's going on?'

'I know. I found him.'

'You *what?*'

'Simon Healy and I found him.' My attention had been caught by a piece of Commons writing paper poking out of the inside pocket of Simon's jacket.

'Brilliant! Who is it?'

I engaged myself in a brief internal conversation about ethics.

'Tony Bagnall.'

The ethical debate over, I pulled the note from Simon's pocket and read it.

'Bugger.'

'Sorry?'

'No one will have heard of him, will they? I've scarcely heard of him. But you and Simon Healy . . . Bloody hell, Peach! You must write something for Sunday.'

'Dan, I'm in the middle of a police interview . . .'

Under a printed, embossed Commons crest and the words 'Tony Bagnall, MP', the dead man had typed: 'I am more sorry than I can say. I have debts to pay that I cannot repay. Give my love to Elise.'

And that was it.

'Call me as soon as you get out of it. And find out everything you can!'

I slipped the note back carefully into Simon's pocket, replaced the phone, and returned to George's room along the corridor in time to hear Simon telling the police that Bagnall had left school when he was fifteen for a job on the railways. 'He got involved in the union, took exams at night school and must have joined the city council when he was in his mid-thirties. He was chair of social services, I think, before becoming leader.'

'And he came into Parliament when?'

'Six years ago, something like that. I'd have to check. He must have been about forty-eight anyway. A vacancy came up for the local parliamentary seat and he was the obvious candidate. Stormed through the selection, as far as I can remember, and increased the Labour majority. But I can't feel he was ever very happy here. He was never likely to get off the back benches.'

'Any particular political interests?'

Simon Healy shook his head.

'He never found a platform here. He was an old-style Labour politician with a belief in a working class which no longer truly exists. His brand of politics was already starting to look redundant when he arrived here. I'm afraid it's only become more so.'

'I see. Did you disturb anything in the room, or remove any objects?'

'Christ, yes! I almost forgot: I found a note.'

Healy went next door, retrieved the piece of paper and handed it over. The inspector read it, frowned, and passed it wordlessly to the sergeant.

'So no other theories about why he might have killed himself?'

'I read the note,' Healy admitted. 'But beyond that, no. He seemed cheerful enough, and had a stable marriage, I believe – but I wouldn't have been the first person to know if he was unhappy.'

While Simon had been out of the room calling Elise Bagnall to break the news of her husband's death, he had also contrived to speak to various of his contacts at the BBC, ITN and the Press Association, so that by the time the police had finished with us, a gaggle of journalists was waiting in an ante-room, ready to set up their cameras and put their questions. Simon and I held an impromptu press conference in George's office, during which the reporters repeatedly demanded to know what we – and especially

I – had *felt*, although in fact the puffy, middle-aged body suspended from the ceiling had already started to seem like something from a dream, half remembered, as if the whole thing had happened to someone else. I scarcely felt anything any more, except surprise that I was here. I think I may have seemed rather inarticulate.

Simon was professional enough for both of us. He related what had happened simply and graphically, interspersed with warm, succinct reflections on the dead MP's career. Tony Bagnall, he said, 'was a man who was not afraid to call himself a socialist, but not afraid of the future either . . . the sort of solidly hard-working MP without whom the House of Commons couldn't function . . . rooted in his community and responsive to his constituents' concerns.'

This all sounded very splendid, despite almost certainly not remotely reflecting what Simon Healy had really felt about the dead man. But it was an object-lesson in how to deal with the press: his tone was sombre, and helpful, and after he'd finished with their questions about Bagnall, he bothered to engage the journalists in conversation about the news that was dominating all the morning's front pages.

Yet another Tory MP was on the point of quitting over a sex scandal.

David Ivison, who'd come into Parliament at the last election after making millions from electronic publishing in his mid-thirties, was reported to have got his secretary pregnant. Unhappily, he already had a wife and three children.

This was the third scandal to have hit the Government since January, and the shocking revelations of Andrew Gunnel, the Secretary of State for Northern Ireland's year-long affair with his colleague, Roads Minister Ellis Fletcher. Both men were married, although as the tabloids had gleefully pointed out, neither had ever had children (the implication being, 'or proper sex').

Gunnel and Fletcher resigned eventually, after initial attempts to rubbish the allegations, then to brazen them out. But the scandal paralysed the Government for weeks and consumed forests of newsprint. Unfortunately, no sooner had it died down than Barry Bianchini, the Home Secretary's PPS, left his wife for a fundraiser who worked part-time in Conservative Central Office.

Lady Hughes, a formidable woman almost twenty years her lover's senior, unfortunately made Bianchini's young wife – whom he had married at eighteen and latterly left in the constituency to look after the children and answer the phone – look pallid and uninteresting.

The cumulative effect of all these transgressions was to create the impression of a government swimming in corruption, its ministers bobbing around in a sea of sleaze like so many old condoms.

No wonder Simon Healy had the air of a man whose time had come. The Prime Minister had to call an election before June. His inability to keep the members of his Government under control – to persuade them it was wisest to keep their trousers done up – made him look weak. Which was unfortunate, because even without the haemorrhaging sewage pipe of his MPs' private morality, James Sherlock would have been hard-pressed to convince the country he'd had a good five years.

The economy was in a worse mess even than when Sherlock had taken over. Experts of all kinds were constantly warning of the dangers posed by the growing underclass of long-term unemployed, living off petty criminality on estates teeming with broken families. Last summer there had been riots. And the Tory Party's response to all this? A barely concealed internecine war over Europe.

'Let me organise George's driver to take you home,' Simon said, when he'd seen out the last of the camera crews. 'D'you think you'll be all right?'

I failed to register what he was saying for a moment, because the door had opened to admit two men, one of whom was distractingly recognisable. We had never met, though I knew who he was, and there was really no possibility of my *not* recognising him, because he brought with him into the room, along with tall-dark-and-handsome looks, a whirling pheromonic storm.

'Helen?' he said. 'It is Helen, isn't it?' He came over and shook my hand. The air crackled with colliding chemicals. 'Joe Rossiter. We half met a month ago at Danny Gould's party.'

He must have bothered to find out who I was. We certainly hadn't been introduced.

I nodded. He was gorgeous. He had a faint accent. Yorkshire, probably. Warm, but slightly edgy, somehow. I looked up at him, met blue eyes. He was slim, athletic, impossibly sexy.

I could remember almost everything about that half-meeting. He had been wearing jeans and a blue shirt, and talking to the political

editor of the *Chronicle*, Frank Threshfield. I'd been at the other
end of the room, half listening to some woman in PR, wondering
who he was, when he'd looked up, caught my eye, and smiled,
devastatingly.

It was the corniest eyes-across-a-crowded-room moment. I dis-
engaged myself from the woman in PR, took a step in his direction,
and collided with Dan, who grabbed my hand and pulled me into
the kitchen.

'I was on my way to talk to someone,' I wailed in protest.

'No excuses. I need help mixing the punch.'

'But, Dan . . .'

'No buts. Anyway, I want to talk to you about Robin Rouse.'

Robin Rouse is the editor of the *Sunday Chronicle* and Dan's
boss.

'Who is that man talking to Frank Threshfield?' I demanded.

'Huh?'

'Tallish, slim, tousled hair.'

'Oh. Joe Rossiter. A lot of women fancy him. Not you as well?'

I shook my head. 'Just curious.'

'Oh yeah, sure. Can't see it myself. I think he looks a bit nerdy.'

'Nerdy!'

'Don't slosh the brandy around. He's Labour's one-man think-
tank, said to have single-handedly written the manifesto. Ferociously
bright, intellectually fearless, so they say. I hate him. I'll introduce
you if you tell me how I can persuade Robin we should hire Teddy
Jacobs.'

'Who?'

'Oh, for God's sake, Helen. You spend too much time writing
about the orgasm. The twenty-eight-year-old right-wing poet everyone's talking about. Everyone in the know,' he added, looking at
me despairingly.

But when we returned to the party, Joe Rossiter was gone.

I'd wondered since if I'd misinterpreted that smile, and in the end
I was forced to conclude he must have been smiling at someone
behind me. Otherwise why had he left?

Seeing him now, though, I didn't even care. I couldn't remember
anyone's ever having had this instantaneous, shocking effect. He
was sexual chemistry on legs.

'Bloody Tony Bagnall,' he said. 'Sally told me what happened.

What did he want to do it for? Horrible. Can I get you anything? More tea?' He glanced down at my cup, in which the liquid had formed a cold scum. 'Possibly not. Brandy?'

I shook my head. He perched on the edge of the desk, facing me, and mentioned conversationally that he knew my work. My heart sank. Much of my recent writing has been for *Femme*, The Glossy For Girls Who Know What They Want, and has exhibited a depressing thematic consistency. It has included features on what people say to each other after sex, where they most like to have sex, and whether they get enough sex.

'Amazing stuff from East Timor.'

'Ah.' *That* work. 'It was a long time ago.'

'George's driver is in Bishop's Stortford,' Simon reported, exasperatedly, coming back in – I hadn't even noticed him leaving the room. 'With George, and the Association of Chief Constables.'

'I can take Helen,' said the other young man, the one who'd come in with Joe Rossiter, and whom, until now, I had scarcely noticed.

'Oh, great,' Simon said with evident relief. 'Thanks, Adam. I'm sorry, Helen, we'll reschedule the interview, if you can still face it.' He caught sight of me, possibly gazing idiotically at Joe. 'Oh, d'you two know each other?'

'Yes,' said Joe Rossiter.

'No,' I said, stupidly, at exactly the same time.

Outside, the tourists were still blocking the pavements, the wind was still whipping up the blossom, and crocuses spotted the grass in Parliament Square like sparkly litter.

Adam Sage swept out of the Commons car park in his battered little car (he explained apologetically that he didn't get paid much as Joe's assistant) with me in the passenger seat.

'What an awful thing to happen,' he muttered, shaking his head, 'for you and for Bagnall.'

'Did you know him?'

'A bit. He seemed a nice enough bloke.'

'I wonder why . . .' I thought of his grey socks, dangling from the ceiling.

'God only knows.'

'Money troubles, maybe?'

'Not that I know of.' He changed gear noisily; the car sounded as though it might well give out before we got to Hackney. 'Awful thing to happen to you – when you don't even work there.'

'Extremely inconsiderate of him.'

'Did I hear you saying you used to be a foreign correspondent? Sounds very glamorous.'

'More desperate than glamorous. I couldn't get a job here as a reporter, so I went to Iraq under my own steam, then to Indonesia. I worked as a stringer for a while, won a couple of awards and then the *Chronicle* hired me. Finally.'

'What were you doing at the House today?'

'Trying to interview Simon.' I changed the subject. 'You work with Joe?'

'Yes. I was in the middle of my doctorate when he pulled me out of Cambridge to come and be his assistant.'

I glanced sideways at Adam. I'd scarcely taken him in, but of course, he was young – no more than twenty-five, I should think – with floppy fair hair and an eager, puppyish manner.

'How are you finding it?'

'Working for Joe? He's brilliant – never thinks in straight lines if he can think round a corner. I've never known anyone quite so intellectually creative. So it's very satisfying.'

'Shall I direct you from here?'

'I'm fine. I know where I'm going.'

He did, too; he drove to Hackney through the back doubles, without taking a single wrong turning, and waited outside in the car while I let myself in.

The house I share with Bobby is beautiful, but located in what even the rashest estate agent would have to describe as a mixed area. I was conscious, looking at it through Adam's eyes, that there were scraps of newspaper and old cigarette packets in the gutters, and that the bright, unforgiving light exposed rank front gardens overrun by straggling privet and starveling weeds.

Hackney, even this relatively salubrious part of it, is an odd place for an American investment banker to have chosen to live. Bobby, though, is probably not your regular American investment banker. Fortunately for me, he is passionate about Victorian gothic architecture and Arts and Crafts furniture. The house is a fine example of the former, and he has filled it with the latter. And he lets me live with him, very cheaply, and cram the south-facing garden with scrambling climbing plants.

I walked in that morning with a sense of relief, which lasted at least three minutes – until I listened to the half-dozen telephone messages waiting for me on the machine. They were all from newspaper reporters wanting to talk to me about my dreadful experience. They all sounded very concerned, in an ersatz kind of way.

I decided to ignore them all; though I called Dan, because I'd promised I would.

'Peach! How are you? *Where* are you?' he cried. 'What a horrible thing to happen!'

'I'm at home.' I felt suddenly tired; I took the phone into the sitting room and flopped on Bobby's plumply cushioned sofa. 'It was pretty horrible. He looked so – *weird*, hanging there above his desk. So heavy, and yet limp. Not quite human, and yet dressed in this ridiculous old-fashioned grey suit.'

'You poor thing. Did you find out anything else? Was there a note?'

'Yes, but no one knows I've seen it, and I don't know whether the police will release it.' I told him what it said.

'Brilliant! I'll get a couple of the news boys onto it.'

'But, Dan, there was something else. Healy told the police he was worried about deselection. His constituency party thought he was out of step with the new Labour Party; they wanted to put up some Asian woman to challenge him.'

'You're brilliant! Peach, you're a star. I've always said so, and I always will.' It was true. Dan had refused to give up on me even when I threatened to turn into a sort of human compost heap.

'I'm terribly tired,' I said.

'I'll let you go. But first, tell me, how did Healy react?'

'Upset. We both were. It was such a shock . . . He certainly didn't say, "Oh, yes, well, we all knew he had troubles."'

'Not that he'd necessarily give anything away. Oh, Peach, I *am* sorry, what a grisly thing to happen. Now you *must* write about this for the weekend.'

'This is the second time in a week you've broken our compact,' I grumbled. 'You may remember we agreed I'd stay off the serious stories. No war zones or dead bodies.'

'The House of Commons is scarcely a war zone. Anyway . . .'

'Anyway what?'

'Nothing.'

I knew what he'd been about to say: that Sam had been dead for
– what was it? – five years, and it was about time I pulled myself
together and got back on track and worked properly again.

'I'll think about it,' I said gloomily.

Chapter Three

I SLEPT FITFULLY, TROUBLED by dreams of being lost in the House of Commons, wandering around the maze of corridors and stairways looking for a dead body. I woke up thinking of Bagnall laid out on some slab. His body would be puckered, white, mottled with veins.

Maybe death gets harder as you grow older. When I was a foreign reporter in my early twenties, I wrote almost breezily about massacres and mass starvation – with drama and passion, sure, but with a certain detachment, partly for effect. Another massacre, another test of my mettle. That wasn't quite what I thought, but it was there, somewhere, below the surface.

I picked up the morning papers off the mat. My photograph gazed out of the front pages at me. 'Tragic girl journalist finds MP's body . . . award-winning reporter Helen Clare, once imprisoned by Saddam Hussein, stumbled upon another body yesterday . . . tragically widowed in Colombia . . .'

And so on.

I sat at the kitchen table in my dressing gown, a pot of tea in front of me, trying not to take too much notice of what they said about me, or to mind that the picture in the *Daily News* made me look as though I'd been having a bad hair day. The person they described didn't sound like anyone I knew. They'd reduced me to a series of types, a photofit in words – a bit of East Ender here, a touch of the tragic widow there, a dollop of dropped-out deadbeat to finish it off.

I made some toast and read an interview with Kate Ivison, wife of the MP who'd been having an affair with his secretary, who seemed most sore about the fact that it was her money that had enabled her husband to set up his electronic publishing business. Then I skimmed through a piece about England's chances in the football match in Milan tonight. After that I tidied the kitchen, threw out the rubbish and made a shopping list. It was difficult then to think of any more excuses not to go to work. So I pulled on a pair of black jeans and the little black cashmere sweater Bobby had given me for my last birthday and caught the bus into the office.

'Dan called,' Sarah said, through a mouthful of pen. 'I wish he wouldn't call me Peach.'

'I know. It's terrible. He does it to everyone.'

'That's no excuse. You might be prepared to put up with it but I don't see why I should have to. How are you feeling this morning?'

'Better.' We'd spoken last night. 'Bobby came home for once, and we drank too much wine and became slightly hysterical.'

'Good,' Sarah said approvingly. 'You need looking after sometimes.'

'You sound like my mother.'

'Your mother is a more sensible woman than you think. Oh, and Simon Healy called. He sounded quite concerned. Said he'd try to get you later.'

I switched on my computer. 'I'm beginning to think Simon Healy is rather a maligned figure.'

'Oh, I can see what's happening. You're setting yourself up to like him so you can write the controversial "It's not true what they say about Simon Healy" piece.'

I smiled. 'I don't think it *is* true. He might want people to believe he's manipulative, but underneath he's a softy. And Hester's very dishevelled and scatty. Quite unsuitable in lots of ways. That must say something.'

The telephone rang before Sarah could demolish this argument. 'Blimey!' she said, putting the caller on hold. 'It's George Dalmore.'

I picked up the phone.

'I know we haven't met,' he said – he'd made the call himself. 'I hope you don't mind my calling, but I wanted to let you know how sorry I was that you found poor Tony Bagnall's body yesterday. If there's anything I can do, anything at all . . .'

'Thank you. But I'm fine, really.'

'I hope Simon made sure you got home safely?'

He sounded young, buoyant, optimistic, even when he was trying to be grave. It was a crucial ingredient of his appeal, I thought, this sense he had that the world was still all before him.

'Adam Sage drove me home.'

'Good. I don't suppose you need any help dealing with the press, since you're a journalist, but if you do, you must let us know.'

I wondered inwardly whether I could enlist George Dalmore's help in getting Joanna Beverley off my back. Joanna is my commissioning editor at *Femme*. 'I'm coping, I think,' I said.

'Good. Well, I won't keep you any longer then. But I mean it: if you want our help, just call. Oh, and Helen?'

'Yes?'

'I really admired your reports from East Timor.'

'Blimey,' Sarah repeated when I put down the phone. I was thinking that if that sort of courtesy was what people meant by Simon's manipulativeness, it was fine by me. Simon had obviously put him up to it.

'So,' Sarah said, through masticated pen, 'what's he like, this person you knew from Dan's party?' I'd happened to mention Joe Rossiter in passing on the telephone last night. Very casually. But Sarah had latched on like an Exocet missile.

'Dark, wavy hair. Rather fine, well-defined features. Tall. Slim. Looks as though he's probably good at sport.'

'Sounds gorgeous.'

'He's all right.'

Sarah made a kind of snorting noise; I smiled in what I hoped was a superior way and turned to the cuttings on Tony Bagnall.

I re-read everything, but it didn't explain why he'd killed himself. There wasn't a great deal anyway: Bagnall had hardly been a figure of great interest to the world outside Westminster. Even his recent election to chairman of the Brussels Group had scarcely caused a stir. I'd learnt more from Simon yesterday.

I finished a piece for Joanna Beverley on women who fall in love too easily, sent off some invoices and had a conversation with my bank manager, who finds the erratic nature of my income a cause of some anxiety. By the time I set off for Hackney Marshes the afternoon was closing in; there was a sense of the day shutting down.

Ryan Stoner had gone out on Friday night for ten minutes to buy his mother an evening paper so she could check what was on the television. He hadn't come back.

They found his body on Tuesday morning, the day before I found Tony Bagnall, lying under bushes on the bank of the River Lea, where it slinks muddily through the marshes towards the Thames.

By then I'd already agreed to write a background feature on the boy for Dan. Even when I took on the piece, it seemed likely he was already dead: three days was a long time for a ten year-old who had never been in trouble to go missing. But little as I wanted to write about a murder, there was something compelling, for me, about this story: Ryan Stoner lived on the council estate where I'd lived when I was his age. Dan said I was the only person who could do the piece properly, and, although he was obviously lying, I could sort of see his point.

I'd already made an appointment to see Mrs Stoner tomorrow, Friday. Now I parked my car beside a derelict warehouse in Waterden Road, close to the river. The wind whipped round my face; I was aware that I'd probably left this outing too late. It was getting dark: an orange halogen glow had turned the late afternoon acidic. I wrapped my coat around myself, and ducked under the iron bar that separated the wasteground from the road.

The tower blocks stood like sentinels around a prison yard, the Marshes beneath them, low and unobserved. Traffic sluiced across the flats, not stopping; on the urban scrub a car seat lay upturned, evidence of a long-moved-on travellers' encampment; a few yards on, a plastic drum, a slab of corrugated iron.

Parts of the Marshes had long been tamed and ordered into football pitches; they looked almost suburban. But the area where Ryan Stoner's body had been found had lain unkempt for years. One day, not too far in the future, it would be carved up by an arterial road; already the cranes were working across the river, their gantries swinging in the dusk.

I made my way through the scrub, trying not to think about rats. My foot crunched on something plastic half-buried in the grass. A

Sainsbury's carrier bag was caught in the branches of a stunted hawthorn. Drinks cans flashed garishly among the nettles.

I scrambled down the steep bank and hesitated. A lone police officer was guarding the place where Ryan's body had been found, an area marked by striped tape, a patch of scrub otherwise indistinguishable from the rest of the riverbank, with its nettles, dock leaves, mud and rubbish.

He looked up as I slithered uncertainly down the steep sides of the bank. He was scarcely more than a boy himself.

'Helen Clare,' I said. 'From the *Sunday Chronicle*.' I fished my press card out of my bag and showed him. 'I'm writing a background piece. I . . . wanted to see the place.'

'Not much of a place,' he said.

'He was strangled?'

'Apparently.'

With his school tie. It had been in all the papers.

'Sexually assaulted?'

'You'll have to talk to the press office.'

'Sure.' Not sexually assaulted, they thought. 'Mind if I stroll around?'

The police officer shook his head. I walked up and down the bank, watching the brackish water churn past the untidy banks, wondering about the man who had found Ryan's body. Out for a walk with his dog. Thinking, no doubt, about something else entirely.

If Ryan had lived, I thought, he might have got away from the Garden Estate. He might have acquired an education, new friends, a different life. Perhaps he'd have travelled, done interesting work, met rich and influential people and not felt intimidated or patronised by them; he might even have reached the point where he felt his background had been an advantage. All this was possible, I knew, although not now for Ryan.

I thanked the police officer, then scrambled back up the bank, through the broken wire-netting fence, and back across the grass to the car. I was glad to get back inside, to feel cocooned again from the rain and wind and squalid little landscape. I slipped a cassette into the machine and concentrated on Courtney Pine all the way back to the City.

*   *   *

'You're sure you got the wording right, about the debts?' Dan asked doubtfully.

We were in a bar round the corner from my office in Smithfield: a place of glass and steel, where the waitresses wore little Lycra wraps round their bottoms, more pelmets than skirts, and served expensive warm salad leaves. The place, Fred's, had only been open a couple of weeks and could hardly have been more improbably situated, but perhaps that accounted in part for its popularity: it was heaving with expensively dressed young people who made me feel I hadn't made enough effort.

Smithfield wasn't like this during the day. Whenever I walked (as I usually did) through the market in the mornings, I had to shut my senses to the gutters bright with blood and the pigeons picking disconsolately among the scraps of decaying flesh. Smithfield was run-down, and, at least until lunch-time, smelt foul. Such offices as there were, like the one I shared with Sarah in an alley off St John's Street, were grimy and decaying. But Fred's was a triumph of plate glass, stainless steel and smooth black granite, dynamically pristine.

'Of course I'm sure,' I answered crossly.

'It doesn't make sense,' Dan grumbled. 'His wife wasn't aware of any money troubles. They lived in a £150,000 house with a £20,000 mortgage in Bradford and had no trouble finding the rent on the flat in Dolphin Square he occupied during the week. The money was never late – we checked. In fact we've spoken to everyone, from ministerial drivers to his cleaner, and no one can understand it. You'd think if there was something seriously amiss . . . But there's no hint of a girlfriend, no suggestion he had his hands in the till. He was a full-time, professional, no-nonsense politician. Liked the job, took it seriously, did it well. Not a high-flier maybe, but that's not a reason to kill yourself.'

I frowned. Dan seemed to expect me to have the answers. I'd only found the poor man's body.

'Elise never moved down here?'

'She hated London: couldn't be doing with the Westminster social circuit. She had lots of friends in Bradford, a nice house and her own hairdressing business. There was a lot to keep her there and nothing to attract her here.'

'Except him.'

'We can't find anyone to say their marriage was in trouble. Which is not to say it wasn't. But as far as the money's concerned, she'd been earning all her life – probably better than him a fair bit of the time. As far as we can see, their greatest extravagance was an annual fortnight in Portugal. Excluding the odd trip to the steakhouse with friends and the beers after constituency meetings.' His voice had grown sarcastic. 'Seems more likely he'd have committed suicide from boredom than bankruptcy.'

'There was something odd about the syntax of that note – "debts to pay that I cannot repay". Surely you'd simply say, "I have debts," if you meant money? He could have been talking about something else entirely.'

'That's why I think you ought to look into this Asian woman candidate angle.'

'Dan,' I complained, 'I'm seeing Ryan Stoner's mother tomorrow, Simon Healy again on Monday, and I've got to finish off this piece you want about finding Bagnall's body. I don't have time.' For someone who regarded herself as a specialist in trivia, I was getting bogged down in a hell of a lot of heavyweight stories.

'Come on, you know more about this Asian woman than anyone else – it's a bloody scoop!'

'I don't even know her name.'

'And as the person who found the body,' Dan ignored me, 'you've got the best possible way in with Elise. And then there's another thing. Bagnall's secretary wasn't there, was she?'

'No . . .'

'There's a rumour doing the rounds of the Commons secretaries she got a call asking her to go somewhere and pick up a package for Bagnall, but when she got there – wherever it was – there was no one there, and no package either.'

'Where?'

'We don't know.'

'How reliable is this rumour?'

'I thought you might like to check it out. Oh, Peach, come on, this is one story you can't avoid – you're already in up to your neck.'

'Send one of the news boys.' Dan's news boys are always boys, even when they're girls.

'We've tried. The bloody secretary woman – June Lennox – is on sick leave, and we haven't managed to track her down. Sends messages to us through the other one – Halliday? – that she doesn't want to talk, too upset. I know: she'll get over it, but by then she'll be talking to everyone. Whereas you have a real opportunity: you're upset too, and you met Halliday. You're all in it together.'

He waved a waitress across and ordered another couple of beers.

'I don't see how I can possibly do it in time to be useful to you.'

'Think about it.'

I drained my glass. Things have changed a lot since Dan and I were at university in Manchester together. I'd been editing the student newspaper when Dan turned up one Thursday afternoon at the start of the autumn term and begged for a reporting assignment. He'd worn glasses then, and orange hand-knitted jumpers made by his grandmother, who appeared not to understand that when you dropped a stitch you were supposed to pick it up. He developed crushes on every girl on the paper, one after another. He'd trail around after them for weeks, until they were driven to explain painfully, in words of one syllable, that they didn't want to go out with him.

Fortunately for his ego, he was also a very good journalist. He took over as editor when I had to step down to concentrate on my finals. At around the same time, he also acquired the habit of putting on clean underwear in the mornings. After he bought a batch of collarless white cotton shirts in the market, a few of the newer girls who hadn't known him in his previous hideous incarnation started getting crushes on him.

I got the first in finals, but he got the job on a national newspaper afterwards.

'David Ivison's gone,' he told me now.

'No. When?'

'This afternoon. Took his time. Thirty-six bloody hours after the story broke.'

'He must have thought he could get away with it . . .'

'Incredible. Knocks up his secretary, thinks it won't make a difference.'

'It happens,' I said. Dan's own morality is hardly exemplary. If his girlfriends don't get pregnant it's mainly because they don't get a chance: he rarely sleeps with anyone more than once. He started wearing contact lenses when he left university and developed a reputation for being attractive to women. I could never see it myself. But there's been no stopping him since. I think this was when the objectionable Peach thing began.

'It's not supposed to happen to politicians,' Dan said severely. 'Your friend Simon Healy will be looking more smug than ever.'

'He's not my friend. I think I've had three lunches with him in my entire life. And I was practically a child at the time. Though he did get George Dalmore to call me this morning.'

'Always one to pay attention to detail.'

'He's very effective.' I toyed with a dish of olives. 'I wonder why he never attempted to become an MP?'

'Decided a long time ago he didn't look the part. Too small and predatory. Funny eyes. Not like George Dalmore, who, our latest great newspaper survey tells us, is the politician most women want to go to bed with. I hope you're not going soft on Healy?'

'Of course not.'

But I had no reason to dislike Simon Healy, who had been, this time as before, perfectly pleasant to me – no, more than pleasant: considerate. I had never been entirely convinced by the media myth of the pocket Machiavelli, and now I was less persuaded of it than ever. Having been the subject of a media myth myself ('Slum girl wins top journalism award'), I suspected Simon Healy's image told less than the whole truth. Perhaps it suited him to be thought crafty and venomous.

'Why should he bother, anyway?' Dan went on. 'He has as much power as Dalmore, fifteen years earlier. He doesn't have constituents to pester him about their gas bills or take offence if he scowls in the street. All the time George Dalmore's hurtling about and performing, Simon Healy's scheming.'

'Maybe he's only scheming about what to have for tea. Maybe it suits him to have everyone thinking he's constantly plotting and manipulating.'

'You *have* fallen for it. Simon Healy was scheming in his cradle. How d'you think he's got so far so fast?'

'Look, I'm the one who used to know him. And all the things people say – that he's ruthlessly self-seeking, and looking for his own advantage – simply aren't true. Not in my experience. You shouldn't believe everything you read in the newspapers.' Dan scowled into his drink. 'You've got a thing about him.'

'I have not!'

But he had. When Simon Healy was being touted as a sort of youthful comet, lighting up the British media, Dan was struggling in the bottom reaches of national newspapers. Simon had been to Balliol College, Oxford, Dan had been to Manchester. It was a boys' competition thing, and Dan still minded. Ridiculous, now they were both so successful.

'So what if I have?' Dan said grumpily. 'Jumped up little man. There's something wrong when a bloke like that gets a girl like Hester Allan.'

There wasn't much I could say by way of consolation. I'd interviewed Hester Allan the previous week and she was stunning. She had tumbling red curls, softly freckled small features, and had been able to wear for the interview a skimpy T-shirt and drainpipe trousers, revealing a stomach that was virtually concave. That was a girls' competition thing, of course.

She also had an air of naïve but appealing enthusiasm: she'd told me about her parents, her cat, the progress of her acting career, the row she'd had with Healy the first time she'd met him, her plans for their wedding in the autumn and what she wanted to do with their flat. Our meeting had lasted two and a half hours, and only ended then because I had an appointment on the other side of town.

'Dan,' I tried again, 'you can't seriously expect me to write about Ryan Stoner and investigate Tony Bagnall . . .'

But Dan's gaze had snagged on some stocking tops, and he wasn't listening.

Bobby was in when I got home, which was unusual: often the only indication that Bobby exists at all is a sprinkling of talcum powder and heap of damp towels which appear intermittently on the bathroom floor. This state of affairs – sharing the house but not each other's lives – suits us both very well. The only drawback for me is the difficulty I have explaining it to my mother, who has never quite got to grips with the idea that I am not married to Bobby but only his lodger. She seems to imagine we hurry home to each other every evening, me to prepare him tempting suppers, he to protect me from the unpleasant characters who roam the East End streets.

Since my mother moved out to Essex, she has made it her goal to conceal, possibly even from herself, that she was born in Stepney. A part of her hated it when I became moderately well-known as a journalist, because occasional scraps of information would slip out about my having lived on a council estate in the East End until I was sixteen. My mother, I think, imagines her acquaintances don't know this. And perhaps they don't. Apart from the fact that her accent very occasionally slips, she gives little away.

I have tried to explain to her the complexities of Bobby's love life. He is, for example, currently having an affair with a married woman who also happens to be his boss. And this is by no means as baroque as it gets. I've tried to make her see there's no room for me. But she doesn't seem able to grasp the point that he's not my husband. If she thinks about it at all, I dare say she imagines that a husband with whom you don't have to have sex is, in any case, in many ways preferable.

For me, however, one of Bobby's several attractions as a live-in landlord is that between the travelling for his work and the shuttling between his women, he's almost never at home. For him, I suspect, the opposite is true: I'm useful primarily because I'm so often in, switching on lights and playing music. I don't have boyfriends, except on the briefest basis, and I don't mind washing up.

Tonight, however, Bobby was sprawled on the sofa in the basement watching the football game.

'Hi,' he said, when I walked in. 'You OK? You were all over the papers this morning.'

'How is it?' I perched on the arm of the sofa. The score was nil-nil but they'd only been playing fifteen minutes. Bobby and I share an enthusiasm for football which can irritate other people.

'The Italians are in control. England can't seem to find their rhythm. Oh, some guy called for you.'

'Uh-huh?'

'Joe someone?'

'Rossiter?'

'Yeah, that's it. Very anxious you should get back to him. I left his number somewhere.' He looked around vaguely then pulled a piece of paper from the pocket of his jeans.

It was a 219 number, the same as the Houses of Parliament. Joe's office, probably. I backed out of the room, still watching the television, then went upstairs and dialled. Joe picked up the receiver immediately. He was still working.

'I called you three times today. I didn't leave messages because I've been in endless meetings. Are you all right?'

'Slightly disconcerted by seeing my career all over the papers, but otherwise fine.'

'What did that bloke say in the *Daily News*? You have a knack of walking into trouble.'

'I'm not sure that's so flattering.'

'Oh, I don't know. And there's a lot more that was incredibly flattering . . . I've got it here. I could read it out to you.'

'No thanks,' I said hastily.

'Look, I wondered if I could – if you'd like to have dinner with me? The only trouble is, I leave for Washington for almost a week on Sunday morning, I have a meeting with George later tonight, and I'm due at Penny Dalmore's birthday dinner tomorrow. But – perhaps you'd like to come?'

'To Penny's?'

'Sure.'

'Can you take just anyone along?'

'You're not just anyone. And it'll be very informal: in their kitchen, a few close friends.'

'I've never even met her.'

'Doesn't matter. She understands. I already checked.'

If Penny Dalmore didn't mind a perfect stranger barging in on her dinner, I certainly couldn't think of a reason to say no. Joe aside, the temptation to attend Penny Dalmore's birthday party would have been considerable. But Joe was not aside. I was interested in Joe. I felt I might have been prepared to spend the evening learning about quantum mechanics if he thought it was a good idea. He was the first man I'd met in five years for whom I'd been able to summon anything beyond a low-level sexual excitement. And as he said, it would be a shame to wait a whole week.

Bobby was no longer sprawled on the sofa when I went back downstairs. He was sitting upright staring at the screen. He looked horrified.

The football stadium was in uproar: many of the England fans were out of their seats, booing, throwing bottles and scuffling with each other; the Italian police were having to clamber over the seats. Young men were being dragged away.

I sank down next to Bobby and stared at the pictures of a group of skinheads with Union Jacks painted on their faces ripping seats from the stands. This was why I didn't go to matches very much any more.

The trouble was spreading. Spectators who were nearby but not involved tried to move away but their exit was blocked. The belligerent atmosphere, aggression tinged with fear, was almost palpable as it fanned through the crowd, spread round the stadium like an upside-down, perverse Mexican wave.

'What happened?'

'The English fans rioted. Don't ask me to explain.'

He caught sight of my expression and relented. 'They started booing Martin Maynard.'

'No . . . Why?'

'Christ knows. He just scored.' Maynard was black and one of England's two best strikers. 'Don't ask me, Helen, I'm an American. They're your people. And they're throwing seats at their own supporters.'

Fifteen fans were taken to hospital, the majority because they'd been hit by missiles raining down from above, a few following scuffles. But these were minor things, ancillary scraps. The instigators – and the police seemed convinced the trouble had been started deliberately – seemed to have vanished.

The Italian police said it was sheer luck no one had been killed, and that they'd had no option but to use the batons and CS gas.

The English police insisted there had been excellent liaison between themselves and their Milanese counterparts; unfortunately, a small group of people, believed to be British neo-fascists, had evaded security checks and travelled to Italy with the aim of causing trouble.

Bobby and I watched until the police had emptied the stadium, leaving behind ruined stands, seats in mangled piles. Where thousands of people should still have been sitting enjoying themselves, there were only a few shredded European flags, their bright stars smeared with faeces. It seemed a dispiritingly apt epitaph for the evening's entertainment.

Chapter Four

THE GARDEN ESTATE WAS thrown up in the mid-sixties, part of the post-war slum-clearance projects designed to decimate those parts of the East End that hadn't already been destroyed by bombers. Arriving to interview Mrs Stoner, I found the place had the power to trip-switch me back to the age of twelve, when I used to make my way home from school along these windy walkways to a flat overlooking a grassy square used by defecating dogs, and, consequently, by no one else.

The Stoners lived in a different block from the one my mother and I had occupied, on the other side of the square. Theirs was low-rise (since our day the council had stopped housing young mothers on the fourteenth floor), and built of an unfortunate combination of grey and red brick, with panelled metal balconies, now, inexplicably, painted a vicious, seething turquoise. The smells were the same, though. As I climbed the stairs to the first floor, I breathed in the familiar, powerful blend of rotting vegetables, rising from communal dustbins, and gravy, drifting downwards from above. The views hadn't changed either: the blasted open spaces, the net-curtained windows of other flats opposite, the 'No Ball Games' signs.

The place was noisier than it used to be: at the end of the road, heavy goods vehicles lurched and rattled eastwards. There was also more anxiety: at least half the flats were sealed like miniature Fort Knoxes, metal grilles on their front doors and windows. Ironic, considering how poor you had to be to live here. Addicts will steal anything.

Mrs Stoner answered her front door. She was dressed in jeans and a T-shirt, which had a picture, like a photographic negative, of an indistinct heavy metal band on the front. A tissue was balled in her fist. She can't have been all that much older than me, with shoulder-length hair cut in layers and a pretty face hardened by harassment.

She showed me into the living room, where she sat in an armchair, pulling at her tissue, and introduced me to her surviving child, Katrina, who was three years older than Ryan.

There were photographs of Ryan on the television, the mantel-piece, the shelves. I thought of my own mother, and of how I ought to call her. I didn't call her often enough.

Ryan was an exceptionally good-looking child, with dark-lashed eyes and clear skin – quite different from Katrina, who had her mother's thin, mousy hair and pale eyes. But Katrina had a steady, intelligent gaze behind her glasses; she sat solemnly on the edge of her chair listening to her mother, her expression tinged with anxiety.

Mrs Stoner spoke rapidly, her eyes darting around the room, her face flushed. She was fighting off hysteria.

Ryan, she said, had never been in trouble; not that it had been easy keeping him *out* of it round here, especially without a husband. The children's father had gone off up North with some woman he met in a pub when Ryan was three; they'd only seen him five times since.

'A lot of kids round here are known to the police by the time they're Ryan's age, but he'd never been picked up for anything.' She clenched her tissue tighter. 'You can't afford to make them soppy, because then they're in even more danger, but you can't have them thinking the boys who hang around in the square doing drugs and talking tough are smart and clever either, which is what they do think, given half a chance. Ryan, though, was a good, sweet boy – very loving to me – and we were a close family. You have to go on hoping that that's what'll matter in the end, don't you?'

I nodded, feeling desperately sorry for her, and asked how Ryan had been doing at school.

'He was a clever kid – well, he got that from his dad. For all his faults, the drifting and all, their dad was clever, and Ryan inherited his brains. He was doing well.' Katrina, it emerged, was also doing well: she had won a scholarship when she was eleven and now travelled into the centre of town every day, learnt Latin and played games on proper sports fields. They'd been hoping Ryan might do something like that too.

'I wish they'd catch him, whoever was responsible,' Mrs Stoner said, dabbing her eyes. 'Knowing he's still out there . . .'

'I don't suppose there's anyone Ryan might have gone off with, willingly?'

There wasn't. Not that she knew of. And yet, it had been late afternoon, early evening, and no one had heard Ryan shouting, as he surely would have done if he'd been *snatched*. There had been no signs of a scuffle.

'He wouldn't have gone with anyone he didn't know,' she said helplessly. 'He knew not to – he'd always known not to. And he wasn't silly: he couldn't have been bribed.'

'Did he have adult friends?'

'We've lived in this flat for fifteen years. People know us, and Ryan was a likeable kid: he'd be on speaking terms with a lot of the neighbours. But I still don't think he'd have gone off willingly with one of them – he knew I wanted to see the paper, for the telly. I don't even think he'd have gone off with a teacher from school or someone from the boys' club.'

'The boys' club?'

'The Lord N'peer.'

I knew where she meant; the Lord N'peer had been in existence when I was a child. It was spelt Napier, although never, here, properly pronounced.

Mrs Stoner was so evidently puzzled that I knew the place, I found myself having to explain about growing up across the square – and, because one thing led to another, I also found myself telling her that I'd won a scholarship, like Katrina, and about how we'd moved out when I was sixteen, after my mother married the doctor.

'I encouraged him to spend time there because it seemed better than mooching about round the flats,' Mrs Stoner said, keen to get back to Ryan. 'They had to do proper activities: table tennis, football, snooker. The bloke there, the leader, manager, whatever, he's called Stewart Saddler. There are others help out, but I don't know their names. Stew, they call him.'

'Ryan got on well with him?'

'Yes, I think so. But that's not to say he'd have gone off to Hackney

Marshes with him, not when he was supposed to be coming home. I think it must've been someone he didn't know.'

'He hadn't been different in the months before he died?'

She shook her head. 'He did some exams – for schools – and hadn't had the results, so he was sometimes a bit quiet. But he was always my Ryan. I'd have noticed if anything was different.'

We looked in Ryan's bedroom. The walls were covered in posters of footballers and pop stars. His pyjamas were still laid out ready for him on the bed. Mrs Stoner got out some old photographs: she wanted to show me how he'd been as a baby. Adorable, with a vulnerable bald head and bright eyes.

'Not much chance of me marrying my doctor,' she said eventually, trying bravely to find something to smile about, as I gathered up my belongings to leave. 'Stuck here with the cockroaches, that's me.'

Outside the front door, I paused to take in the scruffy gardens below. The Stoners had a hanging basket outside their front door. No one else did. I walked slowly downstairs and out into the square.

I was nearly at the main road when I heard footsteps on the pavement behind me. Turning, I saw Katrina thudding towards me, pony-tail slapping on her shoulders.

'I told Mum you'd dropped this,' she said breathlessly when she got close. She was clutching a blue hardback notebook with red binding. She pushed me towards the corner, immensely agitated. 'Ryan *was* different in the months before he died,' she said. 'I think it might have something to do with this.' She pushed the book at me urgently, then glanced over her shoulder. 'He did get quieter – but it wasn't exams. He was upset about something else. He didn't let Mum see – he wouldn't have wanted to bother her, and she would never have noticed because . . . well, she couldn't: he was her little boy. He didn't say anything to me either, and when I asked him if something was wrong he said no. But I could tell. And then after he disappeared I went into his room, thinking there might be some clue, and I found this, hidden under the carpet beneath his bed.'

I frowned. 'What is it?'

'A book he wrote in. Sort of a diary.'

'Did you tell the police?'

She reddened. 'I didn't like them – the officers who came. I didn't like the things they were saying about Ryan, the way they were talking. I thought they might think the wrong things and if

I let them have it that things might come out – about Ryan. I was going to burn it.'

'What do you want me to do with it?'

'Look at it – what is it? – off the record. Tell me what you think, if I should burn it.' She blinked at me in alarm. 'You won't print it or anything? Or show anyone else? You promise?'

'I promise.'

'And you won't tell *anyone*? Whatever you find out about Ryan, you won't tell anyone, without speaking to me first? You promise?'

'I promise.'

She looked at me, as if in two minds, then pushed the book into my hands. 'OK, then,' she said, '*no one.*'

And then she fled.

I sat with the key in the ignition turning Ryan Stoner's notebook over in my hands. Perhaps Katrina was exaggerating its importance. Somehow, though, I didn't think so.

Lorries were thundering past in the road beside me, jolting my small car and poisoning the air with their belching fumes. I couldn't possibly read the diary here; I laid it carefully on the passenger seat and put the car in gear.

When I got home, I made myself a pot of tea in our basement kitchen and took it upstairs to the sitting room. Then I opened the book.

Ryan had begun his diary five or six months earlier and kept it intermittently since. It was three-quarters filled with neat, childish handwriting. I thought initially that most of it was going to be about football: the first entry, for 10 October, seemed typical. 'Today is Dean's birthday. He got a Spurs away strip, and he's going to wear it to play at the Lord Napier tomorrow. I don't think I am going.'

But as I read on, it gradually became clear that, between the match reports, a horror story was unfolding.

October 11, I read, Mum asked if I was going down the Lord Napier, and I didn't know what to say, so I went.

October 15. Stew said he was still thinking whether to talk to Mum. Barsted. Everything was all right before.

October 16. Spurs beat Leeds 1–0. Wicked.

October 20. Stew had a proposal, he said. Dean thinks we should do it, and ask for money.

October 22. Stew said if we didn't do what he said he would arrange to talk to our mums. When Dean asked about money he said we would get some. Katrina was winding me up all evening, saying I am not doing enough work to get into a good school. Sod her. Perhaps I will mess up the exams so I can go to Greenfield with Dean.

October 23. Spurs lost 1–0 to Liverpool (away). The defence was crap. Tomorrow is the big night, ha ha.

October 25. Now perhaps Stew will shut up. I hate him. Dean suddenly said at school we should tell, but it is a bit late now. They wouldn't believe us anyway and then that other stuff would come out. Stew said it will be over soon. We had to go over the Marshes. It didn't last too long, thank God who I don't believe in. He was called John. I didn't see him properly but he was a pervert.

October 26. Oh no. Stew is not going to go away or stop. Now he has really got something on us. Perhaps we should tell, except Stew said we did it willingly. He said next time there would be money. Dean said his was OK, and he wouldn't mind doing it if it meant he could get a mountain bike. I don't want to.

November 2. Mr Morrison told me off for not concentrating. He said I had got useless in the last two weeks, and if I went on like this he would speak to Mum. I have got three exams next week. I told him I don't bloody care about exams or stupid schoolwork and he sent me to Mrs August for telling off. I had to sit outside her room. She said I used to be nice and was I worried about something. I wish she had just shouted.

November 16. I have been doing exams. I cried in one of them. No one saw. I don't think I have passed. I haven't been down the Lord Napier because of the exams. Dean said today Stew wanted to know where I was and if I didn't come back, he would come round and find me. If he wants me to go over Hackney Marshes again, I am not going.

November 22. Stew threatened me about telling. So I went, and it was John again. At least I knew what to expect this time, but it was still horrible. He is all hairy and huge. He doesn't say anything and I can't properly see his face. But he runs his hands all over my face. He says I am beautiful. I'm not beautiful. Anyway, I'd rather be ugly, so he will leave me alone.

I closed my eyes. How had this been allowed to happen? How had Ryan, sweet-faced, clever Ryan, got himself into this mess, meeting some man in the dark on Hackney Marshes? And who, for God's sake, was Stew that he could get away with this, running a boys' club and recruiting for paedophiles?

My tea grew cold as Ryan described in childish prose his seduction into a rent-boy ring; and as the tale progressed, his voice – defiant in October – seemed to grow wavering. By Christmas he seemed to have lost all sense of himself.

He appeared to have met the man John ten times in all. There was no mention of any other client.

John said he wouldn't be here for two weeks [he wrote, towards the end of December]. Last night I had the dream again. [This was a recurrent dream of being chased, running to escape, and colliding with Stew, by which time he was so frightened he woke up.] I don't want Christmas to come because Mum and Katrina will want me to like my presents and everything. Mr Morrison said was I depressed? I think I am, but I'm so depressed I don't even care that I am depressed. Sometimes I quite like being with John. He is kind and friendly, and sometimes the feelings are nice. Dean and I have stopped talking about it. We only talk about Spurs.

And then, ten days before Ryan's disappearance, the tone changed again.

Dear Diary [Ryan wrote self-importantly on March 15],
Stew says it will stop if I do what he says. I am going to do this, because it is not such a big thing to say anyway. He has shown me some photographs.

A week later came the final entry:

Went down the Lord Napier. I wanted to scare Stew so I told him I'd seen John before. He grabbed my arm and said what did I mean. He was hurting my arm, the barsted, so I told him to fuck off and if he made me go over Hackney Marshes again I'd tell everyone about John and him and everything. He said to shut up or he'd kill me. I think he would, too. I really, really hate him.

Chapter Five

BY THE TIME I'D finished reading Ryan's diary it was too late to get to the Lord Napier. But that probably wasn't a bad thing; I ought to calm down before I tackled Stewart Saddler.

I went upstairs and sat staring at the computer screen in the study. I was supposed to be recalling my discovery of Bagnall's body for the readers of the *Sunday Chronicle*. The piece had to be filed tomorrow.

The words swam in front of my eyes; I was haunted by images of a boy and a man on the Marshes. What was he like, this man? How could Ryan have let it happen – go on happening?

I went downstairs and fixed myself a cup of strong coffee, which made my head buzz but didn't help me concentrate on Bagnall. How had Stewart Saddler persuaded Ryan and Dean to go to Hackney Marshes in the first place? Had he taken other boys there before them? Who was he, that he could run a boys' club and do this? Was there no one in authority to monitor him, make sure this sort of thing didn't happen? Who was John? What had Ryan been hoping would stop the sessions on the Marshes?

The questions came and went, the same ones over and over, round and round in circles like a word repeated until it becomes senseless. I would have to see this Stewart Saddler. I would have to go to the Lord Napier and try to understand what was going on. The boys were so *young*. I would have to hand the diary to the police . . . except that I couldn't do that without Katrina's permission. I'd have to persuade Katrina it was the only thing to do.

I could see why she'd been worried; the diary would hurt her mother horribly. But Stewart Saddler could still be recruiting.

I tried to focus on Bagnall's body suspended from ceiling pipes in his office, to recall what I had *felt*; that was what they wanted to know. I tried to think of a way of describing it. Somehow it no longer seemed so shocking. It was difficult to think about anything except Ryan's diary.

It was hopeless. I was getting nowhere. I walked up and down the study. I went downstairs and ate some chocolate. I picked up the evening paper and read about last night's football riots.

It was surprising how much the police seemed to know. They claimed the rioters weren't proper football supporters but almost certainly members of an organisation called the Patriots. I'd never heard of the Patriots but, according to the police, they were loosely linked to the National Front, only nastier. They didn't even pretend to be interested in parliamentary democracy. And they were thugs – though not kids: most were in their twenties and thirties. They hated foreigners and thought immigrants should be repatriated and that multiculturalism was a threat to British identity. They were trained in armed and unarmed combat, and committed to taking their message onto the streets.

They sounded delightful. I went back upstairs, ate an orange, dripped the juice all over the newspaper, then had to throw it in the bin. I sucked at my fingers, not wanting to get juice on the keyboard. The words swam in front of my eyes. I found it hard to think about anything except Ryan; his phrases kept insinuating themselves into my brain, crowding out everything else.

Exasperatedly, I printed off what little copy I'd written, threw on my coat, and went out.

I knew more about Ryan Stoner's death than anyone except Katrina, I thought, as I drove towards the brightly lit towers of docklands. I would have to try to persuade her to hand the book to the police, whatever that meant might come out about Ryan.

A drunk threw a beer can into the road as I turned onto the empty dual carriageway leading down to the *Chronicle*'s offices; it rattled across the tarmac and flattened with a clunk under the wheels of my car. The woman who had sent it spinning into the road lived in a hostel a few yards outside the dockland development's security gates. Drunks were always standing in the street outside the building shouting up to their friends above or leaning out of the windows yelling obscenities down. You had to be careful because they were inclined to wander wildly into the road and you could knock them over.

I gave my name at the security barrier and was allowed in. Brightly lit buildings reared up at me on either side, bordered by riverside walkways, fountains and beds of bright daffodils picked out by spotlights in the darkness. A patrolling security guard in the underground car park watched me into the mirrored lift.

The staff of the *Chronicle* attempted to deal with the glass and marble overload by making as much mess as they possibly could, as if they were mysteriously incapable of functioning without piles of yellowing back copies of newspapers all over the floor or paper and books settling in drifts in the corners. Desks were covered in flat-plans, photographs and scribbled notes that might have been years old or vital to the next edition, and dotted with plastic cups containing cold coffee and plates of congealing canteen food. At ten o'clock on a Friday evening, the journalists were also looking pretty wrecked. Sandra Snugrood, the paper's star feature writer, was running her fingers through her hair in a distracted manner and repeatedly muttering, 'Oh, shit!' dramatically. She looked as though she'd been up for at least twenty-four hours. Dan claimed she deliberately took off her make-up after lunch on Fridays so as to look more pressurised. Robin Rouse was visible in his glass-walled office at the end of the floor, a half-drunk bottle of wine in front of him, his feet on the desk and his shirt sleeves rolled up to his elbows, blinking donnishly at Frank Threshfield, the political editor, as he marched up and down in front of him gesticulating.

'Peach, what a nice surprise,' Dan said unconvincingly, when I appeared in front of his desk. 'We weren't expecting you till the morning.'

'I know you're busy. There were a couple of things I wanted to check with the library.'

'Find yourself a desk.' He looked up from the piece he was editing. 'Were you seeing the Stoner woman today? Only we could do with the copy this week, because unless they find the killer everyone will have forgotten about him by next Sunday.'

It might have been better if I'd told Dan the truth then. It might have saved trouble later. But I'd promised Katrina.

'I've got a colour piece.'

'Can you knock something out? Fifteen hundred words?'

'As well as Bagnall?' I asked, aghast.

'Yes, Peach, it's called journalism. And next week I want you in Bradford. We haven't got anywhere near this suicide yet. The debts don't seem to have been anything to do with money. So what was he going on about? He led a blameless life, as far as we can see: didn't even have any politics to speak of.'

'Except a rather out-of-character enthusiasm for Europe.'

'Was it? Out of character, I mean. Seems to me a fairly typical position for that kind of politician.'

'Oh.'

'Unreconstructed socialism. There's a certain kind of left-winger who still sees the possibility of Utopia in Europe – you know, minimum wages, social chapter, all that stuff.'

'Oh. I hadn't thought of it like that.'

'No, well, exactly. Bagnall's Euro-mania isn't interesting: it's not as if he ever *said* anything, made any important speeches.'

'What *do* you think, then?'

'You should quiz his wife about these problems he was supposed to be having in the constituency. The Party's backtracking on that now, but I bet that's only because they don't want us to think there's any racial tension so close to an election. Seems to me quite likely that Simon Healy blurted out the truth in the shock of the moment. Now, the other thing I meant to ask you was . . .' He frowned. 'What was it? Oh, yes, did you speak to the secretary?'

I had been in touch with Susan Halliday earlier in the day: she had apologised, but explained that she absolutely couldn't help. June Lennox, Tony Bagnall's secretary, had decided she didn't want to talk to the press, which unfortunately included even me. Susan appreciated my point that I was in a slightly different position from everyone else, having actually *found* the poor man, but June wasn't making exceptions.

I had explained to her how upset I was about finding Bagnall's body and my feeling that it might help to know what sort of person he'd been: what it had been like to work for him, for example. I was involved and affected; it was different for me.

I was mildly surprised to discover how easy it was to slip back into proper journalism's half-truths.

Susan said she could see all that, but she'd had her instructions from June, who was at home in the suburbs – Susan was careful not to say which suburb exactly – and ex-directory.

'The telephone call she had that morning—'

'I don't know anything about it. Truly. I've hardly seen her. I'd like to help you, Helen – I mean, this has been difficult for me too – but she's been away ever since that morning. All I know is, she's told the police everything she could, and issued me with instructions to keep the media away. So I'm to refer everyone wanting information for tributes or obituaries or whatever to the constituency chairman, and everyone wanting to know about Tony's death to the police. I'm sorry . . . Look, dear, I hope you won't take this the wrong way, but if you're finding it difficult to come to terms with the experience, have you considered counselling?'

I muttered something to the effect that I thought I'd probably be OK. 'Could you at least tell June I called? And that I wanted to ask her about these rumours circulating in newspaper offices that she had some kind of hoax phone call the morning Tony Bagnall died.'

Susan promised she'd do what she could, but she didn't seem to think it would make any difference.

I fed as much of this to Dan as he needed to know.

'I'll keep trying,' I promised, 'but I don't think I'm going to have any success. I also called Elise Bagnall, and after much persuasion, got her to see me on Tuesday. It wasn't easy: she's had reporters hanging round the house all week.'

'Those news boys!' Dan said despairingly. 'I've taken them off the story. They were never going to get Elise Bagnall to talk to them. Sometimes an investigation needs a woman's touch.'

Dan might be convinced Tony Bagnall's role as chairman of Labour's backbench Brussels Group was irrelevant; I wasn't so sure. Something I'd read in the accounts of David Ivison's resignation had rung alarm bells, and now I wanted to check the files on the other Tory MPs who had resigned their ministerial positions following scandals: Gunnel and Fletcher, Barry Bianchini and Geoffrey Doxat.

I dumped my bag at a spare desk, collected a cup of coffee from the machine, and tapped into the library files.

Re-reading the Fletcher-Gunnel story, I had vivid memories of the salacious thrill that had gripped the country the weekend the news of their liaison broke. I'd been visiting my mother, I remembered, and even she had been distracted from her habitual preoccupation with when I would marry again and whether it would be before I lost my looks.

Some people – Dan claimed subsequently to have been one of them – had always known both men were homosexual. It had been gossip at what Dan called fashionable dinner parties (ones I didn't attend, he meant) for years. But such things are not always easily proved, and sometimes there's even a disinclination to prove them. The press exercised considerable, perhaps surprising, delicacy over Gunnel and Fletcher – tittering at Dan's fashionable dinner parties, but leaving them alone – until love letters (love letters! how could they have been so stupid?) fell into the hands of a reporter on one of the Sunday tabloids.

All hell broke loose. This was unfortunate for Barry Bianchini, the Home Secretary's PPS, news of whose liaison with Lady Hughes might not otherwise have caused such a commotion. As it was, no sooner had the first scandal come off the front pages than Bianchini and Hughes took its place. Forced by the disclosure of the relationship to choose between his wife and Lady Hughes, Barry Bianchini opted for life with his fundraising friend and a setback to his parliamentary career.

The Prime Minister had only just tidied *that* one up, when David Ivison's secretary announced her pregnancy. She'd clearly been hoping the young millionaire entrepreneur would do the decent thing and marry her. In fact, it was rapidly becoming apparent that he had no intention of leaving his wife, although it remained to be seen whether Mrs Ivison would yet decide she was better off on her own with half the fortune.

None of it, though, not even the gay ministerial love letters, would have mattered quite so much if the Government hadn't spent the past four years arguing the importance of personal morality. Morality matters, the Home Office minister Ian Moorhouse was always saying; and what's more, it's the business of the Government to enforce it. So when members of the Government were found to be breaking up families – their own and other people's – with a kind of reckless abandon, it was easy for the press to justify any amount of prurient coverage as the quite proper exposure of hypocrisy.

Not that this was really important right now. I was looking for something else.

And before very long, I found it. I started with the files on Andrew Gunnel who, until his resignation, had been the Prime Minister's closest ally in the cabinet.

With his Old Etonian, diplomatic background, Andrew Gunnel could scarcely have been more different from James Sherlock, who had been educated at a minor public school in Essex and gone straight to work in his uncle's estate agency business. Gunnel had class and a good brain. Sherlock had wealth and political cunning, and he'd convinced the Conservatives he was the man to unite them, even if the unity was precarious, constantly under threat from an increasingly vocal right wing. Gunnel had kept him from veering too far in their direction: without Gunnel, it was said, James Sherlock might have been prepared to concede a referendum on a single European currency.

I made a separate file and copied into it the information on Gunnel I wanted to keep. Then I turned to the others. I was right about David Ivison: he'd made a speech at last year's Party Conference in defence of the European Union. I turned to Ellis Fletcher, Geoffrey Doxat and Barry Bianchini.

I still wasn't entirely sure where this was leading, but there was definitely *something* in it.

And then I drew a blank. Reams of column inches had been devoted to Ellis Fletcher since the revelation of his affair with the Prime Minister's ally. But Europe wasn't mentioned once. The Roads Minister had taken a particular interest in social security and taxation before his promotion to the lower ranks of government, but he'd never said anything particularly striking about either – or for that matter, about roads. He was chiefly interesting, in fact, for having kept so secret his freely indulged predilection for late-night cruising of the capital's gay clubs. His constituency officers had thought their MP was a paragon of domestic virtue, not someone who hung around lavatories and frolicked on Hampstead Heath.

I had no more joy with Geoffrey Doxat, the MP who had been caught profiting from council house sales before the Gunnel-Fletcher story broke. He must have *had* views on Europe, presumably, but he hadn't made them public.

It was Barry Bianchini, though, who blew apart my fledgling

theory. Europe may not have been an important issue for Fletcher or Doxat, but it was all over the Bianchini copy. Unfortunately, all in the wrong context. Bianchini was an ardent anti-European. He'd made speeches about the awfulness of the Common Agricultural Policy when he was still at university. He'd risen through the Conservative Research Department on the back of pamphlets warning of the perils of ceding sovereignty to Brussels. His first act on getting into Parliament had been to join the Bruges Group, and on several occasions he'd voted against the Government over European issues, landing himself in trouble with the whips – resisting cuts in the defence budget, for example, on the grounds that they could be a precursor to integration of Britain's armed forces into a European defence force.

I put my head in my hands, rubbed my face, then got up from the desk. The theory didn't stand up. These men had had to leave the Government because of sleaze, nothing else. I wandered over to the coffee machine and collected another cup of the insipid liquid.

It was clearly time to stop messing about and get back to Tony Bagnall.

An hour later, my account of finding Bagnall's body was pretty much in shape. It finally proved possible to put Ryan Stoner out of my mind if I reminded myself that by not doing so I'd have to stay here all night. By 11.30 p.m. I had something which would only take me half an hour to fine-tune in the morning.

Since my fledgling theory was just that – fledgling – I contented myself with slipping in a line about the coincidence of Bagnall's having been a keen European when so were several of the Tories who had recently quit the Government. I made some slightly frivolous remark about how if the trend continued the Eurosceptics would have no trouble pushing through a referendum on the single currency, which I thought Dan would probably delete when he came to edit the copy. And just in case, I e-mailed the file I'd collated on Gunnel, Fletcher and the rest to myself at home.

'You nearly finished?' Dan asked, perching on the corner of my desk. He was holding a wine bottle and two glasses.

'I've got to drive home,' I said regretfully. 'And I'm exhausted. If I have any of that I may not even reach the lift.'

Visiting the Stoners and reading Ryan's diary had taken more out of me than I'd realised. It was years since I'd lavished so much emotional energy on work.

'Pity,' Dan said, pouring one for himself. 'I was hoping to get you drunk and seduce you.'

'You've spent your whole career sexually harassing me, Dan, and look where it's got you.'

'Nowhere,' Dan said gloomily.

'Precisely.' I picked up my bag and blew him a kiss. 'I'm going home.'

Chapter Six

ON SATURDAY MORNING I returned to the *Sunday Chronicle* and found myself a desk on the eastern side of the building, with a view down the Thames towards the sea. The river snaked away across the marshes, a silvery ribbon in the grey land.

I pushed away the flat-plans, proofs and notebooks that cluttered the desk, logged on to the computer and went through my piece on Tony Bagnall. It didn't take long to tidy it up. Then I wrote the 1500 words Dan wanted on Ryan Stoner, necessarily leaving out all the most interesting things.

On Saturday afternoon I rewarded myself for this effort by spending more money than I could really afford on black silk knickers, suspenders, and a bra with a plunging neckline which promised me a startling cleavage. It felt wildly extravagant, but it had been a tough week. I deserved a bit of *décolleté*.

'Good God, Helen!' Bobby said, arriving home for a shower and finding me in the kitchen. 'What have you done to your toenails?'

'I have painted them,' I said stiffly.

'The house smells like you poured a pint of perfume in the bath. And there's a bag of lingerie in the hall.'

'I'm having dinner with the Dalmores.' I padded to the fridge for some milk. 'Tea?'

'As in George Dalmore, soon to be Prime Minister? Is he particularly interested in underwear?'

'The underwear is Just In Case.'

'Most of the men in your life are lucky if you put on a pair of less than usually ancient jeans. Is this man who merits the red toenails and takes you to dine with the Dalmores someone I should have heard of? And incidentally, honey, the toes betray your origins. Though perhaps in the Labour Party they like a bit of rough? Makes them feel they haven't lost touch with their heritage altogether?'

'You fantasise away,' I told him, sweeping out as grandly as I could in my threadbare dressing gown, hair dripping into my mug of tea. 'I'm going to do my make-up.'

'Go easy on the frosted blue eyeshadow,' Bobby called up the stairs after me.

Bobby had already gone out for some tryst with the woman from his office when Joe arrived to collect me, which was a relief. I'd been dreading having him hanging around eyeing up Joe's clothes and trying to engage him in conversation.

I slipped on my black pumps, picked up the flowers I'd bought Penny Dalmore, and locked the house. Once we were in the car, Joe said awkwardly, 'Look, I hope you won't mind my mentioning this, but this dinner's off the record. I mean really right off: nothing can come out.'

'What are you expecting to happen?' I asked in mock alarm. 'We're not going to have to put our car keys in the middle of the room? I won't have to get off with some septuagenarian backbencher?'

'I doubt there'll be any septuagenarian backbenchers there. I don't even expect anything interesting will be said. It's just that, you know, if anything *did* come up, I've explained that you're there strictly as my . . . friend.'

'Clearly you don't know my recent work. The conversation won't be of much interest to me, professionally speaking, unless it concerns how many times a week people like to have sex and their recent experiences of the multiple orgasm.'

Actually, I felt rather offended. Did Joe seriously think I'd betray his trust by putting Penny's dinner party in the gossip columns?

But of course he hardly knew me.

I changed the subject: 'How did you come to work for George?'

He revved the engine and sped away from the lights in a way I found distinctly sexy. He was wearing a shirt that I suspected was very expensive, with a complicated collar. His profile was intermittently outlined in the street-lamps.

'I was in Washington, teaching philosophy at Georgetown. I knew George a little – I'd met him when I was in my early twenties and working on a book about individualism – but I never imagined his election as leader of the Labour Party would mean anything to me. I wasn't even a Party member.'

'Really? Don't you have to be . . . *committed* to work for the Labour Party?'

Joe smiled. 'Only in the sense of to an asylum. But I *am* committed. I didn't realise at that stage that the Labour Party was what I was committed *to*, or could be, though I liked George and thought he was the best choice Labour could have made. But then he called me and announced he was coming to Washington and wanted to have dinner.'

'And?'

'And he arrived and took me out and it turned out he'd made the trip specially.'

'He wasn't coming to see the President or anything?'

Joe smiled again. 'No. Just for dinner. And to persuade me to come and work for him.'

'You have to admire his single-mindedness.' You also had to be impressed.

'I still said no. I was happy there. I had time to write, lots of friends, a great house-share on P Street. So then *Simon* turned up, took me out for another dinner and announced he wasn't leaving till he'd changed my mind.'

'They couldn't manage without you?'

'Something like that. George was persuasive – you should never underestimate George – but Simon was irresistible. He convinced me Labour really could win next time, and that when they did it would be as a different kind of party, attractive and vital. And that when they won, they were going to put through a radical programme – dynamic and forward-looking. All they lacked was someone to flesh it out.'

'So you gave in?' How was I going to keep my hands off this man all evening?

'Not at first. It was a big risk for me – not very well paid, and I had to uproot – and there was this awful possibility that they might not pull off the changes they promised. But I decided to take it.'

'And now, I suppose, you're about to find out whether it was worth it?'

'Yes.' Joe reversed into a parking space. 'If we don't win the past two years will have been a personal disaster.'

'Interesting, though, presumably?'

'Yes. But bitterly disappointing.'

'And if you do win?'

'Then there are all sorts of possibilities. It's one thing to be adviser to the Leader of the Opposition, quite another to be in power, seeing your ideas in practice, changing people's lives.'

The man for whom Joe Rossiter had put his brilliant academic career on hold lived in a stucco-fronted early Victorian house, one of a terrace whose gardens were all chock-full of bulbs and bursting spring shrubs. Pale pink clematis festooned the Dalmores' fence and clung round the door, and yellow and white tulips jostled in pots on the steps.

Penny Dalmore opened the door, smiling broadly and wearing the draped Donna Karan outfit that had gone down so well with fashion editors at last year's Labour Party conference. She had a good figure, and the woollen two-piece ('wonderfully elegant understatement', as Joanna Beverley had written in *Femme* – amazing that she could recognise such a thing, really) softened her rather horsy features. Behind her in the hall, barefoot and in pyjamas, the two small Dalmores, Dora and Jack, hovered, one of them clutching a teddy bear, looking like a shot from a party political broadcast.

Penny kissed Joe warmly, shook my hand, and ushered us through into the sitting room where half a dozen people were standing holding glasses of champagne.

Everyone seemed to be famous. That was my first thought, and though it wasn't strictly true – some of them were only famous people's friends – they all had the superabundant self-confidence of the famous. When they spoke, it was with the expectation not only that people would listen, but that they'd be impressed. They were the sort of people who when they bored others at dinner parties left the bored people thinking it was their own fault. Penny and George's friends *glowed*, with the patina that people acquire when they're used to being stared at in the street, which attracts attention even while it warns you to keep your distance.

I recognised Nick Llewellyn, the gay chat-show host; Grant Toobin, the alternative comedian; and John Salt, the film director whose latest romantic comedy, *Dangerous Passion*, had got to number five at the American box office. Penny clasped Joe's arm and steered him away from me, and I found myself in a little group composed of Simon Healy, Hester Allan, Adam Sage, and John Salt's wife Katy – who, Penny informed me, was her oldest friend.

'I bet you wish you'd never tried to interview us,' Hester said, touching my arm. 'I tell you my entire life history, and Si introduces you to a dead person. He's supposed to be *good* with journalists. I told him rule number one is not to inflict bodies on people. I think he's grasped the point now.'

'I hope so. My editor at the *Chronicle* thinks because the body turned up while I was working for him, he has some kind of proprietorial claim on it. He's sending me to Bradford next week.'

'Oh no!' Hester's face fell. 'How perfectly miserable!'

'Some people have no consideration – I've *told* him I only do gossip.'

Katy Salt was watching, stony-faced.

'Poor Helen was supposed to be interviewing Si about why he fell in love with me, and instead of telling her how wonderful I am he dragged her off to find a dead body,' Hester explained.

'You're the journalist who found Tony Bagnall?'

'Yes.'

'So *you*'re the person,' Katy went on doubtfully, 'who wrote the reports for the *Chronicle* from Colombia about the drugs cartel?'

'A long time ago.'

'And now you mostly write for – what's that magazine called?'

'*Femme.*'

Katy Salt frowned, as if trying to place it. I knew from a recent television profile of her husband that she produced TV documentaries of stupefying earnestness, but even so she must have heard of *Femme*.

'I'm very sorry,' she said gravely. 'Perhaps one day you'll go back to proper work.'

'Perhaps,' I agreed.

'What does Dan want you to do in Bradford?' Simon's eyes were brimming with laughter.

'Find out why Tony Bagnall killed himself.'

'I can't imagine why. He's had half the newsroom up there for the past week.'

'And they haven't found anything, so now he wants *me* to go up there and not find anything.'

'I hope this doesn't mean Simon and I aren't going to be in the newspaper?' Hester said.

'No, the concept of overwork hasn't reached the offices of the *Sunday Chronicle*. I'm also following up the case of the boy whose body was found on Hackney Marshes.'

'Oh, that poor kid,' Adam said. 'I don't suppose they've caught anyone?'

'No.'

'No clues either?'

I hesitated. 'No.'

'The more I learn,' Simon said, 'the more I'm convinced that Bagnall was simply suffering from depression.'

'But why?' Hester asked. 'People don't get depressed without reason, do they?'

'Sometimes. Anyway, there *were* reasons. Westminster wasn't what he'd expected. He was never going to get anywhere or make much of an impact; his career was effectively over.'

Katy Salt, who had been looking increasingly bored, slipped her arm through Simon's and steered him away. She wanted to find out, she said, what he thought about local government reform as the subject of a documentary.

Hester drew me aside. 'Are you all right? Seriously?' she asked. 'What a clot Simon is!'

I smiled. 'He could hardly be expected to know Tony Bagnall had hanged himself.'

'No,' said Hester doubtfully, 'but he ought to have realised the man was unstable. Just make sure he makes it up to you. Which reminds me: he didn't tell me before I met you that you used to know each other at the BBC. Did he have a crush on you or something? Is that why the secrecy? Anyway, I was relying on you to write something different from the usual.'

'Oh?'

'People – journalists – are so miserable to Simon.'

I raised my eyebrows. 'You think they're unfair?'

'Most certainly. They've got him all wrong: they think because he's powerful, because he controls access to George, he's an intriguer: permanently plotting or something. They don't see his kindness. His generosity. Sometimes I feel I'm the only person who does. But you met him a long time ago. You know what he's really like. Anyway,' she grinned at me: 'I am *dying* to find out: are you here with Joe as in *with*?'

I nodded and she made a face. 'Well!'

I laughed. 'What's that supposed to mean?'

'Nothing. He's great. Very good looking.'

'But?'

'But nothing. He's very committed to his work.'

'Is that so terrible?'

'No. It's just that you always get the impression he'd rather be writing the Labour manifesto.'

I looked at Joe out of the corner of my eye. The way he was standing, the shirt with the inventive collar fell softly against the planes of his body. I could see a rib, the slope of his chest. He was exceptionally attractive. Well, fine, I thought, it's good for a man to care about his work.

'Thing is, I've got one too,' Hester said. 'Workaholics. And you can't reform them. Plenty of people have tried . . .'

She evidently meant with Joe. She also realised it was rather a tactless thing to have said, and promptly reddened, making it worse. 'I'm sure it'll be different with you,' she added unconvincingly.

'What are you two whispering about?' George Dalmore asked, detaching himself from Grant Toobin and Nick Llewellyn. 'I hope you've recovered from your ordeal, Helen. You're certainly looking very well.' He kissed Hester lightly on the cheek and shook my hand, but before I had time to thank him for his call, Katy Salt swept over and linked one arm through his and the other through Hester's.

'George,' she commanded, 'you absolutely *must* come and listen to John's idea for your first election broadcast. It's so important that you get it right . . .'

She swept them across the room, leaving me stranded in the corner by myself. Not that I really minded. I sipped my champagne and remembered I'd been back on the Garden Estate a couple of days earlier. It seemed a long way from there to here. And I didn't feel wholly out of place in either setting. That was something to be proud of. Though I didn't feel wholly at home either.

I covertly inspected the Dalmores' drawing room: yellow striped walls, heavy navy-blue silk curtains, polished wood floors, a pair of Persian carpets. Strategically placed table lamps cast creamy pools of light into the corners, illuminating shelves of political biography and the major poets, maps of George's constituency and photograph frames containing charmingly composed arrangements of Dalmores. Sting's greatest hits wafted contemporarily and undemandingly from the CD player.

It was an incredible achievement for the Labour Party to have found in George Dalmore a leader who was so ordinary. George was rather better-looking, and quite a bit better-off, than most of the people who would be called upon to vote for him; a little more stylish, with a few more and better-informed ideas about how to run the country (most of them Joe's). And that was exactly what was wanted.

It was almost impossible not to like George. He was amiable and normal (apart, of course, from the small matter of being the Leader of the Opposition). An ordinary man, but one with convictions and dignity. He offered the country an idea of itself, what with his elegantly understated wife, his pair of mopsy-haired children, and his tastefully done-up house. He made you feel it was possible to be personally successful and passionate about the state of the community.

It was indicative of how powerful this impression was that in this room, among these people, it was hard to believe that children ever became rent-boys or were left dead by the River Lea.

I watched Joe covertly. He was talking animatedly to Grant Toobin's tall, blonde girlfriend, who I gathered was a scriptwriter. I wondered what was going to happen later. A role for the underwear? But maybe Joe would have to go off and write a bit more of the manifesto.

I was conscious of being on wildly unfamiliar territory. I'd been chary of relationships since Sam died. A part of me found it impossible to believe he could ever be replaced; a part was terrified even to try, in case I found he could. It would have seemed insulting to settle down, have children . . . but this is a position with which my mother has had no sympathy. Having married well herself she felt it was the least I could do: what did she send me to university *for*? It was a constant disappointment to her that I had yet to bag myself a duke.

Penny announced that dinner was served. Somehow – I am still not sure how it happened or which of us arranged it – Joe and I were left in the upstairs drawing room alone after everyone else had trooped downstairs.

He moved towards me. He was smiling, quietly, confidently. He had the look of a person who was used to identifying what he wanted and getting it. I stood there, a little stupidly, waiting for him to come and get me.

He removed the empty glass from my hand and placed it on the marble mantelpiece. His fingers brushed mine. I felt dizzy with possibility. Right then, I thought, I'd do whatever he wanted. He leaned over and his lips met mine, softly at first, but quickly hardening with a kind of must-have desperation. I placed my hands on his shoulders, conscious of the ridiculousness of the situation: this was the leader of the opposition's house, and we were supposed to be making civilised conversation with everyone else downstairs. I was half trying to push him away, half crazy to touch him.

'Later,' he whispered hoarsely, regretfully, after what seemed like minutes but must only have been seconds. 'Later I shall do this again. Properly.'

We pulled apart. We looked at each other. And then somehow I staggered after him downstairs.

Chapter Seven

PENNY HAD SEATED US across the table from one another, which was what I'd hoped, although I knew it would wreck my appetite and give the Dalmores the impression I hated their food.

'Darling, you're becoming redundant,' Nick Llewellyn was saying across me, as I took my place between him and Simon. 'If the Tories go on knocking up their secretaries at the current rate, there won't be anything left for you to do come the election.'

Simon smiled. 'I suspect you underestimate how hard it is for me to organise all these scandals.'

I met Joe's eyes. He was staring at me. I knew what he was up to. He was daring me to look at him, willing me to acknowledge the charge between us. And then he smiled, in a way that was tender but also complicit with lust. My cheeks flamed. I felt helpless, like a foolish young girl and not a sober widow of thirty-two at all. I could still taste the first, sex-promising mouthful of kiss.

'I hope the embarrassments are drawing to a conclusion, that's all I can say.' Nick was waving one of his long thin hands airily, more like a stick insect even than he seemed on television. 'It's becoming awkward. We daren't book Conservative Members of Parliament onto the show for fear that by the time they're due to appear they'll be social outcasts.'

'There *is* another rumour doing the rounds, as it happens,' Simon said, 'but I think it's probably only Westminster hysteria.'

'Are you talking about Moorhouse?' George asked, pouring white wine into the vast fragile glasses in front of us, and catching the tail end of this conversation. 'That really would break the Tories. Or Sherlock, at any rate.'

How was I going to get through this dinner? How was I supposed to concentrate on any of this conversation? I knew what would happen. I would say nothing because my head would be full of Joe, and they would think I was stupid. Oh, what the hell. There wasn't much I could do about it. Never had I been less able to string a sensible sentence together. My head was swarming with maddening, hot images of the tips of Joe's fingers, the whorls running over me, stroking me, stoking up lust. Dreadful.

'That's why I don't believe it,' Simon was saying. 'It's too good to be true.'

'Boys, boys, you're titillating us beyond endurance,' Nick complained. 'What *is* this scandal?'

'Don't ask us,' Simon said. '"Moorhouse," people keep saying to one another. "He's next." But no one quite seems sure why. It's probably the Westminster rumour mill, and only happening because of who he is.'

Moorhouse, I thought. Concentrate on Moorhouse. He was the Home Office minister. He'd spent the past three years co-ordinating the government's ill-fated attempts to turn the tide of divorce and single parent families, a Canute-like effort that had led to his being labelled the minister for the family by the tabloids. He had a very high profile for a junior minister, and it was true that because of his job, any scandal affecting him would have rocked the Government almost as dramatically as the Gunnel-Fletcher episode.

I was doing OK. I could think about this quite clearly. As Simon said, any rumour about Moorhouse would be too good to be true. He was a thoroughly unlikeable character, with a flat, hectoring voice and a smug manner, given to witless attempts to commandeer the Minister of the Family tag in his own speeches and soundbites. There were plenty of people who would have been thrilled to see him get his comeuppance, on his own side as well.

Joe's foot had made contact with mine under the table. I could feel his flesh, his muscles, the bony outline of his ankle rubbing my ankle. I tried to breathe evenly, but the foot was stirring up and pumping hectic messages around my body – lust, ravishment, now! – to every cell.

'Simon, you know everyone,' George said, pausing behind his

chair. 'What d'you know about this dining club called Loyalty? Some forum for discussing European questions? They called today asking me to address them before the election. I wondered if it might be a good place to reassure some of the people who are terrified that Brussels is going to have us all eating straight bananas.'

'Addressing a discussion group on Europe sounds rather dangerous to me, George darling,' Nick interposed: 'I mean, do you actually *have* a European policy?'

'Of course we do,' Joe interjected. I am not sure, but his voice may have been a little hoarse, although I don't think anyone else would have known. He had great aplomb. 'It's not to have too much of a policy.'

'Joe is being frivolous,' George said, moving on with the wine. 'It is true that we like to leave the issue to our opponents. The Tories can't utter the word "Europe" without doing themselves some terrible internal injury. But our policy is balanced. We are against straight bananas and the banning of the great British sausage, and *for* better childcare.'

'When we can afford it,' Joe said mischievously.

'I 'ate all those people who bore on about how great it is to be British,' intervened Grant Toobin's girlfriend, a scriptwriter called Julie Hart. 'I don't know why you don't come out in favour of federal Europe, George. Great British this, Great British that. What does Britain mean to the rest of the world? Football 'ooligans and bad food.'

'Ah, but, Julie,' Nick said smoothly, 'despite your funny working-class accent, you are different from George's voters. You sleep, let us face it, with a celebrity. You're even something of a celebrity yourself.'

'Minor,' said Grant.

'Minor,' Nick agreed. 'But you have an international, élitist outlook. And this is the great irony – and I can say this because I am one of his oldest friends and not intimidated by his soon-to-be prime ministerial status – about George's going about pretending to everyone that he thinks closer ties with Europe are a threat, liable to turn all our dogs rabid and prevent us from eating the chocolate bars that won us the war. He and Penny are élite too.'

'You're such a snob,' said Julie.

'Of course I am.'

'I can't think what you're talking about,' Katy said icily.

'George *knows* Tuscany is nicer than Morecambe. He knows Belgian chocolates are better.'

'Possibly our European policy should be predicated on something more than where George goes on holiday and his taste in chocolate,' Simon suggested mildly. 'Some people think there are issues at stake like democracy and national sovereignty.'

Joe's foot had moved up my calf. When I was with Sam, around the time we married, I remember thinking that one day, when I was old and wearing nightgowns, when my hair was white and thinner, he would have to remember how it had looked dark against clean pillows, and how I had felt when my flesh was firm and clung tightly around my bones. I hoped he *would* remember. But things just don't work out the way you expect.

'Where I come from,' Julie said, 'which as you know, is an 'ousing estate in Sheffield, being British means growin' up thinkin' you won't get a job because you won't get an education, and you might as well throw rubbish down in the streets because where you live is never goin' to look nice anyway and it might just piss off the people 'oo do 'ave the jobs. I wouldn't mind 'avin' to eat straight bananas if some of that changed. It's bleedin' depressin' being British, if you're the wrong kind of British.'

'Oh dear,' said Penny wearily, handing out slices of onion tart – which was better, as Joe pointed out, than you'd get in most French bistros. 'Do we have to discuss Europe on my birthday?'

'So where does that leave me with the loyal diners?' George sat down and attacked his tart, while Penny, at the other end of the table, gamely tried to start another conversation about Hester's latest role as a Glaswegian prostitute in a new television sitcom.

'Loyalty is a dining club run by kids,' Simon told him, 'lots of clever, ambitious, Tory boys not long out of university. They get the more right wing newspaper editors, and cabinet ministers of a certain persuasion to their dinners – right-wingers like Charles Swift – and they have a reputation for being intellectual. They get the more thoughtful end of the business community as well, which would be the chief reason for you to go. But I think actually that might send out too strong a message. Perhaps Joe or Adam or I should go? Though not, I think, to speak.'

Joe, Joe Joe. He had removed his shoe, somehow, and now he'd slipped off mine. His toes were toying with my instep, sliding up my leg. I felt breathless, immodest. I wanted to run my hands all over him. I was sitting here trying to eat this nice onion tart and all I could think about was ripping at buttons and snaps, a tangle of trouser legs and jacket arms, of us shedding our clothes like lizard skins.

'If you want a forum to say your piece about Europe, you could address it in your first election broadcast,' John Salt offered. 'I have, as you know, very strong feelings about that.'

'Oh?' Simon said, in a way that ought to have discouraged John Salt from enlarging, but didn't.

'Presidential,' announced the director of *Dangerous Passion*. 'Let's face it, George: you and Penny are the greatest assets the Labour Party's got. So we want lots of shots of you at home, with the kids in the park, dropping them off at school. And alongside some of the more attractive female members of the shadow cabinet, and Penny involved in charity work. Does Penny do charity work?'

George frowned. 'Well, there's her company,' he said doubtfully. Penny had worked, since her marriage and elevation from her previous job as a Commons secretary, for a PR company specialising in ethical businesses.

'No doubt a charity could be found, eh, Penny?' Nick Llewellyn called up the table.

'What's that?' Penny was concentrating on bringing a second sea bass to the table.

'John thinks a little bit of charity work would be good for your image, darling. What should it be? Handicapped children? P'raps not: could put people off. Breast cancer? No need to show cancerous growths – in fact, it could be an opportunity for entirely legitimate shots of cleavage.'

'You're absurd,' Penny told him affectionately, putting fish on plates, and urging her guests to hand round new potatoes and spinach. 'Don't you take any notice, John.'

'Everybody knows already not to take Nick seriously,' said Katy Salt. 'Now, Simon, if you're only going to tantalise us about Moorhouse, what about Lord Malvern?'

'What about him?'

'This story in the paper this morning that he's thinking of setting up some new political party.'

Simon handed me the spinach. 'Old,' he said, 'an old, old story, as Helen here, being a journalist, will no doubt confirm.'

I wasn't really concentrating. I was wondering about Joe's long thighs, whether there would be hollows on the inside. My breasts hurt. They wanted to make their way out of the very expensive new bra.

Fortunately I wasn't really expected to answer.

'It's a story that surfaces about once a year. It *is* true he thought about setting up his own party once, but he's too bright to waste his time grubbing around at the bottom of the political heap.'

I tried to concentrate on remembering what I knew about Jack Malvern. Married four times. Made a fortune in the 1980s, buying up companies and asset-stripping them, and now controlled a huge range of businesses, from shoes to software, restaurants to mining. An entrepreneur and a *bon viveur*, a modern merchant prince, controlling a territory that superseded national boundaries. He was almost too rich and powerful to be bothered with national politics, but not quite, because of the awkward fact that his companies had to take account of local laws. His chief interest was in keeping these as lax and non-interventionist as possible.

'Why would he *want* his own party?' I asked. I hadn't said anything for ages. I had to make *some* effort. 'I thought he was all cosied up to the Conservatives.'

'He has been in the past, but he can't stand James Sherlock,' Simon explained. 'Not enough emphasis on the free market, not enough enthusiasm for the special relationship. Bit too interested in Europe. But he still wouldn't waste his energies on setting up a new political party.'

'Too easy to buy his way into the existing ones,' said Grant Toobin drily.

'Too busy organising his next wedding,' Simon answered.

'He's not marrying *again*?' Penny said, now bringing a vast, teetering lemon souffle to the table.

'Apparently so. This time he's found himself some glamorous girl straight out of Harvard Business School – a twenty-six year-old investment banker. So my sources tell me.'

I made a mental note, and caught Joe's eye. He was smiling

again. It was the smile of a seducer, of a man who knows he's got some woman exactly where he wants her. It was pointless to try and resist. I hoped this dinner was going to end soon.

Chapter Eight

'SORRY IT'S A MESS,' Joe said, flicking a switch.

'Mess' was an understatement. Not only the desk, but the table, chairs, shelves, sofa were awash: even the *floor* of Joe's house was covered in papers and books. It was hard to see where we might sit down.

'Coffee? drink?'

'Um, coffee, please.'

While Joe was in the kitchen, I tried to detect some order in the arrangements. As far as I could tell, one end of the room was given over to the Irish question, the other to the criminal justice system. There were some faint signs of a more conventional life: the top of a television nudging out above some box files, a dusty spider plant wilting brownly on the windowsill. But the many women who, if Hester was to be believed, had preceded me to Joe's two-up-two-down charming conservation-area cottage did not appear to have succeeded in making any domestic impact. Perhaps they hadn't lasted long enough.

'Were you all right, across your side of the table?' His fingers brushed mine as he handed me a mug.

'I think Katy Salt felt I lacked seriousness.'

Joe sighed through his nose exasperatedly. 'You're a much more serious person than Katy Salt. Silly woman. *I* take you much more seriously.'

I was pleased, but suspected it was only that he was impressed by my (artificial) cleavage. He moved aside some books and sat down beside me on the sofa. This mess could get irritating in the long term, although, clearly, genius requires sacrifices, which may not leave time for tidying up.

'I'm not sure about the Salts.' He frowned.

'How d'you mean?' My mind, I'm ashamed to say, had wandered again, distracted by the sensation of his fingers touching mine. I was thinking about what it would be like when other bits of our bodies touched, when our mouths met and locked together. I was thinking about the blind movement of fingers over material, under material.

Joe, though, was still thinking about the Salts. Or perhaps he was doing this to torment me with anticipation. In which case, he was succeeding. 'George and Penny seem to spend more and more time with them. It's being famous, being recognised in the street. It sets you apart from everyone else whether you like it or not. In the end it forces you together with other famous people and limits your understanding.'

'Dangerous for a politician.'

'Hmmn.' He sipped his coffee. He was actually going to *drink* it! 'So, tell me about yourself.'

'What do you want to know?'

'Everything.'

'Um . . . I was born in the East End, grew up in a high-rise council block. My mother was a single parent. She cleaned offices for a living.'

'And your dad?'

'I don't know.'

He stared at me.

'My mother knows who he was, I hope, but she hasn't chosen to tell me.'

'Haven't you asked?'

'When I was younger. After a certain age you stop asking your parents questions that evidently cause them pain.'

'Aren't you burning with curiosity?'

'Yes and no. He obviously wasn't very interested in us, so I think, well, why should I be interested in him?'

'No photographs, nothing? You don't even know what he looked like?'

'He must have been dark.'

'Dark hair, dark eyes,' Joe said. 'Very good-looking. Arresting.'

Arrested, more like. There had to be some unsuitable history or my mother would have told me by now.

'He would have had fine eyes. Watchful eyes. A mischievous mouth,' Joe went on.

'Mischievous? Now you're trying to get round me.'

'A small straight nose and good skin.'

'The good skin's my mother's. And you're going to ruin it in a minute by becoming completely unconvincing.'

'You know, when I saw you for the first time, at Dan's party, I couldn't believe how sexy you were – that short hair, those dark eyes. You looked so self-contained and *perfect*, somehow, in that red jacket. I had to get out of there.'

That didn't sound quite right. 'Whatever for?'

'I'd only called in for an hour to clear my head before starting work on an article for an American political magazine. The last thing I wanted was to meet girls.'

'Girls?'

'You.'

'I'd hate to be a distraction.'

'It's written now,' he said, and leaned towards me.

I thought I might be swallowed by the kiss: his teeth bruised my lips, and after a few moments his hands were pressing on my breasts.

We made love on the sofa, half sitting, half dressed, his hands pressing deep into my flesh, pinching and mauling. And then he put me on the floor, and then up against the wall in the hall, my back against the cold plaster, legs round his hips, fingers clawing at his chest: all the time he was telling me what he wanted to do next, what plans he had for my body. At last, tired out by our own fury, we ended up in bed. And there we made love again – tenderly this time, with slow relish – and fell asleep wound round each other.

'Fuck,' muttered Joe. 'Fuck, fuck, *fuck*.'

I opened my eyes and blinked sleepily. 'Again?' I murmured incredulously.

Joe grinned, leaned over, planted a kiss on my forehead, and switched off the insistently beeping alarm. 'You are the most fabulous woman I've ever met.'

'Oh, no, it was all you.'

Joe picked up the clock and groaned. 'Six o'clock. How long have we been asleep?'

'Feels like ten minutes.'

'You are unbelievably lovely. And I've got a plane to catch.'

'Oh . . .' I blinked, dredging my memory. 'America. You're going to Washington.'

He got out of bed, long legs pale in the dawn as he rummaged in a pile of clothes on a chair for a dressing gown. Then he came back and sat on the bed. 'Why don't you stay here?' he suggested, taking my hand. 'You might as well sleep, at least.'

'I'm awake now.' I looked around for something to put on and remembered my clothes were scattered in various places downstairs. I had a vague recollection that the very expensive black silk items were no longer intact, having been ripped or bitten off or something.

Joe stumbled down to the kitchen to make tea. It was already light – bright, liquid sunshine glistening on the damp petals of a cherry blossom tree outside the bedroom window – and by the time he came back with a couple of mugs, I'd managed to struggle into a sitting position. 'What are you doing in America?'

'It's a conference.'

'On . . .?'

'Oh, boring, boring . . . Alliances in the Post-Cold War Period, it's called. Does Nato have a future? That sort of thing.'

'Oh.' I wondered if it did, but didn't like to ask. 'Are you speaking?'

'Yes, on Tuesday. And seeing some people in the administration on Thursday and Friday to talk about crime and communities and taxation.'

I nodded, unsure whether crime-and-communities-and-taxation was one thing or three.

'I'm back on Saturday. Can I write . . . send you a fax?'

'Sure. If I can send you one.'

'That would make me very, very happy. I'll try to call you as well, but it could be more difficult. There is one other thing –' He got up and started pulling clothes out of the wardrobe.

'Yes?'

'I'd like you to have my keys.'

'One night of passion, and you've already got me staying in for the plumber.'

'There's no plumber. I'd simply like you to have my keys. Think of it as a gesture of intent. It'll make me feel closer to you. If you want them?'

'You're irresistible. There'll be women hurling themselves in front of you in Washington, clawing off their clothes. The pavements will be littered with half-naked desperate females.'

'I doubt it. And I wouldn't notice them if there were, because I'll be thinking about you.'

We parted on the pavement outside his house.

'I wish I didn't have to go.'

'Well, you do,' I said, in a muffled way, since parts of my mouth were mixed up with parts of his.

'I'd rather spend the week with you, hidden away here, not going out, except perhaps into the garden if it's sunny. We could send out for yoghurt and honey and champagne.'

'How lovely ... I could focus on different bits of you on different days.'

'I'd need a week for your nose alone.'

'It's not that big.'

'It's adorable. I want to make love to you on the kitchen table and the bathroom floor and on the back seat of the car.'

We tore ourselves apart eventually, and I walked home through the quiet streets, past other people's shuttered windows, sleeping lives. The sun was shining determinedly out of a pale blue sky, the air was chilly, and even when I crossed one of the main roads into the City I had only a milk float and an early bus for company.

It was odd, I thought, that you could spot someone at a party like that, and *know* that there was something between you: it felt like – must be what people understood by – destiny. And if we already had this much destiny, what else mightn't we have? Maybe five years from now we'd be – what? – living together, with leading politicians and talk show hosts popping round for supper, Joe thinking his big thoughts in his study ... and me? A cultural commentator, maybe. Highly respected for her insights into contemporary life.

This of course, presupposed that he didn't forget all about me while he was in Washington.

It also presupposed that I'd find a way of getting to the insights into contemporary life from my current activities. There wasn't exactly a seamless flow. Something might have to be done. Without turning myself into Katy Salt, quite, I might have to find a way of focusing less on twenty different ways with a condom. I wanted Joe to take me seriously, and not only because I was a good lay.

The papers had already been delivered when I got home; they lay in a hefty pile inside the front door, spewing sections and supplements onto the mat. I sighed wearily; all this newsprint couldn't possibly be worth reading.

I picked up the *Chronicle*. The front page was dominated by a photograph of George Dalmore, and an opinion poll the paper had commissioned which suggested that Labour was eighteen points ahead of the Conservatives and that George had the highest popularity rating as leader of his party in living memory.

My account of finding Tony Bagnall's body dominated page three; I skimmed through it, noting approvingly that Dan hadn't seen fit to alter anything – which was good because Dan usually liked to alter something, if only to remind you that that was his prerogative. I dropped the *Chronicle* back on the mat, kicked the papers out of the way and promised myself I'd attend to them later. Then I went to bed and fell into a deep, dizzily happy sleep.

At lunch-time I got up, and skipped about the kitchen in my bathrobe and socks to the 'Motown Years' while I made scrambled eggs. At the critical moment, just as the eggs were clotting into sticky cream, the phone rang.

It was Sarah, wanting to know how the hot date had gone.

'Pretty hot,' I admitted.

'What bed and everything?'

'Uh-huh.'

'You are *so* smug. What did you talk about with the Dalmores?'

'Oh, I don't know – all sorts of things. Politics, Europe, exchange rate mechanisms.'

'You don't know anything about exchange rate mechanisms.'

'I looked knowledgeable.'

'Oh no! Be warned. I've sat through lectures on post-modernism, quasars, and even once, God help me, on UFOs, all because I thought I might get laid at the end. It's a funny thing. All my boyfriends have interests; I only have boyfriends.'

'You're so cynical. It wasn't simply sex.'

'Oh my God! You're going to be telling me next you can communicate with each other.'

'I don't think you're taking this nearly seriously enough.'

'OK then, surprise me.'

'It was very romantic. We're compatible.'

'In what way romantic?'

'Um . . . he said he wanted to feed me on yoghurt and champagne . . .'

Sarah emitted a snuffling sound. 'You – the world's greediest girl, and a man whose idea of a good meal is a carton of yoghurt? And Helen, you don't drink champagne. You always say it gives you a headache.'

By the time I'd got rid of Sarah, the scrambled eggs were ruined. I stared at them crossly, thinking how unfair it was of her to say I was greedy and also how at that precise moment I could have consumed most of a supermarket.

She was quite right, of course, to warn me against getting too carried away with the idea of Joe. Not that I needed warning really. People tend to think of me as a sunny, optimistic person. And that's how I am on the surface. But underneath I'm in constant expectation of some really terrible disaster occurring, such as a meteor landing on my head or all my friends dying of mysterious flesh-eating diseases.

It would be nice to think Joe wouldn't turn out to be a waste of good lingerie. I was clinging on to that hope. But when your husband has died a fortnight after you married him and you feel responsible, it's pretty hard to persuade yourself that everything is going to work out beautifully.

I was scraping the scrambled eggs off the bottom of the pan into the bin, and thinking about the oddness of having got caught up in two demanding stories, *and* met Joe all in a few days, when the phone rang again.

'This is June Lennox,' said the woman on the line: 'Tony Bagnall's secretary.' I almost dropped the phone. 'I read your article in the *Chronicle*.'

I dragged a kitchen chair across the floor towards me and sat down.

'Susan said you wanted to speak to me,' June Lennox continued, 'is that still the case, or has the moment passed?'

'No, no, not at all.'

'Good. Why don't you come and see me? When could you manage?'

I thought quickly. I wanted to go to the Lord Napier to see Stewart Saddler tomorrow evening: that was something that had already waited quite long enough. But I could see June Lennox before then. I told her I could manage the morning; and she gave me an address in the outer suburbs of East London – in Woodford – and suggested I come for coffee.

I put the saucepan in the sink to soak and investigated the fridge in the hope that something delectable to eat might have miraculously appeared there since I'd last looked half an hour earlier. I was starving. The fridge yielded up a lettuce, four tomatoes and a spring onion. I was rummaging in the freezer (ice cream, frozen peas, and an enormous leg of lamb) when the telephone rang yet again. This time it was *Femme*'s commissioning editor Joanna Beverley.

'Darling!' she screeched. 'Brilliant Bagnall piece – I absolutely *had* to ring you. Terribly affecting: I'm still reeling, and I wasn't even *there*. But you know, I'd never even heard of him. D'you think he was about to be caught out in some terrible scandal?'

'If so it was very well hidden.'

'How thrilling, though, to have been with Simon Healy when you found him! I'm *terribly* peeved you didn't get that interview for us: we've been after him for ages, ever since he started seeing Hester Allan. She's *so* gorgeous, and he's not exactly movie star material, is he? Though George Dalmore's not bad-looking, I suppose, if you go for that schoolboyish thing, and don't they have someone really pretty dishy there responsible for policy? Joe someone . . .?'

'Joanna, I'm sorry, but . . .'

'Oh God, I know, it's Sunday, you're at home and here I am, rabbiting on as usual about whether people are good-looking or not. But I'm off to Paris tomorrow, and I tried to get you all day on Friday . . . I want to sign you up for this really brilliant idea we've got. You'd be perfect. It's called "The Importance of Being Dumb", and the whole point of it is to talk to women who make money from being bimbos.'

'Uh-huh,' I said. 'What sort of women, exactly?'

'Oh, you know – topless models . . . and . . . that sort of thing. Those weather girl people, maybe . . . You'll think of someone, you're marvellous at research. So long as they're making lots of dosh; we don't want any old tarts. Lots of pix.'

What Joanna really wanted, it rapidly became evident, was women who could be photographed spilling out of the tops of their dresses. I thought of my recently formulated ambition to become a leading cultural commentator.

'Did you know Lord Malvern's getting married again?' I asked her.

'No! Are you sure?'

'So I heard last night.'

'Yes darling, but who from? Did they *know* what they were talking about? People do so like to drop names.'

'It was being discussed at a dinner party.'

'Yes, you said, but who *by*?' She sounded quite tetchy.

'By the Dalmores,' I admitted.

'Oh.' She was evidently taken aback. 'Helen. My! You do have good contacts! The Dalmores. That could be *very* useful. How do you know them?'

'Oh . . . through a friend who knows Penny.'

The information that my acquaintance with the Dalmores was only second-hand evidently cheered her. 'I think it's going to be *such* fun when they get in, don't you? More parties and things, all those actors and comedians and people in and out of Number 10. There could be a whole new atmosphere. Like the sixties or something. Anyway, that's beside the point. Is Jack Malvern sexy enough for us? I suppose he's quite distinguished, in that older man sort of way . . .'

'The interesting thing is that the bride's a twenty-six-year-old investment banker.'

'*Is* she? Oh well, there might be something in that. She sounds like someone our readers might be able to identify with. What does a woman like this see in a man like that sort of thing? Yes, look into it darling, but do the bimbos first.'

How easy was it going to be, I wondered as I put down the phone to Joanna, to progress from cleavages to analysis of the contemporary condition? Evidently, I thought, as I looked one last time in the fridge, I would have to have a plan. I couldn't rely on circumstances to take care of this particular career development. And there was *still* no interesting little quiche. I switched on the answering machine and went out for lunch at a café.

Chapter Nine

JUNE LENNOX LIVED ALONE, in a net-curtained semi in a street of similar, though carefully differentiated, net-curtained semis. Hers was distinguished by a glass panelled front door with chimes and mock-Georgian carriage lamps. Nothing was moving in the street when I arrived on Monday morning, except for a shifty-looking tabby cat which was prowling along a brick wall several doors down. Number 28, June's house, exuded a quiet air of self-containment.

A vacuum cleaner cut out upstairs before June appeared in the hall, visible behind the glass door smoothing down her skirt and patting her hair.

She opened the door – a neat person in her mid-forties, tidily dressed in a straight knee-length skirt and paisley-patterned blouse. Everything about her was in order: her pink carpet and spotless Dralon sofa, the Wedgwood ornaments on the mantelpiece – carefully spaced to avoid any suggestion of clutter – her stiff shampoo and set.

'I'm very sorry not to have been in touch sooner,' she said, as we sat down. 'It was such a shock, Tony dying, and I couldn't face the idea of talking to the newspapers, but I felt guilty about you.'

I said something about its being quite understandable.

'No,' she persisted; 'I felt guilty because I should have been the one to find him. I should have realised. I saw him every day; I simply had no idea he was that unhappy.'

June Lennox poured coffee into bone china cups. She'd worked for Tony Bagnall for his entire Westminster career and a third of her own, she said. Not that they'd always seen eye to eye: 'He was very *Northern*. Professionally Northern, if you know what I mean – bluff and hearty. I resented his manner at first, thought his brusqueness was rude, and that he put it on, which of course he did. But once you got underneath all that he was sensitive and thoughtful.' She pulled an embroidered handkerchief from her cuff. 'He was very kind to me. My mother died, and . . . well, I'm sorry . . . you don't want to know about all that. What I'm trying to say is it was so *unexpected*. I knew him as well as anyone, yet I had no inkling how desperate he was. And the funny thing is, I still can't work out why he did it.'

'He wasn't depressed about his career?' I asked. 'Someone in the Labour Party suggested to me that he disliked the House of Commons.'

'Oh, the Labour Party!' She bit into a custard cream. She had small, sharp teeth. 'Much they ever knew. Or cared. The truth is that Tony was more excited about his career than he had been for ages. Which is not to say he hadn't had bad moments in the past, or didn't still sometimes, over the way things were going and how far he was from having a face that fitted. When George Dalmore came in for instance, he had to face the fact he was never even going to make it into the lower ranks of government . . . "Not smooth-talking enough," he used to say to me. But he'd recently been voted chairman of the Brussels Group – well, you know that, because you had it in your article – and he was excited by the possibilities.'

'What was significant about the Brussels Group?'

'It's a backbench organisation. Named in opposition to the Bruges Group. Cheeky, you see. They stood for opposite things. For more European integration.' She rummaged in a briefcase beside her armchair. 'I've got something for you – a speech he was about to make when he died. His inaugural speech as chairman of the Brussels Group. This will tell you a bit about what he thought, and show you how much spirit he still had.'

She pulled some papers from the briefcase and held them tightly in her lap.

'He wasn't happy with what the leadership was doing over Europe – having their cake and eating it, he told me; and he thought once they were in power they might even consider dropping all the social legislation side of things. So he wanted to use the Brussels

Group to force George Dalmore to commit to European standards on employees' rights and a minimum wage. He wanted George to come out and say what a Labour government's attitude to Europe would be – before the election, not after, which of course is what the leadership would prefer. He spent the last few months of his life meeting like-minded people from all over Europe; he wanted to use the group, you see, as a basis for a campaign outside Parliament, in the country . . .'

'So it doesn't make any sense at all to you that he'd kill himself now . . .'

'No, it doesn't.' June Lennox was resolute. 'He felt there was something to be done and, what's more, that he was the man to do it – and, you know, he was quite a formidable politician, even if his face *didn't* fit. I always thought the party hierarchy was wrong to exclude him. He may not have been classless and smooth like them, but he was effective.'

'What about this threat of deselection?'

'Syreeta Aziz and all that?' She shrugged. 'The people in Bradford would be able to tell you more than I can, but my understanding was he'd dealt with it.'

'Oh?'

'I gathered she'd given an undertaking not to challenge him. He certainly didn't appear to be very bothered by it.'

So that was that. Bang goes the only explanation so far with an iota of credibility.

'What did you make of his suicide note? I presume the police told you what was in it?'

'They showed it to me. I couldn't make sense of it, to be frank, and still can't. You'll know from the papers he didn't have any money worries, and I don't think he had any serious political debts either. I mean, I know the unions work the system and so do politicians: I'm not saying he never did a deal. But he wasn't corrupt: he wouldn't have made promises he couldn't keep.'

'You weren't surprised that it was typed?'

'No. Not at all.' She smiled. 'Tony had a laptop. He loved it with passion.'

'But he'd have had to – what? – take the disk out of there and put it in your machine to print off the note?'

'Well, yes, if he printed it at the Commons. It's conceivable he knew he was going to kill himself when he left home and brought it with him. He had a small printer there.'

She riffled through the pages on her lap, checking the page numbers, ensuring they were all there.

I had to get this over: I asked her about the rumours that she'd received a mysterious telephone call that morning.

But she was more than happy to tell me about it. 'I did have a *very* mysterious call that morning, and I can't get it out of my head that if it hadn't been for that call – if I hadn't gone running off across London – he might not have been there on his own. And then he might not have killed himself.'

'So what was it, this call?'

She sat back, papers in her lap. 'Well, that's the point, I don't know. I *thought*, at the time, it was from Tony's constituency chairman, Mike Soper. The caller was obviously on a mobile phone, and they can make people's voices go funny, can't they, so if I *had* thought he sounded different . . . but, frankly, it didn't even occur to me. I don't talk to Mike all that often, and he had my home number, though I'm ex-directory, so when he said it was him, I didn't give it a second thought. But he categorically denies it was him . . .' She smoothed down her skirt and glanced up at me with embarrassment, as if she felt her failure to identify the call as a hoax somehow impugned her professionalism.

'What did he say?'

'He claimed he had some papers for Tony, something to do with the Brussels Group, and rather than send them Red Star, his brother-in-law was driving them down – he was coming to London anyway – and he wondered if I could pick them up on my way into the Commons?'

'Were these papers something you were expecting?'

'No. This was the first I'd heard about them. But he was most insistent: it was extremely important, and if I wasn't convinced I could check with Tony. So I tried ringing Tony but he wasn't answering at his flat. I guessed he was still asleep, or in the bath, so I left a message on his answering machine. I don't know now whether he got that or not.' She shook her head. 'I was rather irritated, actually, because this place wasn't really on my way into the Commons, although it might have looked like that on the map: I take the tube, you see, and it wasn't anywhere near a station. The nearest station was on the wrong line as well, and I had a lot of letters to get out, but I thought I'd better go and pick those papers up if they were so urgent. I couldn't afford to wait around for Tony to get back to me.'

'Where was this place?'

'A boys' club in Stepney. The Lord Napier.'

I felt sick. I stared at June Lennox.

'I know, improbable, isn't it?' she went on cheerfully. 'I can't think now why I didn't query it at the time, but I was a bit flustered, having my plans disrupted. When I got there – I took a mini cab from the central line – it was closed. Well, obviously: it's a place for schoolkids, and it was nine o'clock in the morning. And there was no sign of this man, Ted Dutton, I was supposed to be meeting, or of anyone else for that matter; the place was absolutely deserted. So I waited half an hour, and then caught a bus back to the tube.'

'Did you tell the police?'

'Yes, I did. I think they assumed it was a mix-up. I'd got my facts wrong or something.'

I wondered whether the police could have made the connection. It seemed unlikely: an entirely different team would be investigating Ryan's murder. And in any case, they wouldn't have the faintest idea about the rent boy activities: there would be no reason for the Lord Napier to set alarm bells ringing in anyone's head. Not unless they'd read Ryan Stoner's diary.

'Mike *does* have a brother-in-law, incidentally, and he is called Ted Dutton, but he was in Manchester that morning.'

'Did Tony have any connection with this boys' club?'

'Not specifically. He was on the board of the Federation of Boys' Clubs. That was something he'd started in Bradford, and carried on when he came down to London. He liked being around kids, not having had any of his own. So he used to visit boys' clubs from time to time, to see what they were up to. But I'd never heard of this one.'

I hope I managed to conduct myself sensibly for the next half an hour. I don't *think* June realised how shocked I was.

I nodded and uttered sympathetic noises, drank another cup of coffee, and talked to her about the House of Commons, where she'd worked for almost twenty years, and which she loved and despaired of in equal measure, hating the way the whips had put Tony's career on hold, loving the gossip and rituals and contact with the constituents. She said she couldn't think what she'd do now: she didn't want to stay knowing it was where Tony had killed himself, but it was her whole life.

I pressed her a little more about what might have possessed Tony Bagnall to commit suicide, though by now I was afraid I might know. I asked her about his marriage to Elise; she claimed the relationship had been strong, in spite of their separate lives. I asked again about the money. She'd have known, she said, if Tony had had difficulties in that direction: there'd have been some sign.

But it was almost impossible to concentrate. My mind was filled once more with images of a boy and a man on Hackney Marshes, the wind blowing across the low-lying fields, rustling in the scrub beside the River Lea. Had *Tony Bagnall* killed Ryan? And then himself? Had he killed himself because Ryan was dead?

When I left the house clutching five sheets of typed, double-spaced A4 paper, my head felt like a washing machine: too many thoughts sloshing about, twisted and wrung. Tony Bagnall and the Lord Napier. Tony Bagnall and Ryan Stoner. What did it mean? What did it make him? Had someone been on to him; had they been trying to tell June?

I sat in the car wondering what to do next: picked up the speech and glanced at it, put it back down on the passenger seat. It appeared only to be the usual sort of political rant. I couldn't believe it was as significant or interesting as June Lennox appeared to think.

Poor June . . . she'd really liked him. And probably hadn't known him at all.

In the end I drove to the park near my house, wanting to be in the open air. The place was almost empty: the day already seemed to be winding down, mournful and slow. I sat down on a bench and watched four ducks fly down on to the lake, landing with a whoosh, a splash and a squawk. A light wind blew out of a gunmetal sky, caught the overhanging fronds of a weeping willow and trailed them across the surface of the water.

There was dog shit on the grass; the swings in the newly renovated children's playground had been vandalised. At my feet a clump of daffodils was stupidly persisting in nudging up through the clayey soil, oblivious to the tower blocks that cast hulking great shadows over them.

Tony Bagnall's speech was not only unfinished, tailing off half way down page five, it was also evidently a first draft, covered with pencilled annotations, arrows and deletions. But it was clear enough what he'd intended to say.

He opened with an appeal to the Labour Party not to turn its back on socialism. This, he said, was a crucial moment in the party's history: a moment when it could be overcome by its enthusiasm for cultivating the middle-class Southern vote and embracing the market economy. A moment when it could sell out, or stick by its principles and prove what it stood for.

Inside Europe, what Bagnall called 'the movement' could hang onto its traditions and help 'the mass of working people'. Outside Europe, the British people would be at the mercy of big business, with no muscle to resist exploitation by here-today-gone-tomorrow international capital.

Bagnall had evidently despised the leadership of his party – people who, he believed, put winning above everything else, who couldn't be relied upon not to turn their expensively-suited backs on European legislation relating to parental leave, childcare, working conditions and a minimum wage. Labour Party members and supporters in the country must recognise the threat before it was too late and register their dismay.

So far, the speech was predictable. It certainly confirmed Dan's reading of Bagnall's enthusiasm for a Europe as the last gasp of the old left. Bagnall couldn't have state-sponsored socialism, so he'd settle for superstate-sponsored socialism. And the European Union, centralising and bureaucratic, seemed to him the last chance for the party he'd grown up with to maintain its integrity. He damn well intended to fight for it.

Had Bagnall lived to deliver the speech, or this part of it, he would certainly have raised awkward questions about Labour's position on Europe, and might well have flushed out some of the internal differences of principle which had been obscured by the overriding desire to win the next election.

But there was a second part, linked to, but not quite following on from, the first. And this was rather more troubling.

In fact, I couldn't really work out what to make of it at all.

'If we do not succeed,' Tony Bagnall had written, 'the consequences may be dire. There are people in this country who will go to almost any lengths to keep Britain out of Europe.' I squinted at the sheets of paper. This second half of the speech was subject to more scribblings and crossings out than the first and it was hard to understand which bits were supposed to follow what.

'These people are fierce nationalists. They believe in white supremacy and the forced repatriation of immigrants. So fervent are they, that they are prepared to use undemocratic methods. They are worse than Jean-Marie Le Pen in France, worse than the Italian neo-fascists, because they don't even *pretend* to care what the majority of the people – the moderate, decent people – of this country want. And they are not all yobs and street thugs. Many of them occupy positions of power . . .'

Here the speech trailed off. In the margin Tony Bagnall had written, '??specifics. ?? must make de Moleyns stick.'

Even after I'd read it through three times I wasn't sure exactly what Tony Bagnall was trying to say. He seemed to be warning that there was more at stake even than the integrity of the Labour Party. But it was all so vague. Who were these nationalists? How would they stop at nothing? Were they something like the Patriots, the group that was supposed to have started the football riot in Italy?

But the Patriots weren't a serious threat to democracy: they were too small and too much despised.

I read it again. Bagnall *seemed* to be saying there was some other, more significant threat beyond the known neo-fascist organisations. Involving people who occupied positions of power. But this might only be a rhetorical flourish, designed to make it all sound more dramatic than it was. And he offered absolutely no evidence.

Actually, it made him sound crazy. It made him sound like a man who was disturbed enough to commit suicide.

I tossed the speech aside in exasperation. What did it matter anyway? Tony Bagnall was probably a child molester, in which case I frankly wasn't interested in his views on British democracy.

Admittedly, the man June Lennox had described, who liked beer and bad jokes, didn't sound anything like a child molester. But what did child molesters sound like anyway? Everyone else. That was the point of them; that was why they were monstrous.

And what else could June's summons to the Lord Napier possibly signify? It was too much of a coincidence.

Someone had found out and was trying to warn him or frighten him – that was all I could think. And when June Lennox left her message on the answering machine on that Wednesday morning he'd panicked. He would have known by then that Ryan was dead. He would have realised from the message that someone was onto him. And that, at last, would explain why he killed himself – and it would explain his note. Debts to pay that I cannot repay. I should think not either. If Tony Bagnall had been John, he'd stolen Ryan Stoner's life months before the child was murdered.

What this neat theory still didn't account for, unfortunately, was who had made the call. I got up from the bench and walked back to the car. Time to go into work.

Chapter Ten

THE TINY OFFICE I shared with Sarah occupied the top floor of a narrow house in an alley off St John's Street, close to Smithfield market. The window frames were ingrained with grime; a partly boarded up door opened onto a linoleum-floored hall. To reach it you had to dodge barrows piled high with carcasses and avoid breathing in too deeply the powerful, meat-sweetened air.

A group of not very successful gay activists occupied the ground floor, and an escort agency the first. The market was a disadvantage, and there was another funny smell sometimes that had nothing to do with dead animals, other than those that might colonise damp plaster. But it was cheap.

Sarah was in and working when I arrived, producing one of her articles of great seriousness and insight, something she does at a rate that would exhaust anyone else.

I dropped her post onto her desk: fifteen letters for her, two for me. She is the sort of journalist I should be, always being invited to cinema screenings and private views, most of which she is far too busy to attend. Like Dan, she finds it hard to appreciate my interest in the G-spot.

'Your mother called,' she said, pen clamped between her teeth. 'We had a nice chat. She's very interested in my cousins.' Sarah has a large family of titled cousins who are always being photographed for upmarket glossy magazines. My mother thinks I should marry one of them. 'She said there's no point ringing her now because she's gone to play bridge. Oh, and your hairdresser called. You forgot your appointment.'

'Oh hell!' I'd been sitting in the park thinking about horrible Tony Bagnall when I could have been sitting in a big chair in front of a mirror being pampered. I'd have to wait at least three weeks for another appointment. By the time Joe got back from Washington I'd look like a St Bernard.

But this was an adolescent thought. Joe was interested in me for my personality, not my overpriced haircuts.

'I thought perhaps you were too shagged out to get out of bed,' Sarah said, frowning at her screen. 'Heard anything from Mr Romance yet?'

'He only went yesterday.'

'So much for the great communicator,' Sarah said sceptically. 'Incidentally, you look daft when you talk about him.'

'I do not!'

'All right then, name one of his faults.'

'This isn't fair.'

'Ha! Exactly. You think he hasn't got any.'

'On the contrary. I am completely clear-sighted about him. He's a workaholic. He's very untidy. He's got through a lot of girlfriends. But that's because he's so interested in his work. And my theory is that they just weren't very interesting girls.'

'It's all lust. You've created this romantic fantasy about what a great person he is to justify your lewd feelings.'

'The brain is the central erogenous zone,' I said pompously, opening my letters and throwing them both straight in the bin. 'And he's got a big one.'

'There's more than one type of cleverness, you know,' Sarah said severely. 'Emotional cleverness, for instance. It's no good being brainy if you're insensitive.'

'We'll have to see,' I acknowledged. 'But I think he has possibilities.'

I switched on my computer and picked up the papers. There was a gruesome story about another racial murder in the East End. Mohammed Abdul, a seventeen-year-old whose parents had come to Britain from Bengal before he was born, was attacked at a bus stop in Stepney at 8.00 p.m. by a gang of skinheads. They broke his nose, jaw and three of his ribs.

Other students at the further education college where he'd recently started on a catering course described Mohammed Abdul as a serious, hard-working young man, shy and gentle, who regarded himself as an East Ender. He died in the ambulance on the way to hospital.

The stallholders on Mile End Waste were already closing down for the day when I left the office and drove east later that afternoon, yanking awnings off their barrows and piling cheap nylon clothes into Transit vans, leaving the wide pavements littered with old vegetables, string and polythene. Windscreen wipers swished against the light rain as I drove with the rush-hour traffic out of the City. It shouldn't have been getting dark yet, but the weather was so dismal, the late afternoon seemed only to be waiting for the dusk. Lights shone weakly through the drizzle out of scruffy shops, illuminating the young black women in short skirts pushing baby buggies, and pensioners with plastic-and-fabric shopping bags trudging home through the gloom, collars turned up against the weather.

I tried to remember what I knew about the Lord Napier Boys' Club. Founded at the turn of the century. Originally a high church chapel and sports club, with its own ground (though both had long since been flattened to make way for high rise council flats) offering the poor people of the area, or the poor young men, at least, the chance to play team games. In return for which they were expected to turn up for services and behave in an acceptable manner.

A manner that suited their betters. Perhaps not much had changed.

I was scared at the prospect of meeting Stewart Saddler. I would have preferred to take Ryan's diary straight to the police. I intended to try to persuade Katrina that was what we should do as soon as I possibly could. But she'd given me the diary so that I *would* see him, and I was pretty sure she wouldn't budge unless I made some effort with this meeting.

I'd have to tread carefully though, not to reveal the existence of the diary or let on that I knew about Bagnall.

It's easier writing about lipstick.

I parked the car behind the long low hut that served now as the headquarters of the Lord Napier Boys' Club. This was why I didn't do this kind of work any more: I didn't trust myself not to make a mess of things, say the wrong thing and send someone off to their death.

I closed my eyes, but the images came crowding in anyway, just as they always did. My last quarrel with Sam in that house in the damp, jungly hills outside Medellin, the air thick with humidity. I thought – we were so close to completing the profile of the man who was threatening the stability of the cocaine cartel – I *wanted* to think – that Sam was exaggerating the threat. I thought the two guys who'd knocked him down in a bar in the town the night before were only trying to scare us.

They'd warned him if we went anywhere near the house we'd be killed and I still don't know why I didn't listen to Sam. I loved him. I respected him more than anyone else in the world. Two weeks earlier I'd married him, in a village half way up a hillside in the Cordillera Central. As he said, we already knew more about Cordoba's trafficking operations than anyone else. We'd tracked him across a continent. We had enough information to write the story and we had pictures, even if they weren't the greatest. But if we could only get a picture of the house, the headquarters, we had the greatest story of the year, of either of our careers. And we were so close.

Sam was all for getting out. It would be madness to go on, he said, and in the end I think I didn't listen to him precisely because we *were* married. I thought he was trying to protect me. I thought his attitude towards me had changed. And he thought, I suppose, that I blamed him for not getting good enough pictures; thought he wasn't pulling his weight on this story, that he wasn't as good a journalist as he used to be or could be; perhaps, even, that he wasn't as good as me.

We quarrelled. I stomped off. He thought I'd gone to Cordoba's house, and perhaps I let him think so. In fact, I'd gone into town, where I bought bread, cheese and a bottle of bourbon as a peace offering. Sam, though, was already dead.

Whether he went to Cordoba's house in an attempt to protect me or because I'd wounded him I don't know. At any rate, someone found him, shot him and dumped his body by the roadside. I never wrote the Cordoba story.

That was why I was a trivia journalist. And that's why I was scared.

Stewart Saddler was already at the club, waiting for the boys to arrive. He emerged from a side-room with an armful of ping pong bats. He had weathered skin and dirty blond hair curling over his collar. I guessed he must have been in his mid-thirties, and he was good-looking, in a battered, rugged-complexioned way. Ordinary, rather pleasant, rough-hewn.

I introduced myself, explaining I was writing a newspaper feature about Ryan's life.

He shook his head. 'Poor kid. It was a dreadful shock. Some of the boys, they pretend they're hard, but they've been really frightened by what happened to Ryan.'

'How long had you known him?' I took some of the bats from him and helped carry them to the green baize tables.

'A couple of years. You want a cup of tea before they arrive?' I nodded and Stewart Saddler unlocked a door across the hall and led the way into a small kitchen fitted with cheap units. 'He came here as soon as he was old enough, at eight, and seemed to love it. He wasn't one of our best sportsmen, but he was good enough to play for the under-elevens football and cricket teams. We insist they do something structured while they're here.'

Was this unremarkable man Ryan's killer? This person I was about to drink tea with? Had he strangled Ryan Stoner? And if not, did he know who had?

'You familiar with the history of this place?' he asked, pouring tea into thick brown mugs.

'A little.'

'Stop me if I tell you what you already know. It was built in a rush of late Victorian enthusiasm for missions to the poor.'

'Sporting activities and the Church,' I said.

'Yes, muscular Christianity, I suppose.' He smiled. React normally, I thought. Just smile; it won't hurt. 'It was a very vigorous institution in this part of the East End for several decades. But things changed after the Second World War. The club had been set up by a group of aristocratic young men, whose descendants eventually lost interest. We still get some money from the original trust, but nowadays we're largely funded by the local authority.'

'And there's less of the religion, presumably?'

'Less of everything. When this institution was set up, it was supposed to transform the lives and values of the people of the East End. Now we're little more than a youth club.'

I'd re-read Ryan's diary before leaving to come here. 'Tonight I met John,' he'd written in January. 'It was freezing with snow on the riverbank. It was vile. Stew said I should go. He said I would be OK. I wish I had never gone to the Lord Napier.'

I shivered.

'Are you cold? I think the heating's on . . .'

'No,' I said, smiling too much now, out of nervousness. 'Well, yes, a bit. So. Um. Are you employed by the club?'

'Yes. It's a full-time job running this place. Open six nights a week, camping trips, sports fixtures; and then there's the equipment and the property. It's not a well paid job, but it comes with a house. And it's very rewarding. We have a lot of kids from troubled backgrounds. They need a fair amount of attention.'

Oh, I bet they do, I thought. I bet they're absolutely the sort of kids you want, pitiful levels of self-esteem and no one to confide in when things go wrong.

'Do you need particular qualifications?'

'I'm a trained social worker. I worked in children's homes before this. But you don't want to talk about me. You want to know about Ryan.'

'Yes.'

The noise level in the hall outside was rising. I wondered how many of those boys making that commotion out there were involved in Stewart Saddler's sex ring, and what had gone so drastically wrong as far as Ryan was concerned. After all, they couldn't *keep* killing kids. Had Ryan become dangerous to them in some way? Because his client was an MP?

He'd written that he knew who John was. He could have recognised Bagnall from the television or the papers. Admittedly, the only reference to Bagnall's election to the chairmanship of the Brussels Group that I'd been able to find was a three-column story at the bottom of page seven in the *Daily Correspondent*. But it had been accompanied by a tiny photograph. It was conceivable Ryan had seen that. Or he could have spotted him on television, sitting on the benches in the

House of Commons, or in the background to some shot in the lobbies.

'Are you all right?'

'Huh? . . . Oh, I er . . .'

'You seemed a bit distracted—'

'Oh, no, no: Please go on . . .'

'So as I say, he seemed an exceptionally bright child to me. A boy you couldn't help liking.'

'Did he seem worried in the weeks before he died?'

'No? Why d'you ask?'

I shrugged, cheerfully inept. 'Oh, I don't know. His mum seemed to think there was something he was trying to tell her.'

'Really? I saw no sign of anything. Not that I would have done, I suspect. I didn't have that kind of relationship with him.'

So how *would* you describe it, this relationship?

'No loss of concentration? nothing like that?'

'Nope.' He smiled, drained his tea and rinsed his mug.

How did men like John get in touch with Saddler, I wondered. Did they all know each other? Meet? Send letters? Use the Internet? How did he co-ordinate it all so that the boys were available when the men needed them?

'I gather Ryan's friend Dean is a member of the club as well?'

'Most kids round here are.'

'Is he here tonight? Might it be possible to have a word with him?'

I swallowed the rest of my tea and handed Saddler the mug.

'We can have a look,' he offered.

We went back into the main body of the hall. Boys aged from ten to around sixteen were playing table tennis, seated round card tables with chessboards and playing cards, kicking a ball at the far end of the room. Saddler called over a small boy who was mooching down the middle of the hall between the tables, hands in pockets.

He wore a black jacket made of some shiny material. His hair was lank, mousey and his teeth were still too big for his mouth.

'This is Helen,' Stewart told him. 'She's writing an article about Ryan, and she wants to ask you a few questions. You don't have to say anything you don't want to, but perhaps you might like to talk to her? Shall I stay with you?'

Dean hesitated. I prayed for him to say no.

''S'all right,' he said.

I suggested we went back into the kitchen, where it was quieter. Dean led the way, walking with a swagger, arrogant and embarrassed.

'Can I have a drink?' he asked, opening the fridge. He took out a bottle of squash, poured some into a glass and topped it up from the tap, splashing himself in the process, then hoisted himself onto the counter, where he sat, swinging his shoes against the cupboard door.

'I'm sorry about Ryan . . .'

'Yeah,' said Dean.

'I wanted to talk about what happened on the marshes.'

'Ryan got killed,' he said sullenly.

'I know. Before that.'

He scowled. 'Wha'd'you mean?'

'The thing you did for Stewart.' I kept my voice low.

Dean stared at me, cockiness draining from him visibly.

'I dunno what you're talking about.' His lips were set in a small, defiant line.

'I know about John and Hackney Marshes,' I said quietly. 'No, don't go.' I caught his wrist as he made to jump off the counter. 'I want to help you, and find out what really happened to Ryan. I think it had something to do with the rent boy stuff on the Marshes.'

'You're making it up,' he said, shaking me off. 'I wasn't no rent boy. That's disgustin'!'

'Ryan wrote a diary.'

'Ain't nuffink to do with me what he wrote.'

'It wasn't your fault,' I said. 'It was Stewart's fault, and John's, and the other bloke's – the one you were with.'

'Shut up!' Dean said fiercely. 'If you don't shut up, I'll call Stew.'

He had me there. That was the last thing I wanted.

Though how in heaven's name did I expect Dean to defy Saddler, when I couldn't do it myself?

'We could stop it.'

Dean shook his head. 'I don't know what you're talking about.'

I fished a photograph from my bag and showed it to him. 'Do

you recognise this man?' It was Tony Bagnall, the photograph most of the papers had used when he committed suicide.

He shook his head. He was perched on the edge of the counter, poised for flight.

'Is this John?'

'I've told you, I don't know what you're fuckin' talking about. I'm getting out of here.'

'Sure.' I fished in my bag. I'd gone wrong somewhere. He jumped down off the counter. 'Look, if you think of anything else, call me on one of these numbers.' I handed him my card. He took one look at it, shoved it in the back pocket of his jeans, and walked away, struggling to recover a little pre-teen cool. Damn, damn, damn, I thought. Perhaps I'd asked the wrong questions.

Chapter Eleven

THE TRAIN SPED NORTH through the outskirts of London: racing across the pastures and water meadows of the stockbroker belt, past slag heaps and pylons towards slate villages in steep valleys. I sat at the window, watching the landscape with a feeling of almost sensuous pleasure. Fields, hedgerows, coppices . . . an earlier shower had drenched the countryside so that the spring sunlight sparkled on the leaves and the grass, drawing the sap to the surface, making the meadows impossibly green.

I was clutching in my lap the fax from Joe which had been waiting in the study when I woke up this morning. He'd already had a hectic round of meetings with people in the administration who were working on healthcare policy. He was missing me. He would always remember Saturday night. I was beautiful and sexy and funny and fun to be with, and he'd try to call me later.

I read and re-read this communication. I felt it would repay close attention, that my appreciation of it would improve with detailed analysis. So it wasn't until we were almost in the Midlands that I was able to bring myself reluctantly to put it aside and move on to the pile of newspapers I'd bought on the station.

These were much less interesting. The *Daily News* had a breathless piece by the showbiz editor about Penny's birthday party, which mentioned all the guests except me, although Nat Connor, lead singer of the band Spoof, was referred to twice, and he hadn't been there. John Salt was described as 'the brilliant director of *Dangerous Passion*' with an enthusiasm that suggested he was the source of the leak, and Joe as 'the whizzkid with the moody good looks'.

The only other remotely memorable piece was interesting mainly because of its author.

There wasn't anything in itself surprising about Charles Swift's appearance in the *Daily Correspondent*. Reputedly the most intellectually impressive member of the Cabinet, Swift took every available opportunity to show off his cleverness. He was always cropping up on feature pages to mount an impassioned defence of blood sports or an Englishman's right to smoke himself to death.

But he usually stayed off the sensitive subjects, which in his case were Europe and the quality of James Sherlock's leadership.

Charles Swift hated the idea of Europe. He was descended from a family of country squires and could trace his ancestry back to the Norman Conquest, which was quite as close to Europe as he wanted to get. He regarded the European Union as a bureaucratic behemoth set up by small-minded foreigners for purposes of meddling; and he particularly hated the Germans, a people he regarded as a race of warmongers who had only ever had one aim, to dominate Europe.

He was right-wing, rude and very far from physically attractive. Grossly overweight, habitually sprinkled with sweat, and with a voice so soft it sounded as though it belonged to a disturbingly articulate small child, he didn't look like a politician for the television age. By rights he should never have got past the selection procedures.

Yet he had not only made it into Parliament and the Cabinet, but he was remarkably popular in the country. Perhaps it was the xenophobia. Anyway, James Sherlock would have been unwise to isolate him. Swift may not have had a high opinion of his leader, but he was less of a threat inside the Cabinet, bound by rules of collective responsibility, than outside, writing articles, making speeches and creating mayhem.

It seemed to be part of the deal that he behaved himself in print. Today, though, he was on dangerous territory, because he was writing about sleaze.

This was most odd. Swift seemed to be implying, or straining to imply, that what he called the 'insidious modern disease of sexual and financial double-dealing' had infected both parties. But it took only a moment's reflection to realise that all the sexual licence and dubious financial dealings had afflicted members of his own party. The MPs who'd slept with each other and had babies with their secretaries, who'd fiddled their tax returns and accepted bribes, had all been Conservatives.

So it was an extremely curious article for a cabinet minister to have written. Perhaps he was trying to suggest that corruption was an endemic political problem, 'a legacy of the permissive sixties', as he put it. (It was a well known fact that Labour had thought up the sixties, funded them, and still wished they were happening.) If so, the attempt backfired. The only scandals to have come to light had been Tory scandals.

So far, at any rate.

And it seemed perverse to remind the electorate of them now, shortly before an election.

I put down the paper. We were racing through a tunnel somewhere in Nottinghamshire. I wondered what Joe's reaction would be if Elise Bagnall were somehow able to confirm my theory that her husband had abused Ryan Stoner. Would he congratulate me for a fine piece of investigative journalism? Or hate me for raking it up before an election?

If I proved that Bagnall had abused Ryan Stoner, I would be fatally undermining an important element in Labour's election campaign. There could be no taunts about Tory sleaze then, because what Bagnall had done would seem far, far worse.

At Bradford Station I caught a taxi to the village on the city outskirts where Tony and Elise Bagnall had lived for the past thirteen years. Daffodils swarmed over the lawn of the hilly garden; the windowsill of a conservatory which ran along one flank of the solid redbrick villa was crammed with pot plants. Elise Bagnall appeared from the side of the house as the taxi drew into the drive, a pair of secateurs in her hand, her elaborate blonde hairdo wrapped in a scarf against the whipping April winds.

'I thought I'd do some cutting back,' she announced as I paid off the taxi driver. She was in her early fifties, I guessed, handsome in a full-blown sort of way, and spoke with a rich, unabashed Yorkshire accent. 'Tony, now, could never understand the gardening. "You're not satisfied, ever" he used to say, not realising that's the whole point.'

She led me inside, shrugging off her jacket, tossing her scarf over a hook and her gardening gloves on the hall table, fluffing up her hair with long fingernails. We went into the kitchen, where she made a cup of tea while I admired the view over the city.

'Aye, it's great. We bought this house to celebrate when he became leader of the council. He said he'd be able to see what were going on all over Bradford.' She indicated for me to follow her into the sitting room. 'Made me laugh, the papers saying I'd have to leave it because we had no money.' She put down the tray and gestured for me to sit down. 'You're going to ask me now what he did mean. They've all been asking – I've had reporters hanging around all week, and I've told 'em over and over I don't have the foggiest. There you go, love.'

She handed me a cup of tea. I sipped it and looked round the room. Immaculate. The house showed not the slightest sign of penury. The shinily-upholstered chintz three-piece suite was new, the television was huge. Two or three of this month's glossy women's magazines lay neatly arranged on the coffee table, one on top of each other with their titles showing.

'Not that we've ever been rich,' she went on, picking a speck from her blouse, 'but we have been careful. Whatever he meant, it wasn't that we didn't have enough money. But there you go – every day someone asks. Even Simon Healy asked.'

'Simon Healy?'

'He came up here on – what day was it? They've all run together in my head. Friday. Said he wanted to see me, having found the body and that.'

'Oh?'

'It seemed to me rather thoughtful of him. He'd had to tell me about Tony in the first place, of course, poor man . . .'

'Yes, of course.'

'I certainly hadn't expected him to come and see me. Tony'd never had much time for him – they had political differences. None of that matters now, does it?'

'I suppose not.'

'He wanted to see if there was anything he could do for me: if I had someone to help me organise the funeral, that sort of thing.

He said he was sure I had enough money, but he thought I might not have enough . . . support. He was very kind. Brought me some of Tony's things, too. His fountain pen, his grandfather's watch. Said June was in no fit state to organise anything, and he didn't expect I wanted to come down. He didn't like the idea of someone I didn't know very well handling them.'

I accepted a slice of Elise Bagnall's home-made lemon sponge, wishing I could square my impression of this woman – bosomy, slightly brassy, far from stupid – with the monstrous idea of Tony Bagnall, child molester.

I had to remind myself again that child molesters don't necessarily look evil, and that Elise Bagnall had spent all her time in Bradford while her husband was doing God knows what in London.

I brought her back to the note. 'Do you have any ideas what he might have been referring to?'

How do you ask a woman if she knew her husband abused young children?

She looked at me narrowly. 'No . . . Oh, I dare say our marriage might look rather distant to you. I know for a fact as some folk thought it was finished when Tony went to London and I didn't. Quite gleeful they were too. But I never wanted to live down South. I like Bradford, and I've got my little business here – and I think it made things easier for him that he could get on with his job during the week. I don't think I'd have seen more of him if I'd gone down there. But that didn't mean we didn't talk when we were together.' She refilled my tea cup. 'We trusted each other, and I think I've been proved right: there haven't been girls crawling out of the woodwork since he died, have there?'

I admitted that there had been no girls.

'So there was nothing wrong domestically. And I think I can safely say I don't believe he made many mistakes. Politically, I mean. I'd have known if he had.'

'I don't suppose,' I said slowly, 'he ever said anything about a boys' club in the East End? The Lord N'pier? That's how they pronounce it down there. It's spelt Napier.'

The effect was electric.

Elise Bagnall froze, cake knife suspended, her lips pursed. The room seemed suddenly suffocating. The idea of the Lord

Napier sat monstrously, squatly, between us, sucking life out of the atmosphere.

When Elise finally spoke her voice sounded quite different. The warm, bustling tone was gone. She seemed drained of energy. 'And who,' she asked quietly, 'told you about that?'

Chapter Twelve

UNTIL THAT MOMENT, I think Elise Bagnall had been treating this interview as one more thing she had to get through, like applying for probate or replying to letters of commiseration from the constituents. She had to see me because I was the journalist who'd found Tony's body. She'd chat to me for an hour, feed me lemon cake, and then I'd be gone.

But all of a sudden everything had changed. She put the cake knife down slowly on the plate and drew her hands together in her lap.

'You've seen June,' she said at last. 'That's it, isn't it?'

I nodded.

'I knew I should have said something . . . I didn't want to alarm her . . . I thought she wasn't going to talk to the press.'

'She hasn't done. She made an exception for me.'

Elise Bagnall stared into the middle distance without speaking. I waited, letting her make up her mind while the silence became uncomfortable.

'What's your theory, then?' she asked eventually. 'What do you think you've discovered?'

'I'm not sure.'

Elise Bagnall got up and crossed to the window. She looked out over the city. 'Perhaps I should have come clean in the first place,' she said, more to herself than to me: 'told the party, told the press . . . I was frightened. And then I spoke to June and I was more frightened still . . .'

'I'm sorry . . . I don't understand.'

She stood with her back towards me for a minute or two, then seemed to reach a decision. She turned back. 'Tony was being blackmailed,' she said. 'But not for anything he'd actually done. He was being set up.'

I stared at her.

'You might well look like that,' she said, running her fingers through her hair. 'That's how I felt at first. Thought he was paranoid.'

'*How* was he being set up?'

She came back towards me and sat down. 'Someone – I don't know who – got some kid to say he'd been abusing him.'

'Ryan Stoner,' I murmured.

'Yes.'

Could this be true, that Bagnall's connection with Ryan – the link I thought I'd so cleverly discovered – was a hoax?

'But why? What had Tony done that someone should want to smear him so horribly?'

'I don't know. I do not know.' She shook her head. 'But he didn't do it – abuse that child. You have to believe that. Whatever you've been thinking, he didn't even know that boy.'

'He had a connection with the Lord Napier, though?'

'Oh yes: that was what was so evil about it.' She was bitter. 'It all looked quite plausible.'

I couldn't work it out. 'Why on earth did someone get Ryan to say he abused him? *Who* got Ryan to say it?'

'Tony wouldn't tell me everything. I think he knew more than he said. It was my own fault, partly . . . I didn't take it seriously at first. Oh Christ . . .' She put her head in her hands.

I waited. And eventually, she looked up. Slowly, she began to explain. 'He started getting these threats, you see. A couple of months ago they began. He was on the Internet, and he got messages through that, the e-mail . . . I never had much time for it myself – the Internet I mean. Or the messages, come to that. I thought it was a joke.'

'But he took them seriously.'

'He was having trouble in the constituency . . .'

'With this woman, Syreeta Aziz?'

'Yes, although it wasn't so much with Syreeta herself as with her supporters. People were trying to persuade Syreeta to challenge Tony; there was a whispering campaign against him. So when he started getting these threatening messages on the computer – saying he must stand down – we assumed it was one of the people who were backing her.'

'What did the messages say exactly?'

'That he must give up the seat and forget going for the chairmanship of the Brussels Group . . . that something unpleasant might happen – to me – if he didn't. At first we laughed them off. But then the other things started happening.'

'What things?'

'He got pictures on the e-mail. He downloaded one or two. They were pornographic, so he stopped accepting them. But then I walked into the room where he keeps his computer and there was this horrible image of a man and a child. I mean,' she shuddered, 'really horrible. Vile. He said it must have been on – what was it? Screensaver, I think: the thing that came up if he left the computer on.'

'But he could get rid of it, surely?'

'Yes, but it happened again. After he'd got rid of it once, it came back. Oh, about a week later. And there was another one – different but equally horrible, on something called wallpaper. Would that be right?'

'When he switched on the computer?'

'Yes. I never saw that one. He only told me, though he wouldn't describe it. He was almost physically ill. Really upset. Said he couldn't sleep for nights afterwards. He couldn't understand why someone would be doing that to him.'

I frowned. 'But surely someone would have had to get into the house to download those images or load them from a disk?'

'Yes. That's what Tony said. We even thought it might have been our cleaning lady – although, without meaning to be horrible, she's the least likely person to be computer literate in the world. And even if she *had* known about computers, she's not the child pornography type, somehow. She's a dear. But then Tony searched the house and we found a broken window catch in the utility room. I can show you if you like . . .?'

I got up and followed Elise down the hall and through the kitchen, into a small room. There was a washing machine, a tumble drier and a washing basket containing a pile of neatly folded sheets. A small window, a metre square, opened onto the garden. The catch had recently been replaced: there was a patch of scuffed, differently-painted wood where the old one had been.

'But you have an alarm,' I said, frowning. 'Surely an intruder would have triggered it?'

Elise folded a clothes airer and stood it up against the wall. 'I'm afraid we had the alarm put in when all this happened.' She gestured back to the sitting room and I led the way. 'We'd never been very security conscious. I don't have a lot of jewellery or anything like that. I only wear the cheap costume stuff. We don't even have a stereo. There's a video, but that would have been the only thing worth stealing until the computer arrived about eighteen months ago – but that's so bulky and tangled up with wires. It would take half a day to unplug.' She smoothed the sheets absent-mindedly. 'Anyway, then there were more messages, telling him to quit, saying people would find out about the pornography. And there'd be more of it. They implied he was someone who *liked* these things.'

'No clues as to who was sending them?'

'No. Tony said you can put any name on messages. And they were always in different names.'

'Did they say *why* Tony should quit politics?'

'No. He didn't know what he'd done – except go for the Brussels Group job. I wanted to believe it was some mad person. But he said they were too slick and confident to be insane. He was alarmed. He took it very seriously.'

I sat down in the armchair again. It seemed so unlikely that someone would break into a house merely to download some pornography from the Internet or transfer it from a disk and leave it on a computer. Unlikely and horrible. And yet I believed Elise. Sometimes you have to trust your instincts.

'Did he ever think about giving in to the threats?'

She shook her head. 'He wasn't the type to submit to bullying. That was always half his trouble, politically. He wasn't even going to drop out of the contest for the Brussels Group job. But then the threats got worse. That was when they let him know they had some kid prepared to claim Tony had been abusing him. They said they were going to "expose" him as a paedophile.'

'Through the Internet?'

'Yes. They said the next move would be to post it on the Labour Party's web site or something. I'm sorry,' she apologised. 'I'm not very familiar with all these computer terms.'

'That makes sense, though.'

'And they were going to get the boy to talk to people in the party. Tony said it didn't really matter who they chose to tell: once the boy came forward everyone would know. They were trying to scare him into leaving politics.'

'And had they done that by the time he died? Got Ryan to talk?'

'They might have done. That might have been what triggered it.' She smiled at me apologetically. 'I keep wondering what on earth it could possibly have been, to tip him over the edge. When he left here that Sunday night – the Sunday before last – he seemed determined to fight it. And the next thing I know, he's dead.' She shook her head.

'So – let me get this straight: they wanted him to leave the Brussels Group and Westminster, or they said they'd expose him as a paedophile? They'd spread rumours on the Internet, then get Ryan to confirm them to people in the party?'

'Yes.'

'But surely, his word against a child's . . .?'

'You believed it, didn't you?' she said. 'Have you ever had any dealings with these child abuse cases? Tony had them in his constituency. Of *course* people want to believe the child. I bet when you came up here, you thought he was guilty. Didn't you?'

I was silent.

'And you didn't even know about the child pornography,' she said bitterly. 'No doubt they would have made sure that came out, somehow.'

'And this is why he killed himself?'

'I suppose he *did* kill himself . . .' Elise said slowly. 'I keep on thinking there must be some other explanation. It hurts to believe he'd commit suicide, that's the trouble: I thought I could support him, keep him going. As long as I went on believing in him, I thought he'd try to fight. But perhaps that call to June Lennox, sending her off to the boys' club, was the final straw. Perhaps when it came to it he despaired of ever convincing people he was innocent.'

'Or perhaps he was alarmed by Ryan's death,' I said. 'Perhaps he thought, if Ryan had spread his allegations first, which we don't know, that he might even be suspected of Ryan's murder?'

She looked at me gravely, knowing it was what I'd suspected.

'Does June know about any of this? The pornography, the threats from Ryan?'

Elise shook her head. 'I was the only person Tony told. As far as I know. But I didn't speak to him for the last two days of his life because he was frantically busy writing some speech for the Brussels Group . . .'

'De Moleyns . . .' I interrupted.

'Sorry?'

'He was going to mention someone called de Moleyns. I've seen a copy of the draft. Did he ever mention someone called de Moleyns?'

Elise frowned. 'I don't think so . . . No, I'm pretty sure he didn't. I'd have remembered – such an odd name . . .'

'He must have thought they were on the point of "exposing" him.'

'Yes; perhaps he couldn't bear it any longer. He said he felt they were always one jump ahead of him, that they were everywhere.'

'Who *are* these people?'

'God only knows. Tony didn't. The bloody establishment, he called them, but that was his answer to everything.' She smiled. 'It was always the establishment.'

'Did he ever mention *any* names?'

She shook her head. 'No. He wouldn't talk about it. Although I had the impression he knew more than he was letting on. He said if I knew who they were it would be even more dangerous. But – that Sunday night, when he left here for the last time – he said he'd found a way of getting back at them. I've thought since maybe he meant by committing suicide. But it hardly seems a very effective form of retaliation.' She smiled bleakly. 'It just doesn't make sense.'

We stared out at the redbrick sprawl of the city her husband had run.

'I'm telling you this in confidence,' she said. 'I don't want anyone else to know. I'm telling you because you were already half way there – more than – and I didn't want you to take away the wrong impression. But if this came out a lot of people would *still* think "no smoke without fire" and Tony isn't here to defend himself. That's why I haven't been to the police. Even though, if someone else didn't actually put that noose round his neck, they might as well have done.'

I sat in the train while the countryside flashed past and went over and over the conversation with Elise Bagnall. Sarah was right: there is more than one type of cleverness, and Elise Bagnall was a clever woman. She gave the impression that she knew what was what; she was *sharp*; she had the measure of people. You felt she wouldn't be easily fooled.

And at least her version made sense of the diary. 'Stew says it will stop if I do what he says,' Ryan had written. 'I am going to do this, because it is not such a big thing to say anyway. He has shown me some photographs.'

Not such a big thing . . . poor kid. And now they were both dead.

I'd been puzzling over why Stewart Saddler would have needed to show Ryan photographs, when Ryan had been with the man at least ten times. It was the one thing that hadn't fitted. But if Saddler had wanted Ryan to say someone else was John; if he'd wanted him to identify a different man from the one he'd actually been sending Ryan to meet, that was another matter. Then he might well have shown him photographs.

It was infuriating of Bagnall to have left so few clues. I could see he might have thought by killing himself he'd spare Elise and the Labour Party the disgrace of the child abuse allegations. But he might have found a way to leave *some* hint behind, beyond a faintly hysterical speech and a single name, de Moleyns.

I still didn't understand why they'd picked him in the first place. He was hardly a front-rank politician. It was an awful lot of effort to go to for a backbencher whom nobody seemed to think had ever achieved anything of note.

I shook my head in exasperation. Something to do with the Brussels Group . . . But it was so *muddy*.

We raced through grimy stations, past rows of redbrick houses. Bagnall had survived the attempt to unseat him in the constituency. He hadn't been frightened off by the invasion of his house and computer. But he must have feared he couldn't survive allegations as serious as those Ryan had made, or was about to make. Even if Bagnall *was* innocent, the accusations would have ended his political career. So he committed suicide to spare himself the misery of trying to face them down, to spare Elise and the party the shame.

But it still didn't quite make sense. He hadn't looked to his wife like a man on the point of committing suicide. Elise had believed in him. And she was a tough woman. He was a tough man. Had he simply *given in*? Why, when he'd told Elise he'd found a way of retaliating?

There was *one* other possibility: that he hadn't committed suicide at all. Elise had said, 'If someone else didn't actually put that noose round his neck . . .'

I sighed through my teeth. Katrina didn't want me to talk about the diary, and now Elise didn't want me to talk about Tony Bagnall. Sam once said I was a good journalist because I was such an incorrigible gossip. But right now the only information I acquired was given to me on condition it wouldn't be repeated. Which is no use at all.

'Dan Dare called,' Sarah announced when I arrived at the office. 'And Joanna Beverley, enquiring after her latest article about women with chests. She wouldn't stop going on about some new shop she's found in Paris. How was Bradford?'

'Elise thinks her husband was being blackmailed.'

Sarah doesn't count. She is trappist in her discretion.

'Is that why he committed suicide?'

'I don't know.' I put down my bags and slid the papers from under my arm onto the desk: 'Possibly.'

'So what had he done?'

'Elise – his wife – thinks nothing. She thinks it was a setup.'

'What?'

I filled the kettle. 'Someone was trying to implicate him as a paedophile.'

'*Implicate* him?' Sarah's voice was plummy with disbelief.

Perhaps because she is so troubled about being the niece of an earl and having had a ridiculously expensive education, Sarah can sometimes overdo the political correctness. She believes coalminers are all good-hearted people; she also subscribes to the hard-line feminist view that children never tell lies about sexual abuse.

I shrugged. There was no point in arguing. Especially as I wasn't allowed to talk about the details. But I could see Elise's point that Tony would have had a hard time persuading people sweet-faced Ryan Stoner was telling a pack of lies.

'Simon Healy had been to see her,' I said instead.

'Why?'

'That was my reaction. Because he's a nice bloke, I suspect.'

'So you're coming round to Hester's view of him as misunderstood man?'

'I don't know.' I put a mug of tea on her desk. 'But I never saw any reason to dislike him in the past, and he doesn't seem to have changed. On the contrary: he took the trouble to talk to me at the Dalmores when some of their friends would happily have ignored me.'

'You may be right.' Sarah grinned. 'And it is about time someone wrote the "Simon Healy is a good guy" piece.'

Chapter Thirteen

THE RISOTTO WAS LUSHLY, creamily glutinous, plump with wine and flecked with wild mushrooms.

'You should do this more often,' I remarked, impressed. 'You're a much better cook than I am.'

Bobby peeled off the oven gloves, refilled my wine glass and sat down across our kitchen table.

'The least I can do. You've had a hell of a week, finding that body and having to go to all that trouble with your toenails.'

'I think it was worth it.'

'So I gathered. And then being bullied by Dan into trekking up to Bradford to find out why the guy committed suicide. And through all this I'm hardly ever around. There's your mother thinks I'm taking care of you and all you ever see of me is an occasional mug on the draining board in the morning.'

'That may be my fault for getting up so late.'

'I wouldn't dream of commenting on your slothfulness.' Bobby tasted the risotto. 'So. Does the new boy cook in return for the black underwear treatment? Will he be able to feed you in the style to which you've become accustomed?'

'God, I've no idea. I've only had one night with him.'

'But he sent a fax this morning. It must be serious.'

'You surely didn't read it!'

'I wouldn't dream of reading your mail. Though it lies around for long enough while you sleep. What's he like?'

'Lovely, I think. It's a bit early to say. But he hasn't made any mistakes so far. You know how you can usually see what's going to go wrong?'

'No.'

'You're hopeless. The bloke says something and you think, "oh *no!*" There hasn't been any of that.' I scraped my fork on the bottom of the bowl, gathering up the last grains of rice. 'Sarah says it's sheer bloody lust. Which it is – except I only ever lust after people who interest me.'

'You're in danger of saying "not like you: you're capable of having sex with a spatula".' Bobby peered under the grill at the red mullet. 'Which would be priggish even if true. I think it's a good thing if you've found someone who . . . interests you. But isn't it affecting your work?'

'I'm not *completely* sex-obsessed. I can think about other things.'

'That's not what I meant. Aren't you supposed to be writing about Simon Healy? And this Bagnall guy? Isn't it all a bit close to home?'

'The Healy piece is only about how he met his girlfriend; it's hardly a major investigation. And no one knows why Bagnall killed himself.'

If he did.

The red mullet were delicious: moist, reeking with fishy flavours. Bobby served them with a green salad. Perhaps, I thought, I could work on his guilt about how little he looked after me . . .

'I heard a great story last night,' Bobby announced, as I tucked in greedily.

'Oh?'

'Which *wouldn't* be a conflict of interest.'

'Oh?'

'In fact, I can't think of anything that would make you more popular with your new Labour friends.'

'I hope it's not about banking.'

'I wouldn't waste a good story about banking on you. No, this is right up your street. Sex. Difficult to believe . . . but . . . we've had a guy over here from New York for a couple of months, working on an international merger. He's going back tomorrow. I had dinner with him last night and he told me that while he's been here – this will offend your delicate sensibilities, I know, but maybe she was interesting – he took up with a high class call girl.'

'Hey, I'm not saying it's a *good* thing to have difficulty getting sexually aroused. It's bloody boring most of the time.'

'All right, then. So this girl – Dillie, she's called, I think – tells him she has another client. And who the hell d'you think it is?'

'I don't know. Someone I've heard of?'

'Ian Moorhouse.'

'No!'

I thought back to the Dalmores' dinner party. Another rumour flying round Westminster, Simon had said, but no one seems to know what it is. Moorhouse and a *prostitute*.

'This woman's *talking* about it?' I said incredulously. 'Would she talk to me?'

'I could ask him.' Bobby looked at his watch. 'I'd have to call him tonight at his hotel. I don't know what time he's flying out tomorrow.'

'And she's talking?' I repeated incredulously.

'I got the impression from him she was pretty pissed with Moorhouse. Sometimes didn't show up or something. And she's a Labour supporter, apparently: thinks George Dalmore's the best thing since the basque.'

'How long has this been going on?'

Bobby held up his hand. 'Before you bombard me with questions, I don't know anything else. But if you're interested, I'll ask him.'

Bobby's colleague wasn't in. So we ate his chocolate pots and collapsed on the sofa to watch television like an old married couple. My mother would have approved. Not that there was any prospect of her dropping in and catching us in this promising position. She thinks our area is unsafe after dark.

'Llewellyn's on,' Bobby said, looking down the listings on the back page of the newspaper. 'He's quite good. Kind of acerbic.'

'He was at the Dalmores',' I said, drawing up my legs comfortably and balancing my coffee cup on the arm of the sofa.

'You're so glamorous, I can't bear it. He's got that John Salt on, the guy who directed *Dangerous Passion*.'

I bit my lip and we switched on. Nick Llewellyn was behind a desk. He'd explained to me at the Dalmores that he'd inserted a clause into his contract insisting that his guests should only ever sit on his right, because his left profile was so much better. He had then turned both ways for me to appreciate the difference, but I couldn't see a thing.

He and John Salt were talking about John's latest project, the first Labour election broadcast, which was an excuse for John to explain why he supported Labour and wasn't afraid of the Party's tax plans, despite being an internationally acclaimed movie maker and phenomenally rich.

'Gruesome,' I said. 'It looks fine unless you know they were having dinner together four nights ago.'

The telephone was ringing. Bobby picked it up, then placed his hand over the mouthpiece.

'It's the interesting guy,' he hissed. 'From Washington.' I took the call downstairs, so Bobby could continue watching Llewellyn in peace.

Joe still sounded incredibly sexy. 'I've sat through endless papers on the relationship between Europe and the former Soviet bloc,' he told me, 'and endured interminable dinners with Japanese delegates. But I haven't stopped thinking about you for a minute. I am going to do *such* things to you when I get back.'

'Oh yes?'

'I'm going to bite and lick every bit of your body: exhaust you with kissing – your arms, your eyes, your kneecaps – and then I'm going to do exactly what I want with you, and you won't have any choice except to submit.'

'I feel weak already.'

'Good, because there's no point in trying to get away from me; I shall pursue you wherever you go. And when I catch you, I shall remove all your clothes slowly, and make you do whatever I want, and leave you longing for more . . .'

It sounded lovely; I couldn't wait for him to stop thinking about geopolitics and catch the plane back to London.

'So I hope you're taking good care of yourself in preparation.'

'In theory, yes. In practice I'm mostly working.'

'What sort of work?'

'Ryan Stoner. Tony Bagnall. I went to see Elise today. Bagnall's wife,' I added helpfully.

'Bagnall and Stoner,' he said. 'They could hardly be more different.'

'Mmn,' I agreed vaguely. I would have to be careful. 'How *is* Washington?'

'You already asked me that. I'm certainly looking forward to getting back and seeing you again. And sometimes I get so exasperated with politics . . . you know, I was talking to a backbench Tory this morning – really decent man called Terence Hardie, who's very interested in transport policy, a railway enthusiast, not a fan of the great car economy. That rare thing, a green Tory. And he's got a bypass planned for his constituency, straight through an ancient wood. But the majority of his constituents want it, so he's having to support it.'

'That's rather spineless.'

'It's politics. He can't afford to upset huge numbers of constituents. He believes they're better off with him than with the Opposition, who'll support it if he doesn't. And it's what local people want.'

'I suppose, in that case . . .'

'But his constituents only want it so they can put more cars on the roads,' Joe said with a patient air, as if I hadn't really grasped the point. 'Anyway, that's the sort of question that comes up all the time in politics. You're constantly being asked to make compromises with your principles in pursuit of power or some higher good.'

'Not you, surely? You don't have to worry about being re-elected?'

'No,' Joe admitted. 'Not me so much . . . Anyway, what are you doing? Perhaps I can think about you during my dinner with the State Department.'

'Watching Llewellyn on television. With John Salt. They're pretending they don't know each other.'

'How incredibly tacky,' said Joe. 'See what I mean about politics? In that case I think I should explain in detail exactly what I'm going to do when I finally get my hands on you.'

I was trailing around the kitchen the next morning, wondering where I'd put the marmalade (on the dining room table) and why I couldn't find the open bottle of milk (because I'd put it back in the fridge) and, above all, why I'd drunk so much wine the previous night.

When the telephone rang it sounded as if a fire engine was tearing through the house.

I picked it up thinking it would be Bobby crowing that he'd already been in the office for two hours. I was prepared to tolerate this if he'd tried to get hold of his colleague with the Moorhouse contact.

But it was a woman. 'Helen Clare?' she said heartily. I moved the receiver away from my ear.

'Yes?'

'I don't know if you remember me? Jean Hammond.'

'Of course.' I'd interviewed Jean Hammond twice in the previous year, but the question was superfluous anyway. The entire country knew who Jean Hammond was; she made a point of being memorable.

Hammond was a Conservative backbench MP and one of the most flamboyant figures in parliament. She wore vivid suits in shades of flame and fuschia, had trenchant opinions and let everyone know what they were. I liked her forcefulness and admired her ability to get things done.

'You'll think I'm hopeless,' she announced, 'but I've only just read your feature on finding poor Tony Bagnall's body. We've met, haven't we? I'd seen that a journalist had found the body of course, when it happened, but I hadn't quite registered it was *you*. All those reports made you sound absolutely terrifying; I had no idea you had such a glamorous past.'

I muttered something about its not having been all that glamorous really.

'You mustn't put yourself down,' Jean Hammond said severely. 'Anyway, I only got round to the Sunday papers this morning and I must say, I thought your piece was very good. But I was particularly struck by one line in it, about all these men who have had to resign because of scandals being pro-Europe.'

'Well . . . not all of them,' I said ruefully. 'Barry Bianchini's a leading Eurosceptic, and I'm not sure Ellis Fletcher or Geoffrey Doxat have any very fixed position.'

'No, but *some* of them – and that interested me greatly. I knew it also interested Tony.'

'It did? You talked to him about it?'

'Oh *yes*. We had several most interesting conversations. The same thought had struck me, and I'd done a bit of digging. And while I was grubbing around I found out that Tony Bagnall was doing the same thing. All in all, I have to say that I think it's *most* odd that he died when did.'

'Odd?'

'I don't want to talk about it over the phone. Let's just say that I think it's *very* peculiar that everyone's accepted this suicide theory so readily.'

My head was aching. The aspirins were taking a ridiculously long time to work.

'But I saw him,' I objected feebly. 'He was hanging from the ceiling.'

Jean Hammond snorted.

'And there was a note.'

'I think Tony Bagnall had uncovered something very nasty. Bit of a coincidence that he should die, don't you think?'

'Well . . .'

'But I'm not prepared to discuss it here. When can you come and see me?'

My diary was two floors up, in the bedroom. I tried to remember what I had organised for the next few days. I was seeing Simon tomorrow and Ryan's teacher today, and I'd have to go into the *Chronicle* at some point . . .

'I've got a hellish week . . .' Jean Hammond continued. 'For some reason best known to my superiors, I'm in Wales for two days, and then there's a health debate, in which I intend to have my say, but I do have a gap late on Friday morning. Perhaps we could meet then?'

'Yes, that's fine I think . . . Shall I come to the Commons?'

'Probably not a good idea, under the circumstances. Can we meet at my flat?'

She reminded me of the address and we agreed a time.

I replaced the receiver on the wall and stared at it.

I was already kicking myself: I should have asked her about de Moleyns.

Jean Hammond clearly thought that Bagnall hadn't committed suicide. But what did she know? What did she think Bagnall had known?

I made another pot of tea. After all, there was no point in rushing this getting-out-of-the-house thing. And I would have hated to spoil Bobby's pleasure when he rang up to amuse himself at my expense.

Friday. Today was Wednesday. Ages. That was the thing about politicians: they were so busy rushing around, they had difficulty concentrating on anything properly.

I liked Jean Hammond, but I knew she was subject to enthusiasms, and occasionally to eccentricities. It was perfectly possible that there was nothing in this theory about Bagnall's being on the point of exposing some . . . some what? conspiracy, presumably.

Still, it made more sense of his death than anything else so far. More than the debts, or Simon's theory about deselection, or the official Leader's Office line about an obscure, sudden and inexplicable depression descending on him like some rogue virus.

I drank the tea and flicked in a desultory fashion through the papers. There had been another football riot at a Cup Winners' Cup match in Belgium. European soccer officials had started to make ominous noises about a ban on English clubs, which was thoroughly depressing news. English football would become more plodding than ever.

I turned inside. George had made a brilliant speech on the future of education in Bristol; Frank Threshfield, political editor of the *Sunday Chronicle*, but writing today in the *Correspondent*, commented that he already looked more like a Prime Minister than the Prime Minister.

My head was beginning to clear. The key question for the morning, I decided, was whether I knew Adam Sage well enough to invite him for lunch. There was an open, faintly naïve quality about Adam. If anyone was likely to tell me whether people in the Labour Party had heard rumours about Tony Bagnall's sexuality, it wasn't Joe and it certainly wasn't Simon. Adam was my best bet.

He *had* driven me home. He had been at the Dalmores. I called his office.

I needn't have worried. He not only remembered who I was but sounded genuinely pleased to hear from me. And when I offered lunch, he said he was free tomorrow.

Chapter Fourteen

I LET BOBBY HAVE his five minutes of hilarity over his hugely funny discovery that I was still at home, still in my dressing gown, and still suffering from the world's worst headache when he called at 11.00 a.m. He was even more insufferable than I'd anticipated: he'd not only been in his office since 8.00 a.m., but swum a thousand metres of the pool at his swanky gym beforehand.

Still, he *had* spoken to his colleague, and he had got the telephone number of the high class call girl. I wrote this down and decided to postpone ringing her for a while. I couldn't believe she'd speak to me. I might as well enjoy the feeling that I was on the brink of uncovering some great scandal for a bit longer.

By now I was beginning to think that there might not, after all, be a techno music combo inside my head. I pulled on a pair of jeans and Bobby's black cashmere jumper, noticing with dismay that I'd worn it so solidly that it no longer looked as chic as I had fondly imagined.

And then I set off for Ryan's school.

This was not the primary school I attended: my mother always had ideas above her station, and I was sent to one a bus ride away. But I knew where it was and what it looked like: Victorian, redbrick, set in a concrete playground; dark, stolid, utilitarian, with separate boys' and girls' entrances. Like a lot of the schools round here, it seemed to have been built for strictness and regimentation, to keep the Victorian poor in order. I half expected to see children in ragged trousers, petticoats and shawls, like some illustration from

Dickens, making their way in cowed, uniformed crocodiles along its disinfected corridors.

This impression could hardly have been more mistaken. Mr Morrison's classroom – Ryan's old classroom – was bright with splashy paintings and models made from cornflakes packets.

Mr Morrison met me as arranged outside the head teacher's office and led me along the corridor. He was a pale, softly spoken man in his late thirties: hesitant; weedy, even. I found it hard to imagine him quelling a gang of boys like Dean, swaggering with insecure, pop-eyed masculinity.

But this impression was wrong as well: Julian Morrison turned out to be surprisingly forthright. He had a sort of missionary zeal – working in Stepney, not, as I had rather arrogantly imagined at first, because he would have had trouble getting a job anywhere else, but because he believed he could make a difference.

He'd liked Ryan enormously, he said. He'd been bright, articulate and outgoing; possibly the most responsible boy in the class. At any rate, that was how he'd been until the final months of his life, when he became increasingly introverted.

I hoped Ryan might have said something – if not confided in Mr Morrison, at least supplied some clue. 'Did you have any idea why he changed?'

Mr Morrison perched comfortably on one of the classroom tables and gestured for me to do the same. 'I thought there might have been something wrong at home. I thought, to be honest, that his mother might have a new boyfriend. We have a lot of transient father figures here, and they're trouble when they arrive and trouble when they leave. But it wasn't that . . . I feel bad now for not looking into it further. Perhaps if it had occurred at a less difficult time for some of the other children in the class, I might have had his mother in. But I know the family – I taught Ryan's older sister – and I couldn't imagine anything too serious had gone wrong. Or perhaps I simply didn't have much time for him. A week before Ryan disappeared one of his friends had all his teeth extracted – every last one – because of decay. Bad diet, you see. Another child's elder brother has recently been sent down for drug dealing. Another's father beat up her mum so badly she had to be hospitalised. We specialise here, I am afraid, in poverty, ill health, unemployment, bad diet, illegitimacy and continuous emotional upheaval. And then the Government asks why we don't perform better in their bloody tables.'

'It must have been difficult for the other children,' I said, sensing that if I let him get started on social deprivation he might not finish.

'I've been encouraging them to write stories and poems expressing what they feel. These kids have so much to put up with that sometimes it seems quite miraculous that their responses aren't blunted, that they remain as sensitive and thoughtful as they do. Give them a couple of years, mind you, especially the boys, and they'll be a lot more difficult. I wouldn't want to teach at a secondary school round here. They're great kids now, though.'

'Ryan never said anything about someone called John, I suppose?'

Julian Morrison shook his head. 'Who is he?'

'Oh, I don't know – someone his mother or his sister mentioned. Do you know much about Stewart Saddler and the Lord Napier?'

'Oh yes. I'm in favour of the place, generally speaking. Some of the staff here think it's rather overpowering, can be a bit of a distraction for the boys. But Saddler gets them involved in things. Keeps them off the streets, sometimes for years. Probably not so good for the ones who don't like sport, but it gives them a sense of structure at least, which is something a lot of them don't have.' He glanced at his watch. 'I'm afraid I'm going to have to kick you out soon. School starts again in five minutes.'

'I don't suppose there's any chance of speaking to Ryan's friend Dean?' I asked suddenly.

Mr Morrison shook his head. 'We couldn't do that without contacting his parents first. I can see why you might want to – and we could certainly try to speak to his mother – but it wouldn't be possible today, anyway. To be frank, you'd be better off going through the family in the first place.' He walked me along the corridor to the exit. He gazed out at the playground. 'Most of our parents have no skills, that's the trouble, no idea what's *meant* by entrepreneurial drive; no energy, even. And the politicians don't help. They've decided state benefits have made the unemployed listless and dependent. So what's their answer? Withdraw the state support. Which is all very well, but it leaves these kids high and dry. I'm sorry,' he turned to shake hands with me, 'I'm ranting. But they make me angry, the whole lot of them. It isn't as if it's going to be any better, frankly, when George Dalmore gets in. He wants the middle-class voters because they'll win him the election, and in pursuit of them he's prepared to abandon these kids.'

I walked towards the car, thinking about the flowers that spilt down the steps of George Dalmore's elegant house, about Simon Healy's sports car, Joe's chaotic room crammed with overflowing files and notes for future, yet-to-be-written books. Mr Morrison was right: the people at the top of the Labour Party understood the middle classes intuitively. George had more in common with middle England than James Sherlock with his millions ever could, and far far more than the Tory grandees like Charles Swift, who had grown up with the idea that they would run things.

But they all, the Labour politicians as well as the Tories, had to make a major empathic leap to be much bothered by the poverty and constant threat of waste against which Mr Morrison did daily, frontline battle.

I stepped into the road to pass three Bengali men in their sixties or seventies, huddled around their shopping bags, talking. They wore off-white tunics and trousers with Western suit jackets. A pair of old white women with perms and trolley-baskets were forced off the kerb as well in front of me; they pushed past on fat varicose-veined legs, grumbling. A young Pakistani entrepreneur in a leather jacket and tight jeans who was pushing a rail of children's clothes onto the pavement caught my eye and grinned, sharing the women's irritation at the usurpation of their pavement by foreign men.

The shopkeeper was handsome. I was still smiling inwardly when I saw a couple of skinhead youths lounging across the road, on the corner, watching him with eyes narrowed in contempt.

I walked on, thinking about Mr Morrison, wondering how much difference he could make to the lives of the children he taught, given that they had to go on to the sink secondary schools and home to parents who didn't have much to promise them. I had the key in the car door when someone pushed a yellow leaflet into my hand.

'March Against Racism,' I read. 'Act now! Fascist groups plan terror campaign in the East End!'

I let the leaflet flutter onto the passenger seat, glad to be out of the smells of curry and uncollected rubbish. It was advertising a march on Saturday to protest against the murders of Mohammed Abdul and another boy, Ali Khalifa, a sixteen-year-old killed by a white gang in Bow one evening last month.

I read the leaflet – for want of something better to do – in a traffic jam on the A13, possibly the ugliest trunk road in the world. The march was being organised by the London Coalition Against Racism and Fascism in response to the murders and to several other racially-motivated attacks in recent weeks. They promised Saturday's turnout would prove that ordinary, decent East Enders wouldn't put up with 'fascist recruitment on their doorsteps'.

I inched the car forward through the pall of exhaust fumes and turned over the leaflet. On the back the London Coalition claimed that paramilitary neo-fascist groups were increasingly presenting a threat to peace and stability in the area, where they were engaged in a recruitment drive, attracting young white men with the promise of martial arts and firearms training and inflammatory promises to rid the streets of immigrants.

'You're very elusive,' Dan observed sourly, when I eventually arrived on the editorial floor at the *Chronicle*. 'I've been calling you for days.'

'I've been working extremely hard on your behalf. Anyway, it can only have been *one* day. You weren't working on Monday.'

Dan edits on Saturdays, putting the paper to bed. In theory he has Mondays off. 'I work every day,' he said seriously. 'And I was trying to find out how you were getting on with Tony Bagnall.'

'*OK* . . .' I said cautiously. 'I've seen June Lennox, the secretary, and I was up in Bradford yesterday talking to Elise.'

'So what's the score?'

'No one knows why he killed himself.'

'That's it? That's all you've got?'

'More or less.' If I started on the blackmail, Dan would never let it go until he knew everything. It was better to leave it. 'George Dalmore's office, for what it's worth, has come to the view Bagnall had some sort of nervous breakdown.'

'Is this the Simon Healy version?'

'Yes. It's also what Dalmore himself thinks.'

'You spoke directly to Dalmore?'

I nodded. Dan was impressed, though he did his best to hide it. He didn't think I had those sort of contacts. 'Depressed about these deselection moves?'

'Possibly.'

Dan tipped his chair back, his palms against his desk. He pursed his lips and considered me. 'Peach, I don't know why, but I have this sense you're not telling me the whole truth. I know you, and you've got a funny secretive look.'

'Ah,' I said, 'well, you'll just have to give me a bit of time.'

'What have you got?'

I burst out laughing. 'That's not giving me time. That's bullying me.'

'I need to show some progress at tomorrow's editorial conference.'

'I'm certainly not telling you simply in order to further your already overblown career. Now, I want to check my messages, if that's all right? Can I borrow a desk?'

Dan waved an arm expansively at the editorial floor. 'Pick one,' he said magnanimously. 'But get this story on Bagnall soon, will you?'

I picked up the bag I'd dumped on the floor beside Dan's chair. 'Incidentally,' I asked, 'does the name de Moleyns mean anything to you?'

Dan knew everyone.

'Never heard of him,' he said.

I sat at Sandra Snugrood's desk, in front of the star feature writer's array of perfume bottles. The general rules about hot desking – no one is supposed to get proprietorial about where they sit – don't apply to Sandra. She has her own inviolate space. Dan says it's the only untouched thing about her.

The office was busy today, however, and Sandra's desk was one of the few not occupied. It had the additional attraction of a special comfy chair, because Sandra has what she describes as ergonomic problems.

I logged onto the *Chronicle*'s computer system, tapped in my password and waited for the signal to come up to tell me I had messages waiting.

Two were from Sukey, my friend in subediting, and concerned

the sports reporter she'd been trying (unsuccessfully) to get off with for the past six months. One was from Robin Rouse's secretary, asking me if I was free to have lunch with the editor and other freelance feature writers in a couple of weeks' time. And one was from Dan. It simply said, 'Bagnall. Be careful.'

'Why did you send me that message?' I demanded, presenting myself at his desk again.

'What message?' He was reading copy on screen and not concentrating.

'The message to be careful.'

He frowned. 'Peach, what are you talking about?'

Sometimes Dan makes me want to scream.

'I just *said*: the mysterious "Bagnall-be-careful" message.'

He finally looked up. 'I didn't send you any message.'

He was telling the truth. This wasn't some obscure idea of a joke. I went back to Sandra's desk and stared at the message again. Dan's log-on was on the bottom. But now I looked properly, the words had been sent at eight o'clock on Sunday morning. Dan may think he doesn't get any time off, but I have never yet known him to be at work at 8.00 a.m. on Sunday.

So someone else had sent this. Someone had hacked into the computer system and sent me a message about Bagnall purporting to come from Dan.

'What now?' he asked testily. I was in front of his desk again.

'Who knows your password?'

'I dunno. No one. Why?'

'If this message didn't come from you, someone must know your password. How secure is this system?'

'Not very. *Christ*, this irritates me.' I wasn't sure whether he meant me or someone hacking into the computer. 'It's a bloody good job we don't have any exclusives on this newspaper; they'd be all over London before we ever had a chance to run them.'

I left Dan muttering to himself and called June Lennox. She sounded a little more cheerful and was pleased to hear I'd seen Elise.

'It must be awful for her. Much worse for her, of course, than for me. It's hard to know you couldn't do anything to help, that you weren't enough support. Especially for a person who simply didn't look like the suicidal type . . . She had no ideas, presumably, about what made him do it?'

'Not really . . . Look, I wanted to ask you – that speech you gave me: why did you think it was important?'

'I don't know that it was, other than in helping you to understand what Tony believed in, what he thought was worth fighting for. To give you an indication of his state of mind. I mean, he wrote it only a few days before he died. It simply doesn't sound to me like the speech of a man who's at the bottom, who doesn't know what to do next.'

'No, you're right, it doesn't. And this name, the one he wrote in pencil at the bottom – de Moleyns. Do you know who it is?'

'No. Not a very nice person, I imagine. But I was rather hoping you might know.'

A pity, that: I'd been hoping she would.

An hour later I was standing outside the gates of Katrina's school near Regent's Park. This was an altogether different prospect from the school I'd visited in the morning. Girls in blue uniforms were already swarming down the front steps when I arrived, pushing long hair off their faces, trailing their fingers across their scalps with absent-minded sensuality.

Katrina appeared a few minutes later, a violin case in one hand, a bag over her shoulder. She caught sight of me and came over shyly.

'I hope you didn't mind my turning up at school like this,' I said. 'I thought it might be simpler than coming home.' She nodded and we fell into step. 'I wondered if you wanted Ryan's book back?'

She was disappointed. 'You didn't think it was important!'

'I thought it was *very* important.'

'I don't suppose,' she said slowly, 'John is his real name.'

'No. I don't, either.' There was a pause. 'But we *will* find him.' I was impressed by how much conviction I could summon into my voice. 'Have you got time for a cup of tea?'

We went to a café round the corner, an Italian sandwich place with a few tables at the back, where tea- and coffee-making machines hissed, and plastic sauce bottles in the shape of tomatoes made sticky rings on the tables. Katrina said it was her first day back at school. 'Mum didn't want me to come, but I couldn't bear it there any longer, thinking about Ryan all day long. It's been a week since his body was found, ten days since he disappeared.'

A week since I'd found Tony Bagnall's body, too.

'I don't want the diary back,' she said. 'Not at the moment, anyway. I worry all the time that mum'll find it.' She looked anxious. 'You haven't told anyone about it?'

'No, of course not. But I do think we're going to have to go to the police sooner or later.'

'Not yet!'

'I don't suppose – if Stewart Saddler got Ryan and Dean to – I don't think . . . What I'm trying to say is, I don't expect the things Ryan wrote about happened only to him.'

'It is what I thought, then.' Katrina's face was tight with effort. 'I thought I might be reading things into it that weren't really there . . .'

'I think it's pretty plain.' There was no kind and gentle way to do this. 'I think other boys are probably involved and may even have been involved over a period of years. More could be involved in the future. Sooner or later we have to go to the police.'

She traced her finger across the formica table top. 'But then they'll arrest Stewart Saddler and they might never get John.'

She had a point. 'And another thing,' she went on, 'I bet they couldn't convict Stewart Saddler just on Ryan's diary. I mean, it could be a forgery or anything. They'd need Dean to give evidence. Or someone, at any rate.'

She was right.

'Unfortunately,' I said, 'Dean won't talk to me.'

'You tried?'

'I went to the Lord Napier. He didn't want to know. Probably not the best place to ask him, of course. But as soon as he realised what I'd come for, he was off. He's scared.'

'He won't talk to me either.' She scratched with her fingernail at a speck of food crusted onto the table.

'He knows there's a diary; I told him. But he says nothing happened. I get the impression you could torture him and he'd deny there was a rent boy ring.'

'We *have* to get him to talk,' Katrina said slowly. 'Don't we?'

'Yes.'

'I could try . . .'

'I don't know what would convince him it was worth doing.'

'No.' But she was thoughtful.

I didn't bother telling her about Tony Bagnall. It was too complicated. And if Bagnall's mysterious 'establishment' had been using Ryan, he must have lied about the identity of his client. Or been prepared to lie. I couldn't see the point of inflicting that on Katrina as well.

A part of me hoped Ryan had changed his mind about shopping Tony Bagnall. That might have been why they killed him. But perhaps he *had* done what they wanted and simply become a liability. Known too much. Poor kid.

I saw them as we were coming out of the café, two men lounging against a building opposite. I wouldn't have paid them any attention if they hadn't been standing in exactly the same positions as earlier. One had a cigarette curled in towards his hand; every so often he flicked ash onto the pavement in a gesture of frustrated, barely-suppressed violence. His companion stood stock still, with narrowed eyes, looking out with loathing. But this time there was no dishy Pakistani shopkeeper. So I suppose, in the absence of the Asian entrepreneur, that they must have been sneering at me.

Which meant they must have been following me.

The car was parked on a meter further up the road. I said goodbye to Katrina and watched her run for a bus and jump on it. The skinheads stirred themselves with unspoken accord and began to walk towards me, very deliberately.

I quickened my pace towards the car, unlocked the door, threw my bag onto the passenger seat, jammed the key into the ignition and crashed the gears . . . which was exactly what I didn't want, to let them see that I was rattled.

They were level with me. I flicked a switch and locked all the doors. They moved on past. I breathed out hard. And then one of them twisted his head round and gave me a brief, hard, backwards look.

I put the car in gear properly this time and moved off. When I reached the corner and checked the mirror, they were still there, and still watching.

Chapter Fifteen

I WAS SERIOUSLY SHAKEN. I hated the thought of being followed half way across London for most of an afternoon. There was something chilling about having been oblivious to the presence of two hulking great blokes behind me.

There was however, worse to come.

I got home from the office at about six o'clock, put down my shopping bags in the hall and went into the sitting room to check the answering machine.

There were books everywhere. All over the floor, falling off the edge of the coffee table: lying where they'd been thrown, half open, pages crushed, on the sofa, chairs and tables.

The place looked more like Joe's house than mine. I clapped my hand to my mouth and backed out of the door. It was as if someone had become violently deranged in my sitting room. As if my coffee table had been the scene of a domestic quarrel involving rabid hyenas.

I went upstairs slowly and into my bedroom. I was prepared for the worst – which was just as well because the place looked as if a typhoon had ripped through it. Someone had turned over my dressing table, rummaging among the contents, leaving the drawers half out and my underwear scattered across the room and all over the bed. Scraps of black and white lace were caught up in the sheets and heaped on the carpet. The bedclothes had slithered onto the floor when the intruders lifted the mattress off its base. Clothes had been pulled from the cupboard and left lying in drifts on the floor.

I sat down and surveyed the chaos. My things, my most intimate things, seemed to have been flung with barely containable fury as far away as possible. They sat in the corners in awkward piles, or in clumps around the skirting board, as if they had been thrown at the walls and slithered down.

I told myself that I was overreacting to think someone was out to get me. Burglars throw things around. This wasn't vindictiveness; it was vandalism.

Except, except . . . Weird messages on my computer. Skinheads following me. And now this.

The computer! . . . I went next door to the study, which had also fallen victim to the enraged book-throwing animals. Dozens of volumes of poetry, history, novels, and politics had been pulled off the shelves and thrown across the floor; files had been wrenched open and the contents flung about. I picked up a notebook which was lying face down on the fax machine and smoothed its crumpled pages. It was years old, probably last opened in Iraq.

I switched on the computer and braced myself for some terrible image to resolve itself from the dots on the screen. But there was no disgusting item of child pornography. Just Bobby's sister's baby in Connecticut as usual.

So it wasn't Bagnall's tormentors. Or if it was, they were up to something different.

I went downstairs again slowly: right down, to the basement. On the half-landing I was aware of a draught coming from the direction of the downstairs cloakroom. I went in slowly, pushing the door open and crunching glass underfoot. A pane was missing from the small window.

The alarm wasn't programmed for this room, or for the hall. So it would have been easy enough for them to get in. But then how had they moved about?

I wasn't thinking straight. The alarm had been on when I came in, surely? If I hadn't had to switch it off, I was certain I would have noticed.

I called Bobby and told him he'd better come home, then the police, then I sat down in the middle of the mess and tried to make out what had happened. The only thing I had that anyone might want was Ryan's diary. But as far as I knew, no one knew of its existence except Katrina.

It was still in my bag, where it had been since she gave it to me.
I picked it up and ran my fingers over the cover. It was starting to
feel like a radioactive substance. A leak waiting to happen.

Bobby caught a cab from the office and was home in ten
minutes.

'What's been taken?' he asked, shrugging off his overcoat.
He put an arm round my shoulder and kissed the top of
my head.

'Very little, as far as I can see. A portable CD player, my laptop
computer and some photograph frames. Plus whatever might be
gone from your room.'

'Have you called the police?'

'They're on their way.'

Bobby looked round, muttering to himself. Despite the devastation, very little was gone from my room. The only things missing
were the laptop, an expensive pocket tape recorder I sometimes
used for interviews and several tapes. It was hard to believe a burglar
would be very interested in the musings of the eighteen-year-old
male star of *LA Teens*.

The gold bracelet my mother and stepfather had given me when
they married was still on the dressing table. So was the ring Sam
had bought me in Brazil. The only thing he, or they, had taken
from here was the stupid tape recorder, which had been in full
view on the corner shelf. So why ransack the room? Why throw
all the books around downstairs?

The police looked round at Bobby's arts and crafts furniture and
said we were lucky we hadn't lost more. The break-in looked like
a professional job. Not like most of the amateurish opportunistic
breaking and entering you got round here. We were fortunate not
to have come home to an empty house.

So little taken, so much mess. An expert break-in, but only
portable electrical items taken: typical kids' trophy.

A scenes of crime officer came round later in the evening and
dusted all the surfaces for fingerprints. By then it didn't surprise
anyone that there weren't any. There was an air of professionalism
about this.

The police explained helpfully that our burglar alarm was of a
type that was extremely difficult to disable: as soon as the cable was
cut the control panel registered that the circuit had been tampered

with and the bell started deafening anyone who happened to be in the street.

'You're sure it was on when you came in?' Bobby asked. 'You're sure you switched it on when you went out this morning? You did have that hangover.'

'It was a hangover, not a brain haemorrhage. I *always* switch it on. I wouldn't have forgotten. I think it's more complicated than that.' I made a guilty, half-hearted attempt to pick up some books from the sitting room floor. Most of them were Bobby's.

He handed me a whisky. 'What d'you mean?'

I took a deep breath. 'Two skinheads have been following me all day. Someone sent me a strange message at the *Chronicle*. I think it may be something to do with a story. I think I may have something someone wants.'

'What sort of thing?'

I hesitated. 'A . . . document.'

'You're not going to tell me, are you?' Bobby said. 'My house is wrecked, my laptop's stolen, and you're not going to tell me why. I didn't know you were going to get a *dangerous* job. I only asked you to move in here because I knew you wrote about shopping.' His expression changed. 'D'you want me to cancel dinner with Antonia? Are you going to be all right here by yourself?'

'I'll be fine. I'll have the glazier for company.'

Bobby is amazingly tolerant, considering.

'Well,' he said, polishing off his drink, 'I'd better get on in that case. I only hope you know what you're doing, that's all.'

Chapter Sixteen

I SPENT THE EVENING writing Joe a fax about being burgled and followed by intimidating men, then fell into bed and slept so fitfully I was unable to get up very early the following morning.

When I finally stumbled into the study, there were three sheets of paper lying by the fax, covered in Joe's large, scrambling handwriting. I took them downstairs and sat at the dining table with a cup of coffee.

His letter had evidently been substantially written before he'd received mine, although he'd scrawled a few lines sympathising about the burglary at the end. The first page was taken up with descriptions of the conference and meetings with old friends from Georgetown; the rest was given over to an extended sexual fantasy involving his back garden and my suspenders.

This improved my mood considerably, and I decided the time had come to telephone Dillie the high class call girl.

She answered in a flat, accentless voice, which might have started out as what my mother would call common and traded up, or posh and traded down.

I explained what I wanted.

'To interview *me?*' she echoed. 'For the papers?'

'If you felt prepared to talk about Ian Moorhouse.'

'I don't know . . .' She sounded bemused. She thought about it for a minute. 'Would there be money in this?'

'The *Chronicle* doesn't pay. It's not that sort of paper. But that's good in a way because it's very . . . respectable. Anything you said would sound very authoritative.'

What was I talking about? The woman didn't want to sound authoritative. She was a whore.

'I suppose I'd become famous?'

'Your picture would be on the front page of every paper in the country.'

Which might be the last thing she wanted. 'Look,' I suggested with an air of desperation: 'why don't we meet? I could explain what would be involved, and you could decide whether you wanted to talk to me.'

'Well . . .' she was thoughtful. 'I *have* got a tape recording.'

'Sorry?'

'Of Ian Moorhouse. I took the precaution of recording him. In case I ever needed it.'

A tape recording? I tried not to sound too transparently over-excited. If she'd recorded him, she must have *considered* payment, and there was no way the *Chronicle* would pay. Still, I made an appointment for Friday afternoon.

I called a minicab to take me to lunch. When it turned up, it was driven by Victor, a burly Nigerian who first drove me a year ago, when I was on my way to the House of Commons to interview Jean Hammond. It had been Victor's first week in Britain and he didn't have the faintest idea where the Houses of Parliament were, or I suspect, *what* they were.

Victor had been unabashed by his ignorance of SW1. He told me cheerfully about his brother, sister-in-law and three-year-old nephew, their digs in Tottenham, and his worries about the political situation at home. We became increasingly lost.

I hadn't wanted to hear his life story. I'd wanted him to get me to my appointment. But in spite of my bad mood, I could see there was something engaging about Victor; and when he came to collect me a few weeks later for a journey to the *Chronicle*'s offices I was secretly rather pleased. By that time, he'd been driving his battered and almost certainly lethal Ford Scorpio around London for four weeks and knew a better way to docklands than I did.

He'd seen the newspaper reports about my having found Tony

Bagnall. 'Why does a man like that kill himself?' he wanted to know as the car lurched forward. 'It doesn't make sense.'

Too right it didn't. 'There are all sorts of theories.'

'Exactly. Because not one of them makes sense.'

'So what do you think?' I was only half-attending.

'In Nigeria, if a politician dies, you assume it's murder.'

'Yes, but that's Nigeria, this is England.'

'And people don't get murdered in England?'

'Not for their politics.'

'Oh no, well, this is not a third world country is it? I forgot. Just looks like one.'

I was quite glad to get out of the car. Victor's a great taxi driver but he does take himself very seriously.

I was meeting Adam in Fred's, the inexplicably fashionable restaurant in Smithfield. He was already there when I arrived, being attended to by one of the barely-dressed waitresses.

He kissed me on both cheeks. 'This is very nice.' His face was anxious. 'I've just heard some really awful news.'

'Oh?' I was starving, and already scanning the menu.

'Jean Hammond's dead.'

I stared at him stupidly.

'She seems to have thrown herself off a cliff at Beachy Head.'

'When?' I didn't believe it.

'Early today. Or fallen. Maybe she fell. She doesn't seem the suicidal type, really.' Adam gulped his wine.

'She was so . . . lively.' I didn't know what to say. Yesterday she'd called me; tomorrow I was supposed to be seeing her; in between she'd died.

'I liked her. She didn't seem like the opposition.'

'No.'

'She was only really a Tory because of her background. It was a sort of noblesse oblige thing,' Adam went on. 'She cared very much about social issues. Facilities for the deaf. Opportunities for women.'

'Yes.' I was finding it difficult to form a proper sentence. When I'd interviewed Jean she'd told me rather gleefully that she'd been brought up to marry a stockbroker and hold village fêtes on her lawn. I'm sure she'd had offers, too. But something, perhaps the death of her father in the Battle of Britain, perhaps the fact that her brothers had both been born deaf, had propelled her into public life.

She would never have killed herself while her brothers were still alive.

'I spoke to her yesterday,' I said. 'I was supposed to be seeing her tomorrow.'

Adam looked appalled. 'Oh, I'm sorry! I had no idea . . . was she a friend of yours?'

'No, no . . . it was work. But even so . . .'

'So,' he smiled, 'it must be true what they said in the *Daily News*. You have a knack of walking into trouble.'

'So it would seem.'

A waitress wiggled over to our table. My appetite had vanished. I ordered seared scallops with leaves in balsamic vinegar almost automatically, though I'd never felt less like eating in my life. I felt way out of my depth.

I mustn't panic. I mustn't be swamped by this creeping sense of unease. But I felt exposed. Fear was beginning to cling around me like an illness. Adam was saying something about my clothes. I had to pull myself together.

'I'm seeing Simon this afternoon,' I heard myself telling him. He'd been saying something about my suit.

Why had Jean Hammond died? For the same reason as Tony Bagnall? Because she knew too much?

'I hope you're going to write a nice piece.'

'What? Oh, yes. I think I probably am.'

'Good. I expect I'm biased about Simon – he and Joe headhunted me when I was still studying and brought me to Westminster and Simon always put himself out to make it easy and comfortable for me: you know, invited me to things and made sure I felt involved and included.'

'That's nice.'

'I don't understand why he gets such a bad press . . .'

'No.'

'Although I suppose I do really.' He tore apart a chunk of ciabatta. 'A lot of MPs don't like him because he's so close to George. And it's not as if he's just taking orders – I mean, it's part of his job to tell George what to do and how to handle things, because handling things – getting information out through the right channels at the right time – can make the difference between triumph and disaster.'

'Yes,' I said feebly. 'I suppose people resent his having that power when he's not elected.'

'Exactly. They think he's not accountable – though he's eminently accountable, actually. I mean, he gets blamed when things go wrong. I suspect the people who don't like him fundamentally don't like his politics. The hard left hate him, and the old right hate him and some of the soft left hate him as well. Is there something wrong with your scallops?'

'No, they're fine.' I forced myself to eat something.

'Someone like Tony Bagnall, for instance, always and only thought in terms of class politics. He would have despised Simon; would have thought he saw everything in terms of niche markets.'

The reference to Bagnall brought me to my senses. This was what I was here for. 'Do you have any theories about why Tony Bagnall died?' I asked, struggling to look as though I was eating normally.

Adam grinned. 'You still trying to make sense of it?'

'You know what editors are like. Dan won't give up.'

'Absolutely no idea.'

'You haven't heard any rumours – about his sexuality, say?'

Adam looked surprised. 'His sexuality? You mean you think he was gay?'

'Not necessarily.'

I was watching Adam carefully and he betrayed nothing. If he *had* heard anything, Adam had nerves of steel.

I'd always known it was a long shot. I could see why he might want to keep it quiet. Bagnall was dead. Ryan was dead. To expose the MP now would only bring disgrace. Still, if he *was* lying, he was doing it very coolly.

'*I* don't think he was gay,' Adam announced. 'From all I've read about him, he was devoted to his wife, even though they had a rather unconventional marriage. But I never knew him. Anyway, it's still not a reason to commit suicide.'

'No, of course not.'

'You're hoping for some scandal here, aren't you?' Adam poured me another glass of wine. I hadn't been aware of drinking the first. 'It won't make you popular.'

'No. I suppose not.'

'I wouldn't stop speaking to you, but some might.'

'You think?'

'You have to remember how much people – Joe and Simon for instance – have invested in winning the election. Even Simon's legendary alchemical skills would have trouble with a sex scandal when we've been saying for months that sort of thing only happens to the Conservatives.'

'You think – if I were to uncover a scandal – they'd want me to conceal it?'

'What do you think?' he asked in amusement.

I got through the lunch somehow. I said goodbye to Adam on the pavement outside Fred's, bought an evening paper and walked the few hundred yards down the road to the office, wondering if the men managing their unwieldy barrows were actually following me; if the articulated lorries manoeuvring into alleyways and belching out carbon monoxide were blocking my path along the pavement purely by chance.

Of course they were. They didn't have *lorryloads* of people watching me. But I was beginning to feel that anything I touched might turn out to be hazardous. Joan Hammond was dead.

I hated the effect this was having on me. Insecurity had settled around me like a clammy fog: I felt so unsteady and easily alarmed. If I saw the skinheads again, I wasn't sure I could trust myself not to panic.

I wished Joe would hurry up and come back. He seemed to have been away for ages. I was too grown-up to believe a man was the answer to all my problems, and I certainly didn't imagine he was going to wrestle the skinheads to the ground and kick their teeth in until they promised to leave me alone. But I suspected his presence might make me feel more stable. And at least I'd have a clearer idea whether he was as much of a sex god as I remembered.

It seemed unfair to have waited so long to meet anyone who even vaguely interested me only for him promptly to disappear half way across the world. How was I supposed to trust my instincts at this distance? Especially when I was so out of practice. He *seemed* pretty wonderful. But at the moment he was as much fantasy as reality. You could probably make anyone seem wonderful if you mooned about waiting for them for long enough.

I ran up the stairs to the office, muttered a greeting to Sarah and sat down on the sofa with the paper.

'Hammond Death Mystery' read the headline, alongside a picture of Jean smiling broadly on College Green, outside the House of Commons.

'Are you all right?' Sarah asked.

'No. No. I'm not. I was supposed to be seeing her tomorrow morning.'

Sarah took her pen out of her mouth and stared at me. 'Jean Hammond?'

'Yes. I had an appointment with her, to talk about Tony Bagnall.'

'Bagnall?'

'Yes, yes!' I cried impatiently. 'She called me yesterday morning. Said she'd had discussions with Bagnall before he died and had some information . . .'

'They think she fell, off the cliff, at Beachy Head . . .'

'Fell!' I shook my head. 'Christ . . . I'm being followed. My house has been ransacked. And now the woman I was supposed to be meeting tomorrow morning has died.'

'What do you mean, you're being followed and your house has been ransacked? Here, I'll make a cup of tea.' Sarah put her pen on the desk, where it leaked a small blue inky puddle, and filled the kettle.

I told her about the skinheads and the burglary. 'I want you to do something for me,' I said, pulling Ryan's diary from my bag, wrapped in brown paper, polythene and tape. 'I want you to look after this.'

'What is this?' She took it.

'It's evidence. I'm afraid someone might guess it exists – or something like it.'

'Does this have something to do with Jean Hammond?'

I nodded. 'Sort of.'

'I see.' She handed me a mug of tea. 'I'm to take this dangerous object and not ask too many questions?'

'It would be easier if you didn't.'

She sipped her tea. 'But you obviously think the people who are after this package *killed* Jean Hammond.'

'I don't know what else to think.' I ran my hand through my

hair in frustration. 'It's as if they're everywhere. Even sending me messages through the computers at the *Chronicle*.'

'And they had something to do with Tony Bagnall's death?'

'I think so . . . Oh hell, I don't know. I'm beginning to think now it's bigger than Tony Bagnall. It's not simply about his death and some cover up. I think he knew something . . . I don't know . . . maybe about the Tory Party.'

'You're not suggesting the Tory Party killed him?'

'No . . . Of course not.'

'So what did Jean Hammond want to talk to you about?'

'She wasn't very specific.' I shrugged helplessly. 'I didn't press her because I thought, well, I was seeing her tomorrow, and you know what she's like . . . I wasn't sure she really had anything. Oh,' I wailed, 'why didn't I take it more seriously?'

'You weren't to know,' Sarah said. 'No clues at all?'

'Oh, something about Europe . . . Tony Bagnall was a keen pro-European.'

'Yes . . .'

'And so are Andrew Gunnel and David Ivison.'

'They're not dead.'

'No, but they're out of Parliament. And now you're going to say Ellis Fletcher and Barry Bianchini and Geoffrey Doxat are out of Parliament as well, and they *aren't* pro-European.'

'I wasn't, but anyway.'

'They thought – Hammond and Bagnall – there was something suspicious about that. Jean thought Bagnall was about to name some people who were involved in a conspiracy – perhaps against those pro-European MPs. It's all very vague.' I gestured helplessly.

'I see,' Sarah said doubtfully.

'I'm wondering now if Bagnall was murdered.'

'*What*? You saw the body. There was a note.'

'Typed. It was meant to *look* like suicide all right . . .'

'My God, Helen.' Sarah was pale. 'What have you got yourself into?'

I picked up the paper and read the story properly. Jean Hammond had gone off the cliff at Beachy Head this morning, probably at around the time I was sitting at the dining table reading Joe's fax.

She'd returned from Wales the previous evening and spent the night at her house in her Sussex constituency. Her secretary had called her there at 10.30 p.m., when, she reported, the MP had sounded cheerful and perfectly normal. No one had seen or spoken to her since.

The first indication anyone had had that something was wrong came when she'd failed to turn up at a meeting with her constituency chairman at 9.30 this morning. According to her secretary, she was to have gone from that meeting to the station, where she planned to catch the train up to London and arrive in time for lunch. She was scheduled to be in the House for Prime Minister's Questions, and later to speak in the health debate.

She appeared to have spent the night at home. She usually rose early; her secretary said she could have been expected to work on constituency business before the meeting with her chairman. But it appeared that what she'd actually done was drive the nine miles from her home to the coast, park her car and go up onto the cliffs. What happened then, no one knew.

She hadn't left a note. No one had seen her on the cliff. The assumption was that she had gone for a walk, strayed off the cliff path, missed her footing and fallen.

I had to rely on other people's interpretations of Tony Bagnall's character, but I *knew* Jean Hammond. I'd talked to her at length, and about quite personal things too, and I was sure she wasn't the suicidal type. There was always some new campaign to take up, some new project to pursue. Besides, both her brothers were still alive.

She liked to walk on the cliffs, I knew; it was possible she'd had an accident. But in my heart I didn't believe it. In my heart I believed she'd been killed.

Chapter Seventeen

I CAUGHT THE BUS to the House of Commons. We rumbled slowly through the traffic, drizzle spattering the windows, tyres swishing on wet tarmac. I sat on the top deck, clutching my shopping bag, the umbrella of the woman next to me dripping onto my ankles. I couldn't stop thinking about Jean Hammond.

Gutsy, flamboyant Jean Hammond, dead. I sat back and closed my eyes. Had the people who killed her killed Tony Bagnall? And exposed Gunnel and Fletcher, Bianchini and Ivison? So why murder Jean but only end the careers of the others?

Because she'd known something crucial, presumably: she thought Bagnall had died because he'd been about to name people. Perhaps she knew the names too. If I intended to go on with this, I'd have to be careful.

They were already letting me know they could get to me: the computer messages; the skinheads, who had meant me to see they were following me; the wanton wrecking of my house. All those things were warnings. And Jean Hammond's death showed that if they chose, they wouldn't hesitate to follow through.

I got off the bus on Westminster Bridge and found myself scanning the street for a pair of skinheads. This was what I hated: the sense that I was vulnerable, a marked woman, not anonymous any more.

I wrapped my coat around me and watched a river bus chug underneath the bridge, its decks empty, ploughing through the mucky water. The expanse of the Thames alongside the Houses of Parliament should have offered a grand vista; but there was something sad about the view across the litter-strewn river to the stained concrete of St Thomas's hospital. And something pointless about a bus used only by visitors. London's river was ersatz, a tourist attraction, its docks derelict downriver, or redeveloped into cheap office space for declining newspapers.

It was a relief to get inside the Houses of Parliament and sit in Central Lobby, glowing with golden light. It made me feel cocooned, safe from the day outside.

I waited for Simon to come and fetch me, wondering what it would be like to spend one's whole life among these mosaics, surrounded by this golden stone. The place would pad you around with security, comfort and dignity, assure you you belonged. It might be difficult, after a while, to remember the world beyond.

Simon flew into Central Lobby and kissed my cheek.

'Sorry I'm late. We seem to specialise in tragic occasions. Awful, this business about Jean Hammond.'

'Perhaps we'd better not go on meeting like this.' I was afraid I might dissolve into tears.

Simon shook his head sorrowfully. 'She was such a vibrant woman.'

I mustn't cry. I mustn't think it was my fault. It wasn't. This was partly why they were following me and wrecking my house and sending me messages: so my defences would crumble.

'Are you all right, Helen? You look rather pale.'

'I'll be fine.' I swallowed. 'I was supposed to be seeing her tomorrow. I feel a bit shaken.'

He turned to me with an expression of dismay. 'Oh, that's awful. You poor thing.' He opened the door to his office. 'What a week you've had.'

'I was burgled yesterday as well.' I intended it to sound amusing, but it came out a bit snuffly.

'Surely not? Oh, how horrible. Was much taken?'

'No, but the place was left in a terrible mess.' I bit my lip. It wouldn't do to collapse in tears in Simon Healy's office.

He gestured to me to take a seat on one side of the round table, which, with his desk, took up almost all the space in the small room.

He sat opposite and poured tea. 'This Jean Hammond death is

very, very disturbing. This may sound odd, but I knew her better than I knew Tony Bagnall. Seeing him there was terrible – I mean, it's not the sort of thing you ever forget. I've dreamt about it, that moment when I saw his feet, every night since. But I was fond of Jean, even though she was on the other side.'

I nodded.

'What were you supposed to be seeing her about?'

'Oh, some new campaign for the deaf. She was going to explain it when I got there.' I blew my nose. 'It's such a shock. I'm sorry.'

'No. Don't apologise.' He squeezed my hand sympathetically. It reminded me how decent he'd been when I was a kid-secretary and he was a television executive from a glittering family. 'It *is* a shock, and it's worse because no one seems to know what happened.'

'What do people here think?'

'An accident. Must have been. She wasn't the suicidal type.'

Exactly what Elise said about Bagnall.

Simon smiled. 'Shall we talk about meeting Hester? That at least is cheerful. We can always come back to Jean later.'

He handed me a cup of tea. I sipped it gratefully and organised my tape recorder and notebook. It was only just over a week since I'd tried to interview Simon the first time, yet in that period the ground between us had shifted subtly. It was partly having found Bagnall's body together. But it was mainly because of Joe. Where we'd been strangers before, now we were almost friends. We pitched up at the same parties. I was on intimate terms with one of his political allies.

I told myself that of course this didn't matter: it was hardly a serious political piece.

Simon leant back in his chair, crossed his ankles in front of him, fixed me with his cheerful lopsided gaze, and began to talk about how he met Hester Allan at the first night of a production of the *Duchess of Malfi*. She'd been playing the Duchess. He was one of a number of politicians invited by the avant-garde director in a bid to drum up publicity for the show, which he'd set at Westminster in a crude attempt to allude to the brutality of politics.

'Unfortunately, it was entirely implausible. MPs don't go around assassinating their enemies, much as they might want to. So at the reception afterwards I told Hester how ridiculous I thought it was to set a play about despotism in a democracy. I'm perfectly prepared to admit that the way we do things at the House of Commons can be cumbersome and self-regarding, but it does impose rules on those of us who work here. We're not above the law.'

They'd had a row.

'Who won?'

'I did.' (She'd said she did.) 'I took her out for dinner and lectured her about all the most idealistic politicians of recent times.' (She'd said he talked about his family.) 'And she had to concede.'

At the end he said: 'I thought your other piece was very good on Sunday, by the way – the boy who died.'

'Thanks. I used to write about quite cheerful subjects. Sex and your star sign. What the cast of *LA Teens* has for breakfast.'

'Did you have to spend much time in the East End to research it?'

'Some. But he – Ryan – lived on the estate I used to live on.'

'I had no idea . . .' He took a biscuit. 'Although, come to think of it, I suppose I did know there was something like that in your background. I'd forgotten. You've done so much since. Has it changed much?'

'Not in essentials. There's less optimism, perhaps.'

'I suppose when they were built those flats were models of social housing?'

'Yes, my mother says we were lucky to get one.'

'I think they were meant to change people's lives.'

'They did change my mum's life. She got a kitchenette. Better than a scullery.'

'I suppose . . .' Simon said doubtfully.

'That was when people still believed in planning,' I smiled. Before chaos theory . . .'

'It must be grim to live there and feel no one has any answers,' Simon reflected. 'At least the Labour Party used to *pretend* it had solutions.'

'You're right,' I said, thinking of Julian Morrison in his bright classroom. 'That's what a lot of people in the East End feel now, I suspect, that the Labour Party doesn't know what to do. And very probably doesn't care: after all, those people haven't got anywhere else to go; they're not going to vote Tory.'

'It's very unfortunate, if that's true,' Simon said. 'Because we do care. I want nothing more, *nothing* more, than to see kids from those estates growing up with a sense of purpose and commitment to society; a feeling they belong, that they have rights and responsibilities and a stake. That's why it's so important to get rid of the us-and-them mentality. So they don't feel dependent on handouts, excluded from the real business of society, bought off. Or sometimes, more painfully for the rest of us, *not* bought off. So that they feel their contribution is not only valued, but demanded. The same as everyone else's. Don't you think that's important?'

I was rather taken aback. 'I do. But how? Kids like Ryan Stoner – well, not so much like Ryan, but older than him – are demoralised and under-educated. They're in no state to start competing with their contemporaries in Japan, say.'

'Exactly!' cried Simon. 'Which is why we have to attack the problem on two levels: educationally and in terms of providing different kinds of jobs, not just in the international economy, to compete with the Japanese, but in the domestic economy too . . .' He caught my eye. 'But I'm boring you.' He smiled. 'And I'm sure you've got to get on.'

I protested that he wasn't boring me at all, but all the same allowed myself to be persuaded to scoop my things into my bag and let him walk me out into Dean's Yard.

I stood there for a moment in the dusk, looking at twigs stiff with buds tossing against the dark sky, and thought about what a long way it was – much further than the few physical miles – from Ryan's school and the Garden Estate to the Houses of Parliament.

I was glad to get home that night. I defrosted some chilli from the freezer, poured it over some rice and tipped half a pot of yoghurt over the top, then ate the whole thing too fast. After that I curled up with a cup of coffee and some chocolate and read the cuttings on Lord Malvern in preparation for my interview on Monday. Anything to take my mind off Jean Hammond. (Who'd come for her? Was it dark? Had she been alone in the cottage? Frightened?)

The telephone rang. I hoped it might be Joe, but it was Katrina.

'I wondered how you were getting on?' she said, her thin voice plaintive.

'I think it's more complicated than we thought,' I said carefully.

I didn't want to frighten her. I didn't want to tell her about the blackmail threats. I didn't want her to be in any more danger than she already was. 'I think Ryan's death was part of something else, something bigger.'

'What do you mean?'

Well she might ask. What could be bigger, for her, than Ryan's death?

'It's too difficult to explain over the phone.'

'Are you still helping me?' Now she was offended.

'Yes! Yes, of course I am.'

'Oh. Well, I just rang to tell you I'm seeing Dean tomorrow. I'm going to try and persuade him to talk to you.'

'Good. If you could, it would make a big difference.'

I could tell she thought I wasn't really doing my bit. She said she'd let me know what happened and rang off. I put the receiver down and stared at it, feeling useless. I resisted the temptation to kick it across the room.

Chapter Eighteen

IT WAS FRIDAY MORNING and I should have been seeing Jean Hammond. But Jean was dead. So I was sitting at my desk in the office reading the cuttings Dan had sent over from the *Chronicle* on Jack Malvern.

I didn't think it would be so very difficult to answer Joanna Beverley's question: what does a beautiful and intelligent woman of twenty-six see in a man like this? I had dozens of cuttings in front of me, most of them accompanied by photographs, and in not one of the pictures did Jack Malvern look anything but devastatingly, shockingly handsome.

He was six foot two and greying at the temples. Nor did he only have looks: Jack Malvern was a multi-millionaire – which, as he would have been the first to point out, meant he was also extremely powerful. Tycoons like himself, he was fond of telling the interviewers who trooped to see him, had more real power than any number of politicians. Just look at the annual sales of General Motors: more than the gross national product of Austria.

The cuttings went back a long way: Malvern had been a newsworthy character almost from the moment he'd inherited his father's small factory in South London, on the back of which he'd launched an assault on a string of electronics companies in southern England, mining companies in South Africa, car components factories in the mid-western United States, software giants in California.

His name had figured in the papers so often partly because he was a corporate raider of startling speed and terrifying acumen, who had bought up businesses – often businesses that looked invincible – and ripped them apart. But he'd featured for other exploits too; he'd always found time between asset stripping to put in frequent appearances at nightclubs in London, New York and Paris and to turn up at the most glamorous parties, usually with a new woman on his arm.

His latest wedding, which was due to take place at his house in the Hamptons in four months' time, would be his fifth. The first wife had been his childhood sweetheart from the small town in Kent where he grew up; the second was his secretary; the third a waitress from one of his clubs; the fourth a wealthy divorcee who had previously been married to one of his friends. The fifth would be a glamorous New Yorker with long chestnut hair and a highly paid job in the bond markets.

The roster of wives, long as it was, still left out the many women who had appeared with him in public when he was between wives or perhaps merely getting tired of the current one. His appetite for swallowing up companies was matched by his appetite for women.

He had the body of a man in his thirties. Once he could have played tennis professionally, and he still found time to get out on the court several times a week, which meant he played to a standard (or so the awed profiles claimed) astonishing in a man of his age. It also meant he had a great body: wide shoulders, slim hips, taut stomach and good legs.

Lord Malvern, then, had everything: looks, money, power, women, property. He owned one apartment on the Upper East Side and another in Knightsbridge; a large house with a prime ocean view in East Hampton; and a manor house with an indoor pool and tennis court in the windswept coastal corner of Kent where he'd grown up. He had bought the last of these for his mother and installed her in a converted oast house in the grounds.

Markets control the modern world, he was given to saying. Markets and the people that ride them. And almost no one rode them better than Lord Malvern.

So he could be forgiven for thinking – as he made it plain he did think – that politicians were rather insignificant people. But he was nothing if not astute, and he knew he needed governments to make the right kind of laws, to allow his companies freedom to operate. For that reason, he had in his time contributed large sums of money to the Republicans in the US and the Conservatives in the UK. He had also, as Katy Salt had remarked at Penny Dalmore's party, considered setting up a political party of his own. But in the end he had too many other interests and too many other ways of getting what he wanted to be willing to start from the beginning with a new party.

In any case, he'd found a hobby. Around the time he abandoned the idea of a political party, he sank more than a million pounds into founding something called the Institute of Heredity and Genetics, which aimed to fund, for example, the search for genes associated with high intelligence. Curiously, very little had been written about the institute. Journalists meeting Lord Malvern seemed to be charmed into breathless purple prose about his urbanity, his business empire, his glittering transnational lifestyle.

There was a knock on the office door. 'For a Ms Clare?' said the delivery man, proffering a huge and expensively disarranged bunch of yellow and white spring flowers tied up with crackly cellophane and string.

Sarah brought them over to my desk and removed her pen from her mouth. 'Mr Romance?'

I raised my eyebrows and took the unwieldy arrangement from her. It was so packed with flowers you had to curl your arms around it as if it were a baby. The scent of freesias and fat hyacinths made me feel dizzy.

I opened the card.

'So sorry to hear about your burglary,' I read. 'With our love, Simon and Hester.'

Sarah was looking at me inquiringly, inky lips pursed. 'Not Mr Romance,' I told her. 'Simon Healy. Well: Hester, I expect.'

The phone was ringing.

'I've had a hell of a couple of days,' Dan was grumbling when I picked it up. 'Why did that bloody woman want to go and throw herself off Beachy Head? ... The editor wants me to pull two features and turn over a whole spread to her: what a great woman, sad loss to the PM, etcetera, etcetera. He's always wanted to be walked all over by a big-boned woman with a voice like a horse. The editor, I mean, not the PM. Though it could very well be true of him too. I suppose, come to think of it, I could have got you to write something. You knew her, didn't you . . .?'

'I've got quite enough to do,' I said firmly. 'Is that what everyone thinks, that she threw herself off?'

'Actually, no: she wasn't the suicidal type. She must have fallen, poor woman. I liked her, actually. She's buggered up my carefully-laid feature plans, that's all.'

'I liked her too.'

'So how's it going? Got Simon Healy and Hester for Sunday?'

'If I write it today.'

'And Bagnall? Can you give me something on that? I ought to let Robin know – I mean, if we've got a big story coming up.'

'I don't know whether it will be a big story or not. But no, I won't have anything this week.'

And next week, the way things were going, I might not even be alive.

'I wouldn't stand for this from anyone else,' Dan grumbled. 'I think you should at least tell me what this story might involve. And then perhaps I could lend you a researcher or one of the news boys. You know, to do some legwork.'

I thought what a relief it would be to tell Dan everything I knew about Tony Bagnall. The connection with Ryan Stoner. The child pornography. The blackmail messages on the Internet. The possibility that his death was murder. The hints of a conspiracy.

But I'd promised Katrina. And Jean Hammond didn't offer a very encouraging example of what happened to people when they tried to talk about it.

'I might have another story for you this afternoon,' I said.

'I'm interested in this one. Besides, you tell me you haven't got time for other stories . . . What is this, Peach? You say you need time, and you're doing something else?'

I told him about my meeting this afternoon with Moorhouse's friend Dillie.

Dan was stunned. 'But that's amazing! If there's anything in it, of course . . . "The prostitute and the Minister for the Family": it'll be the biggest scoop we've had in months. The only scoop we've had in months, in fact. Blimey, Peach, this is the sort of story that could change the result of the election.'

'She may be crazy,' I warned. 'She may have made the whole

thing up.' I didn't tell him about the tape. 'Or more likely, once she gathers what it's worth she'll refuse to talk unless we pay her.'

'You'll talk her into it,' Dan said confidently. 'You're like that. People trust you. I don't know why . . .'

'Because of my attractive personality.'

'This, I have to say, confirms what I at least have always known: you're a great journalist. You get this story, and no one will ever doubt it again.'

I made some calls before I set off to see Dillie. The first was to Hester.

'Thank you so much for the flowers,' I said warmly, when she picked up the phone. 'They're beautiful. Very kind of you.'

It was perfectly obvious Hester didn't have the faintest idea what I was talking about. It also took her some time to work out who I was.

By the time we had resolved the misunderstanding, there was no point in her even trying to pretend that she'd participated in the decision to send me a bunch of flowers.

Fortunately Hester was not a person to be easily disconcerted by such a trivial embarrassment. I would have been crawling with shame in her position.

'That'll be Si,' she said cheerfully. 'He takes much more interest in other people than I do. I never send anyone flowers unless it's to persuade them to do something for me, or occasionally to thank them for having done something for me – which sort of amounts to the same thing. So what did you say? You've had a burglary?'

I told her about it.

'Ghastly, ghastly,' she said airily. 'We were broken into last summer and all my jewellery was taken. That sounds awful, I know. As if I owned the Koh-i-Noor diamond or something. But it was bloody annoying. So you have my every sympathy. I didn't get my stuff back, either. At least you didn't lose much . . . Now, I remember: I've been meaning to ring you anyway . . . Are you and Joe still an item?'

'I think so.'

We seemed to be. I thought of the recent fax, in which the back garden shed had featured prominently and with great inventiveness.

'You must come to dinner. Before the horrible election campaign starts. We won't see them for *months* once that gets going – certainly not if they win, which I *suppose* is what we want. And I feel I'm going to need allies in the years ahead. Other people who don't know anything about European Monetary Union. So I'll give you a ring soon, shall I? Got to go now; I'm late for a rehearsal.'

The second call was to Syreeta Aziz in Bradford. She was in her office and didn't have a lot of time, but said as long as we spoke off the record, she'd tell me what she could about the attempts to have Tony Bagnall deselected.

'A number of constituents – not all Asians, by any means, and from different wings of the party – approached me over a period of months. They suggested that it might be time for Tony to stand down and that I could be the person to succeed him.'

'What did you think about that?'

'I was flattered, naturally, although not that surprised – it's well known I have parliamentary ambitions – and there is a strong feeling in some quarters up here that if any constituency should have an Asian MP, it's this one. But I was also rather dismayed that Tony seemed to have lost support from such different people, from such a range of people. Tony and I weren't political allies – I am much more in sympathy with the leadership – but he was a good constituency MP.'

'Did you consider forcing a contest?'

'Not seriously. I didn't want to be involved in any move to unseat Tony. I knew he'd heard about these whisperings of discontent and that he was upset by them. So I went to see him at home and told him I was having nothing to do with it. I thought that was the clearest signal I could give people that I wasn't happy.'

'Did you have any idea where the impetus to get rid of him came from?'

'No, it was very curious. It happened quite suddenly, and as I say, from different quarters – almost as though it had been orchestrated.'

'Do you think it had been?'

'What?' she laughed: 'Oh, I don't think so. Sometimes things acquire a kind of momentum, don't they? A rumour starts, and people think about it . . . How could it have been orchestrated? By whom?'

Geraldine Bedell

I admitted I didn't know.

'I don't want to sound as though I was very noble,' Syreeta Aziz went on. 'I knew Tony wouldn't stay in Parliament for ever. I don't mean,' she corrected herself hastily, 'I thought he would die. But I did assume he would retire, perhaps at the end of the next Parliament. I felt it was only right that he should have a term on the Government benches. I felt I'd stand a better chance of replacing him if I hadn't tried to unseat him – and a better chance elsewhere – in places where I am not known – if I didn't have a reputation for stabbing people in the back.'

'I see.' That was all remarkably honest anyway. Not necessarily a great deal of help, but straightforward.

'Besides, a contest under such circumstances could have become quite ugly. The papers would have said it was all about race. The racial situation is quite volatile up here, you see.'

The final call was to my mother.

'Hello darling!' She was delighted to hear from me. 'How's Bobby?'

'Fine. How's the bridge?'

'Oh, lovely. You ought to take it up; it's a very good atmosphere. A nice type of person. And you don't have to be a couple. Which would suit you, darling. Have you been out anywhere?'

'I had dinner with the Dalmores.'

'Oh. They're a bit jumped-up, I think. And she looks like a horse. Still, I suppose if he's going to be Prime Minister . . . And how's Sarah?'

'Fine.'

'And her cousins? I see they've got a big party coming up for the earl's seventieth.'

I'd never met her cousins. My mother knew far more about them than I did. 'Fine, as far as I can tell.'

'I went to see Betty's granddaughter yesterday – you know, Karen's baby,' she said meaningfully. Karen was someone I was at school with. 'Such a sweet thing.'

'I'm sure. How lovely,' I murmured. 'I'm afraid this is only a quick call, just checking in. I'm on my way out to interview someone.'

'Oh, anyone interesting?'

'Well yes,' I said. 'Yes. I think she might be.'

Chapter Nineteen

SHE CALLED HERSELF DILLIE DENEUVE. Her real name was Denise Posner, but like Wolverhampton, her home town, it hadn't suited her, so she'd changed it. She answered the door of her flat in Maida Vale wearing jeans and a sweat shirt, her bare toes digging into the thick cream carpet.

I followed her into the high ceilinged sitting room, trying to reconcile the beautiful twenty-three-year-old in front of me with my impressions, evidently grossly ill-informed, of prostitution. Dillie Deneuve clearly didn't operate at the rough trade end of the market. She'd probably never stood on a cold street corner in her life. Or if she had, it was only while she waited for the valet parking service to bring round her car.

Her room was done out in blond wood and off-white, with dashes of black. Like Dillie herself, it was almost oppressively elegant: glass topped tables on improbably slender wrought iron supports, the simplest charcoal line drawings, an abstract sculpture in the pale, smooth ash, white lilies drooping from glass vases.

I sat on one of a pair of watered silk sofas while she went to get the Earl Grey, feeling way out of my depth. Dillie was ten years younger than me, five inches taller and incomparably richer. What's more, she probably had sexual techniques I hadn't even dreamt of.

Men, I thought in amazement, could buy all this, if they could afford the price. They could spend time with this glossy girl who looked like a model and lived in a fantasy apartment entirely furnished in cream. I could imagine that would do quite a lot for a battered ego.

'I'm really not sure I want to talk,' she admitted when she came back, pouring tea into expensive fine china.

So I set about persuading her. If the story had involved anyone else it might be different, I said earnestly, but Ian Moorhouse had gloried in being Minister for the Family.

'Yes, he can't help having been given that job, I know, but he didn't have to take it to such extremes.' Dillie was still clearly worried by my presence in her flat, but I sensed she was open to persuasion. 'I suppose he *has* been rather hypocritical . . .'

'Exactly. He's been incredibly rude about people who don't fit neatly into what he thinks of as ideal families – gays and lesbians and single parents and so on—'

'Yes.'

'And not only rude, he's sought to discriminate against them, to make their lives much harder.'

'I know.'

'It's almost like a moral crusade, which will only give him satisfaction if other people suffer.'

'But he only stays in his own ideal family by visiting me. Or people like me.'

'He's so certain there's only one way of living. But the irony is he doesn't live like that himself. His life is hypocrisy from beginning to end.'

'I *have* always been a Labour voter . . .' Dillie said thoughtfully.

I pointed out that she'd come out of the affair much better if she spoke to the *Chronicle* than, say, to one of the tabloids. No one would be able to accuse her of acting for personal gain.

It wasn't, after all, as if she appeared to need the money. I had rarely been in a room so perfectly beautiful. Where was the personal tat most people cart around with them from place to place?

Why didn't we talk, I suggested, and then she could make up her mind what she wanted me to report?

Dillie tucked up her feet underneath her on the sofa, a move I found faintly shocking. I was nervous of touching anything in case I left grubby marks.

She told me she'd come to London for a weekend jaunt with a friend when she was sixteen and met a forty-three-year-old businessman in a club. She was still called Denise then. This man wasn't bad looking and he'd made a fortune from launderettes. Before she knew where she was, Denise had a job working for one of his friends in the import-export business in Knightsbridge and he'd set her up in a flat nearby.

When he dumped her eighteen months later, probably because he'd found another mistress, she was reluctant to give up the clothes and jewellery and trips abroad. She knew some of his businessmen friends hung around with call girls, so she sought one out and asked her advice.

From there on it was easy. She changed her name, signed up with what she described as 'a sort of employment agency', which dealt only with high class girls and high-rolling clients, and acquired a list of regulars. Sometimes she went to hotels – though only five-star hotels; sometimes she worked at home. Occasionally she accompanied men to Paris or New York or Zurich; she usually spent a month in the Far East in winter with an Arab friend. Now and then there were trips on vast motor launches to Antigua or Spain. She didn't do anything she didn't want to.

Denise had succeeded in displacing herself almost entirely, I thought. Her voice bore no trace of her background, her apartment contained only perfectly beautiful objects, her clothes were classic. She presented a matt surface to the world, whatever personality there was underneath extremely well concealed.

Moorhouse had been a client of hers for three months. Before that he had been seeing another girl, a friend of Dillie's, for a similar length of time.

'You might want to talk to her too,' she volunteered. 'She'll confirm it all.'

Moorhouse had visited Dillie Deneuve in the early afternoon when his staff thought he was taking a constitutional to clear his head in Green Park. He liked her to serve champagne and strawberries, though he rarely drank more than half a glass. For five minutes or so they talked about the weather, restaurants, and any movies she might have seen.

Then they would move into the bedroom. It was all very formal, and rather decorous: he undressed carefully, and being a fastidious man, left his expensive suit and the shirt his wife had ironed for him on a chair. He once told Dillie he refused to let the hired help iron his shirts because she smoked, and he could smell her nicotined fingers on his collars. It was all over rather quickly.

'He told me he'd been visiting prostitutes since he became an MP,' Dillie said, uncurling her long legs, cat-like, and padding across the floor. 'He claimed it was his way of dealing with stress. Curiously enough, that was on the day I'd taken the precaution of tape recording our session.'

I stared at her and she shrugged. 'I never knew when I might want to prove he'd been a client. He was so powerful . . . I thought it might be useful.' She faltered. 'I don't really know what for . . .'

She took a high resolution tape recorder from a drawer and pressed a button. 'I set it at the right place, so you don't have to listen to a lot of unpleasantness.'

Sure enough, Ian Moorhouse's voice floated into the room.

'You're very special. Never anyone quite like you.'

'I expect he says that to all the girls.' Dillie permitted herself a small strained smile.

On the tape, she said: 'It must be difficult, having to pretend.'

'The constituents expect you to behave in a certain way; your wife expects you to behave in a certain way; the office expects you to behave in a certain way. You begin to lose sight after a while of who you really are.'

Dillie clicked the switch and killed the voice. 'There's more in the same vein. You can borrow it if you like. But it kind of makes the point about hypocrisy, doesn't it?'

She sat down opposite me again. 'I think I *do* feel prepared to go on the record,' she said. 'Do you think you'll be able to use any of this?'

Dan switched off the tape recorder.

'There's no doubt it's him. Amazing stuff.' We were in a small meeting room in a corner of the *Chronicle*'s offices, on either side of a long table, the tape machine between us. Behind the floor-length plate glass windows, street lights spread like orange stars as far as the eye could see. Millions of people all over London were negotiating their way home under those lights, getting ready for their Friday night in the pub, thinking about their weekend in the garden, settling in front of their televisions. By Sunday they would all be talking about this.

Dan was in action-stations mode, unsmiling and important. 'OK. Now the lawyer needs to talk to you; I think you should get a draft of your copy to him tonight. You've spoken to the other one . . .?'

'Serena.'

'And she's on the record?'

'And prepared to be photographed.'

'Good, you'd better talk to the picture desk. Is it the same sort of stuff?'

'Yes. Nothing special. No bondage or amyl nitrate or anything like that. But he's been at it for years. One after the other. The girls usually last about six months.'

'My God. You know, I love this newspaper, but there are times I wish I was at the *Globe*. Robin's so fucking high-minded. Keeps taking me aside and reminding me we've got to do it tastefully. And he's got no *idea* what's on this tape. Keeps putting off listening to it.'

I, though, was beginning to be beset by small worries. 'Why *didn't* she go to the *Globe*?' I asked. 'They could have run transcripts – all the huffing and puffing, the whole thing.'

'Because she wanted a quality newspaper. And everyone will run it anyway. It'll swamp the second editions. But it'll be our exclusive.'

'She could have made a fortune.'

'By all accounts she's already got one.'

Dan got up and opened the door. 'You should start work,' he said when I didn't follow. 'So should I. I need to organise features on' – he ticked them off on his fingers – 'escort agencies, the men who use them, political sleaze. And I must talk to Robin. Come on: you say she's a class act; she probably didn't trust the tabloids. They'd have wanted to photograph her in suspenders and a Wonderbra.' He shut the door again. 'Look, Peach, it's no good getting cold feet now. You talked her round. To be frank, I didn't think you'd do it, but she trusts you.' He came and sat down across the table, folded his hands and looked at me severely; 'This self-doubt has got to stop. You are a fine journalist: a *very* fine journalist. But since Sam died you've been hopeless. You hide behind that wry manner and mostly it's quite amusing, so no one minds. But I mind. I mind now, because you've got to get on with your fucking work. So stop sitting there *examining* everything and being so bloody semi-detached and go out and write that story. Please.'

I smiled. 'You win.' I rose and scooped up the tape recorder. 'Mine, I think.'

The newsroom had a subdued, intense atmosphere. Sandra Snugrood, her face bare of make-up, was running narrow, febrile fingers through her hair, bitten fingernails snagging; Dan was sweeping about self-consciously, too important and busy to speak to anyone. Robin Rouse had retreated to his office with a bottle of wine and was blinking at copy on his computer screen. Across the room, fingers clattered on keyboards.

I sat down at a spare desk and opened a file.

The Moorhouse story more or less wrote itself, which, I remembered now, is what good news stories did. I had a decent draft inside half an hour.

I put it aside for a bit; I wanted to give myself a breathing space and look at it again before I sent it through to the lawyer. I sneaked another look at the piece I'd written earlier on Simon and Hester.

This was much less satisfactory. I'd made them sound successful, charming and in love – all of which may very well have been true, but was hardly the complete picture. It was like sticky toffee pudding: warm, and on the edge of sickly. I hadn't got anywhere close to capturing Hester's characteristic tone, somewhere between cutesy and hysterical.

I read through the piece again and sighed exasperatedly. Still, there was very little I could do at this stage. If I didn't file it in the next few minutes, there would be a huge great hole on page thirty-eight. I had to hope that in the excitement about Moorhouse no one would notice how bad it was.

I alerted Dan and the lawyer to the whereabouts of my Moorhouse draft, then called up the MP's cuttings. For the inside piece I'd need more background.

Ian Moorhouse, forty-seven years old and married with two children, was tall, thin and dark, with a hawkish, unhumorous face and the reputation of being one of the least convivial members of the government. A former barrister, he had been a member of parliament for a commuter belt Surrey constituency for seven years, and on the fast track: PPS to the Chancellor of the Exchequer, eighteen months in the whips' office, then the junior job at the Home Office. He threw himself into all of this with gusto, especially the last – using every opportunity to accuse young women of having babies simply to get on council house waiting lists, to rail against feckless young men for abandoning their children, and making himself deeply unpopular with homosexuals by saying if they didn't want to live in families they couldn't be said to have normal human feelings.

Dan leant over my shoulder and poured me a glass of wine. 'The splash is terrific,' he said. 'Hardly needs any work at all.' He perched on the edge of my desk, pouring wine into his own glass. 'You've done a fantastic job to get this story, and written it beautifully. Even Robin can't find anything to object to. I predict,' he raised his glass to me, 'this is going to be great for all of us.'

But I wasn't listening. I'd found something I didn't like. A little more than a year ago Ian Moorhouse had made a speech to a group of business people in which he argued that, but for the European Union, the war in the former Yugoslavia might have spread across the continent. Several months later, in an article in the *Evening News*, he'd said: 'There are those, especially in my party, who believe this country should rediscover what they like to think of as its historic destiny as an offshore island. The truth is that in an age of instant global communication, Britain no longer has that destiny. It only has decline.'

Moorhouse was a passionate pro-European.

Chapter Twenty

'THERE'S A CHILD HERE,' Bobby said drily as I pushed through the front door. He was carrying two cups of coffee into the sitting room.

I followed. Katrina Stoner was sitting on the edge of the armchair, knees together, hands folded in her lap. She looked very like her mother: anxious, beset, ill-at-ease.

Bobby handed one of the mugs to Katrina with a sympathetic smile and the other to me. 'I'll leave you to it, then,' he said in a tone which seemed to suggest whatever I was up to, it should not properly involve children wandering the streets of Hackney at 10.00 p.m.

'Hello, Katrina.'

'I'm sorry.' Her face fell at the sight of my expression. 'You're busy.'

'No . . .'

'It's late, I know. You've been working.'

'It's not that.'

I was worried for her. I was frightened by the cutting about Moorhouse I'd found at the *Chronicle*; frightened that I was being used, manipulated to force him out of government. And if they could manage me so easily, what mightn't they do to Katrina? They could be watching the house. They might think she knew more than she did. I was bad luck. I had no right to get her involved.

'I'm concerned about you. These people, who killed Ryan,

know that I've been investigating his death. I think they could be watching me.'

'Yes. One of them came to see me. At least, I think it might have been one of them.'

'When?' I was appalled.

'Yesterday. Before I rang. I didn't tell you then because you sounded so busy. As though you were trying to do ten things at once.'

I thought back. Yesterday they'd killed Jean Hammond. I cursed myself for being so preoccupied. 'What did this person say? Was he alone?'

This was really frightening. If they got to Katrina – I couldn't even bring myself to formulate the thought of what they might do – I would never forgive myself.

'Yes. He was quite smart. Oldish.'

'How old, could you tell?'

'Fifties, maybe? I'm not very good at ages. He wore a suit and tie. He wasn't from round our area. He had really blue eyes. Really piercing. And he wanted to know about you. He said did I know you?'

'And what did you tell him?'

'That I'd met you. I said you were writing an article about Ryan and you'd come to the house and talked to mum and then you'd come to school to find out if there was anything else I wanted to tell you.' I looked at her admiringly. It was the best answer she could have given. 'I told him I didn't like to keep answering questions. And then I went inside the flat.'

'He was outside?'

'Yeah. He was waiting for me when I got home from school. In a big car. BMW, I think. I was really scared.'

'I bet.'

'Do you think he's John?'

'It's possible.' Or de Moleyns, maybe. Whoever he was.

'So I went to see Dean.'

'And?' What was I going to do about this? How was I supposed to protect her? Because they'd sure as hell be back.

'He says he's willing to talk to you. If you still want to?'

She thought I might have lost interest, moved onto something else.

'Yes. Of course I do.'

'He said tomorrow. He could meet you down by the pub on the towpath by the canal. In Victoria Park. The Princess Alice.'

'What time?' I had the Moorhouse copy to finish tomorrow – if I was going to go through with it. And I didn't see how I could get out of it now.

'Three o'clock.'

I thought quickly. I could probably make it, assuming the copy went well. Joe was coming home some time tomorrow afternoon. Too bad: Joe would have to wait.

'That's fine . . .' I said slowly.

'Is everything all right?'

'Yes, sure. It's these people . . . I think they're really dangerous.'

'I know,' said Katrina. 'They killed my brother.'

I drove her home, feeling foolish. She was angry with me, and rightly, for not being more enthusiastic about her success in persuading Dean to talk to me. But all I could think about was how people around me kept dying. I wanted to keep her as far away as possible from these lethal men, whoever they were, that Bagnall had called the establishment.

Bobby had gone upstairs to bed before I drove Katrina home, but his light was still on when I got back. I banged on his bedroom door.

'What is it?'

'Can I come in?'

'Helen . . . it's bad enough having schoolgirls turning up to ruin my evening without you creating that racket on the landing.'

I put my head round the door. 'I wanted to talk to you.'

'Oh?'

I sat down on the end of his bed. 'What do you know about this colleague of yours who gave you the story about the prostitute?'

He was propped up on the pillows reading, broad shouldered and brown skinned, a scattering of dark hairs on his chest. He put his book aside and folded his arms. 'Did you see her?' he asked. 'How was it?'

'It was fantastic. That's what worries me.'

'What's she like?'

'Beautiful. Stunningly beautiful. But so glamorous she gives nothing away. I got no feeling for what she was like. She's kind of artificial, unknowable. A perfectly beautiful, perfect blank.'

'Sounds rather dreary.'

'And there's something suspicious about the whole thing. I talked her into it too easily. And she had a *tape*, for heaven's sake.'

'You're not saying it's made up? It can't be if she's got a tape.'

'Oh, I don't know . . . No, I don't think it's made up.'

'So what's the problem? Has he denied it?'

'We won't ask him until late tomorrow. Until it's too late for him to get an injunction.'

'So what's the worry?'

I shook my head. 'She didn't demand money. But she had a tape. Why would you make a tape unless you thought at some point you'd sell it?'

'To protect yourself?'

'She convinced me it was reasonable enough when I was there. I thought she didn't need the money. But no one has enough money. And this is a person who sells *herself*, for God's sake.'

'Maybe you're worrying too much about this. A great story falls into your lap and suddenly you don't want it.'

Dan had said much the same thing. And it was true. But why *had* Dillie given me the story? Once she'd recognised its worth she could have taken it anywhere. I wouldn't have been anyone's first choice: it is a fact that the only time I have ever doorstepped anyone was during an investigation into the British and American governments' role in supplying arms to Indonesia for use in East Timor. Meanwhile, London was swarming with journalists who'd spent whole careers waiting for precisely this opportunity, who'd had years in training just so they could give a scandal like this the ultimate treatment when the time came. If Dillie Deneuve had the story she claimed to have, any of Dan's news boys would have killed for it. It seemed unfortunate that a rash remark to another client had landed her with me, a woman who wasn't quite sure she wanted to be a journalist and hadn't broken a story in years.

'Who is this guy?' I persisted. 'The one who just *happened* to have been seeing the prostitute who was seeing Moorhouse, and just happened to tell you?'

'It doesn't seem such an extraordinary coincidence to me,' Bobby said reasonably. 'I told you. He was over here on business, working on a deal I'm involved in. What do I know about him? Harvard, Wharton, Wall Street. Preppy type. Not married. Wine buff. Nice enough guy. What else d'you want to know?'

'Any connections with the far right?'

Bobby burst out laughing. I was quite glad the phone was ringing. It did sound pretty stupid.

'Oh, you are so lovely . . . I got your fax. I want to wrap myself around you, tie my legs in knots around yours. I'll be able to do all of that tomorrow.' It was Joe's last night in Washington. 'How are you feeling now? Any less unhappy about Jean Hammond?'

'Not really. And now there's something else. A story I've written for Sunday's paper.' I told him briefly about my meeting with Dillie.

'But that's fantastic! What a scoop! Brilliant.'

'Is it?' Perhaps he was right. In which case he must think I was very drippy. Every time we spoke I seemed to have a tale of some new disaster. 'I don't understand why she wanted to tell me. Why not someone who knows their way around this kind of story?'

'You persuaded her,' Joe said. 'You heard about it, and you asked her to tell you. So she did. That doesn't seem mysterious to me. I don't understand why you're making it so complicated.'

'Doesn't it strike you as odd that so many of the people who've had to leave office because of scandals have been pro-European?'

'What do you mean?'

'Gunnel, Ivison . . .'

He thought about this for a moment. 'But not Fletcher or Bianchini or Doxat,' he pointed out.

What about Tony Bagnall, then? I wanted to say. And Jean Hammond? But if I started that I might not be able to stop. And Joe wouldn't naturally be sympathetic. He knew I'd been to see Elise Bagnall earlier in the week, and although he hadn't said much about it, he clearly thought it was not only a waste of time but counterproductive. Bagnall was dead, and there was no point in raking over the ashes. Best forgotten.

'Sounds like great stuff to me,' he said. 'Fantastic stuff. I should bask in the glory. Now, what time are you going to be free tomorrow afternoon?'

'Quite late.'

'Oh.' He was disappointed. 'I've promised the Salts I'll call into this thing they're having – a sort of drinks party, a final fling before the election. But you could come. And we don't have to stay long.'

My heart sank. I was beginning to wonder whether I'd ever get to see Joe on his own. Love Joe, it seemed, and you had to love all his political friends as well. It was hard to love the Salts.

I sat at the dining table with coffee and a croissant, spilling crumbs over the papers. Sunshine streamed through the French windows and made dancing shadows of the leaves on the grass; the creamy petals of the camellia dripped heavily over the path to the pond. I told myself there was work to do before I could think about Joe, sex, or anything at all of that nature. There was Dan to face.

He was wandering around the newsroom when I arrived at the *Chronicle*, a slice of toast in one hand, a plastic cup in the other, sleeves rolled up to his elbows.

'Morning, Peach,' he said cheerfully. He was at his happiest on Saturday mornings when the copy was rolling in and he could be at his most pressurised and tense. 'Be with you in a sec. Just trying to organise coverage of this anti-Nazi rally this afternoon.'

'Sure . . .'

I found a spare desk, put down my bag and went to get a cup of coffee from the machine. At least, I think it was coffee.

'You know what I heard yesterday?' Dan demanded, coming over, ticking things off in his notebook. 'Those kids, Ali Khalifa and Mohammed Abdul, who died in the race attacks – you heard this?'

I shook my head.

'They carved – this is vile – Union Jacks on their foreheads.'

'Christ!'

'It's not the first time, either, apparently. One of Sandra's police contacts told her it was exactly the same with that other racial murder – what was the guy's name? – Devraj Patel, six months ago. You remember? The shopkeeper? Body mutilated in exactly the same way. Horrible.'

'Are you going to write about this?'

'No. Not in detail: we have it on a strict no-use basis. At the moment, anyway. The police are terrified of copycat attacks. And retaliation, for that matter.'

It was revolting. 'Do they know who is responsible?'

'It's obviously tightly organised. They suspect the Patriots. But there's absolutely no proof.'

'Surely they must be able to infiltrate?'

'I dunno. I think it's all cells – active units, a bit like the IRA. Anyway, we ought to get on. Just thought I'd brighten your morning with that. Now, we're waiting for Dillie's pictures. And the lawyer's made some notes on your copy; give me a shout when you've had a look.'

'Dan . . .' I began, 'I'm seriously worried about this story.'

He was already on his way over to the picture desk, but this made him turn on his heel. 'Why?'

'It's too easy. She didn't want money.'

Dan sighed testily. 'You can't afford to lose your nerve now.'

'Why did she *happen* to have a tape? Why suddenly decide to talk to the press? Why didn't she even *try* for some money?'

Dan came back over to the desk. He was clearly irritated. 'She didn't try for money because you made it clear that although we don't pay, that lends weight to her story. She decided to talk because she saw an opportunity. She had a tape because she's not stupid and she thought she might need it one day. She's not a media analyst, for God's sake, she's a prostitute. You're crediting her with too much sophistication about all this.' He put his hands on the desk and leant over me. 'And finally, all these things happened because of you. Because you went there and did your job. Just for once Helen, do me a favour, will you? Have some faith in yourself.'

And he turned and swept away.

I switched on the computer. I felt idiotic. Of course Dan wasn't going to give up the story now. It was the *Chronicle*'s first exclusive in years. All I'd done was exasperate him.

A signal was flashing to tell me I had a message waiting; I called it up uneasily.

Perhaps it would only be something from Sukey about her sports reporter.

But I feared not, and my fears were justified.

'Drop the Bagnall story,' I read. 'It's not worth while. Things are only going to get worse.'

It carried Dan's log-on, GOULD.

'Here they are.' He was at my desk, with three pictures of Dillie in his hand. She was wearing a black shift dress, too simple to have cost anything but a fortune. It showed off her cleavage, but tastefully, and made the most of her long, black-stockinged legs.

'Were you in here at six o'clock this morning – 5.54 a.m., to be precise?'

'What do you think?'

'Have you sent me a message this morning?'

'No. So, which one d'you think we ought to use?' He waved the photographs.

'Have you sent me a message about Tony Bagnall at all?'

'Oh, Christ, not again. No, I haven't sent you a message about Tony Bagnall. You tell me to piss off every time I mention Tony Bagnall. You know what I think about Tony Bagnall; I just wish you'd get on with the story. So, have you spoken to the lawyer yet?'

'Did you change your password the last time?'

'Yes,' he snapped.

'You'd better change it again.'

He stared at me, then came round the desk to stand behind my shoulder and read the message on the screen.

'Right. That's it. I'm going to talk to the computer department. System's like a bloody colander – our copy's probably being read by half the newspapers in London right now. Why can't we have something that's a bit harder to hack into? Christ, who else has been getting messages from me?'

'I doubt there'll be anyone else.'

'I sincerely hope not. Something like this could wreck the whole Moorhouse story. Half the bloody subs spend all day in other people's files; not enough to do, that's the trouble.' He flapped the photographs in front of me. 'OK, then, which one of these do you think we ought to go with?'

I picked the one I liked best and called up my copy. I didn't think it was the subs.

But I told myself I had to put it out of my mind. I read the lawyer's notes. She didn't have any significant difficulties and I talked through the minor points she wanted to clarify, then wrote the background piece for page three, wondering all the time about Dillie: where she'd come from, who'd put her up to this.

I'd run as many checks on her as I could – spoken to her sister in Birmingham, her best friend from school and Serena, who was part of the same small and exclusive network of high class call girls.

I believed that she was a prostitute; I believed that Moorhouse had been her client, and that he'd been Serena's before. If this story was the work of Bagnall's 'establishment', and was meant to undermine the Tory party or Parliament, there was nevertheless a substantial amount of truth in it.

But how had Moorhouse got involved with these girls? That was the key question. Had they entrapped him? Or had the establishment come on to the scene later, and persuaded them (paid them perhaps?) to tell the truth.

And why had they picked on me?

Chapter Twenty-One

I LEFT THE *CHRONICLE* at lunch-time. The copy was fine; all that remained for me was to call Moorhouse later.

I caught the train out of Docklands towards the City: a seamless progress from the air-conditioned newsroom into gleaming lifts, marble atrium, and onto the spotless, toytown platforms of the Docklands Light Railway.

I was still thinking about Dillie, even when I was in one of the little bright trains, whirring away from the futuristic glass-and-waterscape to the centre of the city. She was as artificial as the edifices on the Isle of Dogs. The whole story was artificial.

The train sliced through the air on stilts: behind us, the marble and glass of the new city; ahead, the grey solidity of the banks and insurance houses of the old: the dome of St Paul's, the white spires of Wren and Hawksmoor.

I tried to think about Joe. I'd see him in a matter of hours. I'd find out whether he was as thrilling as I remembered. I looked down at the ground, way below: long derelict bomb sites overgrown with weeds; tenement blocks with washing flapping from their balconies, desolate concrete playgrounds where children in saris wandered, carrying babies. Down there the walls were covered in roaring graffiti, windows boarded up. The corner shops looked mean and pinched. Their windows were half-empty, their doorways were dirty; they sold limp processed bread, cigarettes and lottery tickets.

I didn't belong down there. But I wasn't sure I belonged up here either.

I got off at Bank and caught the bus to Joe's house. The front door jammed against the weight of a week's mail: bills, journals wrapped in polythene, flyers for fluorescent home-delivery pizzas, a couple of hand-written envelopes in feminine-looking script.

I went into the living room, put the post tidily on Joe's desk and looked around in despair. The place was a tip.

Whatever had persuaded me that all Joe's house needed was a woman to give it a slightly more homely and cared-for feel? What it needed was a firm of industrial cleaners and half a dozen shredding machines.

Every surface was swimming with newspapers, journals, files, books, documents. Here a heap of them had collapsed; there a pile was still teetering. The place looked desperately in need of a filing system. The only trouble was, if I tried to impose one he'd never find anything again.

I went upstairs in the vague hope that it might be easier to make an impact there. Touchingly, the bedroom looked exactly as we'd left it on Sunday morning: the bed unmade, the duvet thrown carelessly across the pillows. The smell of sex, of Joe and me, was still hanging in the air.

I found clean sheets in a cupboard in the hall. It was hard even to remember exactly what Joe looked like, he'd been away so long. I could bring to mind an eyelid, an ankle or bicep, but somehow I couldn't collate them into a whole, assemble them properly.

An awful lot had happened, I thought as I stripped the bed and dumped the dirty sheets in the corner of the room.

Jean Hammond had died. My house had been turned upside down. My ideas about Tony Bagnall had also been turned upside down – twice. I'd been followed by skinheads. I'd written the Moorhouse story, for what that was worth.

At least I no longer only wrote about how navy blue is the new black.

I straightened up, considered the bed. Mounds of white sheet and tumbling quilt. It was a relief to feel positive again about work, like surfacing from a long illness. I wasn't going to give up that feeling for computer warnings or loitering skinheads. I patted the bed and went downstairs; tipped away the cold sheeny coffee and washed up the cups from the previous Saturday night. In any case, the skinheads seemed to have gone away. No sign of them since Wednesday.

I inspected Joe's fridge indulgently: half a pint of nearly solidified milk and some quietly stinking vegetables. I threw away the food, cleaned the shelves and salad box and went back into the sitting room.

It hadn't become any more obvious how I might clear it up. I picked up a notepad from the floor; half a dozen loose sheets of paper fluttered out and fell on the carpet. Now they were in the wrong order. I tried to reassemble them, which was difficult because I couldn't understand what they were about. Something to do with education policy.

'Oh, hell,' I muttered, putting the notepad back where I'd found it on the floor and shoving the loose sheets inside any how. I told myself it was better to leave the mess; Joe wouldn't thank me for mucking up his work.

I retreated to the desk and tidied up the post. At least I could do that without fear of upsetting some arcane and complex arrangement of filing by furniture. A postcard from someone called Jools (the last girlfriend, I suspected) fell out from between copies of the *TLS* and the *New York Review of Books*. Jools said she was missing Joe and thought they ought to meet.

I replaced the postcard, got my pen out of my bag along with the thick piece of card I'd brought with me for the purpose, frowned and bit my lip.

What would Joe want to read when he got back from the airport?

Jools had very nice handwriting.

Jools, however, was in the past. I was the present, therefore Joe would rather get a note from me. But saying what? Something amusing? erotic? serious? All of those things? Would they all fit onto one small piece of card?

The telephone was ringing. I left it. It might be Jools, or some other abandoned woman.

Joe had said I was witty. We were in bed at the time, so that probably explained it. He probably meant smartass. Or even irritating. Even so, it was an intimidating opinion for him to have expressed about me, because now I felt obliged to be witty on this card. But not too brittle, that was the thing. Warm and sympathetic as well.

The answering machine tripped on and a voice floated into the room.

It wasn't one of the many ex-girlfriends, which was a relief because I hadn't been relishing the prospect of having to listen to some girl sounding rather like myself, desperate to see Joe.

It was a man. Probably some professor of philosophy or . . .

'Joe, this is Jack Malvern's office,' said the voice.

Jack Malvern? I thought. *The* Jack Malvern? The billionaire entrepreneur and Conservative paymaster Jack Malvern? The man I was supposed to be seeing for *Femme* on Monday?

The voice floated out into the room. 'Jack wanted to say thanks for the meeting. Good meeting, we thought. We need to speak about Durham. Jack's arriving in England on Sunday; perhaps you could call him in the country?'

I put down my pen and stared at the machine. It didn't make sense. *Lord* Malvern? What on earth was he doing, having meetings with Joe?

It had to be, though. How many Jack Malverns were there who didn't make their own phone calls? The instruction to call him in the country didn't seem to brook the possibility of refusal. And I knew Lord Malvern was definitely due in England in the coming week because I was interviewing him.

But what was the leading Labour strategist doing with the killer-entrepreneur?

The machine clicked back into position. It must, I thought, be something to do with Labour's charm offensive. The Party was going through one of its intermittent bouts of trying to soothe the nerves of the business community. There had been highly publicised chief executives' breakfasts around the country, and lunches in the boardrooms of all the leading banks.

Jack Malvern, though, was about as extreme an example of the businessman as you could wish to find. Or not wish to find. What common cause could he possibly find with the Labour Party, this man who specialised in paring down companies to the fewest possible employees and offering them minimal benefits and less security?

The Labour Party had changed, of course; but even so . . . if George Dalmore *did* stand for anything different from James Sherlock, it was something to do with keeping men like Lord Malvern under control.

And Joe, surely, *must* stand for something different from James Sherlock. And Lord Malvern.

It was probably simple enough. Malvern was simply keeping his options open. Labour was going to win the election; obviously he'd need to talk to the party about what that would mean for his businesses.

I finished my note. It wasn't witty. Or erotic. Or especially warm. It didn't have much to recommend it at all. But I propped it up on Joe's desk. Then I took one last look around the house and let myself out of the front door. I had an appointment with Dean.

I heard the noise several streets away. Rhythmic chanting; more, and different, chanting, getting louder and uglier all the time: a crescendo of jeering.

I was getting closer: the noise must be coming from Bethnal Green Road or nearby. I remembered – too late – the march. I should never have forgotten in the first place. I'd read the leaflet the day I'd come down to the East End to see Julian Morrison; Dan had been talking about it only this morning. Stupid, stupid.

I thought of trying to get round another way, but I had to get across Bethnal Green Road somehow. There was nothing for it but to plunge on and hope the police had the march under control.

The two Asian boys came tearing out of a side street and almost collided with me. They wore black shiny jackets: one had blood seeping from a cut by his eye, clogging dark lashes. The eye was swollen, but he was running as if to burst, drawing breath into his lungs in desperate, noisy gasps.

They dodged me and ran on, trainers pounding on the pavement. They couldn't have been much older than fourteen, and they were terrified.

An estate bordered one side of the street: four concrete tower blocks, low railings, wide expanses of grass. Nowhere to hide. The other side of the road was more promising, bordered by the backs of garages and yards behind high walls.

The boys ran across the street, scaled a five-foot wall and dropped down on the other side. I stood and watched as they scrambled up the wall, furiously agile, with a swiftness born of fear. I saw one disappear over the top and the other swing his leg across, contemplating for an instant the drop. That was when the skinheads appeared: four white youths with shaved heads, tattoos, jackboots and Union Jack T-shirts, cut back to the armholes to expose their biceps. They must have been cold, dressed like that.

'What's going on?' I asked, obstructing their path as best I could, being daffily female, stupidly getting in the way.

In answer, one, the one nearest to me, put out his hand and pushed me out of the way. A second drew a flick knife.

I backed away, but they weren't interested in me. Their blood was up; they were after the boys. I watched as they pushed past me and ran across the road. I watched, feeling useless, as they scaled the wall and dropped down after the Asian boys on the other side.

I followed. There was a limit to what I could do. I shivered at the recollection of the knife, its bright blade spurting from the young man's palm. At least I could fetch help. I thought I might have to climb the wall, but when I got up close I could hear the skinheads cursing. They'd landed in the alley on the other side and found it empty. The kids had got away.

I listened long enough to be sure the thugs had no idea where the boys were. And then, because I thought the skinheads might find their way through the alleys back into the street and I didn't want to be there when they did, I turned and headed briskly back to Bethnal Green Road.

I could tell even before I got there that the march had collapsed into chaos. Above the chants of 'Racists Out' rose the cynical sing-song call: 'Patriots, Patriots' – the syllables drawn out in an ugly leering challenge.

The nationalists had evidently mounted their own, rival march; and the police – despite riot shields, batons and horses – were fighting to keep the two apart.

I couldn't get through; I was trapped this side of the main road by a phalanx of mounted policemen, who were themselves the second line, behind hundreds of officers on foot. In their helmets and protective clothing, behind their shields, they looked like an army of half-humans, half-robots, fantasy police from the future.

Bottles and cans were flying. There was a smell of burning rubber in the air: the Patriots, or perhaps the anti-Nazis, had overturned two cars and set them alight. Craning past the police, I could see people making Nazi salutes, people being dragged away to vans, missiles raining down from either side. The voices seethed with committed, bloody violence.

And then, all of a sudden, the police charged. One minute they were in front of me; the next they'd surged forward. The street immediately ahead of me was empty, but there was no point in following them. Ahead, at the junction, there was mayhem. I turned and tried to find another way through.

The march had made me late, but Dean was still waiting exactly where Katrina had said he would be, down by the canal.

Approaching the towpath from Victoria Park, I saw him before he saw me: a skinny kid in a dark denim jacket, kicking his foot against the wooden post of the lock gate, shoulders hunched. He was loitering with an air of patient resignation, as though he was used to being kept waiting, used to having nothing better to do.

He seemed startled when I spoke to him. He looked up at me with an expression which seemed ready to be full of distrust and even dislike, but settled into mere truculence when he recognised me.

I apologised for being late and explained about the march. Dean said nothing, just continued to kick the wooden post. I suggested we walk along the towpath.

It was a bright afternoon but chilly, and the canal side was bleak. I wrapped my winter coat more tightly around myself. Dean, in a thin jumper and the jacket, seemed unperturbed by the weather. He walked alongside me, childishly swaggering, occasionally kicking stones off the concrete path into the water.

The canal was murky; it smelt stagnant. Plastic bottles, beer cans and carrier bags bobbed slowly down towards the docks, flecked with scum and slowed by the patches of oil rainbow-shimmering on the surface.

Dean didn't seem disposed to open the conversation, so I said: 'Katrina said you wanted to talk to me?'

Dean didn't answer directly. He kicked a stone. ''Ow d'you know about the marshes 'n'all that?'

'Ryan wrote a diary.'

Dean nodded. He already knew this; I'd told him last time. ''As Katrina seen it?'

'Yes. She found the diary but she couldn't make up her mind

what to do with it. She didn't want to go to the police and so she asked me to help.'

'Is that why Ryan died?'

I looked down at the top of Dean's head. His hair was too long and lank. He wasn't pretty in the way Ryan had been – wholesome, winsome – but I could see his gauche, overgrown boyishness might have an appeal of a kind, the freckles and turned up nose at odds – rather charmingly, almost comically at odds – with the mean manner.

He was almost adolescent, still awkward where he wanted to get on with being grown-up and hard. But you could see the teenager he would become, the lineaments of his adult looks underneath the soft, boyish features and the childish confusion. He wouldn't be like this for very long.

'Not simply because he was going over to the marshes,' I said carefully. 'But it had something to do with that, I think.'

Dean was scared stiff, though he didn't want to show it. We walked on in silence for a bit. I looked at the derelict warehouses on the opposite bank. Dean looked at the ground.

'How did Stewart Saddler get you involved?' I asked eventually.

'We was shoplifting. He found out. Said he'd tell our mums. And the police. He said we could be sent down.'

I resisted the temptation to look up to the sky in despair. The stupid child. So desperate to appear streetwise but knowing nothing.

'Did you think about telling anyone – when Stewart Saddler made these suggestions, that you should go with these men?'

'He said we'd get hurt,' Dean said moodily. 'And there was the shoplifting stuff.'

'Hmmn.'

'And the money,' he added defensively.

I knew from Ryan's diary that Dean had always been keener on the money than his friend.

'Do you have any idea why Ryan died?'

'No. Could I be sent down for this?'

'Of course not.' This was hopeless. The child was a jumble of fears. Idiotic fears, about all the wrong things. 'What we have to do, though, is find John, the man Ryan was seeing on the marshes. And then the police can deal with him and with Stewart Saddler, and with the man you were with.'

'Men. There was three of 'em.'

I looked out over the canal, watching a family of ducks swimming through the rubbish on the surface.

'I told Katrina: I don't want to go to the police.'

'No. Well, you don't have to if you don't want to.'

All he had to do was get me to John.

'Ryan told me something before he died. Stew said he'd leave us alone if Ryan said something, what he wanted.'

'What was that?'

'He wanted him to say the man 'e'd been on the marshes with was someone else. An important person.'

'Do you know who?'

'Not 'is name. He was a politician. I thought – maybe – I thought it might be that bloke in the photograph from last time.'

'It was.'

'Oh.' Dean reflected on this. 'Is that why they killed him?'

'I think so.'

'Did 'e do it, say what Stew wanted?'

'I don't know. You couldn't blame him, you know – if he did.'

'There was summink else, 'n'all,' Dean said, sticking his hands in his pockets and hunching his shoulders. 'That bloke, the one you showed me . . . thing is, I 'ave seen 'im before. I didn't think of it at the time, cos you knew about the marshes 'n'all that and he wasn't never on the marshes. But 'e came round the Lord Napier once, last summer.'

Chapter Twenty-Two

JOE TRAILED HIS FINGERS down my back. 'How did you get on with your Moorhouse story?'

'It's running tomorrow. Great pictures.'

'Front page?'

'Yes. Christ, what's the time?' I scrabbled down beside the bed for my watch. 'Got to call Moorhouse.'

'What for?' He was kissing me, his mouth swallowing my words.

'To get a response.'

'Shouldn't you have done this before?'

'Couldn't risk him slapping an injunction on us . . . Can I use your phone?'

'Sure.'

He released me and watched as I pushed my arms through the sleeves of his white towelling robe and clutched it round myself.

I had Moorhouse's home number but his wife said he was out. I didn't want to explain my business to her and in any case she gave every impression of not wanting to be bothered. She gave me the name of someone in his private office.

This number rang and rang. I was on the point of calling Moorhouse's home again when someone finally answered. The young man on the other end sounded rather bored by a call from the press on Saturday evening, but his manner changed abruptly when I explained myself. He became peremptory and supercilious, and said grandly, and rather threateningly, that he'd call Ian Moorhouse immediately and see what was to be done about me, and about the *Chronicle*. The allegations were outrageous.

Moorhouse called back inside five minutes. He blustered and threatened to call his lawyers, but didn't deny the allegations. He knew Dillie Deneuve and Serena Ashley-Brown. And once I'd mentioned them, he was expecting the rest.

I got hold of Dan, repeated the gist of the conversation and gave him a couple of lines to feed into the copy. I was in the middle of this when Joe came downstairs, dressed, and pointed at his watch.

'Got to go,' I told Dan. 'I'll speak to you soon.'

'Peach, now can we finally get something on this Bagnall story next week?'

'I'm doing my best. I'll explain next week.'

'Good. Oh, and Peach?'

'Uh-huh?'

'You're my very favourite person.'

'Cupboard love,' I said. Joe was kissing the back of my neck.

'We ought to go,' Joe murmured into my hair as I put the phone down.

'I don't have any clothes here.'

'What are those things on the floor?'

'Jeans. I'll have to go home and get something proper to wear.'

'No, you look great . . .'

'I may look great now . . .' I was wearing his robe, which had fallen off my shoulders and come undone at the waist; I was reduced to clutching it rather unsuccessfully around my body.

'In your jeans, I mean. You look fine. You don't have to dress up.'

'If it's anything like Penny's party, everyone will look as though they've spent the afternoon in Bond Street and come home with twenty carrier bags. I've never been anywhere so glamorous.'

'You always look fabulous to me.'

Men were very peculiar, I thought as we got in the car. What was Joe doing with me when clearly what he really wanted was a leading theorist of postmodernism with no clothes sense?

We drove to my house; I couldn't possibly have pitched up at the Salts' party in jeans. Joe waited downstairs while I ran up and changed into the red silk dress and jacket I'd been wearing at Dan's party, when I'd seen Joe for the first time.

'Gorgeous,' he said appreciatively when I came down. 'Though, you know, I think you look gorgeous whatever you wear.'

'It occurs to me if I'm going to spend a lot more time with socialists I'll need a new wardrobe.'

'Rubbish,' he said disappointingly. 'You don't have to take the Salts as seriously as they take themselves.'

He took them seriously enough, I thought; or what were we doing here, on our way to see them, when we could still be in bed? 'I have to spend time with them because of politics,' he went on as we got in the car. 'They're useful to the Labour Party, and to George, and it's a trade. But I certainly don't care what they think of the way I dress, or the way my girlfriend dresses.'

'That's disgraceful!'

He looked at me in surprise. 'What is?'

'Spending time with people you despise.'

'But everyone has to do it, all the time. We can't choose the people we work with.'

'It's 8.45 on Saturday night. You're not *at* work.'

'I'm at work most of the time,' he said mildly. 'It's that kind of job. Why do you keep looking behind us?'

'Because of those skinheads who followed me.'

I didn't feel he was treating my skinheads with the seriousness they deserved. Perhaps it was because I'd tried to make light of them while he was in Washington. I didn't want to seem to be whingeing *all* the time. I'd finally related the full story of being followed from Ryan's school to Katrina's when we were in bed a couple of hours earlier, and he'd seemed rather unconcerned. But perhaps he'd been preoccupied with other things.

'Are you sure it wasn't a coincidence, seeing them twice?' he asked now.

'Coincidence?' For a clever man, Joe could say some pretty stupid things. The same two men in different parts of London at exactly the same time as me? 'They were watching.'

'You're sure it *was* the same people?'

'Perfectly sure.'

I felt irritated. I wasn't the hysterical type. I wouldn't fantasise about something like this. 'And have you seen them since?'

'No . . . But I was burgled the same day.'

Joe fell silent, as if considering whether it was worth pointing out to me that this had no bearing on anything.

'Besides, somebody's been messing about with the computer at the *Chronicle*.'

I hadn't bothered telling him this either. There'd been so many other disasters; I hadn't wanted him to think I was *completely* paranoid.

'What do you mean, messing about?'

'Sending messages.'

'Saying what?'

'Suggesting I drop the Bagnall story.'

'You're not still working on that?' He turned to face me, though I thought he would be better off keeping his eyes on the road. 'I thought you'd established Bagnall had a nervous breakdown?'

'No, that's what *you* established. You and your office. I'm keeping an open mind. That's my job. Like yours is going to parties.'

He ignored this. 'Your job doesn't depend on this particular story. You've got Moorhouse breaking tomorrow. And there'll be others.'

I looked out of the car window mutinously. The Holloway Road was littered with Saturday debris: burger boxes, cheap pink-striped carrier bags, soft drinks cans. A group of youths loitered outside Mothercare looking as if they expected trouble, although the only other sign of humanity in the street was a tramp, picking through a rubbish bin.

'You wouldn't by any chance be trying to put me off the Bagnall story because it might bring a Labour MP into disrepute?'

'Of course not. I just don't believe there's anything in it.'

I didn't say much for the rest of the journey. He was wrong. I *knew* he was wrong; but even if he hadn't been, he still had no right to be so dismissive about my work. I wasn't, however, in a position to explain all this; and he, no doubt, thought I was deliberately trying to make trouble for the Labour Party.

We parked round the corner from the Salts' house – their own road was chock-full of cars – and walked up the driveway hand in hand.

'Darling!' Katy cried, flinging open the door and kissing Joe on both cheeks. 'Welcome home! How was Washington? Nick said you saw the Cartwrights there. And Jools said you seemed to be seeing most of the administration. But I see you've brought . . .'

'Helen,' Joe said.

'How nice to see you again, Helen. We have met, haven't we?'

'At Penny Dalmore's.'

'Ah yes. And what is it you do?'

I hadn't even got my coat off. 'I'm a journalist.'

'Helen's got a big story breaking tomorrow,' Joe said proudly. 'Ian Moorhouse and the call girl.'

'Oh, yes . . .' said Katy, raising an eyebrow. 'I didn't realise you were going to be a permanent fixture. How nice. Jools is in the drawing room, Joe. She's longing to see you. Why don't you come with me, Helen?'

She steered me down the hall. I glanced back over my shoulder: Joe was standing where we'd left him. He shrugged; a gesture which seemed to me inadequate in the circumstances, which called for something more assertive, like leaving.

Who the hell *was* Jools, I was thinking; what did she do? Was she full of insights into contemporary politics? Katy pushed me into a group consisting of her husband and two other men, and said vaguely, 'This is Helen. She's a journalist.'

'We were talking about George's speech today,' one of the men said, offering a sweaty hand and introducing himself as David Kelly.

'Haven't we met before?' asked John Salt.

'At Penny Dalmore's, I think.' I told myself he probably met a lot of people and couldn't be expected to remember them all. 'I'm a friend of Joe Rossiter's.'

'Ah-ha!' said the third man, James, who was short and jowly. 'I suppose you know Jools then?'

'How's the election broadcast going?' David Kelly asked John.

'We go out on Tuesday: final filming tomorrow. Simon exerts a very tight control – not that I don't get on with Simon – but I'd have preferred more shots of Penny and the kids, less of the provinces. We don't *need* to clutter up the film with all that social conscience stuff – and it can be very *drab*, the Midlands.'

'I suppose you'll be looking at some plum advisory position at the Department of National Heritage once we're in government?' the tactful one called James said ingratiatingly.

'What I *really* want is to revitalise the British Film Industry. Could be done inside the Heritage Ministry or outside. The only thing that matters, of course, is to have the ear of the Cabinet, and resources. These positions don't matter. What matters is how close you are to George. Better to be coming in the back door, actually.'

James said he hoped himself to have a senior role in a new Bank of Reconstruction and Development.

I needed a drink. Several drinks. And to separate Joe from Jools. And to get away from these people parcelling out their country's future.

I excused myself and pushed through the crowd towards the kitchen. There must have been more than a hundred and fifty guests thronging the hall and drawing room of the Salts' rambling 1930s villa. Quite how this qualified as work for Joe I couldn't make out. I found it hard to believe we would have been missed.

A waiter waved a tray in front of my face; I took a buck's fizz, swallowed half of it very quickly and scanned the drawing room. The atmosphere wasn't unlike that at Penny's party – a heady mix of politics and show business – but on a grander scale. The Salts, it appeared, knew everyone: in one corner a bestselling biographer was talking to a skeletal fashion model and a female Labour peer; in another, a television dramatist was deep in conversation with an ageing rock star; somewhere in the middle, a friend of the Princess of Wales was gossiping with the editor of the *Daily News* and the Director General of the BBC. It was politics as fashion.

George Dalmore seemed to be the centre of attention, even among all these glamorous people. He was the one they were watching out of the corners of their eyes; he was the one they wanted to talk to, to be seen talking to. He didn't appear to mind this at all. He moved around the room, happy to bestow attention. In this, he had star quality.

I couldn't see Joe. Or Simon and Hester, or Penny, or even Nick Llewellyn. I contemplated the awful prospect of spending the entire evening standing in this doorway pretending I was expecting one of my many friends to rush up and embrace me warmly at any moment.

'Hello again,' said someone at my elbow; turning, I saw Adam. 'Been here long?'

'About half an hour,' I said gratefully, thinking it felt like an entire night.

'Are you with Joe?'

'Possibly. Or I was before Katy Salt carted him off.'

He bit his lip. 'It's a horrible business, being with someone in politics. It's such a bloody time-consuming job. I haven't been able to sustain a single relationship since I joined George's office.'

Thanks a lot, I thought, though I merely said, 'I can imagine sometimes it must feel as though you're going out with an entire political movement.'

'Especially at the moment, with the prospect of being in government in a month or two, if we get it right. Actually to be in power – seeing your schemes changing the shape of the country, having a direct impact on millions of people's lives, modifying history, even – that's something different from what any of us have known. Sometimes it seems worth any amount of sacrifice.'

Joe had said something similar. 'Ends justifying means?'

Adam grinned. 'It does at least explain why we can seem obsessive, why we spend time at parties like this. There's a sense that if we don't grab power in the next six weeks, we never will. The Labour Party will be finished.'

'Really?'

'Don't you think? We can't survive another defeat.'

'Darlings!' interrupted Nick Llewellyn. 'How are you both?'

'We were grumbling about the awfulness of politics,' Adam told him.

'Oh, I *know*. Having to put up with hangers-on like me . . .'

'I was trying to work out whether there's anyone here except me who hasn't appeared on television,' I said.

'No, darling, absolutely not. What's more, at least eighty per cent of them have been on my show. But I happen to know that you *have* been on television. I saw you myself, on *Newsnight*.'

'You have a good memory.'

I could see Joe now, talking to Grant Toobin and a leading liberal bishop.

'Helen!' cried Simon Healy, kissing me on both cheeks. 'There's a whisper doing the rounds you've got a big story breaking tomorrow . . . *Very* good news.'

'There is a story,' I acknowledged.

'What's this?' Nick wanted to know.

'Can I say?' Simon asked me. 'Moorhouse. Prostitutes.'

Nick burst out laughing. 'Horrible little man. So you were right, Simon?'

'No, I thought there was nothing in the rumours. Until Helen proved me wrong.'

'Wouldn't you just know it?' Nick muttered. 'They're *so* sordid, these people.'

'Thank you for your flowers,' I said quietly to Simon. 'Did Hester pass on the message? They still look fantastic.'

'After this Moorhouse thing, I feel like filling your house with flowers.'

'Helen!' Hester herself cried, appearing just then at her boyfriend's shoulder. 'And Nick!' She turned her cheek to be kissed by the famous chat show host. 'I'm fleeing from the most gruesome conversation with a married couple who seem to have been on every activists' committee in the history of the Labour Party and think they're going to be running the country in a few weeks.'

'It's like a bloody job centre in here,' Nick murmured.

'How many posts are there actually going to be for all these people?' I wondered.

Simon said grimly: 'Less than they imagine.'

'Give people a sniff of power and they want more,' Hester complained, turning to me. 'There's an air of *desperation*, don't you think? About these hangers-on?'

'Am I a hanger-on?' Nick asked archly.

'Of course not, darling.' She patted his arm. 'You're a close friend.'

'You can't blame them,' Simon said. 'They've been hanging on, as you call it, for years – through defeat after defeat. They've been canvassing and posting leaflets through doors, sitting at polling stations, attending awful constituency meetings, turning up to conferences and paying money. Now they can scarcely believe it's really about to happen. And they deserve some reward.'

'But you get the feeling they'd sell their own grandmothers for a piece of the action,' Hester complained.

It was true that the glittering people who surrounded the Labour leader seemed to me less glamorous, more venal, the better I got to know them. Hester turned back to me. 'Joe tells me you've got the scoop of the year.'

I inadvertently caught sight of Joe, now deep in conversation with an Asian footwear millionaire and a stunning blonde in narrow satin jeans and a skimpy T-shirt. I hoped she wasn't Jools. She had no hips, let alone cellulite.

Chapter Twenty-Three

JOE KISSED ME AGAINST the car with such passion I thought we might have to have sex in the street. But we did eventually manage to disentangle ourselves, and he suggested driving home via King's Cross to pick up an early edition of the *Chronicle*. I would have preferred bed straight away, or the car for that matter, as long as it wasn't parked in a residential area, but I was touched by his interest in my work.

'Sorry about Katy Salt,' he said sheepishly, putting the car in gear.

'Did she manage to propel you into the arms of Jools?'

'It's finished, you know, the thing with Jools. In every possible sense.' He grabbed my hand and held it, relying on his right hand to control the car.

I disdained to get involved in a conversation about Jools and asked him instead about Washington. It was almost the first opportunity I'd had – we had been otherwise occupied earlier – and he told me about a meeting with the adviser to the Secretary of State, and a dinner with some old friends who were academics at Georgetown, with whom, he said, he had 'talked about the Balkans'. Sometimes I wondered how interesting life with Joe was really going to be.

'What about Lord Malvern?'

'Sorry?'

'Lord Malvern.'

'What . . .?'

'He left a message on your answering machine. Or someone at

his office did. When I was at your house doing the washing up and leaving you that note.'

'Oh. The lovely note.'

'So?'

'Oh well, yes, I saw him earlier in the week. Tuesday, I think.'

'You've told me about all these other people you met, but not him.'

'He wanted to keep the meeting –' Joe hesitated, 'not exactly secret, but quiet.' He revved the engine. 'All sorts of people crawl out of the woodwork when they think you're about to win an election.'

'What on earth does Lord Malvern want with the Labour Party?'

'Reassurance. To be told we're not going to ruin his businesses.'

'Isn't he a major contributor to Tory Party funds?'

'Hence his reluctance to advertise the fact he's seeing us.'

'And somewhere to the right of Attila the Hun and believes in bringing back the Poor Law? Doesn't sound like he'd be a natural soul mate of yours.'

'He believes in the freedom to do business,' Joe said rather pompously. 'So do we.'

'You agree with him about social security as well, presumably?'

From my reading of the cuttings, I knew Lord Malvern advocated the abolition of welfare. People must stand on their own two feet, whether they had shoes or not.

'Of course not,' Joe said slightly irritably. 'We do believe it's possible to create a dependency culture – which is all that he's said, actually. Essentially. So yes, there are things to talk about.'

'Interesting. I'm seeing him tomorrow.'

'Whatever for?'

'*Femme.*'

'But why? I mean, what's the angle?'

I didn't see why he should sound so incredulous.

'Why does a beautiful, brainy twenty-six-year-old fall for a man like this?'

'Oh, I see. Well, you'd better not let him know you know he's been meeting the Labour Party. It'd probably be better if you didn't tell anyone else either.' He stopped the car. We were at King's Cross. First editions of the Sunday papers were piled high on a barrow on the pavement. 'Now. Are you going to jump out of the car and get a paper?'

We sat, heads bent together, poring over the front page of the *Chronicle*. Not a word of my story had been altered. Next to my picture byline and the 'exclusive' tag, Dillie Deneuve gazed up at us with doe eyes.

'Brilliant,' said Joe, kissing the tip of my nose. 'Absolutely brilliant.'

We stayed in bed until lunch-time, making love and dozing. By the time we got up, Moorhouse had resigned.

Joe flicked on the television news while I was making coffee, and there was Dillie, walking through Hyde Park in jeans and a gaberdine raincoat, hair fetchingly windblown. There too was Moorhouse, strolling down the garden path in Surrey in his Conservative MP's smart casuals: corduroy trousers, open-necked check shirt, cardigan. He stood at the gate in front of the clutch of reporters and made a short weaselly statement in which he failed to admit the truth of the allegations but said he was resigning because he didn't want to embarrass the Government. He refused to take questions. His wife, sensibly, was nowhere to be seen.

Joe made bacon and eggs and we turned off the television and ate them hungrily, tossing the Sunday papers backwards and forwards across the dining table. The later editions had all picked up the Moorhouse story, though there'd been little time to do much more than lift our version and change a few words. The *Sunday News* had compiled a short profile of me which, to Joe's amusement, made much of my 'deprived East End background'.

While Joe piled the dishes in the sink, I flipped through the papers for the rest of the news. There were only two other significant stories: the clash on Bethnal Green Road and a series of sporadic outbreaks of violence at premier league football matches around the country.

The police seemed to think the two things might be linked.

The Patriots' presence at the rally in the East End had evidently taken them by surprise. They'd expected a few hecklers, regular troublemakers, but not this disciplined phalanx of nationalists, these armies advancing on one another. Even the Patriots' foot troops (this,

Joe and I thought, smacked of police infiltration) hadn't known till the last minute that their presence would be required on the streets that afternoon. But such was the level of discipline that when they got their marching orders, they marched. They were organised in cells, drilled like soldiers, and could apparently be marshalled in minutes.

The Patriots must have made meticulous plans: you could see that in retrospect. Retrospect, though, was no use. The police intelligence hadn't been good enough, so that what should have been a peaceful march turned into a fiasco. A policeman had been taken to hospital with head injuries; four anti-racist demonstrators had stab wounds. The police made sixty arrests, but yet again believed they had failed to round up the ringleaders. It had taken several hours after the initial charge, the one I'd witnessed, to separate the two groups.

All this was bad enough. But long after the streets had been cleared, when the police could safely have assumed the marchers were at home or in cells, someone pushed a firebomb through the letter box of one of the leading members of the London Alliance Against Racism.

Ahmed Khalifa, the uncle of the murdered boy Ali Khalifa, was fortunately still downstairs when the petrol bomb came through his letter box at 1.00 a.m. as he was about to go to bed. He was able to rouse his wife and four children, who were asleep upstairs, and help them out of the house.

The *Chronicle* had a picture of the children huddled together in a blanket in the street. Their faces were lit by the flames from their house. They looked young and very bewildered.

Once Joe and I had cleared up, we drove to Hampstead Heath and wandered about without any clear idea of where we were going, happy simply to be trailing up hills, along paths, beside the ponds, pausing now and then to admire the view of the city, criss-crossing our route, holding hands.

As we walked, Joe told me about his childhood by the sea in Lincolnshire; about his father, a doctor, who had died in his mid-fifties; and his mother, a nurse, who had given up work when Joe and his younger sister were born. They were a boring family, he said: boringly normal, boringly happy. I thought they sounded lovely.

I reciprocated by telling him how hard my mother had worked to buy me the things she thought I ought to have: new coats every other winter, holidays – and after an hour or so he was in such a benign mood he even agreed with me that the Salts were faintly ridiculous.

When the light was beginning to fade we drove back to Joe's house so he could get to the Dalmores' for a meeting with the election campaign team, from which he had to go on to a session with Julie Hart, who had been roped in to inject some jokes into George's speeches.

I walked home in the twilight, hugging to myself thoughts of Joe – picturing him as a child on the beach in Lincolnshire; sitting earnestly round a table discussing policy at the Dalmores'. But I was actually thinking about him in bed when it happened.

I was walking along a road between the canal and the railway line. It was bordered on one side by iron railings, which fenced it off from the canal, and on the other by corrugated iron partitions, concealing yards and railway arches.

The man seemed to come from nowhere, although he must have been lying in wait behind the iron fence.

For a moment after he grabbed my arm, I was too stunned to move. I was miles away, pressing my face against Joe's skin . . . Then I realised what was happening. I tried to twist out of his way, but he squeezed harder; I kicked out, aiming for his shins, but he dodged my foot, muttering 'bitch', and dragged me sideways into one of the yards.

We were in some sort of car breakers' or scrap metal yard. There was half a car chassis lying on the ground, an exhaust pipe and lengths of multi-coloured wiring.

I absorbed all this in slow motion; I thought with odd detachment how very peculiar it was that his skinhead haircut, which ought to have exposed his features, actually flattened them. He had a nose, mouth, eyes, a leer, but his face was somehow incomplete. It was impossible to see him as fully human; he was simply brutal.

I stumbled and his fingers squeezed into my flesh. I looked around frantically, praying for someone to come into view, and opened my mouth to scream. But he was there before me and his fingers clamped over my mouth, each one pressing into the soft tissue of my cheek like a brace.

He was pushing me so violently that it was as much as I could do to keep upright. My feet trailed behind the rest of my body, rag-doll-like.

After the initial moment of shock I felt real fear. Would they abduct me? Take me off and kill me, expertly and without fuss? Manage things so that no one would ever know how or why I died?

There was a length of rubber tubing on the ground, and those tangled, wildly-coloured wires . . . I felt the thwack of his knuckles on my cheek; my face stung. I watched him with astonishing, focused clarity as he brought his other hand up to catch me somewhere around the solar plexus, before I crumpled, tipping forward.

I was on my knees in the dirt; he lifted me and hit my face again, higher up, closer to the eye. He'd broken the skin; I could tell from the warm blood trickling down my face. I grunted. And that was it. That was all it took. One skinhead, thirty seconds. And then he was gone, with my bag.

Chapter Twenty-Four

MY HEAD ACHED. I didn't need this from Bobby.

'You're mad.' He paced the sitting room. 'First the house gets turned over, now you. What else does it take?'

And you don't know the half of it, I thought. Tony Bagnall. Jean Hammond. Ryan Stoner.

'I've got to cancel my credit cards,' I said, removing the tea towel full of ice cubes from my cheek. 'And they've got my keys: we'd better get the locks changed. In fact we'd better do that right now.'

'You've got to talk to the police. Don't take that off yet . . . You've got to tell them these skinheads have been following you and they've got something to do with your work. Even if you won't tell me.'

'I can't,' I said wearily. 'I'd have to give them the evidence, and it isn't mine to hand over.'

'You've almost lost it twice now. It just happened to be in your bag when the house was burgled, and now you say you've put it somewhere safely. What d'you want them to do? Abduct you and hold you until you tell them where it is? Because they sure as hell don't seem to me like people who are going to give up.'

I sighed, irritably.

'I have to keep picking up the pieces, that's all; what would you have done if I wasn't home?'

'Waited on the doorstep. Called your mobile. I don't know. You *were* here. And I am not handing that diary to the police – not without Katrina's permission.'

I got up and peered at my face in the mirror over the fireplace. 'You'll be all right,' Bobby said grudgingly. 'Facially. Mentally, I'm not so sure.'

I called my bank, the credit card companies, the locksmith and the police, who sent round a couple of officers to take a description. It was hopeless: a suedehead in jeans, Doc Martens and a black jacket. It could have been half the young men in London.

Bobby cooked pasta with a tomato sauce, grumbling all the time, and opened a bottle of good wine – too good for me, he said.

I told him – because it seemed only fair – that I thought someone had been trying to drive Bagnall out of politics before he died and that Ryan Stoner had been part of the plot; that I believed that something had gone wrong and they'd killed both Ryan and Bagnall. I also told him I thought the same people had murdered Jean Hammond.

'They don't mess about, these people,' Bobby said drily. 'Have you got a death wish?'

'What can I do? Someone has to find out what all this is about.'

'Someone, maybe. But you?'

'I'm in the best position. I know more than anyone else.'

'So tell the police. It's not as if you have anything to prove. Your Moorhouse stuff this morning was marvellous.'

'I can't tell the police. There's no proof. They'd think I was mad. Or they'd go off half-cock and arrest Stewart Saddler and congratulate themselves on having destroyed a paedophile ring when that might only be a small part of it.'

'Who the hell's Stewart Saddler?'

'Never mind. I know this story matters. I don't know why at the moment, but I know it does. Bagnall thought it was important and so did Jean Hammond.'

We could have gone on squabbling for hours; fortunately we were interrupted then by a call from Simon Healy, who wanted to congratulate me on Moorhouse.

'An amazing piece of journalism,' he said admiringly. 'Did it take you long to persuade her to talk? To get all that information?'

'No,' I said wryly. 'It all fell into place remarkably quickly.'

'Well, it was clever of you to persuade her to speak about it. And it read very well. You obviously haven't lost your tenacity. Or your flair for telling a story. Which makes me think . . . I've been looking for someone for a while to look into some other rumours. Not quite in the Moorhouse league, but interesting . . . I wondered if you might like to come in and talk to me about them? You may not want the story, of course . . .'

'Sure,' I said faintly.

I didn't bother to tell him my tenacity had just got me beaten up.

I left a message on Joe's answering machine about the mugging and he turned up at midnight, by which time I'd been in bed for hours. Bobby had to answer the door.

Joe insisted on coming in. Bobby refused at first, and agreed eventually only because Joe threatened to stay on the doorstep all night. So Bobby accompanied him up the stairs and hovered outside the bedroom door as he knocked softly and entered. Bobby clearly suspected he'd admitted some mad rapist or murderer.

'I'm too fragile for sex,' I mumbled, stirring and seeing Joe standing over the bed. 'If you touch me I may be forced to scream.'

He didn't smile. He'd switched on the bedside lamp and he looked horrified.

'Oh, you poor, poor thing!'

I was groggy from the painkillers I'd taken earlier. 'Attractive, huh?'

'Oh, I don't know. Even beaten up you look pretty devastating. Can I get in?'

'Only if you promise not to touch.'

He pulled off his clothes and slipped into the bed beside me. He reached over and stroked my hair softly. He made a sound that seemed almost to be moaning.

I stirred once in the middle of the night. God knows what time it was. Joe was still awake and watching me in the darkness, almost as if he were keeping guard. His expression was terribly troubled. I was touched, but I couldn't keep my eyes open.

I spent the following morning at the office in Smithfield cobbling together a piece about party dresses I'd promised Joanna Beverley a month ago and forgotten all about in the excitement over Tony

Bagnall, Ryan Stoner and Ian Moorhouse. I'd woken up this morning with a stiffness in my ribs and a stinging in my face, remembering the piece was supposed to have been delivered yesterday.

'I suppose,' Sarah said testily, standing over my desk and contemplating my bruises, 'once they've succeeded in killing you and realised you don't have the mysterious package – which I haven't opened, though God knows why – they'll come after me. You know what this makes me feel like? That woman who carried a bomb onto a plane for her boyfriend. You have friends and all they do is try and get you blown up.'

'It's not a bomb.'

'It could hardly be more dangerous,' Sarah said, looking at my face. 'It'll serve you right if Mr Romance takes one look at your smashed-up face and decides he can't communicate or share his yoghurt with you ever again.'

'Sssh,' I admonished. 'I'm working. And as it happens, he's been extremely sympathetic.'

Femme had sent me a series of pictures of women in their best frocks, for which I had to produce – preferably witty, although Joanna said magnanimously that they would take merely clever – extended captions. I think this meant I had to mention body parts as often as possible.

I was puzzling over a picture of the Argentine supermodel Coco looking stunning in a strapless gown with a thigh-high split, and had just reached the conclusion there was nothing to say about Coco except that I was jealous, when Joanna called to check that the copy would be coming in today.

'Darling, brilliant piece in yesterday's paper! I always knew you were a real star, even though some people here . . . well, never mind. *Such* good stuff on Moorhouse. And doesn't Dillie Deneuve look marvellous – so sophisticated? We're doing a piece on her for the July issue. Terribly tasteful, of course – trying to get across the idea that prostitutes aren't all sleazy – a sort of social essay-type thing. Lots of pictures of Dillie in taupe, anyway.'

'Sounds great,' I said faintly.

'Now, Helen, you are *very* deceitful . . . When you said the other day you'd been at the Dalmores', I didn't realise you meant you were actually at Penny's birthday party!'

'Ah.'

'Listen, darling, you must write something for us during the election. What I'd really like is for you to spend a week with Penny in the middle of the campaign and report on what it's like from the woman's point of view – what time George comes in, what sort of mood he's in, whether he eats dinner, that kind of thing . . .'

'I really don't think . . .'

'No buts! It's too good an opportunity . . . So is that all right? I'll leave you to sort that out with Penny?'

One way and another, it was a relief to get in the car and drive out of London.

The motorway was quiet. I enjoyed the run out of London, and little more than an hour after I left I was driving through Faversham. Once out of the town, I pulled the car over into a tiny lay-by on a wooded ridge to check the map. In front of me the marshes stretched out to the Swale, the wide ribbon of water that runs between mainland Kent and the Isle of Sheppey; beyond that the island loomed out of the water, a low green-backed hump, with its prison and its wild wading birds.

It was an unlikely spot for Lord Malvern to have chosen. He should by rights have had a house beside the Thames in pop-star belt Berkshire. But he'd grown up in this forgotten corner of Kent; and his mother, who'd lived in a converted oast house on the Prospect House property until her death a year ago, had never had any desire to go elsewhere. So Jack Malvern had bought Prospect House, and perhaps because he never stayed anywhere very long, he ended up thinking of it as home.

The road to the property lay down the hill beside the marsh. I put the car in gear and drove slowly past an Elizabethan timbered farmhouse and a couple of brick cottages, before turning into a lane that led only to Prospect House. To my left were cherry orchards, the blossom out, pink and dancing; to my right the marsh, screened from the road by a row of poplars and willows. Out on the scrubby grass sheep grazed and curlews picked; a heron took off gracefully from one of the dykes, flew a few hundred feet and settled impeccably beside the water.

I passed the church, its graveyard tidied and mown; and then, as Lord Malvern had promised, I was in the courtyard of a pink-washed eighteenth-century manor house.

Prospect House had been a working farm until Jack Malvern bought it fourteen years ago. There was an oast house in one corner of the courtyard, and weathered redbrick barns screening it from the marsh. An old plough rested by the garden gate. But the farm's only role now was to be beautiful, and here it succeeded. To the side and back of the house, narcissi swarmed over lawns; yellow and purple irises waved by the river bank. The place was breathtaking – saved from tweeness by the raw empty spaces of the marsh behind, and from the bleakness of its surroundings by lavish amounts of money.

Lord Malvern came to the front door, wearing brown cords and a check shirt. The most immediately striking thing about him was that his body was too young to belong quite properly to a man of his age. The second was how handsome his face was – the features well-defined, the black wavy hair greying at the temples.

He politely refrained from passing any comment on the state of my face and led me through to a rose-coloured room at the back of the house, overlooking the garden. The chair in which he suggested I sit had a view of the stream, a hump-backed stone bridge and a rose arbour, which was covered at this time of year in scrambling pink clematis. The room itself was comforting, with small dark oil landscapes dotted around the walls. A housekeeper brought us tea.

'Kate hasn't seen the house yet,' Lord Malvern confessed, pouring tea while I set up my tape recorder. 'I don't suppose she'll like it.'

This did not seem to me to augur particularly well for the fifth marriage. 'Funnily enough,' he went on, 'it's almost my favourite place – perhaps it's because it's where I grew up and went to school and did all sorts of important things like kissing my first girlfriend – in a bus shelter in Faversham, as it happens.' He smiled. 'Fortunately Kate loves the house in the Hamptons. That's where we're getting married. So . . . every time I come back I wish I could spend more time here, but more than half my business is in the United States, and when I *am* in the UK I often need to be in London. Anyway, this is probably not of any interest to you at all . . . What can I tell you?'

We talked about his childhood in Faversham, his education at the local grammar school, his absolute determination to expand his father's already successful business.

'I've always been a rather driven person. Work hard and play hard. You know I have an indoor tennis court and pool here? I believe in living to the utmost. Don't you?' He handed me a cup of tea.

'I suppose so,' I said doubtfully.

'I can't stand being – what's the word? – *trammelled*. I'd hate it if I couldn't pursue my interests. Especially at my age. If you believe you've only got one life, it seems to me important to get the most out of it and as far as I can see, that means not being impeded by lack of money or opportunity. So that's what I've always striven for – the opportunity to be an individual. Not letting other people have control.'

'Does that mean having power, or having money?' I asked. 'Which is more important?'

'Money's a means to power – *the* means, I believe. Who was it said if he could be reincarnated he used to think he'd want to come back as the Pope or the US President, but he realised now the only sensible thing would be to come back as the bond market? That's where power is today. Not with the politicians.'

'But didn't you think of setting up your own party once?'

'Sure. It was kind of a sentimental idea, though. I didn't want my country to lose out. And companies, you see – multinational companies like mine – depend on countries to provide them with the means to conduct their business: a legal system that works, people educated and healthy enough to work for them and use their products. And there was a time, not so long ago, when the trade unions in this country threatened to prevent the Government from maintaining its side of that contract with business. I was concerned neither of the major parties would have the nerve to deal with them.'

'So this party of yours would have been an anti-union party?'

'In a sense, yes.'

I knew Labour was anxious to distance itself from the unions, but even so, the party had come a long way if it could find common cause with Lord Malvern. 'I was afraid the unions would stifle economic recovery,' he explained. 'And I knew when that happened the people of this country would lose out – not least as businesses started relocating abroad. As a businessman, of course, I could take my operations elsewhere. But I didn't want to. I like this country. It has a surprising amount to offer.'

'So what stopped you from setting up this party?'

'Events got ahead of me. Mrs Thatcher started to move against the unions, and she was obviously opposed to the stifling regulations the European Union is always so keen to inflict on businesses operating in this country. As you probably will have gathered,' he smiled, 'I am not a fan of the Belgian empire.'

'Do you lobby to counteract the influence of Europe now?'

'The only thing I do occasionally – when I'm in the country – is attend the gatherings of a dining club set up by people with similar views to my own. We discuss the issues. Of course, I have dinner with people who might be influential from time to time – cabinet ministers and so on. But I leave the systematic lobbying to others.'

I wondered if this was the organisation George had asked Simon about at the dinner for Penny's birthday: 'This dining club: is it called Loyalty?'

'You've heard of it? Yes. Set up by a group of very brilliant young people. But that's all I have time for, regrettably. Have you been? It's very interesting.'

'No, I'd like to.'

He didn't offer me an invitation.

I consulted my list of questions.

'How do you see the possible election of the Labour Party affecting this contract you talk about between government and business?' I asked. It wasn't exactly *Femme*-style subject matter, but I was intrigued. I doubted he'd notice. He probably didn't have a lot of time to read *Femme*.

'*Possible* election?' He raised his eyebrows. 'Probable, I'd say. Almost certain. I sincerely hope my companies will be able to work with the Labour Party. I'm a . . . cautious admirer, I suppose you'd say, of George Dalmore. You need guts to do what he's done with that organisation.'

I nodded. There was nothing sinister about that. I asked him about the Institute of Heredity and Genetics.

'Ah, my hobby.' Lord Malvern put his cup and saucer aside. 'Well, that's *not* a political organisation. The important thing to understand about the Institute is that it was established in an open-minded spirit of scientific inquiry, because I felt that genetics was *the* important area of science for the early part of the twenty-first century.'

I nodded. 'The social implications of our recent understanding of genetics are enormous,' he explained. 'Take, for example, the question of why women are less promiscuous than men. A woman can only have a maximum of perhaps twenty or thirty children in a lifetime, whereas there was once some Moroccan king, or so they say, who had nine hundred children. Women invest more, in terms merely of gestation, in their children; it follows that their strategies for getting and keeping a mate are rather different. They want someone who will stick around and help them bring these children to maturity.'

This seemed to me to be a rather convenient rationalisation for Lord Malvern's behaviour. If it was all biology, he presumably couldn't be expected to do anything to curb his tendency to dump women as soon as they began to bore him.

'Then, of course, there's the vexed question of intelligence. This is all rather controversial, of course – you'll know that some of our grants have come in for criticism – but a good many eminent scientists, of all political persuasions, are disturbed by the fact – and it is a fact – that black people score lower in IQ tests on average than white people. From this arises an important question of education. Are we right to try and educate everyone to the same level? Perhaps we should adapt educational programmes to meet the differing needs of different groups. Perhaps it is a mistake to assume we can all become masterminds?'

I opened my mouth to speak, but the housekeeper knocked before I had the chance, and put her head round the door.

'Telephone call for you, Lord Malvern,' she said. 'Teddy Jacobs.'

'I'm sorry, Helen; will you excuse me for a moment?'

He got up and left the room, leaving me staring out at the willow trees and the lily pond and thinking that there were several things I didn't like about his genetics. Perhaps, for a start, IQ tests weren't infallible. Perhaps they only tested how good people were at IQ tests. There might be some bias about them (they were presumably set by white people?) that had yet to be appreciated. And 'tailoring education' sounded like a good excuse not to spend money on black people, or the children Mr Morrison taught, perhaps. And then the less education you offered these disadvantaged groups, the easier it would be in turn to dismiss them as stupid.

Lord Malvern did not come back. Having assembled my argu-
ments about genetics, which I intended to put to him as soon as
he returned, I looked at his paintings. One was a Stubbs. Then I
looked out of the window at the garden. Still Lord Malvern had
not returned. It occurred to me that after two cups of tea, and
with perhaps another half hour of questions ahead of me, I really
needed to go to the bathroom.

I emerged from the rose-coloured parlour and found myself at
the bottom of the staircase. I could hear Lord Malvern's calm,
assured voice drifting from a room along the hall and thought
I'd slip upstairs rather than crash around down here and run the
risk of disturbing him.

I found the toilet at the top of the stairs on the right. It wasn't
until I emerged that the thought even entered my mind that I could
look behind the doors that opened onto the galleried hall.

But then, having once had the idea, I found it impossible to resist.
I don't know what I expected to find – perhaps some background
colour – a book open on a bed, a study full of photographs of his
first wife. Or his fifth: it didn't matter – something that would pull
together my profile.

I crept along the passage and opened the first door on my left
to reveal a pale blue, beautiful, but characterless bedroom. There
was no sign of recent occupation; it looked like a guest suite.

I tried the second door and found myself looking at a four-poster
bed with tapestry hangings. This appeared to be the room Lord
Malvern used; his tennis whites were laid out ready on the bed.
The walls were lined with apricot silk and the furniture was glossy
with age and the housekeeper's attention. But there was nothing
distinctive or memorable here: no photographs or books.

It was the third room that offered what (when I found it) I felt
I'd been looking for.

I turned the handle and eased the door open. A desk stood in
front of me, and behind that bookshelves. There was a lamp, an
extremely old telephone, and an ancient, battered typewriter. I
scarcely noticed them. I was too shocked by the flag draped over
the fireplace. It was enormous, blood-red, and emblazoned with a
fat black swastika.

I took a step forward. Behind the door stood a motorbike.
German. On a side table a helmet sat rakishly on top of a pile

of books. I lifted off the helmet and examined the top volume: Oswald Spengler's *Der Untergang des Abendlandes*, dated 1918, which would have made it a first edition. I knew this book, or I knew its significance. It was about racial domination and the decline of liberal Western society; it had been hugely intellectually influential when it came out and had helped to pave the way for National Socialism. But the book underneath was more remarkable still. It was a copy, again in German, of Nietzsche's autobiography, *Ecce Homo*. The name inscribed on the flyleaf was 'Joseph Goebbels'.

I put the books down hurriedly, as if they burned my fingers. A little cluster of clockwork tin toy cars stood on the table beside them. I bent down and peered, scarcely daring to touch. One was a Wehrmacht troop carrier; another a radio-command van, another an ambulance. All had miniature Nazi crews.

I took a step backwards. Turning by the door, I caught sight of a telegram, framed, hung on the wall. It was dated October 10, 1942, and it was from Heinrich Himmler.

I didn't know what to think. I didn't have a lot of time *to* think. I closed the door softly and went downstairs, as quietly as I could; slipped back into the rose-coloured drawing room; took my seat in the deep armchair overlooking the garden, and waited.

Lord Malvern came back a few minutes later, apologising for having stayed away so long. 'Rather urgent business,' he said, smiling, and asked the housekeeper to bring more tea.

'And now,' he said warmly, putting his fingertips together in front of him, 'where were we?'

Chapter Twenty-Five

'NAZI MEMORABILIA!' I CRIED. 'He *collects* Nazi memorabilia.'

Joe frowned. 'Are you sure?'

'I saw it. Horrible little tin models of Wehrmacht troop carriers. A telegram from Himmler.'

'Perhaps there's some explanation,' Joe suggested, without conviction. 'Perhaps he's interested in the Second World War. Did you ask him about it? He might have a long-standing intellectual interest in the politics of the Third Reich. Like collecting stamps.'

I'd been too *shocked* to ask him about it. All my instincts told me I wasn't supposed to have gone into that room. And if Lord Malvern had a long-standing intellectual interest in the politics of the Third Reich, it certainly wasn't something he'd ever discussed in public.

'It is *not* like collecting stamps,' I protested. 'Not remotely. I don't think you should have anything to do with him.'

'It's not quite as simple as that . . .'

I dropped his arm and walked sideways along the pavement beside him, protesting. 'Perhaps it wouldn't be quite so sinister if not for that Institute . . . But the two things taken together: it's only a short step away from eugenics.'

'We're not talking to him about eugenics. Or his interest in the Nazis, for that matter . . . What's wrong now?'

'I thought I saw the skinheads again . . .' I *had* seen them, up the street, in a doorway. 'No! don't look. I don't want them to know I've seen them. I don't want them to know I'm scared.'

'We're here now,' Joe said, taking my arm and steering me through the plate glass door into Fred's.

'*Are* you scared?' he asked as we sat down. 'Seriously?'

'Seriously.' I was half looking over my shoulder the whole time. 'Wouldn't you be, if someone had beaten you up so your face looked like a bruised banana?'

He didn't smile. 'Then you must go to the police. If you really believe your attacker was one of the skinheads who was following you, and they're still around . . .'

'I can't.'

'Why not?'

'It's too complicated.'

The thought of Katrina made me feel guilty. I'd been so busy with Moorhouse in the last couple of days . . . But I should have been to see her, told her about my conversation with Dean. Not that it would have been especially encouraging for her to see me like this, with the skin below my left eye all mottled and mauve.

'You can't expect me to help you if you won't talk to me about it,' Joe complained.

'You *do* help.'

That was a lie, a relationship-protecting lie. Because he didn't help at all. He didn't *want* me to talk about it. He didn't believe Bagnall's death was mysterious, because he had no interest in acknowledging the possibility that Bagnall had been suffering from anything except the most prosaic, predictable kind of mid life misery; that he'd got so utterly fed up one day he'd decided to end his life.

Now he leaned across the table and touched my face, his fingers gently brushing the bruise. 'I'd like to help you more.'

All right then, I thought: if that's really what you want. And I took a deep breath. 'Tony Bagnall thought he'd uncovered some kind of conspiracy,' I said. 'He talked to Jean Hammond about it. And now they're both dead. I investigate Bagnall's death and men start following me. I get hostile messages on the computer at work. My house is turned over and I'm beaten up. Someone's trying to warn me off. Why they're bothering I don't know; they had no compunction about killing Jean Hammond. Perhaps there'll come a point when they'll just kill me.'

Joe took my hand and gazed into my eyes. He looked worried.

'If it's that dangerous you *must* drop it. You might have been lucky so far, but if they're still following you . . .'

I had been lucky. I hadn't even needed stitches. No one would be offering me any modelling assignments in the next few weeks, but this wouldn't be a radical departure.

'What conspiracy did Tony Bagnall think he'd uncovered?'

I didn't answer. Instead, I said: 'Who is de Moleyns?'

'Who?' He was puzzled.

'I hoped you might have heard of him. Someone called de Moleyns. I don't know the first name.'

He shook his head doubtfully. 'Why do you want to know?'

'He could have been why Tony Bagnall died.'

'You think he's one of the conspirators?'

I shrugged. 'Possibly.'

Our first courses arrived, and in the flurry of sorting out which of us was having the rocket and parmesan shavings and which the Tuscan bean soup, of refilling wine glasses and deciding whether to have walnut bread or ciabatta, I changed the subject back to Lord Malvern and his memorabilia. 'I'm serious,' I said, 'about Lord Malvern. I don't think the Labour Party should have anything to do with him.'

'This Nazi stuff could have a perfectly innocent explanation . . .'

'Joe, he founded an institute dedicated to proving racial superiority!'

'You may be taking rather a simplistic view of sociobiology,' Joe said mildly. 'It's a young science which is popularly misunderstood.'

'Oh yes?'

'Yes. It is, however, taken seriously by all sorts of eminent – and liberal – people. To suggest that only racists are interested in the sort of work that comes out of the Institute of Heredity and Genetics is absurd. Economists are beginning to apply evolutionary principles to technologies and companies. Biological ideas of predator-prey relationships are being taken up by political scientists. Finally, a hundred years on, scientists are beginning to recognise the implications of Darwin's discoveries. This is affecting the way we think about ourselves profoundly – and the more we find out about human genetic make-up, the more that will be the case.'

'I thought scientific racism was discredited by the Nazis,' I said sarcastically. 'I thought since the Second World War civilised people had abandoned ideas of Aryan superiority. But no: here's Lord Malvern. I went to the library when I got back, and you know what? His Institute published a paper a few months ago which claimed one in five black people have IQ scores that put them on the borderline of mental retardation. What do you imagine they'll be suggesting next? Enforced sterilisation programmes? Ghettoes?'

Joe put down his knife and fork and addressed me with the resigned air of one who feels obliged to try to explain nuclear fission to a five-year-old. 'I accept not all the conclusions of sociobiology are palatable to liberal sensibilities. But that's not to say we should shut our minds to it. As I say, it's a young science, and it might yet explain all sorts of things we don't understand, everything from crime to adultery, charitable giving to child abuse.'

I was instinctively mistrustful of any theory that claimed to explain everything. 'So what exactly *are* you talking to Lord Malvern about?' I demanded.

'I told you. He wants to be assured a Labour government isn't going to wreck his businesses.'

'Why was his assistant talking about Durham, then?'

Joe pulled apart a chunk of ciabatta. 'George is giving a speech in Durham – on Wednesday, in fact – in which he will talk about our attitude to business.'

'You let Lord Malvern help you write George's speeches now?'

'Of course not. Why are you being like this? I gave him a preview; I invited his comments. I'm sorry you didn't like him . . .'

'Oh, he's charming,' I said. 'He's urbane, gentlemanly. He isn't patronising. But perhaps he didn't recognise me as one of his underclass. I think his politics are grotesque.'

'You don't know anything about it,' said Joe and we sat in silence for a while. I stared down at my plate; I had unaccountably lost enthusiasm for my linguini in squid ink.

'What conspiracy did Tony Bagnall think he'd uncovered?' Joe repeated eventually.

'I don't know. I honestly don't know.'

It was our first date alone, our first outing without any of Joe's political friends, and it wasn't going well. Certainly not as well as it should have done if he was really Mr Romance. While he was blandly explaining how sociobiology was a young science,

I couldn't help remembering the television news pictures of the Asian family who had been fire bombed on Saturday night: the four stunned children blinking in the television lights, the father at a loss to understand why anyone should try to kill his sons and daughter. Ethnic cleansing in East London.

There was too much racial hatred already for Lord Malvern to be able to throw up his hands and play the innocent supporter of disinterested science, let alone for Joe Rossiter to do it for him.

'I see your Moorhouse story was still all over the papers today,' Joe said, changing the subject in an evident attempt to mollify me. 'The Labour Party's falling over itself with gratitude; everyone's thrilled.'

'I didn't write it for the Labour Party,' I said grumpily.

'No, of course you didn't. But you've inadvertently done us a very good turn.'

I moved my linguini about listlessly. 'I'm still worried about that story. In fact, the more I think about it, the more I worry. It was too easy. Why didn't Dillie want any money?'

'We've been through this before,' Joe said patiently. 'She's a member of the Labour Party. She liked you. And Moorhouse didn't *deny* it, did he? It's true.'

'Yes, I suppose it's true.'

'Then why should you worry? He got what was coming to him. And it's left the Tories reeling. It's inconceivable that James Sherlock will be in fighting spirit for the election: first Jean Hammond dies, now he loses Moorhouse to the worst kind of scandal . . .'

Sometimes, I thought, Joe was hopelessly insensitive. *He* might see everything in terms of its repercussions for the Labour Party, but I hoped I had a wider perspective.

'It's as if they can't do anything right,' Joe went on, obliviously. 'Sherlock was horrified by Jean Hammond's death, and Moorhouse was one of his brightest junior ministers. The Government has been seriously undermined by all this trouble on the football terraces. There's a feeling out there that we're a nation on the brink of some violent eruption. We're certainly a nation on the brink of eviction from European football, and if *that* happened before an election there'd be an awful lot of disgruntled people.'

'Including me,' I said. 'You sound so pleased.'

He shot me a quick, surprised look. Slightly hurt too, as if I wasn't empathising sufficiently.

'Only because at last people can see how much mess the Tories have got us into.'

'Oh, come on,' I said wearily. 'That's just an electioneering form of words, a verbal reflex.'

'Not at all,' he said, offended. 'The country's divided. The Government's fatally split over Europe. James Sherlock can barely bring himself to acknowledge the right wing of his party, and they *hate* him. Meanwhile, George goes from strength to strength, making intelligent speeches full of sensible policy proposals, sounding convincing and authoritative.'

'Talking of the right wing,' I said, 'you know that Loyalty dinner people were talking about at Penny's party?'

'Yes.'

'When is it?'

'Wednesday, I think. Why?'

'Have you and Simon decided whether to go?'

'I don't think I can. Too many other things to do. Why?'

'I want to see what it's like. If you were going to be there I could tag along.'

'I don't think it works like that,' Joe said stiffly. 'I don't think it's a bring-a-partners-type thing.'

'Oh,' I was rather crestfallen. 'But they must want you there. Are you telling me you couldn't get us both in?'

Joe wasn't falling for that. 'No, I'm telling you I don't want to go. I haven't got my diary here, but I'm almost certain that's the night I'm recording a new late-night discussion programme. *Aspects of Philosophy*, I think it's called. I've agreed to appear; I can't let them down now.'

A waitress with long blonde hair and pouty lips leaned over our table. 'Would you like to see the dessert menu?'

'No,' said Joe. 'No thanks. I don't think so. I think we've both had enough.'

He turned back to me and half-smiled. 'Let's go home.'

Chapter Twenty-Six

ROBIN ROUSE STOOD BY the bank of lifts the following morning, waiting to be whisked up to his newspaper. Gaunt and tweedy, he looked as though he belonged in old libraries among dusty books, rather than in these marble halls with their elaborate chandeliers, silent escalators and mysterious mirrored lifts that went twenty floors without stopping. He looked at me, then away, then back again with a frown; then muttered 'Good morning . . . um, Helen,' in an experimental tone. I returned the greeting.

'Wonderful job on Moorhouse at the weekend,' he said as the lift arrived, having reassured himself he'd got the right person. 'Not often we have a story come to us like that out of the blue. You must have very good contacts. I don't know if Dan's mentioned my latest idea –' we got into the lift and he pressed the button for the twenty-fifth floor, 'but it's my belief that Sunday newspapers have become too trivial.' He blinked into the middle distance. 'Supplements and feature spreads are all very well – and readers expect them – but they've allowed us to lose sight of what used to be our greatest strength: spending more time than the dailies on investigative stories.'

I wondered, as we shot skywards, whether to tell him that my very good contacts amounted to a casual acquaintance of my flatmate, a person now half way across the world, about whose honesty I harboured grave doubts.

'I'm looking at the possibility of setting up a crack news team,' he continued. 'A sort of special investigative squad with the contacts and persistence to worry away at stories. We need a political specialist. I wondered if you'd like to come in and discuss it?'

I mumbled something about not having thought of joining the staff of a newspaper again.

'Talk to Dan,' Robin Rouse advised as we reached the *Chronicle*'s editorial floor. 'And come and see me, even if you don't think you're interested. Give my secretary a ring. We'd like to have you here. Nasty bruise,' he added, as he disappeared through the swing doors.

I found Dan sprawled across his desk on one elbow, hand in his hair, having an argument with someone on the telephone. I touched his shoulder lightly and he turned round, saying, 'Yes, yes, yes, I know, but the piece isn't going to work *unless* you can get her to talk.' His expression of irritation cleared as he saw me, and he said, 'Tim, just get the story, will you? I haven't got time for a philosophical debate. Prat,' he muttered as he put down the phone. 'I don't know how half these people ever got jobs.'

He got to his feet, picked up his jacket off the back of the chair, and kissed me on both cheeks. 'You, Peach, on the other hand, are stunningly brilliant, even if more hideously disfigured than you led me to believe. Did Moorhouse's supporters do this to you? Those Tories are so unforgiving. I bet you've never made a minister resign before.'

'That wasn't the point,' I said primly.

''Course it was,' Dan answered, steering me back towards the lifts.

We found a table in an overcrowded wine bar by a square, man-made lake. Once it had been a dock; now it was surrounded by ugly postmodern buildings with bright red and blue window frames.

'You were spotted in Fred's last night,' Dan said slyly, pouring wine into my glass. 'So! Joe Rossiter. That explains a lot.'

'Oh? Such as?'

'How you happened to know what George Dalmore thought about Tony Bagnall. Why you seem different lately.'

'Different?'

'More shaggable.'

'Dan! I think that amounts to sexual harassment.'

'You've been sexually harassing me for the past ten years, simply

by being here. I do hope' – he picked up his knife and toyed with it
– 'you're not stalling on the Bagnall story because you're sexually
entangled with the Labour Party?'

'I'm *not* stalling on the Bagnall story. Nor am I sexually entangled
with the Labour Party.'

'Only one member. One small part,' Dan said lewdly. 'So tell me
about it. The story, I mean. I can imagine the sex, unfortunately.'

'It's not as simple as it looks. I think Bagnall was being
blackmailed. I'm not convinced he committed suicide. But you
tell me something first. What do you know about an organisation
called Loyalty?'

'God, next time I'll take a stone out to lunch, try for blood. You're
incorrigible, Helen . . . OK. It's a dining club. The founders are
all in their twenties or early thirties – that historian who recently
won the poetry prize, a couple of leader-writers, the editor of
that new political magazine, whatever it's called – *Agenda*. So
they're young, but they're also the people who are making all the
intellectual running on the right – the equivalent of your Labour Party
entanglement, if you like, except that there are more of them. And
they've attracted some big names to their meetings – Charles Swift
attends regularly, I gather. Not that they cultivate MPs, generally
speaking – see themselves as the *thinking* right. They're certainly
not wannabe politicians. But they admire Swift, and it's mutual.'

'Aren't they interested in power?'

'Oh, *very*. But they'd argue power's all about media influence,
contacts, pulling strings – and they're probably right. They certainly
make sure they get newspaper editors, publishers, television pro-
ducers, those sort of people to listen to them. They're disdainful
of Parliament; they think of MPs as small fry.'

'So what exactly do they believe in? What are they trying to
achieve?'

'They'd probably say, if you asked, that their agenda is the Future
of Britain. They're pompous bastards. What really worries them is
the possibility – which they believe in quite strongly – that Britain
could become a sort of colony of Germany. What did Swift say
recently? That he didn't believe European integration was about
making Germany more European; it was about making Europe
more German. That's what it all comes down to in the end, the stuff
about sovereignty and monetary convergence . . . And of course

they believe wholeheartedly in the right to earn a lot – especially for clever bastards like them to earn a lot – and keep it.'

'You don't like them.'

'They're young fogeys. They wear dark pinstripe suits and live in listed cottages in the country, surrounded by old books and busts of Churchill and Thomas Carlyle. And they're hedonists, as well, a lot of them – I hear the food's usually good. I'm jealous as hell.'

'Are they all members of the Conservative Party?'

'Some are, some aren't. But they don't really care a stuff about the Tory Party – especially James Sherlock's Tory Party – except as a means to an end. The end being a home for their ideas.'

'Which are?'

'Free market. Nationalistic. Which makes life difficult, because unfortunately for them, the Tory Party *is* the only possible home in mainstream politics.'

I looked out over the empty, square lake. 'How easy is it to get in to one of these dinners? Tomorrow night's, for example?'

Dan shrugged. 'I've never tried. D'you know Elinor Varney?'

I knew who she was: a startlingly attractive, legendarily clever twenty-eight-year-old leader-writer on the *Daily Correspondent*. Our paths had never crossed. 'She's part of it,' Dan said. 'You want to go to this dinner, I take it?'

I looked back at him. 'Mmmn, I do.'

'Are you going to tell me why?'

'A hunch.'

'Oh yeah? Journalism's *supposed* to be all about intellectual rigour, you know.'

'Rubbish.'

'Is this *hunch* of yours anything to do with Tony Bagnall?'

'Yes. You'll have to be patient.'

I told Dan a little – which is to say, I gave him something to be going on with, to mull over. I said I thought my mugging and the burglary were a consequence of my interest in Tony Bagnall, though not that I had acquired Ryan Stoner's diary, nor that Ryan had been used in the blackmail attempt, though he tried to bully and wheedle more information out of me for the next ninety minutes.

'I wouldn't take this from most people,' he grumbled, as he paid the bill. 'You tell me you think Bagnall was being blackmailed, then you turn up with a black eye and announce it's got something to do with a high-powered right-wing dining club. And I still haven't got the faintest idea what's going on. If you weren't such a bloody good journalist I'd make you tell me exactly what you think you're on to. As it's you, however, I have only one request—'

'Which is?'

'Just get the story soon, will you? The rumours are that Sherlock's about to go to the country – any day now, we think. The story's not going to be much use to me after an election.'

'Is Labour going to win?'

Dan shrugged. 'The Labour Party, or so my sources tell me, has conducted a series of polls over recent months which suggest the question hasn't been nearly as clear cut as everyone thought. But I find it hard to believe after the last week or two that Labour *won't* win. It's as if the Tories have pressed some self-destruct button.' He slipped his credit card into his wallet and snapped it shut. 'You know, I almost don't care. I almost don't think it matters.'

'Why not?'

'I don't believe any of them are going to address the real issues.'

'Oh? And what are they, the real issues?'

'Oh, come on. Obvious. The rich are getting richer and the poor are getting poorer. One lot don't need to be interested in this country, the other lot are trapped in it – thousands of young men with no prospect of employment and women bringing up babies on their own.'

I thought about Mr Morrison and about Simon's impassioned speech the last time I'd seen him at the House of Commons. 'Perhaps the politicians simply don't know what to do.'

'Oh sure, but what gets me is they don't even care. James Sherlock, George Dalmore: it's like a bloody beauty contest. Europe and decline: two of the most important issues facing the country, and they never get mentioned.'

'The Labour Party talks about Europe.'

'Only about the fact that it divides the Tories. They don't *debate* it. George Dalmore and James Sherlock snipe at each other like kids in the playground, and we connive at it.'

'You're so cynical,' I murmured, knowing this would please him. 'Now. Do you think you could approach Elinor Varney for me, about this Loyalty dinner?'

'In return for Bagnall for this Sunday?'

It was Tuesday. In some ways I was no nearer to Bagnall than I'd ever been.

'I'll try,' I promised.

'And once the election gets going, how about spending a week with Penny Dalmore, seeing what it's like from her point of view?'

My heart sank. 'Are you serious?'

'Of course.'

'What time George gets in, what he has for supper, that sort of thing?'

'Exactly.'

'Bloody hell.'

'What's that supposed to mean?'

'Well, for one thing, she'd never do it. Not if she has any sense.'

'That's a distressingly negative response. She might do it with you, because she'd trust you. You were at her birthday party. You're sleeping with Rossiter.'

I sighed through gritted teeth. 'I could ask . . .' I said. Though I had no intention of doing any such thing.

'Come back to the office with me.'

We walked across the blowy spaces, catching the spray in our faces from the windswept fountains, back into the marbled tower and shining lifts.

Once more on the editorial floor, I sat at Sandra Snugrood's desk wondering whether I had the nerve to read my messages. They're only words, I told myself. They couldn't harm me. It was the skinheads with knives I should be worrying about.

In the end, I convinced myself I was more or less morally obliged to read the messages of congratulation for my work on Moorhouse. I owed it to the people who'd sent them. And, with any luck, they'd outweigh whatever other unpleasantness there might be. Anyway, they might have got tired of sending unsettling little messages now anyway. They'd moved on a stage, after all.

There were indeed several congratulatory Moorhouse-messages, including one from Robin Rouse and another from Frank Threshfield, the political editor.

But there was also another mystery message. It had supposedly been sent early on Monday morning by Dan.

'Sam Sheridan died because of you,' it said. 'Do not make a similar mistake again. Think of Katrina Stoner. Think of Joe Rossiter. Leave Tony Bagnall alone. You have been hurt once. Next time it will be worse.'

The thought flashed through my mind that it *was* Dan; that he was playing some kind of elaborate game. But even as it registered, I knew it was false. This was deadly serious.

Who were these people, that they knew what had happened between me and Sam five years ago, and could taunt me from out of the ether? No one really knew what had happened, except me. It wasn't something I'd talked about.

Katrina and Joe. I shuddered. It was one thing to go blundering on knowing *I* might get killed, but to be responsible for hurting someone else, for another person's . . . the thought was unbearable.

I deleted the message quickly, as if by wiping the words from the screen I could obliterate the sense of them. A couple of keystrokes was all it took and they were gone. As if they'd never been.

Except that they were still burning into my brain.

I stared past the screen, past Sandra's perfume bottles, feeling icy cold. *Had* I killed Sam? I believed it enough to have been scared of myself for the past five years, to be scared of what other damage I might do.

But it didn't matter, really, whether I believed it or not. It almost didn't matter whether it was true. Sam was dead. And these people were showing they could get to me. First of all they would threaten, and if that didn't work, they might kill Katrina or Joe. And then they would certainly kill me.

'You all right?' Dan was asking. 'I'd say you'd gone white – except your face is so obviously purple and yellow.'

'Huh?'

Dan sighed. 'I told Elinor Varley you were a passionate anti-European. From what I could gather, she'd noticed the Moorhouse story, though fortunately not your work on where celebrities most like to have sex.'

'Ah . . .'

'I've had to offer her lunch. Still, you can go, Cinderella. Oh, and she said you're not to write about it. Chatham House rules. See what I mean about pompous?'

'Thanks.'

''S'all right. But get me the story soon, will you?'

I wanted to go home and hide under the duvet, but I had an appointment for a stupid feature about women who devoted the bulk of their leisure time to going to parties, which I had agreed to do in a rash moment of extreme poverty. Joanna Beverley was turning over an entire issue to summer parties and believed this would be the central feature. It would raise, she said, a number of interesting questions. Did these women see partying as an aspect of their careers? Did they get very tired? And did they have to adopt special beauty routines?

Coco, the Argentine supermodel, was in town, so we were including her as one of our inveterate partygoers. She had never previously been considered someone who did a lot of partying, but she took a great picture.

I was on the way from the Tube to the flat in South Kensington which she occupied when in London, deep in thought about her special beauty routine and whether it would resemble those of the other supermodels I'd interviewed over the years, which seemed to involve consuming bulk orders of crisps and champagne and smoking like a small Victorian industrial city, when I caught sight of a familiar face in a sandwich bar.

It was such an odd, out-of-character place for Dillie Deneuve to be that I stopped on the pavement and stared.

Dillie was collecting a cappuccino from the bar. The afternoon sunshine was coming in through the shop front, so there was absolutely no mistaking her. Besides, she was wearing the same oatmeal cashmere sweater she'd been wearing on television, the morning my story broke.

She carried the cappuccino to a table beside the wall and sat down. Now she had her back to me. Across the table, the seat was already occupied by a man whose face was hidden behind a copy of the *Daily Correspondent*.

Dillie stirred her cappuccino and gazed idly around the room. What could she possibly be *doing* here? Dillie Deneuve was the sort of person who, if she wanted a cup of coffee, would go to – I don't know, somewhere swanky. The Ritz. No, probably even that was a bit brash. Some hotel in Mayfair patronised only by people who were very rich and very discreet. Anyway, she wouldn't come to a place like this – unless, perhaps, she was on business.

The man lowered his paper. And I was almost more shocked by the sight of his face than I had been by Dillie's.

I recognised the pudgy features, jowls and baby-pink lips at once. This was a face I'd seen in the newspapers, on television and once in the House of Commons.

It was Charles Swift.

I was facing him, looking directly into his face, though he was looking at Dillie.

I moved out of his line of vision quickly.

It didn't make sense.

I stood back against the window of the chemist's shop next door. Was *Swift* a client of Dillie's as well?

Surely not. He'd written an article full of lofty pronouncements about the sexual double standards of his colleagues only a week before. And if he *had been* a client, surely Dillie would have told me about him when she told me about Moorhouse? The prostitute and the anti-sleaze campaigner. It was at least as good a story.

I walked away slowly. I passed along a parade of shops – dry cleaner, newsagent, electrical retailer, general store – catching sight of myself reflected in the windows. I looked small and uncertain, frowning slightly. And as I took in this reflection of myself, looking rather vulnerable and ill-at-ease, the full implications of the meeting began to suggest themselves to me.

Chapter Twenty-Seven

WHAT WERE DILLIE DENEUVE and Charles Swift *doing* in that café? That was the question that had been troubling me for the last twenty-four hours. It was such an improbable place for either of them, with those operating-theatre-style kidney bowls filled with crusting mashed tuna and mayonnaise.

I sat at my desk at home trying to concentrate on the interview with Coco, who had proved to have a limited English vocabulary, not much of it relating to parties.

Perhaps they'd sat down at that table coincidentally. I hadn't seen them speak . . . Perhaps they hadn't known each other.

But there had been other tables, empty tables; she'd had a *choice*, and that was where she'd chosen. And she'd been too absent-minded to be quite convincing. There had been something almost studied about their failure to take any notice of each other. Two people whose faces were known. Two people with, in their different ways, striking faces. And not a flicker of curiosity.

My first thought had been that Charles Swift might be a *client* of Dillie's. Was the woman servicing the entire Government? But in that case, why only tell me about Moorhouse?

Which brought me back to the question that had been nagging me for days. Why tell me anyway? There was nothing in it for her.

She deplored Moorhouse's hypocrisy, she said. But that wasn't logical. A whore couldn't be offended by hypocrisy: it was the very currency of her business. She dealt in her clients' deceit on a daily basis, and it had made her a fortune.

She'd always voted Labour. I'd seized on that as well. The revenge of the Labour voter on the foolish, vainglorious Tory. Now all of a sudden it seemed a bit thin.

The whole episode would have made more sense if she'd wanted payment. From the point of view of anyone interested in boosting newspaper circulation, she had a wonderful story. She must have known its value.

There was only one possible explanation. She had wanted to give the story to me.

Had Charles Swift put her up to it? Was he one of them, these people who were creeping into all corners of my life, crawling over my memories, getting inside my computer, picking over my past and even managing my work? But why?

Why would Charles Swift want to damage Moorhouse when by doing so he inevitably damaged his own party?

I called up the Slzbags file, the one I'd sent myself from the *Chronicle*, thinking there might be something I'd missed, something that made sense now even if it hadn't then.

Everything in it was gone. In place of my notes about Fletcher and Gunnel, Bianchini and Doxat were simply two words. 'Drop it'.

We were in an upstairs room at the Falcon, a restaurant which had first been fashionable in the 1930s, and had recently been relaunched to combine a traditional atmosphere with brilliant contemporary cooking. There were about fifty people in the anteroom where pre-dinner drinks were being served. They seemed to be a tweedier, less strikingly fashionable crowd than the people who collected around the Dalmores. If George and Penny's friends thought of themselves as the new establishment, this lot looked more like the old.

I sought out Elinor Varley – a tall woman with black hair and pale skin in a sensible suit – and introduced myself.

'Danny Gould told me all about you,' she said warmly. 'I'm pleased to hear the *Chronicle* is supporting the odd Eurosceptic journalist. About time too. Have you met Richard Openshaw?' She indicated a man standing alongside her, with whom she had been talking, until I came up, about claret. He wore an old-fashioned grey suit, the sort of outfit his father might have worn – or perhaps a person he would have liked to be his father. 'Helen broke the Moorhouse story,' she added.

We shook hands and I told Openshaw I'd been impressed with the first issue of *Agenda*, his new political magazine.

'The party's in a terrible mess,' Openshaw muttered. 'I wasn't fond of Moorhouse and can't think he's a great loss, but even so it's one crisis after another. You wonder where it will all end.'

'All that cheap rhetoric about the family,' Elinor sighed, regretfully.

'Elinor is a great social libertarian,' Openshaw told me with a smile. 'I am more of a moral traditionalist. I had no objection to Moorhouse's pursuit of the socially slipshod. It was his fawning attitude to Brussels I found offensive.'

'Speaking of Brussels,' Elinor said, 'what did you make of Dalmore's Durham speech? Did you read it, Helen?'

'I thought it was tonight.'

'Yes, it is. I wondered if you'd seen a preview.'

'Ah,' I said. 'No: was it interesting?'

'It was. Clearest statement from them yet on Europe. They still sound as if they're trying to have it both ways – he claims he's committed to expanded maternity provision, to paternity leave, a minimum wage, equal employees' rights across Europe. But he did make it very clear that social policies wouldn't be implemented simply on the say-so of Brussels.'

'You think it paves the way for greater Euroscepticism?' Openshaw asked.

'Yes. I do. He was forthright about putting the interests of British business first . . .'

I sipped my champagne. These people were at once more serious and more flippant than the Labour groupies, I thought. They behaved rather as if they all had private incomes (though I knew they didn't), which left as the main business of life eating well, conversing intelligently and developing eccentricities.

I suspected they would have scorned to have the kind of careerist conversations engaged in by the people who surrounded the Dalmores. Of course, practically speaking, the Labour people were expecting their careers to develop dramatically in the near future, whereas this lot were about to become supporters of the opposition. But it was also a matter of *tone*: the Tories, or this type of young fogey Tory, assumed that he, or in a few rare cases she, was born to rule. It would have seemed rather common to talk about it, when you could have been talking about wine, shooting, or Victorian Prime Ministers; it might have opened the way to self-doubt.

The tweedy, clubbable affectations disguised some sharp brains, however, and it was these that attracted people like Charles Swift, who was over there in the corner, to their events . . .

But I got no further with my anatomy of the evening, because I was transfixed by something, or rather someone, I'd seen across the room.

Joe Rossiter had just walked in.

My stomach hung in mid-air for a moment, then lurched. I felt sick with nerves.

He was followed into the room by Lord Malvern, who immediately engaged him in conversation. What the hell was Joe doing here?

And what had happened to *Aspects of Philosophy?*

A couple of other people I didn't recognise – though one of them, I noticed, appalled, had piercing, ice-blue eyes – joined them, which caused Joe to look up. And that was when he saw me.

The shock was palpable. I watched him as he excused himself and came over.

Why, I was thinking frantically, had he lied to me? Was he *with* Lord Malvern or had they merely met outside the door and happened to enter the room together? Since when had Joe hung around with these Tories?

He was wearing a dark suit and expensive pale pink shirt done up to the collar. No tie. Even in the midst of my bewilderment – and fury – I was swamped by desire. I might as well have been at Dan's party again, seeing him for the first time. We might almost have been strangers: never have sent one another faxes, never had those telephone calls from Washington. He was here and I hadn't expected him, and he had the power to send shock waves of sexual possibility through my body.

I took a few steps forwards.

'What are you doing here?' he demanded.

'I might ask you the same thing. I thought you were filming a television programme.'

'It's tomorrow. Who invited you?'

'There's no need to sound so pleased,' I said offendedly. 'Elinor Varley. And at least I gave you warning that I wanted to come. You said you were too busy.'

'You shouldn't be here.'

'Why not?'

'You're not a Eurosceptic.'

I burst out laughing. 'How do you know? You've never asked me. Anyway, are you? And what's going to happen if someone finds out?'

'This is a serious event.'

'You're being ridiculous. Listen, that man with the very blue eyes, who came up to you and Lord Malvern a minute ago. Who is he?'

'Huh?' Joe was looking back at the group, trying to identify which man I meant. 'No idea.'

I wanted to ask him to find out, but I didn't get a chance, because Charles Swift joined us.

'I don't think I've had the pleasure?' he said to me, in the soft, breathy tones of the extremely fat.

'Helen Clare.' I extended my hand.

Joe was scowling.

'And Joe Rossiter,' Charles Swift said, turning to him. 'I think we last met at a conference on the future of industry? A few months ago? And of course I know as much as I am allowed to see of your work. Very pleased to see you here. I hope it is an example of the openness we are always hearing about in the Opposition. Were you responsible for George Dalmore's speech this evening?'

'I had some input.'

'A step in the right direction, at any rate. You're not a regular at these events?'

'No, I think Elinor Varley may have invited George.' Joe had recovered his aplomb. 'It was felt it might be impolitic for him to attend so close to a general election, so I'm unofficially deputising.'

I watched Charles Swift covertly; he had a kind of patrician presence despite his elephantine, lumbering bulk. He looked assured and commanding even though he had to keep mopping his brow and was evidently grossly, wheezily unfit. This air of calmness and consummate authority may have owed something to his exquisitely tailored suit.

'I think we should go in now,' he murmured; people had begun to drift out of the anteroom into dinner. And he led the way, saying something to Joe about the Durham speech and leaving me to trail along behind. Lord Malvern caught my eye as I moved towards the door and smiled broadly; I think he would have come over and spoken to me, but we were separated by a crush of people. I wasn't sorry. He made the back of my neck prickle with revulsion.

We were seated at round tables of eight. I was on Elinor's table, with, among others, a youngish Tory backbencher, a merchant banker in his mid-thirties and a woman in a vivid lemon suit, who was a councillor on the most politicised and right-wing Conservative local authority in the country. They were already engaged in a conversation – bizarrely enough, about offal – when I arrived, and they continued it across me.

'Sweetbreads, fried in butter with onions!' said the woman in the lemon suit, with unnecessary animation.

'Brains, stewed in red wine,' replied the merchant banker.

I looked around for Joe. He was on the same table as Charles Swift and the editor of the *Sunday News*, sitting next to the founder of a publishing house. I tried to catch his eye, but he was evidently engrossed.

The conversation on our table turned to race relations. 'The thing I find really difficult,' Lemon Suit said, cutting into a slab of lamb glistening with droplets of fat, 'is that I am no longer allowed to speak as I find. I am not allowed to *say* that black youths are responsible for the majority of muggings in my borough, even though it's true. All *that* means, however, is that black people don't take responsibility for their behaviour. They are encouraged to see themselves as victims, as not culpable.'

'Exactly. And it's the very same liberals,' said the merchant banker venomously, 'who believe that we shouldn't blame blacks for mugging old ladies and claim they should be excused their criminal behaviour, who most vehemently deny there's such a thing as a criminal gene.'

This went on for two courses. I contributed very little; it took most of my effort to compose my face into an acceptable expression. I was afraid if I relaxed they'd realise I was an impostor.

No one on my table seemed to know the name of the man with the ice-blue eyes. Lemon Suit thought she might have seen him before, at another of these events, but she couldn't be sure. They were always one step ahead of me; that was how it felt. How long before they found out that Sarah had Ryan's diary?

I tried to concentrate on the conversation around me, though it was a dispiriting enterprise and my mind felt as if it was in a loop, going round and round and only ever coming back to the place it had started. They must have deleted the contents of the Slzbags file and replaced it with the warning when they broke in. At least it wasn't child pornography, which I suppose was something to be grateful for. But it was still deeply disturbing.

Joe was talking away to people on his table. I couldn't even see the man with the chilling eyes any more. Perhaps he'd left without eating. I worried about having at some point to speak to Lord Malvern and explain my presence. I told myself there was nothing to feel guilty about; I was as entitled to be here as anybody else, certainly as entitled as Joe Rossiter.

But Joe's presence made me feel uncomfortable. What was I, a supposedly rabid Eurosceptic, doing having an affair with Joe Rossiter? Still, perhaps no one would realise we were having an affair. Perhaps Joe wouldn't say anything to blow my cover. Perhaps no one would care anyway. What was he *doing* here?

After the main course I got up to go to the cloakrooms, as much to get away from the oppressive conversation, the having to nod and agree with assertions which were palpably absurd as because I particularly needed to.

The lavatories were located down the passage from the restaurant, in the cloakroom area where we'd left our coats.

I loitered at the washbasins, admiring the smooth black granite surrounds, the vase of white flowers, the thick pile of towels which were evidently intended to be used once only before being dropped into a basket. I couldn't think why I'd come here. Lord Malvern was half way across the room; Charles Swift was on Joe's table. There was only Yellow Suit complaining that she was unable to be sufficiently rude about black people.

What had I thought would happen anyway? This was a semi-public event involving a large number of prominent people. They were hardly going to start making Nazi salutes or announcing plans to assassinate European Commissioners.

I considered my dress and redid my lipstick.

There was a limit to how long I could dawdle. I emerged from the ladies into the cloakroom.

I heard the two men talking immediately, and something in their tone – something furtive, angry and conspiratorial – made me pause, even before I realised what they were saying.

'Is she here with Rossiter?'

I shrank instinctively into the coats. But they were talking too urgently to sense that I was the other side of the partition.

'No, she's Elinor's guest. Organised yesterday, apparently.'

'This has gone on long enough . . .'

'You know my view.'

I knew now who the men were. One had a soft, breathy voice. The other, I was pretty sure, was Richard Openshaw, the editor of the new political journal, the man I'd been speaking to earlier with Elinor Varley. Charles Swift and Richard Openshaw. Discussing me.

'Did you pay off the prostitute?' Openshaw was asking.

'Yes, although she's part of de Moleyns' set-up anyway. But giving Helen Clare the story was a mistake. I always thought so.'

'Rossiter . . .' Openshaw began.

'We're going to have another bloody Hammond situation,' Swift interrupted, 'and I'm not prepared to let things go that far.'

'She's a long way off . . .'

'How can she be? She must have evidence. She turns up in places she's not wanted. It needs sorting out.'

'Sure,' Richard Openshaw said. 'Sure. After you?'

I heard the door of the gents' swing open and the two men go inside.

I straightened up out of the coats and took three deep breaths. This was *crazy*. Had they known I was there? Was this another attempt to warn me off?

No. It was a conversation I hadn't been meant to hear.

I had to get back before they did.

My legs felt like jelly. I forced myself to put one foot in front of the other, to negotiate the short distance down the passageway into the restaurant; to look at Joe, who glanced up as I crossed the room; even to return his smile. Then I sat down in my place between Lemon Suit and the merchant banker. I was trembling. I smiled blandly around the table.

Another Hammond situation. I knew what that meant. And they'd have to sort me out: I knew what that meant as well. Like they'd sorted out Jean.

I tried to focus – or at least look as if I was focusing – on the diatribe against single parents that was being conducted across me. Anything not to see Charles Swift and Richard Openshaw return.

If they glanced in my direction . . . if I had to meet their eyes they would *know* – it would be written all over my face – that I'd already considered the ways they might kill me.

A sex attack, a body dumped in Epping Forest or by the River Lea? No, probably not the River Lea: too many echoes of Ryan Stoner. Another mugging, only this time more brutal; a car crash; maybe even another suicide? I didn't have much doubt about their ability to engineer any of these things if they chose.

'Giving Helen Clare the story was a mistake.' If I'd wanted confirmation I'd been set up, this was it. But right now that was the least of my worries.

They knew I had the diary, or evidence of some sort.

I experimented with a corner of the chocolate pudding. It was moist and thick with chocolate, but it stuck to the roof of my mouth. I wanted to be at home. No, I wanted to be at my *mother's* home, tucked up in the spare bedroom, in the single bed, under the flowered bedspread she'd bought me when I was eleven. I wanted her to wake me up in the morning with a cup of tea.

I felt a hand on my shoulder, and started.

'Whoa, you're jumpy!' Joe said, smiling. 'You haven't eaten much of that. It's not like you.'

'I've been talking,' I lied.

'Am I forgiven for not being in studio with *Aspects of Philosophy?*' He bent down and whispered in my ear. 'I keep looking over here and thinking about you. I want to tear that dress off you . . . If I go in a minute, will you come with me?'

I squeezed his hand and nodded.

Chapter Twenty-Eight

I DIDN'T SAY MUCH on the way home. I was thinking about those men with their civilised manners, Swift and Openshaw, calmly discussing my death.

What were they proposing? Why had they mentioned Joe? Please, please, I thought, don't get to me through Joe. Not through Katrina, either. How could I have put her in such danger? And I'd have to get the diary back from Sarah. It wasn't fair to leave it with her any longer.

'Was that as useful as you expected?' Joe asked, looking at me sideways as we stopped at traffic lights. Clearly he assumed it must have been a complete waste of my time.

'It was interesting.'

Interesting . . .!

But I couldn't bring myself to tell him about the conversation between Swift and Openshaw. I didn't know how he'd react. And I was afraid that if I spoke the thoughts, brought the monsters out into the light and gave them form and substance, they'd look more, not less terrifying.

'They're very odd, some of those people,' Joe was saying, clearly quite oblivious to my trembling, febrile state. This reflected a quite amazing level of self-absorption on his part, because I was still shaking and shivery; my nerves were feverish. 'I was lectured for an hour by a professor of education who thought school children weren't taught the kind of history that would make them proud of being British. Of course, he meant English really. And I heard what a great and glorious episode the empire was and how multiculturalism was a disaster . . . How *do* you know Elinor Varley, by the way?'

'Oh, through Dan. It's very vague.'

'You have so many friends,' Joe sighed. 'That's because you're nice. And funny. And fun to be with.'

'Elinor's not really a *friend*,' I said hastily. 'More a friend of a friend. But you make it sound as though *you* don't have any friends. Which is obviously not true.'

'I don't, though. Not like you. Not like your relationship with Sarah, or Dan, or Bobby. You have people who support you.'

'So do you. Adam and Simon and George . . .' Though these were, it occurred to me, all colleagues. 'Adam's lavish in your praises. His admiration for you extends even to your sporting achievements and your understanding of the internal combustion engine.'

'Adam's an enthusiast.'

'Well, he's certainly enthusiastic about you . . .'

'He gets caught up in things.'

'There's nothing wrong with that.'

But Joe wasn't really listening. 'I suppose we all do,' he said. 'The Party. Winning.'

I frowned. 'It *is* your work. And given how much time it takes, it'd be pretty miserable if you weren't caught up in it.'

'Yes. Though sometimes, lately, it's felt as though I didn't have a choice.'

Joe kissed me inside the front door when we got home, then carried me upstairs and ran a bath. We made love in the water, and drippingly, on the bathroom floor, tangled in towels. I concentrated everything on him, all my senses: the sound of my cheek softly brushing his chest; the smell of his skin; his arms wrapped strongly around me. When he whispered in my ear, his voice hoarse with desire, I could almost shut out Charles Swift's caressingly menacing tones; when I closed my eyes and concentrated on his ribs and chest and shoulders, I could very nearly banish Swift's lumbering frame. I could almost stop worrying about how arrogant they were, those people, how sure of their power to be able to stand there discussing me within earshot of anyone who might happen to be behind the partition. They thought they were invincible. And that was really frightening, because perhaps they were.

He carried me damply to bed and I clung to him all night. When he turned away, I slid my hand around his ribs, pressed my stomach into his back and my hot face against his shoulder. When he lay facing the ceiling I nuzzled as close as possible and flung my arm across his chest. When he turned to face me, his arms shielding himself, I hung on to his forearms, feeling the fine hairs, the skin and the sinews.

I held on as if I believed holding on could save me. Joe's body was warm – evenly, temperately warm, unlike mine, which was troubled by hot flushes and sudden attacks of shivering – and his breathing steady and regular. He slept as if he had found great satisfaction. I lay staring into blackness, my mind racing, wishing I could absorb some of his peacefulness.

But it was hopeless. Whenever he shifted and I shifted with him, I inadvertently caught sight of the alarm clock beside the bed, its green figures glowing mockingly in the darkness. I lay waiting for indistinct shapes to resolve themselves into known objects: one hump into the chest of drawers, another into a pile of clothes on the armchair. I waited for the crack in the curtains to become visible; for the first aeroplane to fly over the house at the start of its descent to Heathrow, for the twittering of sparrows and the rattle of milk bottles along the street.

The alarm finally went at 6.30. Joe turned to me sleepily and slipped his arm around my back.

'Mmmn. You were very lovely in the night,' he smiled. 'I don't think we can be wrong about this, do you?'

'No.'

'I even think you can't *have* these feelings – not in quite this way – unless the other person has them.' He pushed my hair back off my face. 'I've got to get up, unfortunately: early meeting. You'd think the election had started already. You going to stay here?'

'No. I've got things to do.'

But I lay in bed watching him as he dressed. He was devastating, I thought, watching the hard outlines of his body under the soft material of his shirt.

When he was ready, he sat down on the edge of the bed and took my hand. 'What's planned for today?'

I struggled to remember. Those women who went to parties. Oh: and Simon had some story for me. Wanted me to meet him at the Commons. It seemed so long ago since he'd called.

'Great,' Joe said encouragingly, when I told him. 'You could do worse, you know, than let him feed you the odd exclusive.'

'I know how it works.' Simon fed exclusives to favoured journalists in exchange for co-operation whenever there was something he wanted to get in the papers. It was a deal, and in a way there was nothing wrong with it. Journalists make deals of one sort or another every day, on every story. It's a pity I hadn't remembered that more clearly when Dillie offered herself to me. Every story is a transaction of some kind, and Simon was good at the business. 'It's just that I'm not sure I want to become a glorified public relations executive for the Labour Party.'

'No one's suggesting . . .'

'I suppose you and Simon think because I'm sleeping with you I'm going to start putting out propaganda?'

Though actually, I didn't think Simon was so naive.

Joe sighed exasperatedly. 'It's a *story*. Simon will give you what he knows and you decide what to do with it. You may decide to do nothing; that's your prerogative.' He kissed me softly. 'Anyway, you need something to take your mind off this dangerous obsession with Tony Bagnall and Ryan Stoner. What time are you going to be in the Commons?'

I yawned. 'One o'clock.'

'I'll be there. Come and find me in my office afterwards. And Helen?'

'Hmmn?'

'Take care.'

I pulled Joe's robe around my shoulders and padded downstairs to investigate the contents of his fridge. Matters hadn't improved much since his return from Washington: the fridge now contained half a pint of milk, a bottle of champagne and a lettuce. I smiled indulgently – why was there always a lettuce and nothing to go with it? Did he buy the lettuces with other things which he *did* eat, or on their own? Were they intended to make him feel healthy? I put the kettle on for a pot of tea. While I was waiting for it to boil, I wandered into the sitting room.

I opened the Venetian blind, changing the angle of the slats to let in the daylight. A man with a crew cut, with the wide outlines and taut bulges of a body builder, lounged against the wall of the house opposite. For a minute or two I didn't give him any thought;

but as I bent down to pick up my dress, which had fallen just inside the sitting room door, I became conscious that he was staring straight across the street, watching me.

I walked back to the window and closed the blinds. I stood in the darkened room, my back to the wall, listening to my breath come sharply. I didn't think I'd seen him before. He was short – couldn't have been much more than five foot four – with huge biceps and forearms and narrow eyes. I'd have recognised him.

Behave normally, I told myself. Don't get rattled, because rattled is what they want. I went back into the kitchen, made the pot of tea, put it and a mug and a jug of milk on a tray, and carried it upstairs. I placed it on the bed, crossed to the window, opened the bedroom curtains. He was still there. I straightened the curtains with the appearance of unconcern. He looked up, then glanced at his watch, lifted himself off the wall and walked away down the street.

There was no one else around. I moved away from the window and sat down heavily on the bed, telling myself there were all sorts of explanations. He was waiting for someone. He was watching something else. Have a cup of tea, and a bath, and get dressed.

I would have to go home and change out of my dress into something more practical. And before I saw Simon I wanted to call in at the *Chronicle* . . . I made the bed, tidied up the bathroom, threw the towels in the linen basket and took one last look around downstairs.

Whenever I stood in Joe's sitting room I was overcome by an irresistible urge to pick up all the papers on the floor and throw them in the bin.

I stared in renewed despair. Old newspapers, newer newspapers, magazines; page after page after page of Joe's essays and book chapters and manifesto notes . . . dear, lovely, adorable Joe, I thought. So scatty, but so generous, thoughtful, attentive and anxious about my obsession with Tony Bagnall and Ryan Stoner . . .

I froze. Ryan Stoner. I hadn't told him about Ryan Stoner.

Slowly, I came back into the room. I sat down at Joe's desk.

'Is she here with Rossiter?' Charles Swift had asked last night.

Joe didn't know Tony Bagnall and Ryan Stoner were connected.

I opened the top drawer of the desk. The last time I'd sat here, writing the note Joe was supposed to find when he came back from Washington, I'd heard the call from Lord Malvern's office.

Joe had meetings with a man who collected Nazi memorabilia.

I was pretty sure he hadn't known about Lord Malvern's curious hobby when I told him. He hadn't liked the idea. But perhaps he hadn't been as horrified as he should have been. Like stamp collecting, he'd said. And then he'd tried to blind me with science.

I began to scrabble about in the drawers. I wanted to find something. There had to be something. Proof. Or maybe something that would prove me wrong. That would be better. It would be a document, a note, a telephone number . . .

The drawer contained all kinds of rubbish: calculator batteries, picture hooks, old cheque books, postcards, a bundle of letters tied in ribbon. I pushed them aside, felt the bottom of the drawer with my fingertips.

Computer disks, a spare mouse, keys, Tipp-ex, loose paperclips, staples . . . I moved onto the second drawer, which was full of old foolscap ledgers, bound in black cloth. I told myself it was ridiculous, needle-in-a-haystack ridiculous: I wouldn't have been able to find *anything* among Joe's erratically disordered possessions, even if I'd known what it was I was looking for.

I opened the top book; all the pages were covered in Joe's large, sprawling handwriting. As far as I could tell, they were notes for the manifesto, points he wanted to make about trade and industry. The book fell open at a page about environmental taxes. I tried the second book. Education. Selection. It was hopeless, hopeless . . . even if the thing was here, whatever it was I thought I was looking for, it could be on any of these pages, tucked away towards the bottom of some paragraph . . . I was about to replace the book in the drawer when a slip of paper fluttered out from between the leaves.

It was a single, flimsy sheet of A4, unfolded now, but creased in thirds, as if it had been in an envelope.

I read it, then read it again – although there weren't so many words, and they were perfectly clear.

It was an agenda for a meeting. It didn't say who the participants were to be, although Joe's initials, J.R.R., were typed in the top right-hand corner. But it did say what was to be discussed, and when. Tonight. Moorhouse. Riots. Repatriation. H.C.

*   *   *

Minutes passed before I could think straight. I sat in a haze of confusion at the desk, staring blindly at the pot of ink, the photograph, the tray of pens and pencils, unable to formulate a single thought. Joe, Joe, Joe.

Eventually I slipped the paper back between the pages and carefully replaced the books in the drawer. The photograph of his parents on the desk caught my eye: two young people, not much older than Joe and I were now, and a couple of toddlers. They were on a beach. The kids wore sunhats and clutched buckets and spades; his mother wore a dress, his father shorts and sandals. They looked happy. I thought about our walk on the heath, when he'd told me all about them. I suppose *that* had been true, at least.

Joe had written the Labour Party *manifesto*, for God's sake. He *despised* all those people who'd been at the Loyalty dinner last night.

So what the hell was he playing at?

Chapter Twenty-Nine

THE MEETING WAS FOR tonight at Lord Malvern's house. That meant I had to get through today.

I went upstairs again. The bedroom still seemed full of me and Joe; like ghosts, we had taken possession of the room, and the atmosphere was restive with our presence. I wanted to throw myself down on the bed and weep.

I stood well back and surveyed the street. From up here I could see out without having to disturb the blinds or open curtains.

The man seemed to have moved on. Out of view, at any rate. Perhaps the point was simply to make sure I knew he was there. I picked up the telephone and called Sarah.

'You look awful,' she announced when she arrived an hour later.

'Did you find my car keys?'

'Yes: they were in your desk. And I've left the car where you said.'

'And the tape recorder? And camera?'

'Yes, I've got them. And I spoke to Silvio.'

'The package as well?'

She patted her bag. 'In here. I think it's time you told me what all this is about.' She stuck her head round Joe's sitting room door. 'He's a slut,' she informed me.

'I know.'

She looked back at me sharply. 'Come on. Let's get out of here.'

In the car she asked: 'Where now?'

'Home, I think. I should change out of this ridiculous dress.'

She put the car in gear. 'So what happened?'

'You remember when I was burgled, we couldn't understand why the alarm hadn't gone off?'

'I think so . . . there was some dispute with the engineers.'

'They said the alarm hadn't been disabled, it had been switched off. I thought they were trying to tell us it was invincible, which I was sure couldn't be true. I also thought they were trying to suggest I hadn't switched it on when I left in the morning. But I had. I always do. Anyway, I know now why it didn't go off. The engineers were right: the burglars weren't so sophisticated that they could outwit the alarm system and leave no trace. They simply walked up to the control panel and punched in the code. Joe had told them, you see. And then, when they left, they punched it in again. I suppose that amused them, leaving it like they found it. Except for the devastation, of course.'

'*Joe* was behind your burglary?'

'He didn't actually throw all the books about. He was in Washington. But he knew the code. He'd seen me setting the alarm the first time we went out together. He watched me punch in the numbers as we walked out of the house. And it's not as if they're difficult to remember: we chose them because of Bobby's niece's birthday. Christmas day.'

'Why would Joe want to raid your house? For the package?'

'It's Ryan Stoner's diary. It proves he was a rent boy, and that he'd been asked to claim that Tony Bagnall was his client.'

'Hang on a minute . . . you're saying Bagnall was a paedophile?'

'No,' I answered patiently. 'He wasn't. But someone wanted him out of politics.'

'Why?'

'He was about to launch a major campaign to persuade people of the benefits of European integration. First of all his enemies tried to get him deselected by his constituency, then they tried to blackmail him. But he found out who they were. And that's why they killed him.'

'But why is *Joe* one of his enemies? He's not an anti-European, is he?'

'No. That's what I don't understand. Not that it's something we ever talked about . . .' What *had* we talked about? Sex. How much we liked each other. What we wanted to do to one another's bodies. 'I'd *say* he's broadly in favour of Europe. But there's no doubt that it's partly because of him they knew so much about what I was up to. He knew I'd been to see June Lennox and Elise Bagnall, and even though I didn't tell him what I'd discussed with them, it would have been easy enough to work it out . . .'

I felt sick. I'd spent the night clinging to someone who had lied to me and arranged for my house to be vandalised, who'd listened to me talking about Tony Bagnall and Jean Hammond and never tried to warn me he was on the other side.

I kept going over the phases of our relationship. That Sunday afternoon I'd been mugged by the canal: had he known when he said goodbye to me outside his house I was about to be attacked? Had he thought about it while we were on Hampstead Heath, given the skinhead some signal after he kissed me goodbye, sent me on my way?

'What now?' Sarah pulled up in front of the house.

'I'd better take the diary.' She handed it to me, still wrapped in its brown paper and polythene. She passed over my tape recorder and camera.

'Where are you going?' she asked, her forehead furrowed.

'I can't tell you. It's not safe. I've caused enough trouble already.'

'Helen . . .'

I ignored her. 'Would you mind waiting until I get inside? And then I think you should probably disappear for twenty-four hours. Go and stay with one of those cousins of yours who own half of Lincolnshire.'

'You're not serious?'

'I am. Whatever you do, don't go to the office.'

I scanned the street: houses, front gardens, the man from number six with his dog, post box, cars, my car . . . nothing out of the ordinary.

The house was silent, the burglar alarm still set. All the doors that were supposed to be closed were closed; the rooms were possessed by an air of remote and shuttered calm. I went into every one before I waved Sarah off: the only movement was of dust, swirling in the shafts of light coming through the trees at the back of the house.

I changed into a pair of jeans, the black jumper and a warm jacket and picked up the phone and dialled for a minicab. I had no intention of hanging around here. The body builder might have reported back by now; they might have decided what to do. How long would they wait? Once they'd made up their minds they'd move swiftly. They were decisive people. They planned, then acted. They didn't screw up.

The car company said they could send a car right away.

'No,' I said; 'I only want Victor.'

'He's not free right now, love.'

'It *has* to be Victor.' I couldn't take the risk.

The man on the switchboard hesitated while he considered how abusive to become.

'It's very important,' I said; and perhaps he heard the edge of desperation in my voice, because he answered grudgingly, 'I'll see what I can do. Where you going?'

'Hampstead.' The wrong direction. 'Can Victor come to the door?'

'Bloody hell, I hope you give good tips, lady.'

While I was waiting I called my mother. Just to say hello. She was still telling me about the bridge club when Victor arrived: six foot tall and built like a prize fighter. He grinned broadly.

I glanced up and down the street. The body builder was nowhere to be seen. I locked the front door and walked out to the beaten-up Scorpio sheltered by Victor's bulk.

'Hampstead, then?' he said, when we were in the car.

'No. The House of Commons.'

Victor frowned. ''S'funny, they told me Hampstead.'

I passed him a twenty pound note. 'If anyone asks, Hampstead's where you took me.'

Victor shook his head and muttered something about English women not understanding what it meant to be liberated. 'Sure hope you know what you're doing, hon.'

'Yes,' I said. 'So do I.'

Simon Healy came down to collect me from Central Lobby, kissing me on both cheeks.

'Haven't got much time I'm afraid,' he apologised. 'We're expecting the election announcement any time. Good: you're fairly warmly dressed. How about lunch on the terrace?'

I would have to tell him about Joe. In case I didn't survive this evening, I would have to tell him Joe had meetings with Lord Malvern at which they discussed the repatriation of immigrants. Not to mention how to get rid of me.

Simon handed me a tray and I followed him along the self-service counter.

'What would you like? I'm having a salad, I think.'

I had a salad too, and we emerged onto the terrace and found a table overlooking the river. One or two other hardy souls acknowledged us, nodding or waving forks in greeting.

Simon looked at me expectantly. I'd hardly spoken since he met me upstairs.

'Do you feel optimistic? – about the election?' I asked simply to make conversation. I had to say *something*. I had to find a way to tell him about Joe.

'Reasonably. The Tories are weaker than we expected – riven over Europe and damaged by a series of scandals, of which your Moorhouse story has been one of the best. And we're pretty strong: full of ideas, energy and purpose – largely, it has to be said, thanks to Joe.'

He smiled at me conspiratorially, knowingly.

Knowing nothing.

Perhaps however, this was my opportunity: 'How could you be sure Joe would be the right person for the party, when you asked him to come back from Washington?' I asked carefully.

'No one had written about social policy issues as imaginatively or as cogently as Joe – not on the left, not for years. He was obviously one of the most interesting, radical thinkers around, and that was what we needed.'

'But supposing,' I said desperately, 'his radicalism had led him in the wrong direction? He wasn't a member of the party . . .'

'I'd read enough of his work to be fairly certain where it would lead him,' Simon smiled. 'But I never worried about him being pluralistic in his thinking. That was the *point*. I mean, before his ideas actually become policy they have to be filtered through the party – through me and George and the National Executive

Committee and Conference.' He poured sparkling water into my glass. 'I'm afraid we really ought to get on, talk about this story. It's going to be a hectic afternoon. But I wanted to offer you this tip-off: you were so brilliant on Moorhouse. And this needs a similar level of investigation.'

Moorhouse hadn't needed any investigation, I thought bitterly. All it had needed was for me to come to the notice of Charles Swift.

I bit my lip. I'd blown it. Simon was preoccupied and wanted to get through lunch as fast as possible so he could move on to the important things like the general election. But I *had* to tell him. Someone had to know.

'Tell me,' Simon gazed out across the river, 'have you heard of Robert Maddock?'

I frowned, trying unsuccessfully to dredge up the name.

'He's a Tory backbencher. Came in at the last election, now PPS to the Home Secretary. Before that he was Chair of Housing on Paddington Council. Which is the part of his life I think might repay investigation.'

I gazed at the brown river sluggishly churning past the mother of parliaments. A faintly fetid smell, of rotten vegetation or effluent, rose from the water and sat in the nostrils, mingling on the tastebuds with the quiche.

'There's a council officer, whose name I'll give you in a minute, who's done some preliminary research. He claims Maddock masterminded a policy of selling council homes to Tory voters in the part of the borough that has now become his constituency, so securing himself a safe seat.'

'How come?'

'A number of the key figures in his selection happen to have benefited from this policy. He also, supposedly, helped people jump the queue for home improvement grants. The sums I think were up to about twenty thousand pounds – and again, the beneficiaries were party members, Tory voters, or – so our source says – waverers whom Maddock believed could be bought. While all this was going on, the parliamentary seat was held by a sixty-seven-year-old Labour MP, Alf Gough, who wasn't in the best of health, and who was – between ourselves – useless. Ten years ago, the seat had been relatively safe for Labour. By the time Gough left, it was very definitely a marginal. That was partly because Gough was hopeless, partly because of changes in the social make-up of the constituency. But if what our source says is true, Maddock hastened those social changes considerably. And since Gough was obviously going to quit – that was clear at least five years before he did – Maddock had plenty of time to get to work, transforming the constituency into a Conservative stronghold.'

'It's a good story,' I acknowledged. 'But it'll take a lot of work.'

And there may not be time. Those men Bagnall had called the establishment – Charles Swift and his friends – might dispose of me before I ever got started. Those people might even achieve their aims, whatever they were.

I tried to imagine myself delving through reams of council documentation, struggling to get to grips with the normal running of housing departments, let alone how Maddock's operation had been different. It all seemed very remote. I couldn't see it happening. Something more significant was going on than the misdemeanours of a minor Tory MP.

'There's something I need to talk to you about,' I said urgently. 'It's about Joe.'

'Oh?' Simon looked surprised.

'This is probably going to sound absurd, but . . .'

I had lost Simon's attention already.

George Dalmore had emerged onto the terrace. He looked agitated – for George, at any rate, who was habitually composed – and he was speaking even before he reached us.

'Sally said you were out here. Hello Helen,' he smiled broadly. 'Great work on Moorhouse.'

But he had already turned back to Simon. 'The word is that James Sherlock's going to make the election announcement any time now. In the next hour. We need to get going, I'm afraid.'

Simon was on his feet. 'Helen, we obviously need to finish this conversation. What are you doing later?'

I hesitated, considering the possibilities. 'I'll probably be at home.'

Simon glanced at his watch. 'Will you be there at five o'clock? I'll call you then.'

'Sure,' I said.

'Were you intending to call in and see Joe now?'

'No. I . . . I've got to be somewhere else.'

'You should grab your opportunities while you can,' Simon said cheerfully. 'After this, you'll be lucky if you see him at all.'

But as it turned out, I saw Joe immediately. He was coming towards us along the corridor as Simon and George swept towards the leader of the opposition's offices and I made my way out of the building. His jacket was slung over his shoulder and he was carrying a file under his arm.

His face brightened as he saw me. 'Helen!'

I had to struggle not to flinch.

'We were just talking about Helen's talent for turning up at moments of crisis,' George said.

'Infallible.' He bestowed on me a great smile. Then he said to the others: 'Are we having this meeting now?'

'I need to talk to Simon for ten minutes. Why don't you and Helen go and have a cup of tea?'

'I've only just had lunch,' I demurred hastily.

'Come down to my office,' Joe urged. He was smiling slightly, the skin around the corners of his eyes crinkling. He had a faraway, hopeful look – a look I knew. It belonged to a man who thought he might be about to get a quick bang up against a bookcase.

'I think Helen has to be somewhere,' Simon interposed.

'No she doesn't,' Joe said. 'I know for a fact that her meeting with you was her only fixed appointment for today.'

'Go on,' George encouraged us. 'After this there's absolutely no possibility of your having any of Joe's time. I shall be monopolising him completely.'

'Come on,' urged Joe. They were all staring at me. 'Just for five minutes.'

Chapter Thirty

'IS SOMETHING THE MATTER?'

'No. Why?'

'You seem distracted.'

I had to get out of there without arousing his suspicion. That was all that mattered. Whatever I had to go through, that was the crucial thing, the point I had to keep at the forefront of my mind.

He locked the door and came towards me, smiling. He wasn't locking me in; he was ensuring we had privacy. There was no need to be scared. Yesterday I would have wanted this. Having sex on his desk in the House of Commons would have seemed as exciting to me then as it evidently did now to him.

'What do you think of the office?' he asked, though I suspect he meant something else entirely. He was inviting me to hurl myself into his arms, choose a particular part of the office against or underneath or on top of which to make love. Perhaps several places.

'It's like Simon's,' I said. 'Except, um, more philosophy books.'

I looked around frantically, planning my escape. At least he'd left the key in the lock.

He was much too close to me . . . How could he think of such a thing? What kind of person did he imagine I was, to offer myself up to him for a quick shag in the middle of the afternoon in the House of Commons? On the day a general election campaign was starting?

I stood my ground, resisting the temptation to back away. I made myself meet his eyes, resisting the other temptations – to look away in embarrassment or break down and demand what he knew about Ryan Stoner, Tony Bagnall and Jean Hammond.

'I want to make love to you on the desk,' he murmured. 'I want to force you down on your back and stand astride you and . . .'

I inched away. 'I'd get pencils in my back.'

His mouth was in my hair. 'Or up against the door, pushing up your jumper, pulling your bra aside.'

I felt if I kissed him I might be ill. I thought of the skinhead's fist, grinding into my cheek. The bruise was still vivid and speckly underneath my eye. 'So,' I said brightly. 'The election at last. Exciting.'

He withdrew slightly and looked at me with a hurt expression. '*Something's* the matter. What is it?'

'Nothing.' I tried to sound as though I didn't know what he was talking about. 'What do you mean?'

'You're not . . . It's like you're absent.'

I held my breath and ran my fingers from his shoulder to his waist. He frowned. 'Don't. Don't do that if you don't mean it.'

'Of course I mean it.'

'What's happened? Something's different. Normally you've got your clothes off before I've even made up my mind.'

I stepped back, stung. 'That's unfair.' Was that how he saw me, as some kind of rampant, out-of-control sex-fiend? Had I behaved in a hideous nymphomaniacal manner throughout our brief relationship?

Well, yes, obviously I had. And I daresay it *was* pretty undignified. But I'd thought we were in it together.

'So what's changed you?' he was demanding. I had to remind myself he was the one who was rapacious now and he was only being so hurtful because he wasn't getting his own way. 'Why didn't you look pleased to see me in the corridor? Why did you practically have to be frogmarched down here? Why can you hardly bear to touch me?'

Because you stood by and let some skinhead kick me in the face, I thought. Because I would be happy if I never saw you again. I inched sideways, nearer to the door. Now I was closer to the exit than he was.

He looked at me, up and down, assessing me dispassionately, perhaps deciding whether to say what was in his mind, shatter the illusion for ever.

'This is still about Tony Bagnall,' he announced at last.

I shook my head, too fast for denial, trying to shake the sounds away.

'You hadn't told me about Ryan,' he said slowly. 'I realised as soon as I'd said it. I thought perhaps you hadn't noticed. But I never did give you enough credit.'

'Is that why you started seeing me?' I asked quietly. 'So you could keep an eye on me, make sure I didn't find out too much? Stop me if I did?'

'Of course not.'

'Why are you doing it? How can it possibly be worth it?'

'You wouldn't begin to understand. What are you doing?'

I was at the door. I'd taken my chance while he was speaking: covered the few paces across the floor, seized the handle. Now I was fumbling with the key, my fingers stiff and shaking, about as useful as a bunch of carrots.

Joe was behind me.

'Helen . . .' He had hold of my arm. He was trying to pull me away from the door, to prise my fingers off the lock.

I fiddled with the key: pushing, pulling, feeling it clash against the inside of the lock. Finally, after what seemed like minutes but can only have been a couple of seconds, it turned. I twisted the handle and yanked it towards me, and the door flew open into the room, jerking us both off balance. Joe almost fell; it took him a second to recover himself. But by then I was already outside in the corridor.

I fled, pounding down the empty passageway, my heart thudding in my chest, breath coming in unreliable, painful gasps. I heard him running after me, feet muffled by the carpeted floor but coming closer; I could hear his breathing in my ears, as I had heard it before, but differently.

I remembered the way out to Dean's Yard; I knew there would be a police officer there, and cabs; I threw myself against the door and emerged into the sunshine.

Only then did I allow myself to turn and see whether Joe was behind me.

But he'd given up. He'd gone back. To his meetings, his election preparations, his important job at the heart of Government.

I caught a cab and directed the driver to Clapton bus garage. No one followed me out of Dean's Yard. But the traffic was tangled and confusing around Parliament Square, and it was impossible to tell whether any of the vehicles that crawled onto the Embankment were tailing us.

I sank well down in the back seat, rebuffing the driver's few desultory attempts at conversation in a way that, in other circumstances, would have been ungracious.

There was a bus waiting on the stand, slowly filling with passengers, but I didn't move yet. I got the cabbie to park outside the garage and paid him so I could be ready. Only when the bus driver put his vehicle in gear did I jump out and run. No one got on the bus after me.

I sat hiding uneasily behind a copy of the *Daily News* as the bus jolted and wheezed towards Bethnal Green. I looked out of the window at the traffic, and every now and then, surreptitiously, at my fellow passengers. They were mostly pensioners and women trying to keep squirming toddlers under control: struggling people. Old people, harassed people. Shoppers on their way to the market: young women with buggies; older women whose legs were mottled with varicose veins. I took most care over the younger men: one black and two white. They looked as though they were probably unemployed: all of them seemed to have the weary resignation of the dispossessed. They didn't look sharp enough to be killers.

At Mile End station I got off and walked down a side street, past telephone boxes covered in prostitutes' stickers: line drawing women with teen-magazine long hair and improbably big busts promising French lessons and chastisement.

I stopped outside a café, looked in both directions, then pushed open the door. A bell tinkled. I glanced around the room, taking everything in: the formica tables with chipped tops, the dense, damp fug generated by the spurts of steam from Silvio's tea urn mixing with cigarette smoke and old fat.

Two middle-aged men in donkey jackets. Silvio behind the counter, grinning broadly. Sam and I used to come here all the time. It was some indication of how besotted we were with each other that we thought it was charming.

I bought a cheese roll from Silvio and looked inquiringly towards the back of the shop. Silvio nodded. I slipped through the curtain of plastic fronds that screened the shop from the passageway, and down the hall. Once there, I slipped down my jeans, and with fumbling fingers, quickly attached the tape recorder to my thigh. Then I slid the bolts on the back door and stepped outside.

A cat jumped from the sloping roof of the old outside toilet into the narrow back yard, landing at my feet, making me jump, and began to prowl greedily round the dustbins. I slid back the bolts and pushed at the wooden back gate, leaning all my weight against it. The gate was stiff; when it gave I almost toppled over.

I was in a narrow alleyway. Weeds sprouted from broken concrete. I looked both ways. In one direction, there were high fences, gates, a few broken sheets of corrugated tin dumped on the ground; in the other I could see the road. No one was watching.

And parked a little way up the road was my car.

I drove east through the Blackwall tunnel, out through the docks on the other side, past waste ground where the air was thick with old, stale smells from the molasses factory, like overcooked vegetables or someone's congealing roast dinner. I drove past rows of nearly identical semi-detached houses lining the road, stretching away as far as the eye could see; through the scrubby landscape bordering the Thames estuary; past the pylons that marched inland from the vast power station on the Isle of Grain. I drove over the Medway bridge, over the river, curling out past Rochester to the sea, and on, on into the rolling countryside of Kent.

I thought, all the way, about Joe. How could I have been so stupid? Why hadn't I *seen* what was in front of my eyes? Why did I never think it was suspicious that one minute he'd implied I was paranoid about the skinheads and the next he was telling me I should give up the Bagnall story because it was too dangerous?

How could he have told me he believed these feelings couldn't be faked, when he'd done nothing but fake? I slammed the heel of my hand against the steering wheel in frustration. How long had I been insulating myself?

I should have been more suspicious about the call from Lord Malvern. I should have thought more carefully about the way Richard Openshaw had referred to him, 'Rossiter', so casually in the cloakrooms, when he was discussing me with Charles Swift.

I'd never have imagined I could go on wilfully ignoring the obvious for so long.

The traffic thinned the further I drove out of town, so that by the time I turned off the motorway the road was clear ahead and behind.

I drove through Faversham and out of the other side, reached the hill overlooking the marshes, where I'd stopped to check the map before, and took the car slowly down past the Elizabethan timbered farmhouse and the pair of brick cottages. Where the cherry orchards ran out and the lane turned left to run alongside the marsh, a stony track led straight on towards a scattering of farm buildings and the sea. I bumped along it for a quarter of a mile to where a five-barred gate opened onto a field and a footpath. The car tyres crunched noisily over the rough ground.

I parked behind an old wooden barn and got out, walked round the building twice to check the car couldn't be seen either from the house or from the road. And then, having satisfied myself it was visible only to someone walking across the marshes from the sea, I wrapped my jacket around me and made my way back on foot down the track.

The sky was cloudy; the only lights came from a couple of cottages on the low brow of the hill inland, and, glimmeringly, behind its protective surrounding covert, from Prospect House. A lamb was bleating out on the marsh.

I was walking along the lane when I heard the car coming and saw its lights swivelling in the darkness half a mile away as it turned down the hill. A clump of trees and straggly hawthorns lay ahead of me. I clambered over the low fence and crouched in the undergrowth, waiting until it had passed: a Jaguar XJS, long and sleek and quiet, rolling smoothly down the lane.

I emerged from the bushes, shook off the dirt and prickles and padded on down the black track to the gates of Prospect House, guided by lights from upstairs windows. With my back to the gate post, I gazed over at the pink-washed house. The Jag wasn't the only car parked in the old farmyard: peering round the gate, I also made out Lord Malvern's Rolls and a dark green BMW.

*   *   *

I fiddled with the tape recorder, then lifted the camera to take a picture.

The man was bulky enough; I don't know how I didn't hear him, except that he moved with a fighter's deftness and grace. But I *didn't* hear him. And I certainly didn't see him.

The first I knew that he was there was when the blow came down on the back of my head.

Chapter Thirty-One

THERE WAS A THUMPING pain behind my eyes. Something was gnawing into my flesh at wrists and ankles. My neck was stiff from lying so awkwardly. I tried to move my hands but they were tied behind my back.

I was lying on something soft. The lights were low . . . lamplight, it had to be: the warm, reassuring glow of table lamps. I was reminded for some reason of George Dalmore's sitting room, of the night I'd been there for Penny's birthday party – how comfortable it had been, how elegant. How interesting and glamorous it had seemed to be a part of that crowd. All that anticipation, all that excitement about Joe, that sexual promise. I shuddered.

This room was comfortable too, I suspected. They'd left me on something soft, cushioned, covered in silky material; not very wide, with a back. A sofa. And that was . . . that thing across the room, black, red. I shifted my head slightly, gritting my teeth against the pain skipping like a stone on water down my spinal cord, and brought it into focus with effort. A high-backed armchair. Not the swastika.

I was in Lord Malvern's drawing room. There was a fire flickering in the grate. Out of vision, to my right, I suppose, were the men.

My nerves were throbbing, especially behind my eyes, where they seemed to be smashing against my retina. I wondered if there was any way of working out how long I'd been unconscious. It might have been minutes or hours. I tested the inside of my mouth, running my tongue around the gums, across the palate, over my lips, none of which tasted stale enough to suggest I'd been there any great length of time. But my head was hurting and objects were still swimming in and out of vision and that made it difficult to think about anything clearly.

I'd been hit. I remembered that much at least; I'd been outside. And I'd been hit on the back of the head.

I shut my eyes again. Someone had hit me, brought me in, tied me up and left me in this room with these men.

These men. I hadn't seen them, but their voices registered; a low murmuring audible somewhere below the pounding of blood in my head. I was going to pass out again . . .

I dreamt I was caught up in some violent street disturbance: shouting, simmering violence, ugly faces. I was jostled, jeered at. A mass of people was forcing its way between the houses, trying to get to a couple of Asian boys. The road was too narrow. They were pushing and punching; I was hit on the back of the head. In a minute, too many people would converge; there would be nowhere for the viciousness to go. They'd start overturning cars.

Lord Malvern was saying something about the criminal gene. The uselessness of rehabilitation. The criminal gene was commonest.

The criminal gene was commonest in those of African descent.

This was not part of my dream, I realised, shifting slightly; this was part of Lord Malvern's mad world view.

I struggled towards consciousness. Lord Malvern was mad, but Charles Swift was madder. Swift supplied the intellectual ballast, I remember thinking. Lord Malvern made wild assertions, but Swift proceeded slowly, making breathy, silvery-voiced references to Nietzsche and Adam Smith, to boot camps for criminals, to abortion for foetuses that carried the gay gene.

What the hell were they talking about? I wished my head didn't hurt so much; I wished my brain would *work*. They sounded almost as if they were having a manifesto meeting for Lord Malvern's political party. But that didn't make sense, because Lord Malvern had dropped the idea of a political party.

I thought about Jean Hammond's violent death, dragged from her bed at dawn, thrown over a cliff. Who had come for her? Not these men, obviously. The skinheads who watched me? The one who beat me up and snatched my bag? The bodybuilder who had waited and watched outside Joe's house?

The curtains were drawn in this room, the lamps cast a tawny glow over the rich carpet and the polished mahogany table and a fire flickered in the grate.

They were talking about the Patriots: using the Patriots for something. Trouble in the inner cities. Football matches. Policing.

It didn't make sense. I drifted off again, I think. At any rate, when I next registered, they were talking about the economy. Stability, the family, order, social cohesion. Punishing disruptive elements . . .

I tried to shift slightly and jarred my shoulder. I must have grunted with the pain because I heard a chair scrape back and Lord Malvern was standing over me.

'Ms Clare. How unwise of you.'

'What am I doing here?'

'I have absolutely no idea. You tell me.'

'Someone hit me.'

'My security guard. You're nothing if not tenacious. Do you know Charles Swift?' Swift looked up and acknowledged me briefly. 'Walter de Moleyns?'

The other man looked up. He had ice-blue eyes.

'You won't have met – although, as you may have realised, Walter knows a good deal about you. You gave your husband a very hard time in Colombia, if I may say so, considering you were so newly married.'

'You don't know anything about it.'

'I think you'll find we know quite a lot. Most unwise, sending your husband off to his death.'

'I didn't send him.'

I don't know why I was bothering. Sinking to their level.

'Ah well, hardly matters now. We won't keep you long.'

And with that he returned to the table, collected his papers, nodded at the others and strode out of the room. Charles Swift lumbered to his feet and followed him. Walter de Moleyns went too, cold blue eyes not even bothering to meet mine.

Once they'd gone I realised there was a clock ticking across the room. But there was no telling the time: I couldn't see the clock and I certainly couldn't move. I had to lie and listen to the clock hammering into the silence.

I wished now I hadn't been quite so scrupulous about Sarah. It was stupid not to have told her where I was going.

What were they going to do? Kill me, obviously. Get someone else to kill me. Lord Malvern wouldn't dirty his own manicured hands.

They probably already knew how they were going to do it. I cursed my stupidity. I couldn't have made it easier for them if I'd stuck my head in the gas oven at home. I had delivered myself into their hands. I'd given them time and a range of options.

How long would it take for their henchmen to arrive? Which ones would it be? The one who'd gone for me in the park? The skinheads who'd followed me from Ryan's school to Katrina's? The one who'd mugged me down by the canal? How long would I have to sit here listening to the ticking clock, noisily disrupting the silence?

I shook myself. I had to think about something else. Try to work out what they were doing round that table. Ignore the clock. Not think about time running out.

Escape; I had to think about escape. But my hands were tied and there was a rope round my ankles which was secured to the foot of the sofa.

I slid off the sofa onto the floor with a thump, jarring my back. They would have heard me hitting the floor. The only reason they didn't come and investigate, presumably, was that it didn't worry them. They knew I couldn't get away.

The sofa had bulbous feet, like a Chesterfield, and the rope was secured above the place where they fattened out. Hopeless. It had been expertly and thoroughly fastened.

Thinking about escape only made me panicky. One not very tall, rather slight woman. I might have been able to outmanoeuvre Charles Swift, but de Moleyns looked agile enough, and Lord Malvern was an athlete. In any case, it wouldn't be them. It would be some musclebound skinhead.

I mustn't panic. I must try to think straight.

Oh Joe, Joe, how did you let this happen?

And then the door opened and Simon Healy walked in.

Chapter Thirty-Two

ONLY HOURS EARLIER SIMON HEALY and I had sat on the House of Commons terrace talking about Robert Maddock, the man whose reams of incomprehensible council documentation were supposed to keep me out of trouble. It scarcely seemed credible now that we'd looked out at the river eating civilised little salads and discussing anything so trivial as my next assignment.

'Don't you have an election to organise?' I asked him sarcastically.

'You should have given up.' He pulled out a chair from the table and sat down facing me. 'None of this need have happened.'

'So that's what Robert Maddock was about. An opportunity for me to leave this alone. And what Moorhouse was about too, presumably. A distraction.'

Simon looked at me lopsidedly. 'I underestimated you.'

I smiled inwardly at the thought of my idiocy in trying to warn him about Joe. Perhaps if I hadn't been besotted by Joe, and ready to be half in love with everything around him, with his world, I might have seen Simon for what he was.

He leant back on his chair, tilting the front legs off the floor and made a regretful, sucking noise with his mouth.

'You're a beautiful young woman,' he said. To smile and smile and be so sentimental. 'You had such a lot to lose . . .'

One question was bothering me: 'Does George know about these people?'

Simon didn't hesitate. 'No.'

'So what's in it for you?'

He shrugged. 'Government. The chance to be in government.'

'These people are giving you money, aren't they? They're funding your election campaign. How much?'

Again, he merely smiled.

'Millions, then, I suppose. And what else are they doing to make sure a Labour government gets elected? They're exposing or – I don't know – even *creating* scandals to discredit the Tory Party.'

'You seem to have it all worked out. It's a pity you persisted so long. You're good; you could have had a great career.'

I looked away; I didn't want his compliments.

'Yes,' he acknowledged. 'They uncovered, or on occasion even fomented, scandals. Walter de Moleyns, the man whose identity you – sadly from your point of view – did not discover, is a senior figure in MI5 and so has access to a great deal of information about all sorts of people.'

Unbelievable. I'd realised what was happening. But even now, hearing Simon admit it, it was incredible. These right-wing Tories were undermining their own government. They *wanted* to see it fall.

'They must really hate James Sherlock,' I said wonderingly.

'They do. And everything he stands for. They think he's ruining their Party, dragging it towards European federalism.'

'But what good do they think it will do, having their Party in opposition?'

Simon lowered the chair legs onto the floor, picked up an ashtray which was lying on the table beside him and twisted it idly in his fingers. 'A period out of office gives them the chance to reconstitute themselves. Quite a few people on the right of the Conservative Party actively want to lose the election. Defeat will inevitably trigger a leadership challenge, which the right is bound to win – not least since Andrew Gunnel, the party's most persuasive pro-European, is now out of the picture.'

'But in the meantime,' I objected, 'they'll have to live with a *Labour* government. Isn't that worse? These people – Malvern and Swift, and de Moleyns too presumably – are rabid right wingers. Why would they want Labour in power? How can they be sure you won't – I don't know – sign up for a single currency? You must have promised them something.'

Simon's composure was astonishing. But I suppose it didn't exactly matter that I knew all this now, given that I was about to die.

'Withdrawal from Europe,' he said.

I stared at him in stupefaction.

'You're not serious.'

'Why not?'

'But you can't do that! I mean, wouldn't there have to be a referendum?'

'You think we couldn't manage to get the result we needed?' He looked at me in amusement. 'You're still underestimating us.'

'But it's completely undemocratic! Don't you stand for *anything*?'

Simon folded his hands, rather as if I had raised a nice point of political philosophy and he was giving it proper consideration. 'Certain things must change in this country, if we are to remain a force in the world and not decline into a kind of upscale third world nation. A Labour government can make such changes. And if the price of that is getting out of Europe: well, it's by no means certain staying in is desirable. Opinion is divided.'

He sounded like Joe when he'd been justifying sociobiology. In their frantic pursuit of power, there were, apparently, no moral or intellectual limits these two were prepared to recognise.

Bagnall had been right to call his enemies the establishment. Perhaps it had been an automatic verbal reflex; perhaps 'the establishment' was how Bagnall always thought of people to whom he was opposed. But Swift, Malvern and de Moleyns were about as establishment as you could get.

Their assumption that it was up to them to run Britain was unquestioning. The landowner-politician, the businessman and the spy; they were a powerful coalition and they didn't trust newcomers, or even oldcomers who didn't have their own highly specialised perspective on Britain. They'd always had influence, and they didn't intend to stop now, simply because the political tide might be turning against them.

If they couldn't maintain and extend their power by democratic means, they'd do it by undemocratic means. They'd get rid of the unhelpful Tory Party and buy up, stitch up Labour.

'That's why you had to get rid of Tony Bagnall,' I said

slowly. 'He was going to launch a public campaign to promote Europe.'

'That's not why he had to be killed. Initially he was just a bit of a nuisance. We tried to force him into retirement, as I think you know, but he'd developed an inflated sense of himself and refused to go quietly. The reason he died is that he found out about our friends down the hall. Or he was close to finding out. We were never quite sure.'

'You knew, didn't you,' I said wonderingly, 'that we were going to find the body the morning I came to interview you?'

'Yes.'

'Did you kill him yourself?'

Simon burst out laughing. 'What do you think? Look at me. He weighed fifteen stone. It was the young man who relieved you of your bag who put the gun to his head. A friend of his – I can't remember if you've met him – helped with the noose.'

'You wrote the note.'

Simon picked up the ashtray. 'I wrote the note, and I misjudged you. I thought it was clever of me to arrange for a journalist to find the body and see me finding the note. But it had to be a journalist who would be satisfied with explanations about threats of deselection. And you hadn't written anything serious for years . . .'

'And Jean Hammond died because Tony Bagnall had told her what he knew . . .'

'Yes. I liked Jean.'

I withdrew, involuntarily, back into the sofa. The man was loathsome. How had I got him so wrong? How could I have allowed a little kindness, a little flattery more than ten years ago to blind me to his egomania?

'So de Moleyns organised all the scandals,' I said slowly, 'or at least made sure people knew about them.'

'Yes. There's a lot of disillusionment in MI5. No role, you see, now the Cold War is over. No communists to spy on. The Irish peace process. De Moleyns hates the Irish peace process. Anyway, he was able to identify the – how shall we say? – pressure points for certain MPs whom it was felt that Parliament might be better off without.'

I shook my head: 'it was felt'. So much certainty.

'And entrap them? Is that what Dillie Deneuve did?'

'Dillie Deneuve is part of – a network, I suppose you'd call it – of people in the sex industry on whom Walter de Moleyns can call.'

'I saw her in a café in Kensington. With Charles Swift.'

Simon raised his eyebrows. 'He would have been handing over money, I expect. He is inclined to be careless.'

'Stewart Saddler too?' I murmured. 'Was he part of de Moleyns' "network"?'

'Yes. Not all the MPs who were involved in scandals were entrapped, of course. Bianchini was already involved with his fundraiser, Lady Hughes, and no one *forced* David Ivison to get his secretary pregnant. But because of Walter's . . . privileged position with regard to information, it was possible to make use of these things.'

'What I haven't ever understood,' I said, 'is whether they were getting rid of pro-Europeans, or simply creating an atmosphere of sleaze around the Tory Party?'

'Both. Getting Andrew Gunnel out was a priority, because he was a potential leadership contender and the Tories' most persuasive pro-European. To do that we had to bring down Ellis Fletcher as well, because they were lovers – even though Fletcher has no very fixed position on Europe.'

'Bianchini?'

Simon smiled. 'Bianchini upset the pattern; he was intended partly to confuse anyone like you who'd noticed that the scandals were removing prominent Europeans. He was, as you realised, a Eurosceptic. But what you didn't consider – and I'd have expected this of someone like Dan Gould, but I'm surprised at you – was Lady Hughes's position. Very pro-Europe. And becoming increasingly influential at Central Office. Of the two of them, she was probably politically the more significant.'

I bit my lip. Bad mistake.

'Geoffrey Doxat came earlier,' Simon continued blandly. 'He wasn't part of the campaign. A happy accident, is how you'd describe him, I suppose. But the aim, in any case, as you have guessed, wasn't simply and solely to reduce the influence of Europhiles in the Tory Party. Anything that contributed to a sense that sleaze follows Sherlock around was desirable.'

'And Ryan Stoner?' I asked quietly.

Simon shrugged. 'There was never much hope for Ryan once Saddler had picked him to finger Bagnall.'

I shut my eyes in despair.

Simon though, was not similarly troubled. 'Ryan did complicate matters for himself, mind you,' he added cheerfully. 'He decided after all he didn't *want* to identify Bagnall as his abuser.' He sighed. 'We were perhaps relying rather heavily on his youth, impressionability and ignorance. It turned out he watched the television news more than we thought. And he recognised the man he had really been meeting on the marshes. After that he imagined he had a bit of power.'

'Charles Swift,' I said.

Simon rubbed his temples. Even he found this distasteful. 'Charles Swift has some unsavoury habits. He makes rather heavy use of Walter's . . . facilities.'

'Swift takes rent boys onto Hackney marshes. Malvern collects Nazi memorabilia. And de Moleyns runs an underground sex ring. How can you have *anything* to do with these people?'

He misunderstood. 'A year ago our private polls were telling us we probably weren't going to win. Another defeat would have finished the Labour Party.'

'But how can you believe you can even *begin* to change the country,' I wailed, 'when to do it you entangle yourselves with people who are so corrupt? Absolutely corrupt. And they want absolute power. They don't care about democracy. They want to run the country for their own purposes, regardless of how people vote.' For personal advantage, according to a bizarre political philosophy based on their own weird interpretations of dubious scientific data.

'They're prepared to help us get a Labour government.'

Simon was evidently mad. He sat there, looking at me complacently, one eye askew, legs crossed at the ankles, thinking he was in control. Did he really believe once Labour was in power they'd let him get on with whatever he wanted to do? Of course they wouldn't. They'd want more. They'd *never* give up, never let go.

Fragments of the conversation between Malvern, Swift and de Moleyns were drifting back to me. References to the Italian neo-fascists and Jean-Marie Le Pen. Deals. With the Labour Party, with Le Pen.

'I've been lying here listening to them. And you know what they've been saying? They *hate* black people. They want to "repatriate" them.'

'Cranky,' Simon agreed.

'No!' I couldn't believe he was so complacent. 'They're fantastically dangerous. Malvern believes in the existence of a criminal gene – and what's more, he thinks it's more prevalent in black people. You're a politician: you know what the implications of that are.'

'Dreams. Games. You think he stands a chance of ever doing anything more than holding secretive meetings with his rich friends to slaver over their dangerous ideas?'

Well, yes, I did. Mainly because Simon seemed to be doing everything in his power to ensure it.

'How many of them are there?' I demanded. 'It's not just those three, is it?'

'Those three are the prime movers. I think you'll find, however, that their influence is quite extensive.'

'Oh, I can see that,' I replied sarcastically. 'It extends right into the heart of the Labour Party.'

Simon smiled. 'They need some organisational muscle. They tend to feel they're above the running around.'

'So who else is involved? All those people in Loyalty? Elinor Varley and Teddy Jacobs and that awful woman I sat next to in the yellow suit?'

'The dining club is, if you like, the public face. Which is not to say that everyone who attends the dining club is privy to the . . . full prospectus. But the dining club is a way of disseminating ideas.'

I was groping for something else I vaguely recalled from the conversation between Malvern, Swift and de Moleyns. 'They run the Patriots, as well, don't they?' I said. If Loyalty was the respectable public face, the Patriots were the unrespectable one.

'Very astute.'

'They're thugs, Simon! It's like a private police force. Like the brownshirts.'

'I think that's an analogy those most closely involved would appreciate.'

'I'm sure! And that's all been part of it too, hasn't it? The trouble at football matches, the violence in the East End, the racial tension

– all designed to create an atmosphere of instability, to discredit Sherlock's government?'

'The Patriots are at least *political* thugs,' Simon said, almost to himself.

'What's that supposed to mean? You're saying it's a *good* thing they're nutters, as well as being violent?'

'It makes them more controllable.' He held up his hand to silence me. 'I'm not suggesting any member of the Patriots is capable of intelligent thought. The truth is that most of them are entirely devoid of strategic vision. But because they have a set of beliefs, they can be managed.'

'Their so-called beliefs are an irrational hatred of black people and a feeling that it's all right to beat them up.'

'Sure. They're spoiling for a fight, and left to themselves they'd be completely directionless. But they haven't been left to themselves; Walter's genius has been to impose tight military discipline. And so they become a powerful political tool.'

I looked at him in amazement.

He shrugged. 'They've developed links to Loyalist paramilitaries and got involved in gun-running. They have contacts with continental neo-fascists. They are violently opposed to immigration. All those things have been and will be used to increase their own power and destabilise the Conservative Government. They'll make a useful contribution to the campaign to distance us from Europe.'

This was supposed to make me feel better?

'So let's see,' I said sarcastically; 'you're working for a triumvirate of madmen with links into the establishment through their personal contacts and through Loyalty. These people also happen to have their own, highly militaristic private police force which they intend to bring into play at a moment's notice to destabilise the democratic process. And in pursuit of power – in pursuit of some cranky idea of what Britain ought to be – they are prepared to lie, corrupt children and commit serial murder. Is co-operating with them the only way you think Labour can get into government?'

'No, but if they *want* to give us money and help us be *sure* of power, who am I to turn them away?'

'Simon!' I exploded. 'Do you have any notion what you're unleashing, giving these people a route to power? Nationalism and

Nazi-worship, that's what. They're secretive; they only acknowledge the rules they set themselves.' They had no interest in the well-being of the people of Britain; they only wanted to line their own pockets and pursue their idiosyncratic, white supremacist politics. If Simon thought that having once inveigled their way into power they'd gracefully give in when things didn't go their way, he was a fool.

They'd tolerate a Labour government for as long as it remained their puppet. For as long as it remained anti-Europe, anti-immigration, fiercely nationalistic; for as long as it allowed the Patriots to roam the streets dispensing punishment.

If once the Government started to show independence of spirit, the killings would start all over again.

He caught my expression. 'That Britain would be better off outside Europe is a perfectly valid view,' he remarked. 'Other small, relatively affluent countries – Norway, Switzerland – have concluded they're better off outside Europe. Really, I had no idea you were such an ardent supporter.'

'I'm not.' I was an agnostic; I'd scarcely even *thought* about Europe. But that wasn't the point. 'I object to the plotting of the country's future by a handful of unelected power-crazed people. I thought Britain was supposed to be a democracy.'

'The democratic niceties will be observed.'

'You think?'

Simon looked at his watch. 'Do you wish to shout at me any further? Only, as you observed, I have an election to run.'

I stared at him hopelessly. He looked small, young, even rather vulnerable. His eyes, which were so often said to make him look shifty, tonight looked like a disability.

I suddenly felt very tired. God knows what time it was. I'd only had a cheese roll to eat all day. There was no point in arguing with Simon.

It was all very simple. Labour would win the election. Everyone thought for better or for worse that that would change something. But the truth was that the old establishment had no intention of letting go. If Charles Swift, Jack Malvern, Walter de Moleyns and their friends couldn't hold on to power legitimately, they'd do it illegitimately.

Simon rose and took a deep breath. 'Well,' he said, 'in that case I'll see you later.'

But I could tell he didn't mean it. Simon Healy wasn't expecting to see me ever again.

Chapter Thirty-Three

I THOUGHT MANY TIMES about how they might kill me. They'd do it soon, that much was sure; they wouldn't wait till morning. It would be efficient, and like Jean Hammond's death, even like Ryan's, it would have a certain logic, be explicable. Sarah would have her suspicions; Bobby and Dan might be able to work something out between them. But none of them would know where to begin to find out what had really happened.

I didn't have to wait long for them to come for me. Only ten or fifteen minutes after Simon Healy left, the door opened again.

There were two of them: tall, well-built, with skinhead haircuts and a vicious certainty. The youth who'd mugged me for my bag came in first: cropped fair hair, pale lashes and eyebrows, milky blue eyes. He had a baby face, ugly with indifference. He met my eyes and his didn't flicker.

The other was older, I guessed: taller, and dark; he seemed to be in charge. He was wearing a tight T-shirt that exaggerated his pectorals and seemed ready to split around his biceps. An eagle was tattooed above his elbow. I wondered if he was the man who'd put the noose round Tony Bagnall's neck, whether this was the pair who had come for Jean.

The younger, pudgier one was carrying a scarf. I told myself, suppressing panic, they wouldn't strangle me here in Lord Malvern's house.

They did everything in silence, moving swiftly, drilled and confident, like a couple of crack soldiers on an important mission, chock-full of patriotic self-belief. They probably didn't think of themselves as criminals at all.

And that was all I remembered before the cloth came down over my face. I went to scream, not because I thought it would do any good – the house was a mile from the nearest cottage, the marsh was desolate – but because I wasn't going to go down without a fight. I opened my mouth, took in a great lungful of fumes, and passed out.

My head hurt more than before. Someone was hitting it, bashing it with a hard object – a brick? No, a lump of metal. And there was a strange noise. Rumbling. Or a sort of churning, maybe.

I opened my eyes. It was pitch dark. I felt sick, woozily nauseous, the sort of suppressed sickness that might be caused by reading in a car.

A car. We were bumping over rough ground, an unmetalled road. My head was being knocked against the floor of the boot. I felt sick from the movement and the chemical residues in the gag. My right arm was in agony. I tried to move it and realised they'd untied my wrists, although the pain where the ropes had bitten into the skin was so intense they still felt tangible in the darkness. I experimented with flexing my feet. They were still bound.

I thought frantically. I could bang on the roof of the boot. Except there was no one to hear. I couldn't hop away with my feet tied together, and there was no point in beating at them with angry, impotent little fists. There were two of them and they probably had knives, if not guns. Not that they needed weapons, the size of them.

The boot space was airless, fume-laden and maddening. I felt groggy from the gag. They were probably relying on my being too woozy to fight back. And no doubt they were right.

The car jolted to a halt. I heard footsteps crunching on stones – big stones, not gravel. I waited, expecting the boot to open. Nothing happened, except for a rumbling sound, something heavy being dragged over concrete.

My sense of time fell apart. I lost all track. Joe, Simon, Lord Malvern, Charles Swift.

Eventually, when I'd given up waiting, the boot did open. I kept my eyes closed; I didn't want another blow to the skull. But I could tell where I was, more or less. Even through the gag there was a powerful smell of seaweed, and I could hear the waves pounding on the foreshore, sucking the stones back, chewing them, dashing them onto the land again.

We must have crossed the marsh to the sea wall.

I think they believed I was still unconscious. The darker man picked me out of the boot and tossed me over his shoulder in a fireman's lift; I might have been a bag of feathers for all the effort it cost him. Relief flooded through me at the idea of being out of the car, then quickly gave way to despair.

Up against him in this intimate way, smelling his pine-forest deodorant and feeling the hard outlines of his muscles against my body, I knew they could do anything with me. I could beat this man's solid chest with my fists. I could kick at his thighs with my feet. But it would only make matters worse. I had to wait for a moment when fighting back had some point, until defiance was useful. If that moment ever came.

The wind flicked my hair against my face, stinging my bruised, still-broken skin. This was the lowest point of the day or night – around three o'clock in the morning, I guessed: the time when people most often die. It was hard to sustain hope here, with the sea grinding on the stones.

That's when I heard him. 'Lay her in the bottom of the boat,' he commanded, his voice thick, stiff with anger.

Joe. What was he doing here? Come to make sure they finished me off properly, that there was no possibility of my surviving to wreck his brilliant career?

I twisted my head to see him. Handsome profile in the moonlight. I wanted to hurt him.

I thrashed against the man's shoulder then, recklessly abandoning my resolution to surprise them later. I heard the click of a switchblade and heard Joe say coldly:

'There's a knife at your throat. I shouldn't move.'

I sensed, rather than saw or felt the six inches of cold steel below my right ear. They were going to kill me, drown me, I was pretty sure. I wanted to say something smart, to tell them to get on with it, use the knife. But I'd only sound ridiculous if I tried to speak through the gag. And actually, as a way of dying, having my throat slit seemed one of the least attractive options.

They put me in the bottom of the boat, face down, just as Joe ordered. So: not content with betraying me, he'd come to oversee my murder. The dark one stood over me with the knife while Babyface pulled at the outboard motor, nagging it into life. It caught, and the boat moved, slipping off the ramp and softly clattering across the bay, towards the open sea.

There was water in the bottom of the boat. I had to turn my head to keep my face out of it – only half an inch, but it was filthy, and enough to drown in. There was nothing I could do about the way it was seeping through my clothes. My thin jumper was already plastered to my skin, the smell of wet wool competing with the petrol fumes and the fishy, barnacled smell of the boat. I shivered in the stiff breeze. The black water was choppy and flecked with white in the moonlight.

How would they handle this tomorrow? Simon would see to it: it would be easy for them. They had my car, my tape recorder, my camera. They could concoct almost any story they chose.

I lost track of time. Five minutes? Hardly any more. But far enough out into the bay. Too far to swim. I'd be dead from exposure before I ever got near.

It was Joe who spoke again. 'OK,' he said neutrally, and Babyface fiddled with the engine again until it cut out. We sloshed about on the choppy waves.

Swim or give in? Why *bother*, when there was only one outcome?

The wind was cold, whipping round the tiny boat, blowing through my clothes to my skin, muscles, bone.

So. Another suicide. With Joe on hand perhaps, to talk about the terrible quarrel we'd had.

I was still groggy from whatever it was they'd used to knock me out. My limbs felt heavy and the pain in my cramped feet was excruciating. The blood was beginning to seep back to my wrists, stinging the stiff muscles. The skin was raw where the rope had cut into it. How long had I been tied up? Must have been several hours. Now it came to it, I knew I stood absolutely no chance against these men. Not only was it one against three, not only were they all taller and stronger than me, but I was half-drugged. I struggled for some clever, courageous thing to say when they took the gag off, something that would stay with Joe for the rest of his life. Except that now that it really counted, now I had an opportunity for cutting last words, my mind was blank.

The dark one bent and cut the rope that tied my feet. This was it, then. He moved forward to untie the gag. For an awful moment I thought he was going to slice it off with the knife, but he slipped the weapon into his belt and fumbled with the knot at the back of my head with stubby cold fingers. But he never finished. There was a thud, and he grunted, fell forwards. The boat tipped precariously; for a moment I thought it was going to spill me into the sea. And then I realised that *he* was in the sea, the man, a great dead weight hitting the waves and sinking. He was already unconscious.

I twisted round and sat up, still barely understanding what was happening. I was prepared for death. I had already given up hope. Yet here was Joe with a wrench in his hand, staring at it stupidly, as if unable to believe he'd killed a man. But that's what he'd done: knocked him out cold, sent him flying forwards out of the dinghy.

Joe gazed after him into the black bobbing waves.

Babyface gave a cry of surprise and lunged forward from the motor towards Joe. I saw the knife and felt a spasm of pain as he stepped on my shin. But I'd already lifted my other leg. I aimed furiously at the soft places between his legs.

I failed to knock him back screaming in pain, which is what I'd intended. My foot flailed wildly in the darkness and merely collided with his shin. But that was enough in the rocky little boat. It tripped him up. He was throwing himself and his knife at Joe's chest, and I made him fall so the knife only grazed Joe's shoulder. I heard Joe yelp with pain. But he wasn't dead. He hadn't even fallen.

Babyface toppled awkwardly against the side and the boat rocked again, barely righting itself; the knife clattered onto the floor.

I groped for it frantically. Out of the corner of my eye I saw Joe lift the wrench again. But Babyface recovered himself quickly and dodged him, picking me up easily by the waistband of my jeans. For a moment I was hanging in the air, waving my arms impotently at Babyface, trying to reach his body. For a moment I felt weightless while the wind rushed around me, and then I was flying. He hurled me into the water.

My body, stiff from being tied up for so long, hit the sea like a dead weight. The cold was shocking. Salt water rose through the gag, up my nose and filling my mouth; I was gasping.

Wave after wave hit my face and made me choke, ran into my nose and down my throat. I coughed, struggled for breath and had no idea which way I was supposed to be going. And all the time the icy water was clogging my clothes and seeping into my body, chilling me slowly. I trod water, then tried a crawl, limbs thrashing numbly through the water.

I was being eaten alive by cold, on the point of passing out. I only dimly registered the object prodding me. I was nearly delirious: a fist? No, more like a pole, a boathook. I summoned the last dribble of strength from somewhere, gripped it and held on. I was being towed through the water; I was kicking against the side of the boat. Someone had hold of my hands.

I fell forward, into the bottom of the boat. Joe was stripping off my clothes, pulling a sweatshirt over my head, helping my legs into jogging pants. I slipped my limbs gratefully between layers of fleece and wrapped a tarpaulin round myself.

We were alone in the boat.

Chapter Thirty-Four

I SAT HUDDLED IN the stern, hands in my armpits, head bowed, while the little boat puttered back to the shore, Joe steering. I looked up at him, at his slim, athletic body, his handsome face, and felt absolutely nothing.

'Quick,' he said, 'into the car. I'll get the heater on.'

They were the first words he had spoken apart from the inarticulate, pained little cries he'd emitted when he was rubbing my hands and my back to try to return the circulation.

He offered me his hand. I took it and allowed him to help me onto the concrete jetty. I was amazed how warm he was. My teeth were still chattering.

He bundled me into the car, switched on the ignition and turned the heater onto full power. I flexed my fingers experimentally. They moved in all the places they were supposed to move. I was going to be all right.

Joe dragged the boat onto the land and got into the driver's seat. 'We should get out of here.'

I nodded. He put my car in gear and crunched softly over the gravel track. He didn't switch the headlamps on. When we were past the barn, close to the lane, he got out of the car and scanned the marsh and the road ahead.

We rolled quietly past the orchards, away from Prospect House. But as soon as we were clear, as soon as we came level with the brick cottages, he hit the accelerator and we roared away, towards the town and the motorway.

Only then did either of us speak.

'Are you all right?'

'I think so.' I couldn't understand why I didn't feel more. The only emotion I seemed able to register was a remote surprise, almost as if I was observing myself from a great height. 'How come they let you come out on the boat?'

'They never imagined I'd save you.' He paused. 'Simon never had any idea how seriously I felt about you. He sees everyone in terms of their usefulness.' He smiled grimly in the darkness. 'Mostly that works to his advantage. Occasionally it leads him seriously to misjudge people. He thinks that's how everyone else operates as well. And let's face it, Hester's not someone you'd throw everything over for. I honestly think he couldn't contemplate such emotion.'

I watched the silent houses fly past in the darkness. Streets of semi-detached villas, their curtains closed, their inhabitants asleep inside.

'Besides, it was a kind of punishment,' Joe said. 'I promised I'd stop you and I failed. I let them think I was taking the consequences, that I was determined to make amends.' He paused. 'They'll come after us,' he warned. 'We've got a couple of hours. But that's all.'

'I know. What happened to Babyface?'

'Huh? Oh, he went into the water when you did. I hit him on the head . . . It was . . . well, never mind. Not pleasant. I knew he was dead.' He swallowed hard. 'But you'd gone further than I thought. I had to start the engine again to reach you.'

We were already at the motorway junction. 'Where do you want to go?'

'Tell me one thing. What does George know about any of this?'

'Nothing.'

'Are you sure?'

'It could never have happened if George had known,' he said bitterly. 'George is too principled.'

'In that case,' I said, 'I think we'd better go to London.'

Joe drove very fast. The roads were empty; he handled my car expertly. In other circumstances the drive through the darkness might have been exciting.

I stared out of the window. It still seemed faintly surprising to be alive.

'How did you get involved?' I asked eventually, so quietly I wasn't even sure Joe had heard me.

'Through Lord Malvern. He approached me – oh, I don't know, about nine months ago. He explained he was having difficulty communicating with the Conservative Party. That was how innocent it was. He didn't get on with James Sherlock and felt the Tories were fatally divided and directionless. On the other hand, he admired George. His only serious worry about Labour was whether once we got into government we'd be too pro-European. We've made a conscious effort in the past couple of years to meet business half way; so I met him and we talked. He said he had friends with similar views. And he held out the prospect of money.'

'You mean he bribed you?'

'No. I mean he said if he could be satisfied with our position on Europe the campaign funds that would have gone to the Tories might come to us.'

It sounded like a bribe to me.

'And what did you have to do?'

'Fudge the issue a bit. That was all I thought it entailed. For a long time, that's all I thought it was.'

'But you knew later. You stood by while I was followed. You let a homicidal skinhead beat me up.'

'Yes, I knew – but I was trying to help you. The whole time I was trying to help you.'

'You have a funny way of going about it. Why didn't you tell me the truth? Why pretend I was paranoid when those skinheads were trailing me all over London?'

'Because if I'd told you you were right you wouldn't have given up.'

'I didn't give up anyway.'

'No.' We sat in silence for a minute or two. 'I didn't know anything about the mugging until afterwards. I would never have let . . .'

'But you gave them my burglar alarm code,' I pointed out coldly.

'I was trying to save your life.'

'Oh yes?'

'I thought if I could stop you working on the story you'd be safe. I guessed you had some evidence from Ryan's family. I thought if you lost that, you'd have to stop.'

'And you let all those people die,' I murmured.

'I tell you, I didn't know about the people dying until it was too late. I didn't know what our involvement with those people entailed. I didn't even know there was a "those people" until Bagnall and Stoner were dead. I was in Washington when they killed Jean. They didn't tell me.'

I thought back to the morning Simon and I found Tony Bagnall's body, when Joe had strolled into George Dalmore's office. His presence had knocked me sideways. Of course, I'd partly fallen for his looks. And the fizzing sexual chemistry had had something to do with it. But mainly what I'd fallen for was the heady optimism, the sense those people had had in that office of being on the brink of something.

Joe had seemed assured, authoritative and idealistic.

The idealism of course, caused a lot of the trouble in the end. He'd been carried away by a belief that the world could be perfected.

'I really did believe the country could be turned around,' Joe said hopelessly. 'I knew – with our ideas – a Labour government could make a difference.'

I had no such illusions about Simon. Simon had just wanted to run the country.

'Was Adam involved as well?'

Joe was astonished. 'Adam? No. Just Simon and me. It was mainly a Tory plot.'

As we drove through the outskirts of London and swept down to the Blackwall tunnel, he told me they'd planned to claim I'd committed suicide. They would have made out that I was slightly unstable. She blamed herself for Sam Sheridan's death, they'd have said; she was never the same after that. She wrote all those features about sex and celebrity. And she had a lot of difficulty with relationships.

We made one stop, to collect the package I'd hidden in Silvio's back yard. That only took seconds, but all the same, it was dawn when we arrived outside George Dalmore's house in London, and already possible to discern that the tulips in their pots on the front steps were a different colour from the aubretia spilling over the garden wall. The white stucco front glimmered in the grey light.

'What are you going to do?' I asked.

'Leave the country. I daren't stay here. As soon as they realise you're not dead they'll come after me.' He looked at me anxiously. 'Don't leave it too long before you get yourself somewhere safe. Really safe, I mean. They'll have people in customs and immigration and the police . . .'

'I know.' I had no intention of hanging around. 'Take my car.'

'Yes? I'll probably go via Heathrow. In which case . . .'

'I know. I'll go another way.'

I opened the car door. Joe got out too and came round to my side. We stood on the pavement awkwardly.

Then I turned slowly, opened the gate, and walked up the steps to the Dalmores' front door.

Penny answered after a minute or two, wearing a pale blue floor-length dressing gown. She blinked at me, panda-like, through smudged mascara.

'Helen!' she exclaimed. 'What are you doing here at this time of night?' She peered into the street. 'Is that Joe? Are you both coming in?'

'Could I, please?'

'Sure . . .' She looked doubtful. 'George has got his early morning meeting in – I don't know – an hour or so . . . Is Joe not coming in with you?'

'No.' She looked doubtful again, so I added: 'It's urgent. I need to make a phone call.'

The car company answered immediately.

'Oh, it's you again,' the switchboard operator grumbled. 'You realise this is way off our patch? No . . . all right then, you're in luck. It's OK. Victor's here. He says he'll do it.'

It was that easy. An hour later I was in the Channel tunnel.

Chapter Thirty-Five

I STOOD AT THE window, drinking hot coffee, pungent and dark. It was as well it was strong because I'd had no more than five hours sleep in the last two days.

The meadows were chaotic with spring flowers: they seemed to stretch half way up the mountain. The air was so clear it made you gasp. I watched a Swiss woman, the woman from the bakery, urging her small son along the lane. He wanted to dawdle and pat a dog that leapt up and down excitedly behind a garden gate.

I turned back into the room. The hotel was fantastically expensive. But it was discreet. And it had all the equipment I needed.

I put the coffee cup down on the desk, next to Ryan's diary. Then I sat down and re-read the story I'd written.

Everything was there. Names, dates; large chunks of the transcript of my conversation with Simon at Prospect House. I'd slipped the tape recorder off my thigh in the boot on the way down to the sea and hidden it underneath the mat, with the spare wheel. They hadn't searched the car. There should have been time for that, I suppose, when I was dead. I'd removed it when Joe and I arrived at the Dalmores'.

The story was very long. Dan would cope, I thought. He'd enjoy the prospect of cutting my copy.

I slipped the disk out of the laptop the hotel had lent me and took it through to their on-line terminal. If I sent this on the Internet no one had to know where it came from.

And by tomorrow it wouldn't matter. The story would be on the front page of the *Chronicle*; and Simon Healy, Stewart Saddler, Lord Malvern, Charles Swift and Walter de Moleyns would have been arrested. George Dalmore and James Sherlock would have already begun the painful process of rebuilding their parties.

I wondered where Joe was, on which continent, and whether he too was planning to go out for a walk somewhere, and if he was thinking about George and Simon and what it was like to have killed two men. And I wondered whether he'd left enough of himself behind to make a difference.

I watched and waited while the copy transferred from one microchip to another. The tops of the mountains were just visible: jagged, thick with snow. Tomorrow I would go out for a walk, up through the meadows, as far as I could get.